MW00587557

THE WICKED NORTH
Hearts Touched by Fire, Book 1
Copyright © 2016 Gina Danna
The Bitter End Publishing
All rights reserved

Cover Design and Interior Format

THE
WICKED
NORTH

GINA DANNA

DEDICATION

It is time to honor the dead. To give respect and remembrance and to save the hallow grounds of our ancestors who fought in this terrible war, The War of the Rebellion, 1861-1865. Though the war itself was four years, the trouble that came to a head in April 1861 in the attack on Fort Sumter, had been brewing for generations. For the people who lived through it, died for it and those who survived, each for the North and the South, need to be remembered. This war forged our nation, defining us as a true republic, much to the dismay of Europe who hoped our self-governing system destroyed us verses making us stronger. It is not a time, now, to destroy memorial statues and markers depicting the War on either side or destroy our history just to appease modern correctness, for what we do not learn from the past, we are doomed to repeat.

Therefore, I honor the soldiers who fought in our Civil War, both North and South. Rest in peace and know you will *not be forgotten*!

"**F**ind out where your enemy is. Get at
him as soon as you can, and strike him as
hard as you can. And keep moving on!"
~ General U.S. Grant

PROLOGUE

Virginia, June 1862

Emma Silvers was not afraid to shoot Yankees.

She leveled the .57 caliber Enfield rifle at the line of blue coats standing before her porch at Rose Hill that evening. She counted ten men, fully armed and wielding torches. They reeked of wet wool, sweat and gun powder–a noxious mixture combined with the scent of pink roses surrounding the house. Bile rose in her throat. She swallowed hard.

The officer took a step forward. In the dim light, she couldn't discern his face, though she saw him flinch as she pointed the muzzle at him.

"I want you off my land, now," she demanded, her voice remarkably even despite her pounding heart. At twenty-two years and virtually alone, she knew one able-bodied man could easily overwhelm her. With no able men and few slaves remaining, she only had bravado left.

"Now, ma'am," the Union officer began. He spoke like a gentleman, but, dressed in blue, he was an imposter as far as she was concerned.

Jeremiah, just behind her right shoulder, cocked the

hammer on his rifle—a welcome sound to her ears. *Good boy*, Emma thought. If the Yankees didn't believe she was a threat, she hoped the armed slave boy next to her got the message across. She wasn't allowing any soldiers on her property again.

The rifle felt heavier by the minute, making her muscles ache, and she feared she'd drop it. The weapon was foreign to her hands, but as the war raged closer to her home, she learned to use it. She wasn't very good at it, but, as close as the Yankees were, she was bound to hit one of them. She didn't want to pull the trigger. The gun's recoil would knock her off her feet, throwing her aim off. With so few bullets left, she'd hate to lose the shot.

The light streamed through the open front door across the officer as he stepped onto the porch. She saw his face and the nose of the gun slipped. Jack Fontaine, that good-for-nothing traitor! How dare he come here, especially after what had happened last summer? Rage took control and gave her the added strength to pull the muzzle up to his chest as she cocked the trigger.

"Emma, please," he said softly. He looked at her the same way he had that night months ago, his green eyes glowing like emeralds in the light. She remembered those eyes, those mesmerizing emerald eyes. They were all hers the night she had lost her heart to him. The night he had betrayed her. Her anger flared. No. Not this time. Not again, she vowed. Gritting her teeth, Emma narrowed her gaze.

"Get away from me, Jack, or I swear to God, I'll blow a hole through you and send you straight to hell!"

Inside the house, a babe wailed. Emma instinctively turned. Jack reached for her and she panicked, squeezing the trigger. The rifle exploded, throwing her backwards, pain shooting into her shoulder. But instead of falling, she found herself in Jack's arms as they wrapped around her, shielding her back from the impact of the wooden floor.

The patrol stormed onto the porch and into the house. Lying in his embrace, his body shielding hers as his troops marched past them, Emma couldn't breathe. Her eyes were wide open. She felt the heat of him around her. The scent of him invaded her senses. Warm, masculine, and spicy rolled into one. She fought the heat in her belly, but it was hard as his eyes locked onto hers, his lips only inches away.

She closed her eyes. Behind her, the wailing continued, and she heard the thud of soldiers' boots inside. Her jaw tightened as she glared at him. "Get off me, Jack."

"I can anticipate no greater calamity for the country than the dissolution of the Union. It would be an accumulation of all the evils we complain of, and I am willing to sacrifice everything but honor for its preservation."

~ Col. Robert E. Lee, USA, in a letter to his son Custis, January 23, 1861

CHAPTER ONE

May 1853, West Point

Jack Fontaine bent over his horse's neck, shortening the reins, his thighs holding his stance as they raced down the countryside late in the afternoon. The Riding Hall was straight ahead, the end of their race. Jack bent low to his ride's body, and the bay's black mane whipped across his face as they raced to the building.

His horse, Windswept, made excellent time and the distance narrowed, but he could hear the thundering of hooves coming close. Jack didn't have to look to see it was James Ewell Brown Stuart, a classmate of his, the class of 1854. Stuart was closing in, fast and furious on his white steed. The duo had stayed behind them for most of the race until now. Moonstruck was soon alongside Windswept, and the two riders turned to face to each other, laughing as they made the final turn to the stable yard.

Waiting near the stable doors, young cadet John Sappington Marmaduke stood, waving the air with his uniform hat. The thundering hooves passed him before they slowed to a trot and down to a walk.

"Yes! Moonstruck!" Marmaduke exclaimed, following the horses as they circled to the distant post.

Stuart laughed the loudest. His hand slapped Jack's shoulder as they walked the two horses around the stables, cooling the animals down.

"You see, laddo," Stuart stated flatly. "Never underestimate this beast!"

Jack laughed as he rubbed Windswept's neck. "Perhaps, but you cut that turn short back there..."

"I daresay you can't take losing to me," the winner stated, mirth still marking his lips.

"Stunning race, stunning!" Marmaduke declared as he reached them.

Both riders slid off their mounts and in uniform precision, threw the reins over their horses' heads as they led them back to the fence around the pasture. Taking the saddles and bridles from their mounts, the men motioned to the two young stable lads who scampered to the horses. Jack and Stuart walked into the tack room as the boys rubbed the beasts down and gave them oats.

"You were cutting it close," Marmaduke said. "If Mr. Trenton returned and found you racing those two, the demerits would've been high."

"I don't know, Jeb, what ya' think?" With a lopsided grin, Jack turned to his co-conspirator. "Thinkin' we're getting friendly warning here or someone lookin' to get a bribe?"

Stuart laughed and swung the saddle up to the peg on the wall. "Don't rightly know, meself. Could be he's wanting a piece."

Marmaduke colored at Stuart's remark, not looking to start a fight. Jack knew Marmaduke, two years behind them, wanted to join in their wild excursions. Truth be told, there'd be hell to pay if the master of horses found them racing across the fields. He opened his mouth to speak when a movement caught his eye. He turned and found his roommate, Charles Silvers, trying to hide in the corner behind a wall of tack. In his lap was his mechanical engineering book.

Jack sighed. "Charlie, what are you doing here?"

The boy looked up and gave a half smile. "Ah, Jack, you know I can't concentrate with all the ruckus in the parade field."

Stuart joined Jack. "Silvers, my man, whatever is the cause?"

"He's studying, Jeb, can't you see that book?" Jack elbowed the cavalryman. "You and I should be doing the same with finals approaching."

Stuart snorted and walked off. Jack smiled. Stuart was studious and excelled at West Point. For Jack, his parents made education a top priority, so he had many tutors teaching him as he grew up in Louisiana. Hence his studies at the Point weren't as difficult as Charles', who barely scraped by.

Charlie Silvers was typical of many students at the Point. Political connections got him in the door. The Virginian planter's son excelled in drawing and reading, with basic mathematics good enough to manage a prosperous farm like his family's Rose Hill plantation. But Charles wanted adventure, and the Army promised a ticket out of the Commonwealth.

Jack shook his head and turned to leave. "Watch your timing, Charles. You can't be out after call."

The man scrambled to his feet. "Jack, please, I need your help."

Jack stopped but didn't turn around. Charles fretted at the end of every term and begged Jack for help. This time, Jack wanted payment for his services. Summer was coming and he didn't have arrangements to last till fall. He refused to return home to the sultry, hot hell of his father's house.

"Charles, for my time, I'd better be duly compensated."

"You will, I promise." Charles was behind him, and Jack could hear the rustling of book and lecture notes in his roommate's hands. "Come home with me this summer. We're having quite the celebration with my sister's introduction to good Southern society. I know it'll stretch to cover our time off, with plenty of ladies and drink." He grinned.

Jack's lips twitched. Charles might have hit the ticket. "Your sister?"

"Yes, Caroline," Charles replied. "She's the oldest, turning seventeen this spring. My parents are having a week-long party for her. Everyone's coming." He walked closer, and his voice dropped. "And, I daresay, it will be quite the party."

Jack laughed. The man was desperate, offering his sister's celebrations as an enticement. Well, why not? Anything was better than his home.

"All right, come on then," Jack stated. "And, Charles, I better be having a good time, you hear me?"

Charles laughed nervously. "No problem on that, Jack. No problem at all."

Rose Hill Plantation, King Charles, Virginia

June in Virginia was lush, green and inviting to the study-weary Jack as he neared Charles' home, Rose Hill, just north of the James River. The closest city was Petersburg, a growing railroad hub for the state. The capital, Richmond, was a day's ride by horseback. And horseback was still the easiest form of transportation in the South as railroads seemed non-existent there in comparison to the North. Granted, he could have taken the train and left with Charles when their tests were finished, but he preferred to ride his horse. Time to relax and not think about the Point—that was Jack's objective. That and forgetting the letter he received from his mother, begging him to reconsider and come home for the break.

At the top of the hill, Jack halted Windswept and looked down at the fertile farmland below. Charles' house, named after the wild roses growing in abundance around the two-storied white clapboard mansion, was one of the older homesteads in the area. Charles boasted his family had arrived two hundred years ago. Jack gazed at the cotton fields and the gang of slaves working the crops. He shook his head at the sight. Just like home...

Inhaling deeply, he twisted in the saddle and flexed his back after the hours of riding. Windswept sidestepped and snorted. Exhaustion seeped into Jack's bones, but the time to relax was still an hour away. Nudging the stallion on, he rode toward the copse of trees and the creek that fed them. His mount deserved the water, and Jack wanted to stretch his legs so they would not be cramped from days in the saddle.

As he got closer to the trees, it wasn't a creek he'd seen

from above but a stream, large enough for small rafts and with a bridge across it. The water rippled and he stopped in the cover of the trees. Someone sat on the small boat platform. He looked closer and saw a young lady wearing a blue chintz dress. Her bonnet lay next to her on the decking, with her white gloves, black stockings and black square-toed boots beside it. She sat on the edge, her skirt and petticoats pulled high enough to expose her naked calves as her bare feet splashed in the cool water. The sleeves of her dress were unbuttoned and pushed up, and her collar, unpinned, lay open. Her auburn hair, plaited in one long braid, fell down her back, the strands under the sunlight shone like copper. Pretty, young and risking her reputation if discovered.

Jack smiled. She might be Caroline, but she looked a mite younger than seventeen to his eyes. To protect her privacy, he leaned back in the saddle, signaling to Windswept to step back. The stallion took one step, but with fresh water so close, he shook his head and sidestepped forward. The commotion of the leather and bit and the horse blowing through his nostrils caught the girl's attention. She looked back toward him, her eyes squinting, brows furrowed, but she didn't move.

With a mental shrug, Jack sat upright in the saddle and loosened the reins. Windswept took advantage and moved to the stream.

At the bank, close to the dock platform, Jack slid off the horse.

The young woman gave him a look, her lips twitched, but she said nothing. Her honey brown eyes stood out against the splatter of freckles across her nose. She had high cheekbones and a narrow chin with rose lips pink in the light.

"Sorry to disturb you," Jack stated. He took his hat off. "Jack Fontaine at your service."

She stared, appearing rather indifferent to him, his horse and his presence in general. Her lips tightened and she narrowed her eyes. "I'm not Caroline."

Jack smirked at her tone. "All right," he said calmly. "Then you might be?"

"Someone," she stated flatly, turning her eyes back toward the stream.

Jack's lips curved to a half-grin. Most ladies he knew would have been mortified to be caught barelegged by a man...stranger or known...and rapidly try to cover themselves up. The young lady had dismissed him as a nobody. And that fascinated him.

"Well, Miss Someone," he said with amusement. "This is the Rose Hill Plantation, is it not?"

Her gaze darted back to him, and, if he heard correctly, she huffed. His grin widened.

She pulled her legs out of the water. Her dainty feet and shapely calves made him wonder about the rest of her. Crunching the brim of his hat, he dampened his thoughts. At nineteen, his mind wandered too frequently to places it didn't need to go, but she was—intriguing.

"Yes, of course," she answered. She stood and her dress fell over her bare legs, hiding them from his sight. She grabbed her boots, stockings and gloves in one hand and her bonnet in the other. Shoving the straw hat on, she told him bluntly, "Just keep heading straight and you'll find Caroline...along with all the other men."

"Thank you, Miss..."

She didn't look back at him, just walked off the landing with a snort.

Jack smiled. This summer may not be as boring as he feared.

———∞———

Emma Silvers stalked off to her mare, tethered in the woods, away from that Yankee-sounding man on the deck. Her bare feet did not like the twigs, dirt, stones and bugs she walked on, but her dignity prevented her from stopping and putting on her boots until she heard him leave. Hiking her skirts higher, she stood on the stump next to Angel and mounted the grey mare bareback, astraddle like the men did. She took the back way to the house to avoid Mr. Busy-body.

Riding up to the rear entrance, with many of the house slaves and children scurrying about in their chores, Emma slid off Angel, dropped the reins and flattened her skirts.

"Miss Emma," Sally scolded her from the landing at the door. "Your mama…"

"Not now, Miss Sally," she interrupted. Sally was her mother's favorite house slave, and she had helped Emma and her brother and sister in their growing years. Emma loved her but didn't want to be lectured by a house slave about the right way for a lady to act. Hearing it from her mother was bad enough.

Gathering her skirts, Emma ran up the servant staircase in the back to the second floor. She went to her room and threw her hat and gloves on her bed.

"There you are."

Emma closed her eyes as she plucked at her bodice buttons. *Caroline.*

"Yes, here I am," she stated blandly.

"Everyone has been looking for you." Caroline walked straight into her sister's room and sat on the settee. Caroline

studied her sister and shook her head. "Down at the
stream again, huh? You know you're not to go there alone,
especially this week. We have too many guests, too many
young men about for it to be safe."

Shoving her gown off, Emma responded, "I know your
only concern is not about my safety but about you losing
the center of every man's attention if they have to search
for me." She felt nothing but disgust. When children, they
had been so close, but not now. In the past year or two,
her sister had become a self-centered creature. Of course,
their parents doting on Caroline was out of control as far as
Emma was concerned and made her sister intolerable. Now
her actions had become even worse—Caroline's debut into
society had meant introductions to eligible suitors, but,
heaven forbid, she had a younger sister! Only two years
younger, but Caroline still considered her no more than a
child in so many ways. Emma bristled. She was not a child
and grew tired of Caroline's snotty treatment.

Caroline had already turned her attention from Emma.
She stared out the front window to the circle drive below
and the horseman arriving.

"Oh my, my," she fluttered. "What a gorgeous arrival."

Emma wanted to gag. But she couldn't help herself and
went to stand next to her sister.

Below them, dismounting an attractive bay horse stood
the man from the stream. What did he say his name was?
Jack. Jack Fontaine. He stood tall, broad shouldered in
his dark grey jacket. His matching grey pants molded to
him, displaying long, muscular legs. He took off his riding
gloves and black hat, revealing his dark brown, almost black
hair. A smile reached his square jaw as he handed the reins
to the slave and bounded up the stairs to the house. He
moved fluidly, like a feline. Searching her memory, Emma

thought he had emerald green eyes. Yes, a handsome man. She sighed out loud without knowing it.

But Caroline had heard her. Her sister turned, "Remember, they are all here to help celebrate *my* birthday, not yours. Don't you forget it. Just keep quiet and whoever I don't want, maybe he'll still be around in the next two years. Or you can just have old Billy Bealke," she laughed as she flounced out the door.

Emma frowned. Billy lived at the next plantation down. Heavens, they were second cousins! She liked Billy, but that didn't mean she'd want to marry him.

Yanking the ribbon out of her hair, Emma ran her hand through the braid. She only vaguely noticed Jenny, her slave, moving about behind her, setting out her clothing for dinner. She took out her frustration about the tedious week ahead on her hair, brushing it with violent strokes. It was all about making Caroline happy. Heaven help her!

**"It is well that war is so terrible,
or we should grow too fond of it."**
~ *Robert E. Lee to Gen. James Longstreet at
the Battle of Fredericksburg, 1862*

CHAPTER TWO

Jack stood under the sycamore tree with Charles and Charles' father, John Henry, as the slaves followed the directives of John Henry's wife, Margaret Silvers. Inhaling on his cigar, Jack couldn't help but smile. The festivities were to begin this afternoon. Guests were arriving, but the men took a moment to smoke, away from the commotion in the house.

"So, Jack," Charles' father began. "You're from down the Mississippi, Charles tells me."

"Yes, sir," Jack answered. "My family's land is along the great river's coast, up from N'Orleans."

"Hmmm, sugar?"

"Among other interests," Jack replied flatly. His father's investments increased by the hour, most of them not the type to speak of in polite company.

The elder Silvers studied Jack as he puffed on his cigar. Jack knew the man wanted to question him about his father's political views. The latest conversations among men tended to the current debate over tariffs and the new territories in the West and Texas, but Jack's short reply gave him no opening. Skirting the conversation meant not being backed into a political box. Jack had spent too much time up North to fall into line with his father's views.

"I understand I have you to thank for Charles' tutoring this past term," the patriarch of the Silvers clan finally stated.

Jack glanced at his friend and roommate. Charles grinned. "Yes, father, Jack is a great friend."

"Yes, indeed he is," John Henry agreed, gazing on their guest.

Jack pursed his lips and nodded. "It was nothing more than to clear his mind of distractions."

"Daddy!"

The men looked up at the feminine voice calling across the lawn. John Henry shook his head. "If Caroline doesn't learn to contain herself, I believe her mother will throttle her."

Fascinated by the man's failed attempt to sound stern, Jack blew the smoke clear from his eyes.

The young woman hurried across the green grass, tightly holding her skirts up to clear her booted toes. The long tiered skirts, belled out in the current fashion of a caged crinoline, made for quite a sight as she came toward them. A whirl of green and cream silk surrounded the lady, who released the material upon reaching them. Caroline was petite, with blonde hair swept away from her face, dangling in curls at the back. Dressed appropriately from her neck to her ankles, she looked the height of fashion. Corseted in the waspish-waist style, she gave the impression of being a vulnerable, delicate young lady. Caroline's creamy white skin, unmarked by freckles or blemishes, was like porcelain—so desired by fashionable women. The Southern Belle. Jack knew all about those women.

"Caroline Silvers," her father said. "I really…"

"Daddy, I need to talk to you," she interrupted boldly.

With a tilt of her head, she saw her brother and then Jack. Her gaze didn't wander from their guest. Blue eyes sparkled deviously in a calculating gaze. It destroyed her delicate doll image.

Jack recognized that look. It spoke of determination and dominance to get her way. He'd bet her lilting voice, light as it sounded, could be irritating when it turned demanding.

Clearing his throat, John Henry took his daughter's hand and turned toward Jack. "May I introduce Miss Caroline Silvers, our birthday girl? Caroline, Mr. Jack Fontaine."

She held her hand out to Jack and smiled. "How do you do?"

He took her hand and brought the back of it to his lips, a lazy smile on his face. "Very well, Miss Caroline. Happy birthday."

"Thank you," she smiled back at him as he feathered a kiss on her hand.

"Caroline, what brought you blazing out here?" her father interjected.

"Well," she looped her arm through her father's as she began her tale of woe, directing him back to the house. She glanced over her shoulder at Jack and gave a small grin.

A hand slapped him on his shoulders. "My boy," Charles stated with amusement, "I told you it wouldn't be dull."

Jack eyed the departing lady, her skirts and curls dancing for him as she walked away. Jack knew women like her. Pretty, daring but also demanding and spoiled. His mind fluttered back to the young woman he'd met at the stream and her direct dismissal of him. Lips curling in a smile, he punched Charles' arm.

"I'm thinking I need a drink before this all begins," he told his host. Charles laughed.

Emma stood at the side of the ballroom floor, shifting uncomfortably on her feet. For Caroline's birthday celebration, the opening festivities began with a fancy ball and dinner. Because these events were hosted at Rose Hill, Emma couldn't avoid them. Her mother demanded she attend. Almost sixteen, Emma was too old to be indulged like a child and too young for a beau. She knew the Carson girls down the lane were her age, one of them even married, but her mother said they were "below" the Silvers. Because of the Silvers' station in the community, Emma had to wait until she was Caroline's age to be introduced to Society. Her father really preferred for them to be a year older than seventeen, but Caroline's impatient brooding prompted him to relent. He hoped Emma would wait. Glancing at the dancers before her, and the gawking men surrounding Caroline, she'd gladly wait.

But, until that time, she had to attend all of Caroline's celebrations. It was her first ball, and her mother had had a new gown made for it, as well as new clothes for the other engagements. While Caroline's excitement about her new wardrobe could be heard across the entire plantation, Emma quietly acquiesced to what was expected of her. Her dresses were the latest in fashion but designed for a young miss. Emma's neckline wasn't cut as low as Caroline's, nor was anything made in the white or cream silks her sister had. Emma's new corset cut into her middle more severely than her previous one. Its stiff boning constricted her movements and her ability to breathe. Complaints got her nowhere. She was told it made her look more ladylike.

Caroline fluttered her fan and twirled among all the stuttering, imbecilic males vying for her attention as Emma scowled. Being a lady was a nuisance. She'd never compare with supposedly sweet, angelic and naïve Caroline. Caroline was none of those things but acted the part. Emma knew she wasn't as pretty, her coppery brown hair looked dull compared to Caroline's blonde tresses, and her body didn't have the waspish, petite form of Caroline's. For one thing, she was four inches taller, and she'd never be small waisted. Her hands weren't dainty, and she had freckles on her nose despite her mother's attempts to scrub them away. Plus, she'd rather read a book or ride Angel than put up with all the pomp and circumstance. Caroline could "oooh" and "ahhh" her way out of any problem, but Emma stuttered like a fool if she tried that approach.

"Miss Emma, may I have this dance?"

She didn't see Billy coming. Or William, as he liked to be called. The Bealke's farm was across the ravine near Malvern's Hill. They were cotton growers, like the Silvers. The two families had blood ties through her father's side. Billy's father was her uncle once removed, whatever that meant.

Billy smiled at her, his hand waiting. At eighteen, he was closer to Charlie's age, but he didn't go to West Point. He'd run the family farm soon. A tall young man with tawny hair and blue eyes, he was solid from working in the fields with his father and their few slaves. Emma and he had grown up together and she liked him. But marry him? No.

Emma smiled in return as she accepted his hand and they walked onto the parquet floor. They took their place for the Sir Roger de Coverly. She scanned the four couples in the dance, her curiosity piqued. The two lines formed for the dance placed the gentlemen opposite the ladies. Two dancers down from Billy stood Jack Fontaine. The blasted man gave her a quirky smile. Her eyebrows raised, her gaze caught in the light of his eyes, those brilliant green orbs.

She blinked hard, tilting her head away from him. He was here for Caroline, not her—she must ignore him.

The dance started, and, as she followed the steps with Billy, their movements took her close to Jack. That piercing gaze always seemed to be on her when she glanced up. She could hardly wait for the music to end, and, when it finally did, she grabbed Billy's hand to leave the dance floor.

"Emma, Emma," he called, laughing. "Slow down."

"Billy, please, I'm so thirsty," she pleaded, aware Jack was only steps away.

He took her to the refreshment table. "Emma, what's wrong?"

She gave him a half-smile as he handed her the punch cup. "Just all the excitement of today," she gulped the lemonade. It was tart and sweet and cold. She stopped mid-swallow, realizing how unladylike she was behaving by gulping her punch.

Billy laughed. Charles came up and nudged him. "Billy, ole boy..."

Their voices were drowned in the noise. Emma closed her eyes, letting the coolness of the glass cup seep through her white cotton gloves.

"Good evening, Miss Emma."

The male voice was loud and clear. It sounded amused—and familiar. She opened her eyes to find the green-eyed panther before her. Her throat tightened. Inhaling deeply, she lifted her head and forced herself to remember her manners. "Mr. Fontaine, how nice to see you again."

A wicked smile came to his face, his eyes slanted. "Yes, it is so nice to see you again." He leaned slightly forward and dropped his voice. "I'm enchanted to meet the water nymph I thought I must've dreamt of, only to find you are real. You know, I had to ask your brother who you were."

She glared at Jack. Not having been properly introduced, she could have walked away except this was a family celebration, and he apparently was Charles' friend. "Well, I'm of little concern if you're among Caroline's admirers."

He looked over her shoulder at the dancers lining up for the next dance. "Yes, lovely Miss Caroline. I do admire beauty," he looked down at her, "but I saw my fairy first."

Her anger mounted. *Water nymph? Fairies? Was the man touched?* And he did admit to Caroline's beauty. With a disgusted harrumph, she turned on her heel to leave.

He chuckled. His hand touched her elbow. "I had come to ask you to dance."

She spun around. "What? Is Miss Birthday Girl's card filled?"

"I have no idea," he replied. His hand opened the card on her wrist before she could think straight. "Ah, they're going to dance the windmill." He looked at the formations on the dance floor. Taking her cup and placing it on the table, Jack directed Emma to the dance floor, "I see there is an opening for one more couple."

They formed a square with the other three couples. One couple was Caroline and her dance partner. Caroline glared at Emma. It wasn't Emma's fault she picked up the dance steps better than Caroline, enough so their instructor referred to her as floating with grace. Being one step ahead of Caroline in mastering some of the graces only led to more anger from her sister. But now, Emma was flabbergasted. She couldn't deny Jack now without appearing vulgar. Tightening her lips, she narrowed her gaze on the grinning green-eyed rake.

Caroline watched Emma, and Emma felt the scorching fire in her eyes. Mr. Fontaine was about to discover that

Caroline would not appreciate his having asked her sister for a dance.

———∾∾———

Jack found the dance enjoyable with the cute young miss as his partner. Emma's fluster amused him, knowing she had no excuse for not dancing with him. He also knew Caroline stared daggers at her while smiling at him throughout the rotations. Women, young and old, were all alike. Except for his partner. She was different, or perhaps it was her indifference to the festivities that he found refreshing. He congratulated himself for taking Charles up on his offer to visit.

At the end of the dance, he offered Emma his arm to escort her off the dance floor, but she shot him an evil glance and stalked off on her own. He chuckled as he followed her.

"Why, Mr. Fontaine," purred the blonde Caroline as she glided up to him and tucked her arm through his. "I knew the college men up North were taught a fine education, but I had no idea dancing was part of it."

He kept the smile pasted on his face but inwardly grimaced at the sound of Caroline's voice. West Point graduates made the best trained officers in the US Army. Not only did Jack and his classmates learn about warfare but also how to be gentlemen—and that included dancing. "Of course, Miss Silvers, we are not only soldiers but gentlemen."

She laughed. "Oh, do call me Caroline."

"Miss Caroline," he bowed his head to her. Out of the corner of his eye, he saw Emma near the refreshments. She rolled her eyes. Yes, this summer would be quite pleasant.

The celebrations lasted well beyond a week. Jack always found it amusing how the South's hospitality continued for so long. Of course, in an agricultural community such as this, with people spaced far apart, what other diversions were there but to visit and entertain?

More fancy dinners were arranged. A few more dances. Musical quartets played. Lawn parties and teas. And for the men, Charles' father arranged hunting matches and horse races. The men laughed with the ladies at dinner and danced and played Graces and other lawn games. Jack enjoyed the archery matches, the one sport dominated by the ladies. He considered it comical that Society found it acceptable for ladies to shoot arrows, but not bullets. While both can prove deadly, the latter was considered unladylike.

But who did he find at the gun shooting match? Emma. He was surprised to see her, as she had avoided him after the first evening's celebrations. In fact, he hardly saw her at all in the brief moments he freed himself of her sister.

Caroline was very pretty, very feminine and, as he suspected, very spoiled. She clung to his arm at various functions. If it weren't for Emma's occasional appearance and the bored expression on her face when she saw him with Caroline, he might have enjoyed Caroline's enticements. Jack was there only for the summer and he wasn't interested in wooing anyone. But why did Emma's dismissal bother him?

On this day, Jack had risen early to go to the stable and saddle Windswept. The thoroughbred nickered to him, rubbing his muzzle on Jack's arm.

"Yes, boy, today, we're goin' for a run," he told the

stallion as he groomed him and put the saddle and bridle on. Leading the horse out of his stall, Jack, reins in hand, grabbed a lock of the horse's mane and leaped into the saddle.

The morning air was crisp for summer in Virginia. Jack inhaled the slight breeze and closed his eyes. He found himself alone and savored the experience. The Point kept him with his class. On this trip, Charles was his companion at all times. The Silvers family planned a busy schedule to keep their company entertained. It made him relish moments like this—peaceful, only a man and his horse. He exhaled and scanned the horizon. Finding the copse in the distance, he nudged Windswept at a fast walk and then into a trot.

It felt good to be independent, just him and Windswept. Charles' sister pursued him constantly. Last night had been more than he could handle. After dinner, the older adults left Jack, Charles, Caroline and three of their neighbors in the parlor. They considered playing various games but finally picked charades, with the winner to get a kiss from whomever they chose. All fun and laughs.

But Emma was absent. Jack missed her not being with them. Later, he did catch a glimpse of her on the staircase, bent down and watching. He grinned up at her...about the same time Caroline won the match and came to him for her kiss. As she reached up to meet his lips, Jack saw out of the corner of his eye Emma pull back and stumble up the staircase.

Kissing Caroline in the parlor games was fun, he had to admit. But a shudder washed through him as he could still feel her pressing on his lips, her tongue set to enter his mouth. She was too bold and he didn't comply. Obviously, she wasn't pleased but withheld from making a scene over it. Still, it racked his nerves, and now Windswept picked up on the tension of his rider and increased his speed.

As Jack reined the horse toward the trees near the stream, the area where he first met Emma, he slowed his mount. Something about this area drew him. Maybe her presence in his memory. Maybe because its trees concealed him from anyone else who might follow—like Caroline, though she wouldn't be up yet. He grinned. She was typical of the wealthy girls he knew, wasting all morning on their beauty sleep. Military life had changed Jack from ever wasting the day away in sleep. Reveille early every morning, drilled into him for the last three years, eliminated any chance of him sleeping late.

Reaching the first of the trees, Jack slowed Windswept to a walk, but the stallion shook his head, sidestepping, his ears twitching.

"Whoa boy," he said in soothing tones, petting the horse's neck. Looking beyond his mount toward the stream, he saw another horse and rider. Sun speckled through the tree leaves, blinding his vision. Squinting, he only saw white, no doubt from the horse, but the rider was a blur.

At a slower pace, he went closer, eyes wary. Could it be Caroline?

At the water's bank, a white horse sipped water as its rider sat straight, looking away from him. A lady, dressed in a blue riding habit, sitting sidesaddle, her skirts draping the left side of the horse. Her back was upright from her corset. Prim and proper, her small pillbox hat at a slant on her head, a hatpin keeping the blue contraption in place. Beneath it, a spill of copper-colored curls fell across her shoulder. Emma.

As Windswept's hooves crunched on the sticks, she glanced in Jack's direction. He saw the surprise on her face as her hands drew back, pulling her horse's head up and back stepping.

"Why, Miss Emma," he drawled, riding closer. "What a surprise to find you up so early."

Her eyebrows furrowed. "Mr. Fontaine, what are you doing here?"

Jack laughed as he halted Windswept parallel to her. Tilting his hat back to view her better, he smiled. "I do believe there's a horse race this morning."

"Yes, I suppose there is," she replied. Her gaze darted around. She looked spooked.

He eyed her carefully. Emma was stunning and poised in the way she sat on her horse. Her seat was perfect, and her hold on the mare displayed confidence.

Her mare was slightly smaller than his horse, with the dish-shaped muzzle unique to her breed. Emma sat on an Arabian, the same breed as Jack's horse. He was impressed. Windswept's nostrils flared, his ears twitched as he tried to get closer to the mare. Jack smiled. Emma's mare was in heat. He could use that to help him in the race.

"Beautiful horse," he commented. He wanted Emma's attention on him. Frankly, she looked ready to take off and he didn't know why.

She blinked at him. "Yes, she is."

"An Arabian?"

"Yes," she answered as his horse sidestepped closer. "Her name is Angel." Her head turned toward the house.

Jack looked and saw other horses saddled and hitched at the rail. Charles, his cousin Billy and several others were coming. But a glance back at Emma made him tilt his head at her panicked look.

"Not to worry," he reassured her. "I have control over Windswept."

She blinked rapidly and looked at his horse, as if she hadn't seen it before. What was wrong with her?

"You need to leave me," she stated frantically.

"Why would you say that?"

"You can't be here with me, alone," she hissed.

This was the liveliest he had ever seen her—and the longest time he had seen her since first arriving. But she was correct. He shouldn't be alone with her, here by the trees, hidden from view. Society and her family, especially Caroline, would find it unacceptable.

He grimaced. On horseback and fully clothed, he couldn't have "compromised" her if he'd wanted to. Jack laughed to himself. As if she'd let him get that close.

"Why do you not like me, Emma?" He'd say anything to get her to stay a moment longer. There was something about her that drew him to her. What, he didn't know, but he hoped if he talked to her, he might find out.

She looked back at him and shook her head, appearing amazed at his question. "I don't dislike you."

"But you avoid me."

Her lips curled in disgust. "You talk like a Yankee," she sputtered. "Well, you did at the first, a lot, I might add, though not as badly now."

He laughed out loud. "Believe me, ma'am, I'm Southern born and raised." He bowed from his saddle.

She grunted in disbelief. "Charles said you were from Lou's'ana."

He gave her a lopsided grin. "Just north of N'Orleans, on the river."

She didn't return his smile but got her horse to step back. "You really need ta' be goin' on, sur," she stated forcefully.

Jack looked at the field below them. Riders came at a trot in their direction. "Will you root for me to win?"

Emma glared at him as if he was an idiot. "I believe you have Caroline's support for that."

He smiled. She was jealous. How interesting. "I may have Caroline's but I'd like yours as well."

"Caroline would not like that," she stated flatly. "For one of her followers to want..."

"I am hardly following her," he replied. He wasn't, but he'd admit, she was attractive and lively enough that he liked being with her.

"Really? You're here to win her favor, are you not?"

He frowned. "I'm here at your brother's invitation. Not for your sister."

She studied him. "I thought you were like the rest of the..." she stopped. He couldn't help but wonder what that might have been. "Most of the men who've attended this week will be askin' to court her."

"I'm not here to court anyone." He snorted. "Like your brother, I have one more year till graduation and a commission to fulfill. Tell me," he leaned closer, dropping his voice. "Do you think the lovely Miss Caroline would take well to becoming an army officer's wife?"

Her lips curved in a smile. They were pink and plush, ever so ripe.

"No, I don't believe she'd be that willin', unless you were stationed around Virginia or maybe Washington."

He nodded as if he considered her words but twitched his lips as he asked, "And what about you? How would you take it?"

Sitting up straighter, her seat fully in the saddle. "It isn't anything for me to worry about, now is it, Mr. Fontaine?"

Squeezing Windswept with his legs, he made the stallion move closer to her. "At least, give me a token to show your favor in the race."

Tilting her chin down, she said, "No, I believe you'll want Caroline's."

"Please," he insisted. "I'd rather have yours."

Her eyes darted to the riders closing the distance. Nervously, she yanked her handkerchief from her sleeve cuff and handed it to him. "Here, now please go."

He took the lace-edged cloth and inhaled the lilac scent on it. Putting it in his pocket, he grinned at her. "Thank you, my darlin' sweet Emma." And he rode off with a smile.

The horse racing that day was a competition by elimination. Jack patted his mount's neck, praising Windswept for their third win. It was down to the final race, and he edged the horse closer to the starting position. Next to him stood Charles' and Frederick Johnston's horses. Windswept flicked his tail in anticipation as Jack scanned the crowd for Emma. Oh, he found Caroline without a problem. She sat on a roan-colored mare, a rather placid-looking beast, off to the side, rooting Jack on. His lips tightened. He eyed the crowd again and finally, close to the finish line, with Billy and her father, Emma sat on Angel. *Perfect.*

Suddenly, the gun fired, starting the race. The horses leapt into a run, galloping for the line ahead. Jack bent over his horse's neck, shortening the reins, riding him close. Windswept set the pace and as they got closer to the end, Jack felt a hitch in his horse's step. He must have picked up Angel's scent. Natural instinct kicked in fully, increasing Windswept's speed. As they flew over the finish line in the lead, the crowd roared and clapped, the ladies' white handkerchiefs fluttering furiously.

Jack trotted his horse down to a walk as he returned to

the finish line. He threw his leg over the saddle and leapt off Windswept, handing the reins to the waiting groom. He was congratulated by the senior Silvers and other gentlemen. Caroline was there, dismounting and excitedly waiting for him. As she jumped up to kiss him on the cheek for winning, Jack laughed but looked for Emma.

Still sitting on Angel, she gave him a slight nod. Jack grinned at her fully. Caroline, whose hand had laced under his arm, noticed his sudden grin and realized it wasn't for her. Turning her head, she found it was for Emma. Her lips thinned. She glared at her sister. How dare she even look at Jack, Caroline fumed to herself. Emma's eyes caught Caroline's and her shudder was visible. As she turned Angel's head, nudging the horse away, her sister's lips curled derisively.

Caroline squeezed Jack's arm, her face turned amiably toward him, pleased his gaze was back on her as it should be. He squeezed back as he gave her a half-hearted smile.

Jack would have to remember that morning with Emma, as it was the last time he would talk to her, really talk to her, for the rest of the summer. And he soon found himself missing her.

"We have devoured the land and our animals eat up the wheat and corn fields close.

All the people retire before us and desolation behind. To realize what war is, one should follow our tracks."

~General William T. Sherman, on the campaign near Atlanta, 1864

CHAPTER THREE

Caroline stood still in her room while Tilly adjusted the white collar insert in her bodice. As Tilly worked, Caroline's rage grew because of Emma's refusal to heed her warning and stay away from Jack Fontaine. He was the man Caroline decided would be hers. A shiver raced through her at the prospect of being Mrs. Jack Fontaine. And the last thing she needed was Emma sidling up to him. Silly girl, she thought. Emma would pay for disobeying her. She pursed her lips, her mind weaving a way to get back at Emma.

She stared out the front window, watching her father with Charles and Jack ramble down the lane on horseback. They were off to Richmond—for what, she didn't know or care. Her foot tapped the floor as her patience evaporated.

"Finish already, Tilly," she snarled.

"I'm be almos' dun, Miss Ca..." Tilly timidly voiced as she struggled with the last flap, but Caroline pulled away from her.

"Just be gone!"

Tilly scampered out of the room as Caroline paced. Plans for the day included her going with Emma and their mother to the Williams'. *Harrumph!* It was the last thing she wanted to do. As she paced, she heard something outside the window. She stopped and stepped closer to it, biting her lower lip.

Below, Billy Bealke walked to the stable. Her mind flittered at an idea forming, and a slow smile spread across her face. The sound of the bedroom door opening startled her. She grabbed a book lying on her trunk and sat next to the window.

"Caroline, are you ready?" Her mother said, walking into the room.

She buried her nose in the book, appearing intent until she realized she had opened it upside down. With a momentary cringe, she slammed the book shut before her mother noticed.

"Yes, mama?" She asked, masking her surprise in a lazy drawl.

Margaret Silvers crossed her arms, her eyebrows furrowed as she looked at her daughter. "Now you know we're heading to the Williams' this morning."

Caroline sighed and lowered her shoulders. "Mama, please, I'd rather not go."

"Caroline Ann, you know..." her mother argued.

"I know, mama, I know, but I'm so tired," she faked a yawn, covering her mouth with the back of her hand. "Why can I not stay home and rest today?"

Margaret eyed her daughter warily. Caroline worked hard to effect an exhausted appearance, though without a looking glass, she didn't know whether it was at all convincing. She watched her mother's expression slowly soften as she stepped closer, placing her palm on Caroline's forehead.

"You don't feel flush. With your daddy and Charles gone, that leaves Billy the only man here to keep you safe."

"Oh, mama, please," Caroline grunted. "I'm not a child. I just need to be gettin' some rest, maybe catch up on my correspondence."

Cupping her daughter's chin with her hand, Margaret smiled sympathetically. "All right, dear. I'll tell Billy to stay till we return, but you be kind to him, you hear me?"

Caroline gave her mother an innocent look. "Mama, you know I wouldn't be doin' anything bad. I like Billy."

"We all do, especially your sister," Margaret said as she turned to leave. "I'll have Sally make you a tonic to help you rest."

Caroline smirked as she watched her mother leave. "Thank you, mama. Tell Mrs. Williams hello for me, you hear?" When the door closed, Caroline's heart jumped with anticipation. She glanced out the window and saw her mother talk to Billy as he stood next to the carriage. Her smile grew more devious as he assisted her mother into the vehicle. Now Caroline would see just how much Billy Bealke cared for Emma. On many occasions, she had noticed her sister's shy smile for him. With a grunt, Caroline twisted her lips. They looked like little sweethearts, all quaint and gay. Well, so did she and Jack—until Emma had barged in. Cute, young Emma thinkin' she could have Caroline's men made her want to scream. It was her birthday, not Emma's!

A knock at the door interrupted her thoughts. "Come in."

The door slowly opened and Tilly stepped in, holding a cup and saucer.

Caroline looked at her. The tonic. She didn't need that.

"Oh, put that thing down, Tilly," she ordered as she threw open her armoire doors again. With a yank, she loosed her sky blue satin and velvet riding habit and threw it at the slave. "Here, get me out of this dress and into that," she ordered.

Tilly, easily cowed, timidly walked to her. *Stupid girl*, Caroline thought. But she wouldn't hit her just for doing her mother's bidding by bringing the bland tonic for a problem that didn't exist. The slave started to unfasten the hooks on Caroline's bodice.

Within minutes, Caroline was out of her caged crinoline and into the riding habit. Tilly hooked the longer side of the skirt up and fluffed the fabric to make it look a little fuller, though without the hoops, it didn't stay that way long. Caroline's patience began to wear thin as Tilly pinned the straw hat on her head.

As soon as the hatpin went in, Caroline grabbed her gloves and hurried out of the room and down the stairs.

"Jemmy," she yelled as she neared the door. The dark young slave boy was at her side. "Go fetch Guinevere and saddle her for me..."

"Yessum," he said, hurrying ahead of her to the stables.

"And be quick about it!"

It took her a few minutes to round the house to the stables. Her steps slowed and she lifted her chin, swaying her hips as she got closer. Billy stood in the corral, his shirt wet with sweat, his trousers furry with horse hair. Instead of leaving the birthday celebrations to return home and help his father with their farm, he had stayed to work with her father's colt. Caroline smiled. Billy loved to work with horses.

"Why Billy Bealke, you're a sight," she cooed as she came to the railing.

He held a ladle in his hand, sipping water from it out of the trough next to the corralled outdoor arena. Seeing her, he quickly replaced the ladle and wiped his mouth with the back of his bare hand. He had such nice hands, large and callused, his fingers long. She shivered.

"Miss Caroline," he greeted. Polite and dull. "You thinkin' about a ride?"

Jemmy walked up with Guinevere saddled. He offered her the reins and she took them with determination. "Why yes, I was thinkin' how the air might be better after a ride." Her voice dropped. "Wanna come with me?"

Billy looked at her, wiping his hands on his pant legs. A big man, broad shouldered, with a taut chest under that dampened shirt. Through the fabric of his pants, Billy's legs looked muscular. With dirty blonde hair, brown eyes and a slightly crooked nose, Billy wasn't exactly handsome, but he wasn't bad either.

"Miss Caroline, I thought you were tired or at least, that's what your mother told me." His eyes studied her. They looked deeply into her eyes before lowering. Caroline lifted her shoulders back, tilting her breasts toward him and smiled as his eyes fixed on them.

"I'm feelin' too locked in," she drawled.

"No, I think we need to stay here. Your mama asked me to watch over the place. You know she doesn't trust the darkies..."

Her face tightened. "Jemmy," she called as she stepped to the horse's side. The slave ran back to her and lifted her onto the sidesaddle.

"Caroline," Billy's voice strained. She loved watching his emotions cross his face, they were so revealing.

Taking the reins, Caroline said, "Billy, I'm going. If you're to keep a watch on me, to keep me safe, you best be gettin' yourself a mount." As he went for Guinevere's reins, she backed the mare out of his reach and turned her away.

Caroline heard Billy curse and storm into the stable. With a satisfied grin, she slowed her mount.

Within minutes, the thundering hooves caught up to her. Working to erase her broad smile, she glanced at him. "So nice to see you've joined me."

His lips tightened as he controlled the bay he sat on. "This isn't funny, Caroline."

"Oh, Billy," she sighed, bringing her hand up to her face and fluttering it like a fan. "I just wanted to go to the water and enjoy the shade."

His laugh was hollow as his gaze remained on her. "Okay, but not for long."

"Of course not," she soothed and then nudged her horse into a canter.

The mid-morning sun dappled the shady grove. Caroline stopped at the riverside and waited for Billy. He rode up behind her, slid off his saddle, and lifted Caroline off hers.

"Thank you, sir," she replied sweetly. His eyes locked onto hers, and she wanted to laugh in satisfaction as they turned dark with want. Yanking the hatpin out of her straw bonnet, she threw the hat onto the dock as she turned to the water.

"Isn't it so pretty up here?" she asked in an innocent tone.

"I suppose," he muttered. She looked at Billy's face and read the hunger she saw there.

It took a few seconds to control her desire to smile. But when his eyes trailed down her bodice, she felt herself tense. Her nipples ached, and a pool began to form between her legs. She returned Billy's stare and her eyes raked down his body as well. His breathing was shallow, and she noticed the bulge of his arousal.

Caroline turned and bent over, her buttocks before him as she took off her boots.

"What are you doing?" He asked, his voice low and strained.

She lifted her skirts and removed the garters above her knees and slid her stockings off. "I'm goin' ta' cool off," she replied, gathering her skirts as she stepped into the water.

He gulped audibly.

"Caroline," he rasped. "Don't be doin' that."

She was in the water up to her knees. Her skirts floated around her as she turned to look at him. His face showed his torment, as lust struggled for the upper hand. Poor Billy, just like every other man—so easy to make them putty in her hands. Just how far would he go, she wondered. He'd always had a liking for her sister. But her sister had somehow attracted handsome Jack Fontaine, and Caroline wasn't about to let that go. Emma needed to learn how it felt to share Billy's attention. And that thought had determined Billy's fate, right then and there.

Caroline smiled wickedly as she started to unbutton her bodice. "What, darlin'? Don't do what?"

Billy growled and kicked off his boots. With one long stride, he joined Caroline in the stream but didn't stop her.

Caroline's breathing quickened, and she wondered whether to continue. But she hesitated only momentarily. Emma was going to pay for taking any of Jack's time from her. Caroline decided to take some of Billy's time—and more—from *her*....What she was doing was dangerous, but that only added to its attraction. While Billy wasn't as handsome as Jack, the two men equaled each other in age and muscles. Billy was a bit less polished, but he would do, she thought. She opened her bodice. "Do you like what you see?"

He moaned and took her into his arms, kissing her hard, his tongue forcing into her mouth. When she parted her lips, his tongue dove in as his hands skimmed across her breasts, down her hips and around to cup her buttocks. Her arms went around his neck as he lifted her, placing the apex of her thighs against the hardened member beneath his pants. His bold embrace, the way he flattened her against him, thrilled and surprised her.

He stopped kissing her and looked into her eyes, still holding her tight. "Caroline..."

She smiled, her hands holding his face. "Oh Billy, I want you."

"But I'll have to marry you." He sounded resigned.

She giggled. His not wanting to marry her actually lifted a weight off her shoulders. "Why, Billy? All we're doing is playin'. No one will ever know," she whispered.

He stared at her. She felt him hesitate so she wiggled her hips, rubbing harder against his erection.

With a deep groan, he carried her ashore and laid her on the ground. Lifting her skirts, he ripped his buttoned pants and drawers open in a quick movement. Her hand held his hardened shaft and stroked the silken flesh once. His eyes caught hers as he tipped her legs wider, separating the split pantalets.

"Yes, Billy, yes," she pleaded as the moist head of his arousal nudged her lips below.

"Oh, Caroline!" He exclaimed as his cock plunged into her.

Emma sat in the Williams' parlor, listening to her mother and Mrs. Williams talk on and on about Caroline and her would-be suitors. As exciting as it was for them to gossip, there'd be no wedding proposals because her sister was too young. In her mind, Emma could hear her father saying over and over how he would not grant any engagements for another two years.

In a year and half when she turned seventeen, Emma would refrain from all this nonsense. It would lead nowhere, and, besides, there was always Billy. He was nice and he was her friend. Not exactly what she thought she'd want in a husband, although he'd be more loyal to her than that nonesuch Jack Fontaine. But the memory of Jack caused a delightful shiver down her spine, and that frightened her.

When Emma and her mother returned to Rose Hill later in the afternoon, Sally said that Caroline was resting. *It was four o'clock in the afternoon—whatever was she doing sleeping at that hour?* Emma wondered.

Walking out to the stables, she found Angel. "Hello there, pretty," she petted the horse's muzzle and the mare's head dropped as she nickered at her.

Billy walked along the barn aisle but didn't stop to greet Emma, and she thought he couldn't see her behind Angel. She ran her hand down the mare's back to her rump and rested it there as she looked at her cousin.

"And good afternoon to you, too," she mocked.

His step faltered. Surprised, Emma wondered why her voice had startled him so.

Billy turned, trying to clear his thoughts. "Sorry, Emma, didn't see you there. Good afternoon."

She thought his voice sounded odd and noticed his cheeks turned red. Was he blushing? She dismissed the idea.

Sunbeams streamed between the slats of the barn's roof, and the heat must have colored Billy's face.

"I'm thinkin' about taking Angel for a ride. Care to join us?" She smiled at him.

With a quick shake of his head, he said, "No, no, I's got some work to be doin' with that new colt."

She frowned. He'd never turned down a ride with her before. "Oh, yes, how silly of me to forget."

He grinned as though he was relieved. Then his smile became hopeful. "Maybe tomorrow?"

"Yes, definitely."

Whistling, Billy walked away.

How strange, Emma thought as she began grooming her mare.

**"It's just like shooting squirrels, only
these squirrels have guns."**
~ A veteran Union soldier, instructing new
recruits in musket drill

CHAPTER FOUR

March 1854

Leslie opened the letter with her eyes closed and
inhaled. She opened them and smirked. "Vanilla?"

Jack hummed in agreement, his fingers playing absently
with the loose tendril of curled ebony hair, releasing it on
her bare back. Sated, they laid on the mattress, bedsheets
mussed from their lovemaking, their bodies covered with a
sheen of moisture.

Leslie was on her stomach, propped up on her elbows.
Jack was on his side next to her, his fingers tracing the line
of her back to the swell of her buttocks.

"Jack, stop that," she chided as his fingers skimmed the
wetness between her legs.

Moaning, he fell on his back. "Sorry, my dear, do
continue."

March at the Point was still cold outside. It had been
snowing the previous evening when Jack arrived at Mrs.
Turnbull's Hospitality Inn, the local brothel. Leslie was his
favorite and the one he wanted when he needed a break
from school. Many cadets went to Benny Havens' pub, an

off-limits retreat Jack also enjoyed. It was near the Point and, of course, forbidden by the administration. But Mrs. Turnbull's was close behind in location and attraction.

"My Dearest Jack," Leslie read aloud. "Oh, my darling, the winter is so long without you." She paused and turned to him. "Winter? Just how bad can winter be in," she flipped the letter over, "Virginia?"

He gave her a lopsided grin. "It can be cold there too, Les. Even snow."

She snorted. "Do they get a foot of snow like we got last night?"

"Generally, no." It was one thing he despised about the North. He doubted he'd ever get accustomed to the cold, snow and ice. Back home, in southern Louisiana, it seemed balmy in comparison. "In fact, though, it's dreadfully cold." He snaked his arm around her waist, pulling her closer to him.

She laughed. "Stop it, Jack. How I can read this if you keep interrupting me?"

He growled into her shoulder blade.

"All I can do to get through these long months without you is to remember your kiss...," Leslie raised an eyebrow.

He shrugged.

With a clenched fist, she turned to hit his chest. "Oh pray, do tell!"

Her position gave him the advantage he needed to scoop up her hips and wiggle his body underneath hers. He let her continue to read the letter, but in the glow from the fireplace, her body glistened, and another part of him stirred.

"Jack," she chided, sitting across his hips, his hardened cock snuggled between their bodies. She still held the letter. "Let's see what else she has to say."

He gave her a wicked grin as his cock twitched. She ignored him and read out loud more of the simpering letter he'd received the previous day. Caroline's words coming from the whore's mouth seemed comical to him. His fingers wandered up her sides to her breasts. Reaching underneath her hands that still held the letter, he cupped both globes and pinched her nipples.

Leslie dissolved with laughter. "Signed with all my love, Caroline." She looked at him. "Love? Caroline? But that hankie you carry has 'ES' embroidered on it."

ES—Emma Silvers. His body hummed when he thought of her. He had kept the handkerchief, her token, because returning it was virtually impossible afterward. He carried it with him, in his pocket, every day. Leslie found it last time he was there, and he refused to answer her probing questions about it.

He raised his hips, his arousal nudging her most sensitive part, drawing her attention just as he planned. She slickened, and he wanted to be back inside her. "Enough, Les."

"Oh Jack, Caroline is not who you want to hear from, is she?"

"Yes, she is." He lifted her hips and then lowered her, impaling her with his erection.

She moaned as the letter fluttered to the floor. He liked when she rode him, her breasts swaying above his face and her long black hair feathering his fingers as he held her hips.

"That's it," he coaxed, his bollocks tightening with each thrust. "Come for me."

Her head fell back, and she uttered a deep groan. He felt her sheath tighten around him.

A loud pounding thudded on the door. Jack and Leslie ignored it and continued.

"Fontaine!"

Jack's eyes rolled backwards as he pumped his cock higher.

"Fontaine, open up!"

"Go to hell, Stuart!" He bellowed. Leslie giggled—a sound that hitched with his next thrust into her.

The door opened slightly. "Jack, the Colonel wants you in his office," Jeb Stuart's voice came through the open door. "Now."

Jack stopped moving. "Now? I'm busy."

"I realize that but thought you'd like to know." Stuart muffled a laugh.

"Dammit!" Jack lifted Leslie off him and rolled off the mattress to grab his pants. Looking up, he saw the door was still ajar. "Thanks, you ass!" He kicked the door shut, hearing his fellow cadet's boots departing as his laughter echoed along the hallway.

Jack pulled the great coat tighter around his neck as the winter gale swept across the field on his way to the superintendent's home. Snow crunched under his boots, making him wish he was still in Leslie's bed, her hot body keeping him warm. Whatever the Colonel wanted him for, Jack couldn't fathom, but it'd better be worth it.

Still on his mind was the letter. It was one of many he had received from Caroline this school year. His last year at The Point. After spending the summer with Charles' family, he felt a part of them. It felt good, unlike how he regarded his own family. The birthday girl had taken every opportunity to be with him and Charles, dragging most of the other guests along with them. By the time he'd left in August, he had grown to enjoy Caroline's company and asked whether he could write to her. He grinned as she enthusiastically accepted. An odd compulsion prompted him to also ask Emma on one of the rare occasions when he saw her. After first hesitating, she told him yes.

Caroline wrote constantly.

Emma never wrote. And that bothered Jack more than he cared to admit.

Caroline was the prettier sister, the more outgoing and vivacious. Her lively letters reminded him of summer and carefree days. He'd even laughed out loud at some of her tales.

And that kiss. They played parlor games on numerous occasions, and several of them included a kissing component. Caroline knew every one of them. Her lips were soft and willing. Definitely made the game enjoyable, to say the least. But Emma never participated. Jack didn't think she was too young for them and knew she watched, hiding rather poorly in the shadows of the staircase. Either her parents wouldn't let her play, or, he suspected, it was because of Caroline. The woman wanted no competition. A wicked thought raced through him—he wanted to kiss Emma and see whether her plump little pink lips tasted as good as they looked. That thought made him huddle deeper in his greatcoat. The cold must be getting to him.

At the Colonel's house, the butler let Jack in, taking his coat and escorting him to the front parlor to wait. Still chilled from the walk, he went to the fireplace, trying to thaw. He heard steady footsteps coming down the wood-floored hallway to the parlor. On the heel of his sodden boot, Jack turned, standing at attention.

Brevet Colonel Robert E. Lee walked into the room with a bundle of papers in his arm. Dressed in his Army blue uniform, he took a seat at the large stuffed chair.

"Son," Lee stated warmly, pulling the side table in front of him and dumping his papers on it. "Take a seat."

Jack went to the armchair across from Colonel Lee and slowly sat. Lee had entertained the cadets, including Jack, in his house several times, but Jack had never been summoned alone, much less on a Sunday afternoon. Lee was a religious man, and, though recruits were required to attend Sunday services, Jack hadn't gone this morning. Instead he was with Leslie. Surely he wasn't being reprimanded over missing Sunday services.

Lee fumbled through his papers until he found what he needed. Withdrawing a sheet, he looked up at Jack. The Colonel, graduate of the class of 1829, made it through the Point without any demerits and was assigned to the prestigious Corp of Engineers. The perfect soldier. Jack fought the urge to tug at his collar. The intensity of the dark-haired Lee's eyes made him uncomfortable.

"Ahem," Lee coughed. "I didn't mean to interrupt your afternoon, Cadet Fontaine."

Jack's eyes closed. Damn, the Colonel must have been assessing his appearance and saw his hair was still a mess from romping with Leslie. Part of Jack feared that the man knew why he looked rumpled. Not good. Lee wasn't the type to condone his men laying with whores. Jack swallowed the knot in his throat.

"I understand, Jack, the Army has you to thank for Cadet Silvers' improved grade."

Jack frowned and then blinked. He had been called here because of Charles? The fact that the Colonel knew about Charles didn't surprise Jack. Lee was familiar with most of the cadets and felt at ease with them. Charles being a fellow Virginian helped, plus the fact that Jack and Charles were in the class of '54—the same class that included the

Colonel's son, George Washington Custis Lee.

"I have tutored him, yes, on occasion," Jack replied.

Lee gave him a half-laugh and settled back in his chair. "Jack, I called you here for another purpose, though I did want to say thank you for that. Charles is a good man and should do well—that is, if he can pass the final exams."

Jack sat more erect and looked straight ahead. "Of course sir, I have no doubt he will do so."

"Good, good," the Colonel stated. He brought the paper in his hand closer, reviewing it one more time. "Son, I understand your grades are starting to slip some."

Jack grimaced. He had allowed them to slip on purpose—not to failing level, but they weren't as high as they had been the previous three years. And it hadn't escaped Lee's notice. He was involved with his students and always investigated when their grades fell. He also wrote the students' parents to apprise them. No doubt he had written Jack's parents. "I don't think my grades will continue on a downward spiral, sir."

Lee smiled. "That's what I want to hear. But, there is a letter here I wanted to talk to you about. A letter the War Department has received from your father."

Jack felt a jolt of fear run up his spine. He gritted his teeth, preparing for what he knew would come. And the reason for his drop in grades...

"Your father requested that you be stationed at New Orleans Barracks upon graduation."

His heart thudded. He knew this would happen. That man would do anything to make him return home. Still sitting rigidly, Jack tightly clasped the arms of the chair.

Out of the corner of his eye, he saw Lee was assessing his reaction.

"I see," Lee finally said, folding the missive up again. "You realize, Jack, the Army is not prone to listen to the desires of family requests, despite any political pull they may have."

Jack looked to his commander, his gaze boring into Lee. His father had strong political influence with the senators from Louisiana and the Secretary of War, Jefferson Davis, a family acquaintance. No doubt the man had called in favors—damn! "Sir, I'd prefer not to be stationed there."

Lee laughed. "No, I suspect that's why you've let your grades drop. You'd rather go to Jefferson Barracks and west, fighting the Indians?"

"Yes, sir," he answered with quick determination.

With a slight shake of his head, Lee's gaze turned warm. "Well, Jack, pull your grades up. Despite your father's connections, I do not think New Orleans Barracks will be your home."

Jack stood. He felt drained as his tension began dissipating, and he fought to maintain his posture. "Thank you, sir." At Lee's nod, Jack turned and left.

July 1854

The class of 1854 assembled on the parade grounds, center field. Wearing dress uniforms, they stood in formation before the review stand. The other classes grouped in similar fashion behind them. Jack's stance was like the rest of the cadets, perfectly straight. He dared not look at the people watching from the sides of the field—families of the graduates. His mother was to be here, but he prayed his father wouldn't attend.

After the ceremony, the graduates were congratulated by Lee and several dignitaries from the government and the Army, with families applauding from the sidelines.

"We did it!" Charles exclaimed, slapping Jack on the back.

Jack smiled. Only by the skin of his teeth had Charles made it through exams. Stuart came up to them, a cigar already clenched in his teeth. With the formal festivities finished, he pulled his red silk neck scarf out of his collar and let the ends of it flutter in the wind. "Beauty" Stuart, in all his flamboyancy, grinned. Even with the man's numerous demerits, he had graduated thirteen in a class of forty-six. Jack had placed at number eighteen. Both ranked much higher than Charles at forty-fifth place.

"Gentlemen," he said, handing each a cigar. "To us, the Class of '54!"

"Huzzah!" Jack and Charles both exclaimed, accepting their cigars.

"Charles!" A distant yell. The men turned to find Caroline Silvers heading toward them, followed by her sister and parents.

Stuart backed away, and Jack wanted to join him.

Charles handed Jack his lit cigar and wrapped his arms around his sister, swinging her around in a circle.

"I'm so glad you could make it," he looked up at his family. "All of you."

"Congratulations, my boy," the elder Silvers stated, grasping his son's hand and shaking it.

"Oh, Charles, I'm so happy for you," his mother said, leaning to kiss his cheek.

Jack watched Emma. She stood back a bit. His eyes roved over her, drinking in the beauty she had become. Her auburn hair still retained copper highlights, her brown eyes were warm when she hugged Charles. She had grown a good six inches, he guessed, taller than her sister but still shorter than he and Charles.

When she turned to offer him her hand in congratulations, he saw her face had become more angular, with high cheekbones and freckles sprinkled across her nose. Her full, heart-shaped lips beckoned to him. Lips he so wanted to kiss...

"Congratulations, Mr. Fontaine," she said flatly, extending her hand.

"Thank you," he murmured, fighting the urge to bring her hand to his lips. Off to the side, he saw Caroline frown at him.

"He's Brevet Second Lieutenant, Emma," Charles corrected her.

Emma scrutinized Jack. "Really?" They stood for a minute, neither moving. Her hand in his, their eyes locked.

"Jack!" Another feminine voice called to him. He recognized it, and the spell between him and Emma broke. He released her hand reluctantly.

Emma quickly turned back to her family, who were deep in discussion.

He hated that she had dismissed him so quickly.

But deeply inhaling, he turned to find his mother, his sister Cerisa and older brother, Francois. "Mama," he greeted her with a smile.

"My dear Jack," she said, kissing his cheek.

"Brother," Francois said, extending his hand, a smile across his Creole face. Dark-haired with pale blue eyes, Francois looked like their father, Pierre Fontaine. His brother had followed their father in the family business, which was a relief to Jack. He couldn't abide his father's rules and rigid, old-fashioned beliefs, nor did he want anything to do with the family business. Jack had hated his father ever since the man had insisted he learn some of the family's "business practices." To avoid his father, he had attended West Point.

His refusal to obey his father's commands and his break from family tradition had alienated the two men. Jack's distance from his family for the last four years had been a relief. He'd rather deal with the Army than his father.

"Father?" Jack asked tentatively, trying to conceal his hope that Pierre had not come.

His mother, Marie, shook her head. "Jack, you know he's too tied up in contracts to take this long a journey." She smiled at him warmly, trying to convey by her expression that he should not be angry—or happy—because of his father's absence.

Jack smiled at her, taking her hands in his. "Of course, I understand. I'm so glad you are here." Pierre hadn't come because he believed Jack had refused his efforts to have him stationed closer to home. Jack couldn't help but laugh inwardly. His father must have finally realized he couldn't control his son any longer. Or so Jack prayed.

"War is cruelty. There is no use trying to reform it. The crueler it is the sooner it will be over."

~ Union General William Tecumseh Sherman

CHAPTER FIVE

July 1854

Windswept and Galahad flew up the dry dirt drive toward Rose Hill, dust clouding them and their riders on the last leg of the journey from West Point. As the two horses closed in, both riders pulled on their reins, sitting back in the saddles.

"I got you on that one, Jack," Charles cried triumphantly, throwing his leg over the saddle horn and jumping to the ground.

Jack gave his friend a wry grin and laughed. "Yes, I do believe you won—this time."

Charles grinned in return as he threw both horses' reins to the slave who waited at the front of the house for them. Jack trailed Charles as he threw the front doors open. "Momma! Momma where are you?"

He stopped at the double doors to the right and opened them. Feminine laughter drifted out as Jack's friend walked right in.

"Charlie, we didn't think you'd be home till tomorrow."

Jack slowly entered the front parlor as Charles hugged

his mother. His gaze went to the other person in the room, Emma. She sat on the settee, a book in her hand, smiling at her brother. Jack was drawn to her smile, and his mouth twitched. Her hair was pinned up, swept back, and held by tortoise combs, giving him a clear view of her lovely neck. The cream-colored gown striped with yellow made her bronze hair and the freckles on her nose most appealing. Her sister had written to him, but why hadn't Emma sent him a letter? At the very least, to answer the one he sent her.

"Charles?" The shrill voice came from the hall.

Charles turned. "Sis!" He opened his arms and Caroline hiked her skirts, running toward him.

"Caroline, control yourself," Margaret Silvers' voice was low, reprimanding her daughter for her outrageous behavior, but to no avail. Charles picked up his sister and twirled her around.

When Caroline's feet touch the floor again, she turned toward Jack. "Mr. Fontaine, how nice to see you again." She held out her hand for him to kiss as she grinned.

Jack smiled as he drew her hand to his lips. "Miss Silvers."

Out of the corner of his eye, he saw Emma roll her eyes. As Caroline fluttered her eyes at him, he released her hand and turned toward Emma.

"Miss Silvers," he greeted as he also drew her hand to his lips.

She regarded him. "Mr. Fontaine."

"Mother, when's dinner?" Leave it to Charles to want food right away.

"We shall eat now," Margaret said, offering her arm to her son. Caroline took his other arm and chattered constantly.

Jack looked at Emma, offering his arm to her.

It was obvious that Emma's contempt for Caroline's

behavior hadn't tempered. Maybe it was even a bit more evident now that she was older. It made Jack smile wider.

———∾∾∾———

Dinner at the Silvers' was a lively affair. Caroline's and Charles' voices grew louder as each course was served. And when John Henry joined in, his deep booming voice caused Caroline to talk louder still. It was the most animated time Jack had spent in ages. Not that the mess hall at The Point was quiet, but the cadets droned in comparison to this bright and noisy exchange. If he had gone home, the meal would have been painfully quiet and long, the friction between him and his father intensifying between courses. But dinner with the Silvers was entertaining.

Emma, though, hadn't joined the conversation. It took her brother several tries to get her involved, but her voice was stern, almost as though everyone was bothering her. During the meal, her manners were impeccable—delicately holding her fork and taking small bites. When her mouth closed around the tines, it lit a fire deep inside him. And when she swallowed a piece of meat, his mouth went dry. He shifted in his chair. The Army had better assign him soon.

———∾∾∾———

After dinner, some neighbors arrived. Emma sighed as she fiddled with the folds on her skirt. She'd have to spend even more time around Jack. Her gaze lingered on him for too long. No doubt Caroline would be on her about "staring" at Jack even though she knew Caroline wanted all his attention for herself. His and about half the county's.

Thank heavens Billy arrived, along with the Anderson twins and Abigail Somerton. The twins were a delight.

Timothy and Edward Anderson were tall and handsome. Their height was not as impressive as Jack's, nor did they have his charisma, but they were good natured, always in a festive mood. They were also Charles' friends, hailing from the Anderson farm just down the lane. Cotton growers, like the Silvers. Abigail Somerton was Caroline's age, a stunning redhead whose personality fit the stereotype— fun, outgoing and short tempered.

In the glow of the candlelit room, Emma marveled at how Billy had grown. A year older than Caroline, he tended to his father's farm with the hope that he'd inherit it when the elder Bealke passed. All those years working outside with horses had made him tan and muscular. His attentions were on Emma most of the time, and he was always there for her when her sister ranted on and on about any issue that she didn't like.

Emma pasted a smile on her lips. With her parents occupied, the younger generation had found a way to amuse themselves—parlor games. Emma, at seventeen, now was old enough to play them too. Standing there, she felt her legs begin to shake. Caroline had taught her how to play, but Emma worried that she wasn't talented enough. That's why she lost so often. Her hands felt clammy. She hoped her sister would keep her cruel, vulgar remarks to herself and not embarrass Emma about her inexperience.

Perhaps Jack would distract Caroline, making her forget about her sister. With a sigh of resignation, she wondered whether it was possible for him to get any better looking. In his black jacket, white shirt, sapphire blue waistcoat and black trousers, he was dashing. His broad shoulders, narrow waist and corded legs could hold any woman's attention. His dark brown hair was slightly tussled, and those green eyes glowed in the firelight. Emma stifled the excitement growing in her because of his presence.

"Now's the time we've been waiting for," the elder Silvers girl said. Her tone conspiratorial, she lowered her voice. "We all have forfeits to redeem. How shall we begin?"

Emma remained quiet. She had lost the game five times already, hence she had five forfeits. Caroline told her forfeits were the best part of the evening because for them to be satisfied, it usually involved kissing the men. Her stomach twisted in anticipation. Jack was here. He was part of the reason she lost the first three rounds in the conundrum game. But if Caroline picked that game, Emma would have to share his lips. No, she wouldn't do that. Emma opened her mouth to suggest a way to pay off the forfeits, but she found herself speechless. Kissing couldn't be that vulgar, could it?

Jack's eyes roved over her. His grin turned wicked when it reached the bodice of her pink and white silk gown. His eyes sparkled like emeralds.

"I suggest," Caroline began. "That we must kiss each corner of the room."

Abigail squealed. The men nodded. A tingle reached down Emma's spine. A kissing game. She was excited and frightened at the same time. Biting her lower lip, she watched her sister place Billy in one corner, Edward and Timothy in the next two corners and Jack in the last. They were the "corners" to be kissed in exchange for a forfeit.

Charles clapped his hands. "I do believe I shall forego kissing the corners." He laughed.

"No, Charles, you shall be our north star and stand here," Caroline stated, placing him in the center of the room. She smiled, pleased with herself.

Emma twisted the ribbon handle of her fan. Her forfeits numbered the highest in the room. Her sister stared at her. Would she make her leave? This game was meant for Caroline to kiss the Andersons and Jack. Emma lifted her chin and straightened her shoulders as she returned Caroline's stare. She would not leave just for her sister.

Caroline's lips pursed, and Emma heard the muffled stomp of her sister's foot, but when she wouldn't back down, Caroline sighed. Loud enough to be heard. So ill mannered, Emma thought, grinning. She won the right to stay.

Abigail went first. She started with Timothy. Caroline cheered her on, and when their lips met for a quick kiss, Caroline turned to Emma. "I know you're still a baby. This is your first experience with men. Just go up to them and give them one of your sweet baby kisses on their cheeks, you hear me?"

Emma's lips twitched. Order her around, would she? As always, Caroline wanted to be the center of attention. These last few months, her self-centeredness had grown. Of course, Emma had turned of age, her own debut not far away. If Caroline didn't get a man soon, Emma might surpass her. What a pleasant thought, though now, Caroline was first and trying to remain there. Emma smiled. "Yes, sister."

Caroline's eyes twinkled, and she grinned from ear to ear. "Wonderful. Now do be careful. Men often try to get more." She giggled and turned to go to Timothy.

Emma stood, waiting for her turn. She was in a good mood for her first time playing parlor games, and, despite her nerves now, she was determined to stay that way. How dare Caroline ruin it for her?

Abigail walked to her third corner, where Jack stood. Caroline stretched and gave Edward a kiss after he taunted her for trying to steal one. Both of them laughed at his accusation.

A knot tied in Emma's stomach as she slowly walked to Timothy.

"Do I get to be the first you kiss, Miss Emma?" He gave her a lopsided grin.

She stood before him, uncertainty washing over her.

"Come here, so you can kiss me," he coaxed.

She took a step and he met her by leaning closer. He had to be six feet tall, and she'd have to stand on her toes to reach his cheek. She pressed her hand on his arm and stretched upward, lightly kissing him at the corner of his mouth.

"Too afraid to kiss me? I do declare," he teased her.

She nodded with a small grin and went on to Edward. The twins were almost identical in looks and height.

Edward held out his hand, his lips curved in a devil-may-care grin. Without any hesitation, she leaned up and gave him a kiss.

Next was Jack. She walked to his corner, gazing into his glowing emerald eyes.

"Emma," he whispered.

She heard voices behind her. The others had already finished. She was the last. Turning her head slightly, she looked for Caroline. She caught a glimpse of her sister in her buttercup yellow dress, talking to Abigail, Charles and the twins.

"I'm right here, Emma," Jack said, drawing her attention back to him.

He was too handsome. She wanted to both kiss him and avoid him. A tingle in her belly spread up to her nipples.

When Jack smiled his devilish smile, Emma felt as though

she would turn into a puddle at his feet. Her mouth went dry as she stood there, frozen.

"Why didn't you ever write to me?"

The question rattled her, bringing her back to her senses. "I sent you a letter, but I never received one from you."

He quietly chuckled. "I sent you a letter, hoping you'd respond."

"I never received any correspondence from you," she said.

"Hmm, I never got yours either." His low drawl reached inside, soothing her. "But," he continued, "I believe you owe me a kiss."

She opened her mouth, but not a sound came out.

Jack stood still. She fidgeted. The silk dress clung to her breasts and her narrow waist. Her cage crinoline maintained a respectable space between them, regardless of how much he wanted her closer. He put his hands at the waist of her skirt and felt her tremble. She bit her lower lip. Oh, how he wanted to soothe that lip.

With a gentle tug, he pulled her closer. The motion unbalanced her, and her hands sought his arms. When she still didn't lean up to kiss him, he brought her even closer, his eyes fixed on her lower lip as her teeth released it.

He wouldn't meet her halfway. This could be the only time he'd have the advantage, and he didn't want to waste it. Because Emma's feet were slightly lifted from the floor, she gripped his arms tightly.

He brought her to him. As he kissed Emma, his tongue traced her lower lip before his mouth enveloped hers. He wanted her to open her mouth, and he prodded the crease between her lips, coaxing her with his tongue. She parted her lips but pulled her head back as his tongue invaded her mouth.

She tasted like strawberries and wine. It was an intriguing taste and he wanted more. She felt soft and warm against him. He knew he was pushing the limits of the game and propriety, but when he glimpsed her eyelashes feathered on her cheek, he almost growled. Abruptly, Jack released Emma and set her on the floor, his hands remaining at her waist. He could feel her shiver as she looked into his face, her eyes wide open. He smiled.

Within a second, she raced away from him as fast as she could in a ladylike manner. Jack smirked. She had enjoyed his kiss. With his head cocked to the side, he walked to the sideboard and poured himself a brandy.

When Emma had stepped away from Jack, she did everything within her power to control her nerves. Her lips felt swollen. His hands had left an impression on her waist—an impression that wasn't his to make. Her next and last corner was Billy's. He grinned at her as she tried to maintain a steady gait, but the memory of Jack's kiss tingled down her spine, making her feel hot and cold simultaneously. *Stop it!* She gave her head a small shake and stopped, inhaling a large breath before returning Billy's smile.

But she wanted to kiss Jack.

No, what he did was take advantage of the situation. How vulgar of him! Why did she crave more?

"Is something wrong, Emma?"

Conflicting thoughts clouded her mind, and she didn't realize she was already in front of Billy. Politely dismissing his concern, she said, "No, no, nothing is wrong."

Billy's head lowered slightly for her. "Kiss me, or pay a higher price forfeit."

Emma was curious about what the higher price might be, but, after Jack's advances, she ignored it. Composing herself, she met Billy's lips part way.

He didn't play with her lips nor press to enter her mouth. In a very gentlemanly manner, he gave her a quick kiss and bowed away. No fire came from his lips as it had from Jack's. If anything, she was gravely disappointed that Billy hadn't tried to kiss her like Jack had. She should have been glad, but she wasn't.

Like a good girl, she placed her hand on his sleeve and let him escort her back to the others. Caroline enticed them all to start charades. Jack was with them, a devilish grin on his face that Emma had the sudden urge to slap. When his glance fell her way, excitement raced through her veins, and she had the strangest sensation her nipples were tightening. Tamping down the fury of emotions Jack caused, she spent the rest of the evening at Billy's and Caroline's side and away from Jack.

✺

For the rest of the week, Jack spent a great deal of time with Charles hunting, fishing, horseracing and flirting with Caroline, who always appeared at the most opportune moment without Emma. Jack noticed Emma's absence from many of their amusements, and he was disappointed. He simply refused to believe she was purposely avoiding him. That kiss had lit a fire inside him. But without Emma there, Caroline had all of his attention. As sweet and demanding as he remembered, at least she liked him enough to be with him, and, after four years among only males, the company of the fairer sex was most enjoyable.

He knew his and Charles' assignments would arrive before long, ending their time with the ladies. A couple of weeks later, when a rider appeared at the house, Jack and Charles recognized his uniform and realized their freedom was over.

"Well, my friend, I do believe our furlough has just ended," Charles muttered.

The rider jumped off his mount and climbed the stairs to the porch, handing them the missive from his pouch. With a salute, he jumped back on his mount and left.

Charles broke the seal. "To Jefferson Barracks, 6th Infantry."

Jack took the orders. "Report to General Harney by July 30th." With a heavy sigh, he slumped onto the cast iron bench. "And I'm to go to Texas. Mounted Rifles."

Charles folded up the message and looked at Jack. "I'll go tell mother we'll need to leave tomorrow."

Jack nodded. With a weary snort, he stood up. It was time to move on and take up his position in life. Thankfully, his father's determination to have him assigned to Jackson's Barracks in New Orleans and home had failed. His lips curved up as he leaned against a pillar and gave a low chuckle. Old man Fontaine outfoxed by his own determination.

Pushing off from the column, Jack strode to the barn. He needed, no, wanted to ride. To enjoy his last day as a free man. He saddled Windswept and leaped onto the stallion's back. The horse snorted approval at the change in his routine and stomped his way out of the barn.

Jack headed him off at a gallop to the grove of trees near the pond where he had first met Emma that fateful day. He hadn't seen her much lately, and she wasn't in the mansion so he wondered whether she was out there.

Directing his mount toward the running stream, Jack

caught a flicker of white among the trees. A grin spread across his face. Surely that had to be Angel. Emma was close.

"Whoa, boy," he said as he sat back in the saddle, gently flipping his wrist down to control the horse. Throwing his leg over the saddle horn, he leaped to the ground, dropping the reins. Ahead of him, he found Emma in the shade on the edge of the deck though, this time, she hadn't taken off her shoes. She just sat quietly.

"Emma."

"Mr. Fontaine." Her voice was flat. She must have seen him coming.

"Don't you think we might be beyond proper names?"

She wouldn't look at him but dangled her booted foot above the waterline. "I suppose after you virtually ravished me there in front of everyone..."

"Ravished you? It was a kiss, Emma, and you liked it as well."

"Yes, but it was my first time, unlike you, who've probably sampled many women's kisses." He watched her face flush as she spoke the words.

"You make me sound like rogue," he commented with a chuckle. "I rode out here to let off..." *some steam.* But he left that unsaid.

She turned with a slight smile. "Did you ride out here to apologize or to try to take it beyond a kiss?"

He stepped forward. "Would you like me to?" The words were whispered, hopeful. Heaven knew his body craved more. He could feel himself tensing under her gaze.

She shook her head. "You'll be leaving soon, and I wouldn't dare threaten dear Caroline's chances."

"Actually, our orders just arrived," he stated as blandly as he could. He was aroused, although he knew it was for naught. "We'll leave for St. Louis on the morrow."

"Poor Caroline. You'll leave her here with me, won't you?"

"I'm not asking for her hand in marriage now, no," he answered. "I need to get the lay of the land in the Army, and being encumbered with a wife isn't the way I want to do it."

She shrugged indifferently.

He took another step closer, as though she was a doe poised for flight. And he had noticed her looking at her horse, which was behind him.

"Emma, I'd like you to write to me," he almost pleaded, sounding like a fool. Perhaps he was.

"Jack, really, why?"

He took one more step. She was within arm's reach. "Being in the company of only men, I find a letter from home soothes the soul."

Her nose crinkled as she thought about it. "Fine, I'll respond to every letter you send me."

He laughed openly. Behind him, he heard his horse nicker. "I'll write. You just make sure you are taking care of the posts, not Caroline."

He watched her exquisite neck as she swallowed, nodding agreement as she quickly moved beyond his reach. He laughed and followed her to her horse. He lifted her easily and placed her sidesaddle. She gave him a quick smile and nudged her horse on.

He stood there and watched her gracefully ride away. It hadn't taken long for him to realize that Caroline never gave Emma his letter, and she had kept the letter Emma had written to him. Because of Caroline's interference, each thought the other had chosen not to respond.

Cursing under his breath, Jack approached Windswept, picking up the reins and jumping onto the saddle. It was time he told Caroline the news. Ah, sweet Caroline, he mused. She was charming, petite and pretty but he wasn't getting married now. Not till he knew what frontier life was like. For Caroline's sake, he couldn't just take her away from civilization. And what of Emma? He shook his head. What was he thinking? For now, he would remain an unmarried soldier.

Squeezing his knees, Jack reined his horse back to the house. He knew the message he had for Caroline would not be well received.

"I claim not to have controlled events, but Confess plainly that events have controlled me."

~ Abraham Lincoln, 1864

CHAPTER SIX

Lieutenant Jack Fontaine rode out the next morning, beginning the long trip to Texas. The route was of his own making. He'd follow Charles to Louisville, then go on to St. Louis and Jefferson Barracks.

The November air felt cool and crisp. Windswept stomped his hooves, but Jack wouldn't turn around. His gloved hand gripped the reins as he tried to dampen the feeling of loss threatening to overtake him.

General Harney would not allow him to take his horse, claiming the animal was unfit for rough, dry Texas. That had been his first disappointment. The next one came as a delay to his departure because of a yellow fever epidemic in New Orleans. The week-long postponement had grated on his nerves. His alternate transportation would take him right past Bellefountaine—the empire of Jean Pierre Fontaine, his father. The longer it took to get past the tyrant's location, the more it ate at Jack's sanity. He would have ridden horseback to the Texas wasteland and his assignment just to bypass his home, but it would have been against orders. Regulations. *Damn!*

Jack finally turned to his trusted companion and pulled an apple out of his pocket. Windswept took the fruit, slobbering as he munched on it. Jack stroked the horse's neck, trying to stanch his sadness.

"Jack." A hand clapped down on his shoulder.

"Charles, come to see me off? I feel honored," he joked before they both broke into laughter.

"Ah, yes, to sail down the Mighty Mississippi," Charles sighed. "It'll bring you closer to N'Orleans."

Jack shifted. Yes, the river would take him to the Gulf and then to Galveston, Texas. If he could just find a way to avoid the banks of his father's plantation, he'd feel better. It was the last place he wanted to see.

"You see that pretty sister of yours, you tell her ol' Charles wishes her well," his friend chuckled.

Jack's eyebrows furrowed as he focused on Charles. At their graduation, Jack's mother, sister and brother were in attendance, his father thankfully absent. But the introduction of Charles to his sister had been, well, brief. For him to remember her now..."My sister, you say?"

"Well, you'll be down about there," Charles shuffled.

"Yes, and I be prayin' we've no reason to stop." His voice was harsh. "I don't plan on visitin' Bellefountaine anytime soon."

Charles frowned. "I don't get you, Jack. You've barely seen your folk in the last four years. You never talk about home or..."

"Nor do I intend to. Charles, just drop the subject."

His friend's eyebrows rose, but he kept quiet. Good, Jack thought. He hoped the old man had no knowledge of where he was going, but Jack didn't think he'd be that lucky. Old bastard...

"...doubt there'll be much for ya' there."

Jack's mind snapped back. What was Charles talking about? "Whatever are you babblin' on about?"

"Women!"

Only Charles would measure an assignment using the availability of the fairer sex as his guide.

"I just said I doubt you'll have any pretty ones in ole Texas! Nothing but Mexicans and savages. And I'll be here, with all the lovelies," he patted his chest, smiling smugly.

Jack rolled his eyes. "I think I'll be fine, but thanks for the concern."

"How many pretties did you get to write to you, Jack?"

He smirked. "A few."

"My sisters too?"

"Charles," he warned.

"Oh, I don't be doubtin' ya', not at all. You know Caroline'll be writing," her brother laughed. "But little Miss Em? Uh oh! You sly fox!"

Jack turned again to Windswept, patting his muzzle. "Charles, leave me be."

Charles' laughter rang loud, and Jack couldn't help but join him. He'd miss the Virginian.

The whistle from the steamer blew as the boat approached the dock below. Its shrill tinny sound quieted the two friends. Looking at the paddle wheeler, Jack sighed, and he stroked Windswept one more time. The horse lowered his head as Jack pulled him closer to whisper into the animal's ear.

"What you be tellin' my new mount?" Charles queried. Did Jack hear tension in his friend's voice?

He laughed and tossed Charles the reins.

"Just told him goodbye," he said as he shoved on his hat and picked up his bag and rifle. With a nod to Charles, he went down the path that would ultimately lead him to Texas.

Jack's luck had held after all. The paddle wheeler went past his father's plantation and onto New Orleans without stopping. From there, he took another boat to Galveston. Reaching his destination, Jack didn't find it at all appealing. It was a dry dirt town, its only amenity an elaborate billiard hall and saloon adjacent to the Tremont House. His mood lifted upon finding his old cadet mate and friend, "Beauty" Stuart, seated at a table, flirting with the ladies.

"They'll let just anyone into these places, huh?" Jack nudged the Virginian.

"Fontaine! Great to see ya' here," Stuart exclaimed, removing his plumed hat from a chair. "Off for the Rifles, heh?"

Jack took the shot of whiskey Stuart offered and downed it, enjoying the burn of the alcohol after the numbness of traveling for days. "Yessur."

"Good, good," Stuart abruptly stood. "Let's be getting a move on. We've got to git you a mount, boy. The Rifles are a ride, to be sure."

"Really? Where we goin'?"

"Heard they're about four hundred and fifty miles west of Laredo, in Indian country." The Virginian's mouth broke into a broad smile.

Jack laughed. He was beginning to feel at home already.

With a deep breath, Emma fought to keep from throwing the needlework into the fireplace. *Dratted design.* Tatting handkerchiefs was the last thing she wanted to do today. She'd rather be out riding, but in the last few months, her mother had kept her busy, "learning how to be the mistress of the house." *Posh!* Pulling the needle through the linen, she found the thread to hook and yank out...

"Emma, be careful," her mother scolded as she peered over her shoulder. "If you take too much, it will pucker."

Caroline's snickering drifted to Emma, and Margaret Silvers frowned at her.

"Now, Caroline," her mother admonished. "It took you a time or two to accomplish this. It is Emma's first time..."

"She'll never get it," Caroline stated.

Emma glared at her.

"Caroline Ann," her mother's stern voice stopped Caroline's giggle.

Emma didn't give a hoot about a handkerchief with fancy holes in it. But she bent her head over the cloth again and looked for a thread. Losing her count, she glanced up. Her mother was talking to Sally, and her sister sat on the edge of her seat, working diligently. *Wasn't that a joke?*

With a sigh, Emma put down the linen and stretched her fingers, giving her a chance to look at the clock. It was almost four. Where was Mathias with their post? She'd swear...

Her hand went to her mouth. She hadn't uttered a sound but feared she might. A glance at the window showed how pretty it was outside, and being cooped up in this parlor with handwork was driving her mad. Oh, where was Mathias? She hoped there was mail for her.

Jack Fontaine. She swore she wouldn't fall under his spell. He was only after Caroline. But he had written her two weeks ago, telling her of his trip to Texas. He'd described the rolling lands of Tennessee, the big river city, St. Louis and Jefferson Barracks where Charles was—with Jack's horse, he complained—and then the riverboat trip south. It sounded so exciting. Things she'd never see...particularly when her role was to tat linen cloths.

"Ma'am," the low voice of Mathias came from the doorway.

Caroline's head popped up from her needlework at the same time Emma's did.

"Good boy." Margaret took the bound letters from him. "Why don't you go see Merry, tell her to give you a biscuit?"

"Yessum," the boy said as he scurried out of the room as fast as his bare feet would take him.

Emma started to rise but stopped as her mother looked at the floor where the slave boy had been standing.

"Now, you see here, Sally, that boy brought in all that—"

"Momma," Caroline interrupted. Emma stifled the hysterical laugh forming because of her sister's impatience.

Margaret Silvers' hazel-colored eyes narrowed on her two daughters as she inhaled, as though to take in more air to give her voice volume. "Caroline, there's no need to be rude."

Caroline's mouth twisted, and she stomped her foot on the floor. "You was only talkin' to Sally, momma."

"Still..."

Emma slowly stood, reluctantly backing her sister's stand. This was one of the few times she'd side with her because she, too, wanted to know whether she had mail.

Her mother's lips thinned. "You two will sit and return to your needlework until I am ready to go through the mail."

Emma slumped down onto the settee and picked up her project. She heard Caroline *harrumph* loudly, plopping onto her chair, the cotton of her dress and petticoats crushing loudly against the satin-covered seat.

"I don't know what *you're* hoping for," Caroline muttered to her sister.

Emma's nerves were too wound up for her to sit calmly as Caroline began talking about Jack Fontaine marrying her. But despite Emma's resolve to remain quiet, she snarled, "A letter. What else would I be lookin' for?"

Caroline replied viciously, "You really don't think my darlin' Jack will be writin' to you? Heavens, when he was here, you said barely a word to him. In fact, you were downright rude, avoidin' him and such."

Emma swallowed the knot forming in her throat. Caroline was right. She had avoided him after that kiss. But that was only for self-protection. If Caroline wanted him, Emma knew she didn't stand a chance.

"Girls," their mother interrupted. Margaret pulled the ribbon holding the letters as she began to rifle through them. "Caroline," she said, handing a letter to her. "And Emma."

Emma took the envelope from her mother and quickly opened it.

Dear Miss Emma, I write in hopes that you are in good health, the scrawled handwriting stated. With a quick glance down, her heart fluttered at the signature, *Your good & obedient servant, Jack Fontaine, Lieutenant, U. S. Mounted Rifles.*

Clutching the letter to her chest, Emma felt excitement course through her. She opened her eyes to Caroline's spiteful look. She knew that face. "Momma, may I be excused?"

Margaret smiled and nodded. "Yes, I believe we'll return to your project later."

Emma took the letter and left for her room. Dumping her sewing on the dresser, she went to the window seat, opening Jack's letter again.

Dear Miss Emma,

I write in hopes that you are in good health. I made it to Texas

and my unit in good time. The air here is much drier than Virginia.
Vast lands of open ranges with little foliage to break the heat of
the sun.

I have a new mount, Goliath. He stands at over sixteen hands
and is coal black. He'd tower over your pretty Angel. But he is
good, well natured and has the agility for this land.

We have had several run-ins with the savages. They raid the
settlers here something fierce...

With a resounding thud, Emma's door flew open and hit
the wall. Caroline stood there, her face grim. She walked in
without asking and sat on Emma's bed, glaring at her.

"Just what do you think you're doing?"

Emma snorted. "I'm reading my letter. What in heaven's
name got you into such a snit?"

"You got a letter from my Jack, didn't you?"

Caroline's snarl made it perfectly clear to Emma she was
to stay away from him. She folded the letter as she stood,
gritting her teeth. Caroline's possessiveness had only gotten
worse since Charles and Jack had left. In fact, any man that
came to the house was for Caroline only, she stated.

"He wrote me a letter, yes," she stated carefully.

"You are not to write back to him." It was a cold
command.

Emma responded, "He asked me if he could write to me
and for me to write to him. There's no harm in that."

"Of course there is," Caroline spat. "He's not for you."

Emma frowned. "Caroline, it's just a letter."

Her sister stood, fire in her eyes as she tried to intimidate
Emma. "Perhaps, but don't be thinkin' he'll want you."

"Want me? This isn't a ball or, or courting, Caroline."

Caroline straightened her shoulders, her hands clenching.
"No, it's not and don't push him for more. He's too old for
you. And when his time in the West is finished, he'll be

asking for me—not you!" She threw her chin in the air and stormed out of the room.

Emma sank down again on the cushioned window seat. Now she knew why he had told her not to let Caroline take her posts or retrieve them. Caroline's animosity made her shudder. Despite the avid attention of most men who came to the house and Caroline's flirting ways, she'd decided Jack was the one. To her, Emma was a threat. Whatever happened to the sister she'd played with as a child? What would the woman do to keep Jack to herself, she wondered?

<hr>

Spring 1855

Jack sat back in his saddle, chewing a piece of straw as he took a last look at the terrain of western Texas. In his few months there, he'd dealt with Indians, or "mustangers" as Jeb called them, with their uncanny ability to capture and train wild horses to trade for Army bread. The beauty of the land was inspiring, from the colorful fauna to the low and vast sky at night. The cry of a panther sent a chill down a man's spine when he was resting on the range. There was never a dull moment, but despite the work, the loneliness of the frontier seeped into him.

His friendship with Jeb was particularly beneficial that spring when Secretary of War, Jefferson Davis, organized the 1st and 2nd cavalries. Jack was the 2nd lieutenant of the 2nd Cavalry, under the command of Col. Albert Sidney Johnson and Jack's former West Point commander, Lt. Col. Robert E. Lee. Jack knew it had been Lee's influence that opened the position for him on the roster of the 2nd. Another step away from his father's influence, or so Jack hoped. Deep in his gut, he knew his father had maneuvered to bring him to

New Orleans, but the new cavalry units had the Secretary of War's hand involved, and his father had no influence in the Mississippian's sphere.

Charles was ecstatic when Jack and Jeb arrived in St. Louis. Although Charles reluctantly admitted he hadn't made the cut for the Mounted Rifles, he didn't seem envious of Jack's move to the cavalry. However, Charles bemoaned the tedious affair of being a foot soldier, stuck eight miles away from the bustling town of St. Louis.

Time together at Jefferson Barracks was short for Jeb, Jack and Charles. Jeb's unit moved its headquarters to Ft. Leavenworth, Kansas in the summer of 1855. Jack's unit remained at Jefferson Barracks. The 2nd Cavalry was often referred to as Jeff Davis' Own or Jeff Davis' Pet because the Secretary of War had handpicked its officers, many of them West Point graduates.

Jack finally felt as though he fit in. William J. Hardee of Georgia, graduate of the Point in 1838, was an excellent teacher of cavalry tactics. Earl Van Dorn of Mississippi, who graduated with Longstreet, grew up just across the river from Jack's family. The man himself had become Jack's savior when things at Bellefountaine turned ugly and Jack needed to escape his father's rule. Van Dorn's connections had helped Jack get into the Point, and now, serving under him in the 2nd Cavalry, Jack meant to show him how valuable his help had been.

But his stay at Jefferson Barracks did not last long after Jeb's departure. The 2nd Cavalry was sent to western Texas soon after.

"Thought you enjoyed Texas," Charles chortled at dinner.

Jack grunted. The next day, his regiment was to leave. He downed another shot of whiskey, savoring the heat along his throat. "Texas is fine. Just, I don't know..."

Charles eyed him above the rim of his own glass. "You mean to tell me that you're finding Army life not the challenge you thought?"

"It's not that," Jack replied. "The savages always set the schedule and change their location, so the challenge of staying on top of them and curtailing the violence is hard enough." Frankly, it was damn lonely out there, but he wouldn't say that to Charles. Being in St. Louis meant his mail came on a more regular basis. In Texas, it was anybody's guess when it'd arrive, particularly on the uncivilized plains.

"Oh, I get it," Charles snickered. "You'd be worried about missing Caroline."

Jack quickly downed another shot. Caroline. Missing her wasn't possible. He had a saddlebag full of letters from her. They made his nerves prickle at times. He was glad to get mail. It never failed to break the monotony—the dull routine of drills, inspections and time that filled the day. Even gambling got old. But Caroline's long stories of every little thing she did could grate on a man's nerves.

"No," he laughed. "I don't think I'll have the chance of missing her. Her letters always come through, like a homing pigeon." He shook his head.

Charles cocked his head. "Emma?"

Jack quickly looked away. Emma. Her letters were short, very rare and hardly personal. Not happy about her brevity, he couldn't really complain either. He had plenty of other beauties who wrote. No, the problem with Emma was she invaded his dreams. They had shared only one kiss, but the impression of it and the feel of her in his arms remained strong. How many times had he awakened from dreams of her naked, in his arms? He even tried to wash the desire away with whiskey and whores, but that didn't work. All he got for it was a bad headache and frustration.

Charles gazed at him. With a half smirk, Jack replied, "No, I hear from her, too. Not as much, mind you. Perhaps it's melancholy."

"You? Melancholy? I doubt it," Charles chuckled. "Thought you never wanted to go home again."

His eyebrows raised. Charles had figured it out. Jean Baptiste Fontaine had destroyed that longing years ago. Jack was just surprised he'd been that transparent about his feelings.

"Jack, both my sisters like you," Charles continued. "I'm sure you'll hear from them again. And perhaps you'll get lucky and get leave or reassigned back East." He poured a shot for Jack and himself. Pushing the glass to his friend, Charles raised his. "To freedom!"

Jack raised his glass and downed the amber liquid. Perhaps if he drank enough tonight, he'd sleep without dreaming of Emma, but he doubted it.

**"I, John Brown, am now quite certain
that the crimes of this guilty land will
never be purged away but with blood."**
~ John Brown, 1859

CHAPTER SEVEN

Harper's Ferry, Virginia, 1859

Robert E. Lee stood behind his desk at his home in Arlington, organizing for his return to Texas. His leave in 1857 to head back East because of the death of his father-in-law, George Washington Parke Custis, had extended into two years of various assignments for the War Department. But now, his time home was over. As much as he hated to leave his wife, he had his orders.

He wiped his brow on the warm October morning, supervising his slaves with the luggage. Parks, one of Custis' slaves that Lee had inherited, dropped the trunk, spilling papers, ink and books across the parquet floor. The man glanced at his new owner before slowly bending over the mess, his movements sluggish. Anger flared through Lee. His distaste of the peculiar institution of slavery grew daily, especially with those slaves he inherited from Custis. The lot of them had to be the worst he'd ever seen, rebellious beyond reason, despite Lee's care of them.

"Reuben," he said, straining to keep his voice even.

The elder slave appeared at his side. "Yes, massa."

"Parks here needs to be reminded of his position," he stated loudly.

Reuben retained his stance, not flinching from his owner's command, but both knew Parks would never change, no matter how many chores or whippings he got. The abolitionist who had come to Parks, Reuben and the other Custis slaves spewing trash about them being free because of their master's death had left an indelible impression on them. And Lee had spent the last twelve months showing them otherwise. Reuben, however, knew his place. He gave a curt nod and grabbed Parks roughly, pulling him out of the room.

Slavery left a bad taste in Lee's mouth and he so wanted to throw all his darkies out, let the world treat them however it would, but he couldn't. He sighed heavily. It was his duty to care for these ill-begotten ignorant people, but he hated it.

"Samson, get this," he pointed to the mess on the floor.

"Yessum."

"Colonel Lee?" A voice from the hallway drifted in.

Lee turned. "Jeb Stuart! What a pleasure to see you."

Jeb tilted his head, the feather from his overly plumed hat hiding the face of his compatriot.

Coughing loudly through the plume, Jack waved the hat off Stuart's head. "Pardon me, Beauty."

Lee smiled. "Jack Fontaine. To what do I owe this honor, gentlemen? Is there anyone left in Texas, or am I to see the 2nd here as well?"

Stuart's mouth thinned. "No sir, we've orders from Washington for you."

Lee took the slip and opened it. He inhaled deeply and looked at his two former students. "Gentlemen, I'm to leave immediately, so I beg pardon for the departure." He grabbed his hat and started for the door.

Jack stepped next to him. "Sir, we'd like to go with you on this."

"Yes, perhaps as your aids," Jeb offered.

Lee stopped and gave them an appraising glance. Yes, he remembered them well. Both good Southerners and the type he could use for this. "You gentlemen know what's afoot?"

"Yessir," Jack answered sharply. "Captain John Brown and his group have taken Harper's Ferry Arsenal. They claim to be willing to arm slaves and help them fight for freedom."

Lee caught the distain in Jack's voice, sounding as if this was a minor incident. "Sir, you do realize he's stolen federal property."

"Yessir, I do."

"And his type will bring havoc to the nation over our God-given right?"

Slavery—a peculiar institution—godsend of the labor-needy South but abhorred by abolitionists in the North. Lee knew he wasn't alone in hating it, but, without a viable alternative for laborers, slavery remained. It was costly for Lee and most of his fellow Southerners, yet they wouldn't let the lot go free without some form of compensation, a notion abolitionists refused to address.

"Yessir."

"You realize it is our duty to save these peoples' souls by helping them through this life and in the ways of the Lord," Lee pushed. He had to make sure the Louisianan before him, who he knew had some aversion to going home, understood that slavery was God's answer to the black race.

Jack swallowed. Slavery. The biggest political nightmare

in the United States. He hated it. It held back their great nation from modern thinking. Jack had seen this time and time again. His father was a walking example and worse. To keep everything the way it had always been. Tradition, patriarchy, all the trappings of feudal England gripped the South, and Jack swore it would kill it.

But men like the Colonel considered it to be righteous. Jack felt the strength of Robert Lee's beliefs, and who was he to deny the man's integrity? His respect for the man outweighed the arguments of Northerners who knew nothing of the South. Yet, did Jack want slavery to continue? Tradition?

Ever since that spring years ago, of himself obeying his father's command and the look on Fanny's face, the fear...

"Yessir, we both do," Jeb answered for him.

Jack knew Lee's eyes remained on him. He had taken too long to answer. It should have come naturally to him to agree. After all, he was a Southerner. A shudder from the past swept over him, of that day behind his home on the Mississippi. After all these years, he prayed that being away from home and his father, the nightmare would fade, but he felt Fanny's fear invade him again. He hated himself for following his father's orders, like the good son he was told to be. But the act had destroyed any love he had of family.

Jeb flicked his hat into Jack's face. The feather hit his nostrils, and it snapped him back to the present. "Yessir. Always." His late reply brought a flash to Lee's eyes. Anger? Distrust?

"Then gentlemen, we must depart."

— ❦ —

Caroline sat on the edge of the bed and stretched her legs, flexing her feet. She sighed. As she arched herself, her blonde hair cascaded down her naked back and tickled the hairs on Billy's outstretched arm.

"You come here," he growled, his arm snaking around her waist to pull her back to him.

She giggled when he leaned over her shoulder and tugged on her earlobe with his teeth.

"Billy, I do declare, you're getting better and better," she teased him.

He rose above her, kneeling over her body. Ah, yes, Billy'd grown to be so luscious, she could barely contain herself with him. All those years of working on his daddy's farm made him lean, his muscles hard like marble.

"I'm going to have you, Caroline, till you scream my name again," he growled, his eyes dark.

Caroline's mouth twitched. Her hand touched his chest and skimmed over his toned stomach down to his hard, thick member. When she wrapped her fingers around it and squeezed, he closed his eyes and held his breath. Oh, she loved this. He was so easy. All it took for him to come running was a note to meet her wherever she said and at whatever time. Her power over him gave her such satisfaction and was worth more than those dreary housekeeping lessons her mother tried to teach her. She had learned through Billy that she could control men just by tweaking her finger, promising them she was theirs.

Billy grabbed her hand and gave her the look saying he was in charge. She laughed, because she knew better.

"No, little missy, you are going to scream for me," he stated again as he bent over her, kissing down her stomach to the spot between her legs.

Caroline loved to scream for him. At this little shack in the woods, near the edge of her family's property, no one would hear them. Only her slave, Tilly, knew she was here. The little ninny even acted as their lookout. And she was good about it, or she knew Caroline would have her whipped if she failed.

She gasped when he licked the folds of her sex. Spreading her legs farther, she sighed, "Yes, Billy, harder."

He inserted one finger, then two while his tongue played with her swollen nub. When she moaned, he looked up at her. "Aren't you the good sister, helping me to learn all this?"

She laughed. She had said she'd teach him how to please a woman so he'd be good for Emma. But as the "lessons" continued, she knew he wanted her and not Emma in his bed. A tiny voice inside reveled in satisfaction because he favored her now, but a bit of guilt tugged at her. She loved the attention she was receiving from all her men callers, but she wanted to wed Jack. Until then, Billy could fulfill her needs. Too bad she didn't want him all the time...

He suddenly stopped and moved up to nibble her breasts. He'd ignited such a fire inside her she didn't want it to end. But when he bit her nipple, her eyes flew open.

"Ah, you see, you're in my clutches," he whispered and turned her over. He lifted her pelvis and shoved a pillow under her. He nudged between her legs, his manhood resting on the crest of her anus.

"Billy, what are you doing?"

"You'll like it," he growled, spreading her cheeks and sliding his shaft into her slick canal, filling her. She gasped. He felt different inside her this way, with her hips tilted higher and her face buried in the mattress. His hand wrapped around her hair, pulling her head back.

"Oh, yes, yes!" she cried.

His free hand squeezed her hip. "Say it. Say my name."

"Yes, Billy, oh yes," Caroline screamed and shattered against him.

"Oh, Caroline!!!" he shouted as he climaxed and withdrew, his member falling onto her buttocks and spilling his seed across them.

Emma sat on the window seat in her room, staring outside at nothing. To avoid another afternoon of embroidery work, she had claimed she had a headache. Who cared what her pillowcases looked like? Nearly twenty, she supposed she should be building her trousseau in happy anticipation of marriage. But in fact, she feared she might never wed.

Caroline would get married of course. She had several gentlemen callers, and Emma cringed every time one of them showed up to fawn over her sister. Naturally, Caroline enjoyed their ludicrous endearments. She was the pretty Silvers girl, so petite and dainty, always outshining Emma.

Several of Caroline's callers paid their respects to Emma as well, though she knew they did so only to be polite. Billy was her only friend and companion. They knew so much about each other, having grown up together. Billy, four years her senior, would have a substantial farm from his father's holdings, and he had been tutored for the last few years, so he was learned as well. If he asked for her hand, there was no reason to turn him down. She sighed. No reason except for the green-eyed man who wrote to her periodically. Whenever she felt Billy would be a good husband for her, Jack invaded her dreams, and she awoke tense and excited.

But as Jack's letters became more infrequent, her dreams about him did too. Granted she hadn't responded to him quickly. It was hard to concentrate on writing with all the tension brewing around her. The meetings her father held and the men ranting in the library about politics grew so loud and vicious they could be heard through closed doors.

A light sound at Emma's door interrupted her thoughts. "Enter."

The door opened, and Annie, her slave, slipped in. In her hands, she clutched the *Richmond Post*. "I's got it 'fore your daddy done seen it," she said slyly, handing the newsprint to Emma.

Emma took the paper and opened it. The headline covered half the page.

Execution of John Brown & Scenes
at the Scaffold
December 1, 1859

She read the article, her blood racing as fear rose. The fact that some deranged man could think of arming slaves, believing they'd give their blood for freedom appalled her. She glanced up at Annie. The slave was making herself busy, straightening the perfume bottles and knickknacks on the dresser. Was Annie miserable being a slave? She received everything she needed to live—food, clothing, shelter—wasn't that enough?

Emma opened the paper again and read the articles about the upcoming elections. The Southern viewpoint of states' rights aligned with Emma's beliefs, although she didn't fully understand the arguments for and against. Who could she ask? With Charles gone, her father never discussed politics with the family, and the few times she asked why his meetings were so loud, he soothed her by saying they were dealing with issues beyond her worries. Perhaps if she wrote Charles...

A flicker of activity outside the window caught her eye. She turned in time to see Caroline's buggy returning from town. Though she claimed she would take Emma, Caroline told her she'd no doubt find it boring and useless because she was going to the apothecary. Emma frowned and looked at the clock. Four hours at the apothecary? It wasn't that far away...

Hooves pounding down the lane called her attention back to the window. It was Billy. She smiled. Folding the newsprint, she handed it back to the slave.

"Now, you be careful takin' that back."

"Yessum," the slave dutifully bowed and left.

Billy's arrival was well timed. She could ask him more about the debate she'd read about without worrying he'd tell on her. And it'd be nice to have some company. That is, if Caroline would stay away...

"We have shared the incommunicable experience of war. We felt, we still feel, the passion of life to its top. In our youths, our hearts were touched by fire."

~ Oliver Wendell Holmes

CHAPTER EIGHT

Charles City, Virginia, May 1861

It had happened. The nation was now divided. Captain Jack Fontaine of the 2nd US Cavalry pulled the reins, sitting back in the saddle and bringing Goliath to a halt. He looked at the rolling green land as a wave of despair threatened to wash over him. Shifting in the saddle, he removed his hat and ran his fingers through his hair. Did he dare continue to the Silvers' home? Would he be welcomed?

His mission in January had been simple. Escort the new president, Abraham Lincoln, to Washington, DC. Threats to the newly elected official demanded a covert entry into the capital city. On the trip back East from Illinois, Jack got a close look at the changing nature of the country. South Carolina had seceded in December, soon to be followed by Georgia, Alabama, Mississippi, Florida, Texas and his home state, Louisiana. News reports revealed the rapid deterioration of the nation as men left the military and government to head home and offer their services to the newly formed Confederacy. He shook his head at the idiocy of many of his brethren in the Army for resigning their commissions for this farce. But as the attack on Fort Sumter showed, it wasn't a farce after all.

Despite the upheaval in the newly elected government and the secession of some states, a message from his father had reached him in Washington. His father demanded he come home. Jack simply wadded the note and threw it into the fire. He would not go to Louisiana, but he had requested leave. He felt the need to return to Virginia. Caroline's letters sounded panicked, or maybe overwhelmed, with the idea of Virginia leaving the Union. Emma wrote nothing, and that irked him. And what of Charles? He knew his commander, Robert E. Lee, was waiting for Virginia to make a decision. Jeb told him over the holidays at Jefferson Barracks that he'd go with his state and had already sent his wife home.

But what would he, Southern-born Jack Fontaine, do? His loyalty was to the country as a whole. It was an obligation enforced by an oath he'd made when entering West Point. But as the middle states teetered, he felt pulled to consider leaving to support the South, and the internal conflict unnerved him.

From his mount, he could see Rose Hill, and all looked normal. The slaves working in the fields, the horses in the pasture and smoke rising from the house chimney. The scene he remembered from years ago, when he was only a youth on leave from West Point. But now he was twenty-five and supposedly mature. He snorted. Goliath heard him and shifted, lifting his head from the grass, ears forward and alert.

Enough musing, Jack, ride on.

He squeezed his legs and the horse stepped forward.

Concentrating on the fabric, Emma pinned another tuck in the bodice and felt the metal poke into flesh.

"Ouch! Thought you knew how to at least pin!" Caroline screeched.

Emma bit back a grin. "I do. Now, hold still or I might stick you again."

Her sister groaned but stood still. Emma restrained herself because giggles threatened to take control of her, and she would definitely drive the pin into flesh. How she got involved in this was beyond her reckoning. But Caroline pleaded with her to fix the tear in the silk ballgown. Taking a deep breath, Emma held the fabric together and pinned.

"There, now, let me get my thread," she said as she reached for the spool. Emma wasn't thrilled to be doing this, but after working with needle and thread the last couple of years, her skills had improved, making her the more talented of the two at sewing. Sadly, neither of them would ever be as good as their mother. After the woman had died last winter, Emma reluctantly found herself the mistress of the house and was saddled with all the responsibilities that had been her mother's. It was irksome because this was the year she was to come out. But Caroline had no skills for running the house, so it had fallen to Emma. Actually, it wasn't that Caroline lacked the skills—she had them but avoided using them. In that regard, she excelled, which irritated Emma to no end.

"Why, look what I see before me," the male voice from behind said.

Caroline jumped and squealed before Emma had a chance to turn.

"Charles! You're home!" Caroline raced to her brother.

Emma set her sewing needle down and smiled at him. "Charles, whatever are you doing here?"

"And you're not wearing that dreaded Yankee blue!" Caroline added.

Charles laughed. "No, no. I'm going to offer my services to the good old state of Virginia."

"Whatever do you mean?" Emma had read the newspaper headlines. She knew of Fort Sumter's surrender and the new president's demand for the states to ante up militia to put the rebellion down. But that was the last she'd learned.

"Why, we're all seceding, sister," he drawled.

Caroline bounced again. For being older, she behaved like such a child.

"Father is in the library," Emma quietly said.

"How's he holding out?"

She shrugged. Their father felt the loss of their mother more keenly and often retreated to his library for days at a time. Only immediate business ever got his attention now. The attack on Fort Sumter and its aftermath had made him a little more visible but only because Emma persuaded him to meet with the neighbors who visited, worried about the state and such. But she feared for his health. He looked gaunt and sickly in color. Maybe with Charles home, he'd get better. She hoped.

Charles patted her shoulder. "I know it's been hard on you."

Her vision blurred, and she felt slightly relieved, as if his presence would make everything all right. But that was just an illusion because the flames of war licked across the land, and, despite everything, she knew her brother would fight. A knot of fear formed in her throat, and it took all her strength to swallow it.

"Massa Charles," their butler Sammy interrupted. "You've gotta visitor."

Charles frowned. "We expecting someone?"

Emma blinked her tears aside and shook her head. "No."

"Charles."

Emma flinched. She knew that voice.

"Jack! Good God, man, what a surprise," Charles exclaimed. His voice was nearly drowned by Caroline's scream of excitement as she lifted her skirts and ran to Jack.

Jack laughed and picked her up, giving her a peck on the cheek and setting her down.

Emma stood stock still, her senses reeling. Jack Fontaine had just sauntered into her house and back into her life. She scanned him from head to toe, relishing the sight of the man she couldn't completely shake from her dreams. His dark hair gleamed in the sunlight, emerald-colored eyes dancing in amusement. He wore civilian clothes of brown jacket, white shirt, green waistcoat and dark sable pants. Tan from the last few years in the sun and riding for the cavalry, his face was more chiseled, shoulders still broad, waist narrow and legs long and muscular. When Emma glanced back up to his face, she found him staring right back at her, a wicked smile on his lips. She felt the heat rising up her neck to her cheeks, embarrassed to have been caught looking him over.

"Miss Emma," he said softly.

"Jack, what a surprise," she replied, trying to recover her composure, but he had caught her in the middle of the day, wearing nothing more than a plain workdress. It wasn't suitable for receiving company. She smoothed the worn skirt. Well, what did he expect, appearing at this hour without any warning? She straightened her shoulders.

"Caroline, why don't we allow the gentlemen a few minutes," she said. Caroline had looped her arm through Jack's as she chattered rapidly.

Caroline gave her a nasty look, daring her to push the issue.

Charles laughed. "Jack, come, let's get my father and open a bottle, huh?" he said, tugging him away from Caroline.

———◆◆◆———

Jack exhaled a sigh of relief at his warm welcome. With the rift in the country, he wasn't sure how the Silvers would act toward him. Seeing Charles here, in civilian clothes, had steered Jack away from commenting about the military. And when they entered the library, he knew his decision to travel in street clothes had been wise. The elder Silvers sat at his desk, newspapers and other papers strewn across the desk in disarray.

"Father," Charles said as he and Jack stood before the desk.

John Henry's glassy-eyed stare at the desktop broke as he blinked, his gaze inching upward.

"Charles?" he voice croaked.

"Yes, father," Charles went to him, grabbing his hands. "I'm home."

His father smiled weakly as he embraced his son. "I'm glad you're safe."

"Father, Jack Fontaine is here as well," Charles pointed, and his father looked past him.

"Mr. Fontaine," the elder man's voice still sounded gruff but was gaining in strength. Jack wondered what had waylaid the fine statesman he had met years before. "Nice to see you again."

"Yes, sir, the pleasure is mine," Jack replied, glancing at Charles.

Charles' eyebrows inched up for a second before he turned back to his father.

"You boys need to stay home now," John Henry
continued more strongly. "There's war a coming."

Both men nodded. Charles walked to the cabinet and
pulled out a bottle. "Let's drink for peace, shall we?"

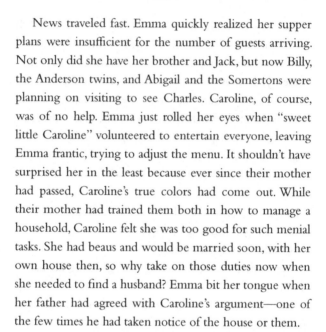

News traveled fast. Emma quickly realized her supper
plans were insufficient for the number of guests arriving.
Not only did she have her brother and Jack, but now Billy,
the Anderson twins, and Abigail and the Somertons were
planning on visiting to see Charles. Caroline, of course,
was of no help. Emma just rolled her eyes when "sweet
little Caroline" volunteered to entertain everyone, leaving
Emma frantic, trying to adjust the menu. It shouldn't have
surprised her in the least because ever since their mother
had passed, Caroline's true colors had come out. While
their mother had trained them both in how to manage a
household, Caroline felt she was too good for such menial
tasks. She had beaus and would be married soon, with her
own house then, so why take on those duties now when
she needed to find a husband? Emma bit her tongue when
her father had agreed with Caroline's argument—one of
the few times he had taken notice of the house or them.

So it was left to Emma to pick up the reins, despite
having skills that didn't come close to her mother's. She'd
just have to muddle her way through and hope for the best.
After making arrangements with the kitchen, she bathed
and changed just as the last of the guests arrived.

This was her first attempt at hosting a party—impromptu
as it was—and she began to relax as laughter drifted from
the various conversations at the dinner table. She glanced
down the long rectangle, ablaze with candlelight, and her
stomach jumped when she noticed Jack looking her way.

She hadn't seen him since his surprise appearance that afternoon. Granted, she had been busy with preparations and cleaning up, but his glance set her nerves flittering once again.

Seated across from Jack, Caroline did her best to keep his eyes on her. It irked Emma. Caroline was the oldest and should have taken her place at the head of the table as the new hostess of Rose Hill, but she had shirked her duties to remain the center of Jack's attention. Emma sighed, barely able to contain her frustration.

"Are you all right, Miss Emma?"

She looked up and saw the concern on Billy's face. Good Billy, always looking out for her. She returned his smile, nodding.

The final course, cheese and fruit, was set before them. The house slaves, dressed in their newest frocks, poured the sweetened blackberry wine. Emma exhaled. All had gone well.

Her father clinked the side of his wine glass, calling for attention.

"Ladies and gentlemen, in celebration of my son returning to us, we shall adjourn to the parlor together for further amusements."

The table slowly cleared as people moved to the front room. Emma watched her sister on the arm of Edward Anderson. Annoyed at Caroline's lack of manners, she remained to talk to her staff about cleaning. When she stood and turned, she came right up against a wall of solid flesh. She gasped, her hand splayed across the fine cotton shirt and silk waistcoat.

Two strong hands caught her elbows to stabilize her.

"You all right?" His silky voice sent a warm rush over her, and, with it, his touch kindled a fire deep inside her.

Emma's breath hitched as she looked into those sparkling green eyes. "You surprised me," she sputtered.

He gave her a low chuckle. "I just wanted to thank you for a lovely meal."

His voice was mesmerizing. She was frozen in place, her hand on his chest. The heat radiating from him filled her, seared her, enticed her. Those lips—oh yes, she remembered his lips. She had dreamt of them for months on end. When his curved upward and twitched, she refocused, yanking her hand off him.

"I'm so pleased you enjoyed it." She sounded stiff, even rude, but her thoughts were scattered. "Perhaps we should join the others."

His smile deepened. He released her and turned, offering his arm to escort her into the room. "But of course."

She returned his smile and lightly placed her hand on his sleeve. It was going to be an interesting night.

Jack sat back after his failure at charades. Of course, his third glass of brandy probably hadn't helped. More important was his sense of peace, something he hadn't enjoyed in the last four years in the Army. He truly felt the Silvers were more like his family than his own was. The drink relaxed him further as the lively group before him laughed while continuing the game.

However, his substitute family presented somewhat of a problem—specifically, Caroline and Emma. He admired them both. Well, perhaps that wasn't the right term. He liked them both. Caroline was the belle of the ball among Southern ladies, all frills and lace, batting her eyelashes at him and every other man there.

"Ooops!" Caroline squeaked, landing in a heap on the

floor after trying to act out her charade. The room erupted with laughter. Her father helped her up.

"I think you failed, my dear," John Henry told her softly.

The door to the room opened, catching everyone's attention.

"Mathias, what is it?" His owner demanded.

The man stood, wide eyed, holding a folded scrap of paper in his hand. "A message, massa, from Massa Lawrence, sur."

John Henry yanked the paper away from the boy and opened it. The room was so quiet, a pin drop would have been loud. The elder Silvers inhaled, closing his eyes. When he opened them, they sparkled and a grin spread across his face.

"Virginia's done it. We've joined the Confederacy!"

The crowd burst into shouts of joy and began hugging each other. Jack stood still, his heart thudding wildly. Everything in his life had suddenly changed again. Charles jumped with excitement. Even Billy Lawrence got a slap on the back in congratulations for living in such a free-thinking state. Jack pasted a smile on his face. His leave would end and he'd have to report for duty.

Across the room, he saw Emma in Billy's arms as he swung her around the room. He didn't like it, not one bit. Why couldn't that man go after Caroline? The thought brought him up short. Billy had released Emma, and she stood, laughing, but it didn't reach her brown eyes. Her gaze found his. His heart skipped a beat. She was so pretty, always had been from the moment he first met her. Tonight, at this very second, she looked beautiful. Her rich brown hair, a dark sable, was falling from its pins because of Billy spinning her. Her buttercup gown glowed like honey, dripping in cream lace. Taller than her petite sister, she was stunning. Her breasts rose with every breath, appearing to almost spill out of her bodice. Her ivory skin was flushed with color. And those plump ruby lips. She licked them and his body tightened.

He wanted her. That kiss years ago continued to haunt him. Would she grant him another, before he left to betray their home, the South? His hands clenched. He should leave now, before succumbing to the temptation she represented.

<hr />

"Huzzah!"

The word buzzed in Emma's ears. She tried to regain her balance after Billy's wild spin. This meant the War would affect her personally. All she had to do was look at each male face in the room and know she was doomed to lose her family and friends over a cause she didn't understand or want to.

Caroline succumbed to the enthusiasm of the moment, even hugging her sister. But Emma wasn't happy at all. Charles and Billy were already spouting about killing some Yankees. She turned and caught Jack watching her. He had such a strange look on his face. As though he could read her mind—he knew war meant tragedy and that it wasn't something to be celebrated. The intensity of his stare burned into her. Would he depart without giving Emma another kiss to remember him by? Would she allow it? When he finished his drink and left the room, she went out another door.

She heard his boots stomping down the hallway, toward the back of the house.

"Jack!"

He didn't stop.

"Jack, wait!"

He was too far ahead of her, and now, she couldn't see him or hear his boots. She stopped, stifling a sob in her throat with her fist. He was gone.

She wanted to sink to the floor. But an arm circled her waist, pulling her into the dark drawing room. A gasp escaped her as she heard a sultry "shhh" in her ear.

"Jack?" she whispered.

He spun her around and brought her closer. "My sweet Emma," his voice gravelly as he caressed her cheek with his knuckles.

Her heart pounded wildly. Heat radiated from him to her. Her breasts were crushed against his chest, his stomach against her stays.

"Kiss me, Emma," he whispered as he tilted his head, his lips brushing hers, teasing her.

He was too tempting to resist. Her mouth met his as she raised her arms, encircling his neck. He growled as his tongue played against her lips, seeking entrance. When she parted them, he invaded her mouth, his tongue tangling with hers. It was a passionate assault, and she met it just as forcefully.

His hand cradled the back of her head, and the other held her waist in his embrace. She tasted the brandy on his tongue, inhaled the sandalwood, spice and musky smell of him. Her fingers threaded through his hair, feeling the softness of those dark locks.

There was a thud as her back hit the wall. She could barely breathe but wouldn't let go of him. He broke the kiss, murmuring her name as he nibbled down her neck. He pressed into her, smashing her crinoline to the wall, flattening it. Through her petticoats and silk skirt, she felt the hardness of him against her lower abdomen. It excited and scared her, but she didn't utter a sound except to gasp as he kissed her neck and moved back up to her mouth.

"Emma," he said, pulling his head back, staring into her eyes. All she saw was the black depth of his. "Emma, you know this means war..."

"Yes."

"You know I have to go."

"No, please," she begged. She didn't care if she sounded pathetic.

A sad smile played at his lips. "You know I do."

She fought the tears that threatened to form. "Kiss me, Jack. Kiss me. I've always wanted you to kiss me again."

He groaned and recaptured her mouth. She played with his hair and around his neck, digging in under his collar to the bare flesh. She felt the vibration of his growl in her mouth.

He slid his hand up along her bodice and across her breast. His fingertips traced the lace fiche and dipped below it, skimming her skin. He looked into her eyes as his finger scraped her nipple. She felt it tingle and harden. He kissed her neck as he freed her breast and bent his head, taking the rosy nub into his mouth, suckling lightly. Desire uncoiled fast and hard inside her. She shifted her hips slightly and felt a dampness between her thighs.

He released the nipple and pulled her other breast free of the bodice, suckling on it as he squeezed the other. The pressure inside her was building. She groaned, perhaps too loudly because his mouth covered hers again. His hand fell to her waist, leaving her breasts exposed, the hardened nubs rubbing against his silk waistcoat, abrading them.

"Oh, Emma," he moaned. "I want you." He cupped her rear, lifting her against him so she could feel his desire. His hardened member pushed against the spot between her legs, and she felt her petticoat stick to her wetness.

"Jack, please," she begged before she knew what she was doing. She was on fire and needed him to put it out. Her skirts crushed under his grasp as he pulled them up and his hand went under them, skimming her thighs. With his other arm around Emma and her back to the wall, her hips flattened, causing her legs to spread apart. Her body was begging for some kind of release she didn't recognize, but she instinctively knew Jack could provide it.

With the palm of his hand, Jack reached between Emma's thighs and cupped her mound through the slit in her pantalets. She gasped. He stilled, breathing against her neck.

"Oh, God, Emma," he muttered as he moved his fingers across her wetness.

Her mind reeled at first, but she moved her hips as her body dictated. She could hear the slick sound of wet flesh. Then his finger entered her, and she wanted to scream in ecstasy.

———✦———

Every nerve of Jack's pushed him further although he knew he should stop. She was a virgin, for the love of all that was holy! But he couldn't stop himself. His shaft was so hard it throbbed with the need to be buried inside her. Her body had responded to his at every turn. He so longed to taste the nectar coating his fingers.

He pulled back abruptly, removing his hand from beneath her skirts. She was breathing hard. So was he. Fearing it might repulse her, he slowly licked her juices off his fingers.

They were alone. She was ready for him. Nothing was stopping him from taking her but himself. He closed his eyes, tried to steady his breath. When he opened them, he drank in her disheveled beauty and smiled.

He gently recovered her breasts, his breath hitching.

"Emma, you know I love you. I want you."

She let out a breath. "I want you, too."

"I can't take you here, not like this. You deserve to have the vows spoken first," he said, looking into her eyes. "I'll speak to your father before I leave."

Emma smiled shakily. "If you leave now, he'll think you're no better than a damn Yankee."

Jack's face turned stony. "Emma, that is what I am."

Her expression crumpled before she said, "Then it's best I go."

She didn't denounce him, but she didn't say yes, either. He wouldn't push her. Not here, not now.

Caroline drank another glass of wine, squealing "Long live Virginia!" till she was almost hoarse. Looking for another bottle but finding none, she decided her sister, the maudlin "mistress of the house," needed to rectify that. But Caroline discovered Emma was gone, as was Jack. The realization quickly sobered her, as a chill went down her spine.

She suddenly remembered that game of forfeit years ago and the kiss those two had shared. It had lasted too long for a parlor game and was too unseemly for public display. She had absolutely no doubt Emma had forced herself on Jack, and he, being a good Southern gentleman, didn't say anything about it.

And now that they were missing from the soiree, Caroline became angrier with each step she took. It made her skin crawl to think her sister was off having a dalliance with her intended. Caroline quietly walked down the hall, listening at every door for sounds from them. She wanted to scream. But then the click of a door unlatching stopped her. It was just ahead. The hallway was dark. She quickly found a nook in which to hide. Tucking herself into it, she watched as Jack stepped through the doorway, looked up and down the corridor and motioned behind him. Caroline's hand flew to her mouth as she saw Emma slip her hand into Jack's. He bent and kissed her lips, muttered something that Caroline couldn't hear and released her hand. Her sister went in the opposite direction down the hall.

Jack turned in Caroline's direction, and she watched as he straightened his waistcoat and jacket, stifling her outrage over the implications of why he'd need to do that. Her mind raced as her anger flared. How dare that woman believe she could have him? Emma, sweet and demure Emma, who Caroline had feared her parents favored. She'd often seen her mother instruct Emma in how to be the mistress of the house, bypassing Caroline completely. And her father? He was always protecting darling little Emma. Well, that girl obviously didn't need any protecting after disappearing into a room with a man and spending far too long alone with him.

Caroline composed herself, focusing on one thing—giving Emma another lesson. Obviously, she was too stupid to see that Caroline was determined to get what she wanted and deserved. Emma could have only what she didn't want. Like responsibility for running the house. The perfect little job for Miss Obedient! As for Billy, well, she'd let Emma have him later...

Where Jack was concerned, Caroline thought she had taken care of everything when he first asked her and Emma to write him at school. She burned the letters Emma wrote to him, of course, and kept those from Jack to Emma. She was prevented from intervening the second time, after Jack had asked them to write again, and that angered her.

But what she had just witnessed made her resolve to keep Emma from Jack once and for all.

Jack's footsteps approached, and she had to act. Steeling herself, Caroline inhaled and pasted a dazzling smile on her face. Stepping out from where she had concealed herself, she ran right into him. She slipped on purpose so he would have to catch her.

"Caroline?"

"Oh, Jack," she sighed sweetly. "You scared me."

He stood her upright and frowned. "What are you doing away from the party?"

She gazed up at him, feigning innocence. "I was looking for Emma. We're out of wine."

He cleared his throat. "Well, I don't think you'll find her here in the dark." He turned her back toward the front parlor.

"Perhaps, though I found you here, and I saw her walking the other way."

He stopped. "Are you trying to tell me something?"

"Oh, no," she smiled, playing with one of her hanging curls. "But if you want help getting her, you'll need my assistance. Daddy won't take kindly to you Yankee types snooping around her skirts."

"Caroline," his voice sounded tense. She'd hit a nerve.

"Jack, I'm not stupid. I know you want to keep your pretty command in the Union. And you'll be heading back North now that war's begun. My father won't support your cause without my help." She winked at him. She saw the flicker in his eyes as he considered what she said, and she knew she'd won when he swallowed hard. Oh how she'd like him to swallow something else...she shivered with anticipation.

"All right, Caroline, I need your help then."

"I am tired and sick of war. Its glory is all moonshine. It is only those have neither fired a shot nor heard the shrieks and groans of the wounded who cry aloud for more blood, more vengeance, more desolation. War is Hell."

~ William T. Sherman, 1879

CHAPTER NINE

The gleam in her eyes should have warned Jack. It was barely visible in the dark hall, but he caught it. His heart thudded madly from wanting to protect Emma and placate Caroline. As he led her back toward the others, his head was foggy from drinking and Emma's scent, which still lingered. He blinked and tried to steady himself, only vaguely aware of Caroline's chattering.

"...just follow my lead," she whispered outside the door to the parlor.

Jack nodded.

"Jack, there you be," Charles slurred, shoving a glass of amber liquid into his hand.

Jack smiled at his friend. This might be the last time he'd see him. He raised his glass to cheer for Virginia, feeling a tug of regret that his duty called him to the federal side. Those in this room, his family, his home and the South were his heritage. But when he thought of his father, the brandy curdled in his stomach.

Jean Baptiste and tradition. He'd heard about it throughout his childhood. The Fontaines had been here since the French and would remain so by blood. Even if that blood meant pain and torture for a young girl, "sacrificed" for the family. Jack felt anger rolling through him just as Billy smacked his shoulder with a laugh.

He turned.

"You lookin' kinda quiet, there, Jack," the young man said.

Jack scoffed and raised his empty glass. "Just noticin' I's be needing another," he drawled.

"Here, let me," the syrupy sweet voice cooed next to him.

He looked down and found Caroline pouring his glass full. She looked up at him, her gaze hooded as she bent her head and took a sip from his glass. What was she doing? But she flitted away before he could ask.

The rest of the night ebbed and flowed. He put his glass down only to have it thrust back into his hand as they raised another toast. He had a long ride ahead, but first, he must rest before speaking with John Henry about Emma. Emma. He closed his eyes, remembering her touch, and he swayed off balance, barely able to stop his fall. His thoughts were clouded by the whiskey. Shaking his head, he tried to clear his mind.

The world slowly began to spin. Stepping toward the side table, he set his glass down and vaguely heard it hit the floor as the room exploded with another roar for the South. He turned to bid everyone good night, but then everything went black.

∼∽∼

Emma made it to her room, her chest heaving with each

breath as she closed the door. She went to the window, grabbing the frame as she struggled to concentrate.

"Miss Emma..."

Emma's heart leapt at the timid whisper of her slave, Issy. With her hand at her heart, she fought to breath evenly. "Issy," she stammered. "Leave."

Issy looked at her, the whites of her eyes showing in the moonlight pouring through the window. She nodded and scampered out of the room.

With her hand skimming over her neck and down, past her bosom to her waist, Emma's eyes closed, remembering Jack's touch. She touched her breasts, and a shiver racked her body as her nipples tightened. The pool between her legs returned at the memory of Jack's kiss, his groan as his fingers slipped inside her. It was wicked, wanton behavior, but she couldn't deny her longing for him.

Her legs buckled and she plopped onto her mattress, falling backward on the downy softness. Despite her wine-induced haze, she knew what had happened. Jack had compromised her thoroughly. And he had spoken of making her honorable by marriage. Yet, had he asked her to marry him? No, but his words hinted at it. She sighed, closing her eyes. Yes, she would be all right...

———⌇⌇———

Click.

Jack heard the sound. Metal, like a gun's hammer locked into place, the chamber loaded. Naw, he was nowhere near any guns, not yet anyway. The pounding inside his head hurt terribly. His mind slipped back to the place he had been, hoping the pain would stop. He drifted, holding Emma, naked in his arms. She laughed when he pulled her closer so he could nibble at her neck again. That beautiful, elegant neck. He nuzzled her hair, burying his nose in it, kissing behind her ear and tracing her neck with his tongue.

She still wore that contraption of metal and lacing. He was puzzled. When did she put that back on?

"Jack."

It was a male voice. Plus the smell of metal. And sulfur. He recalled one other time he had heard that metallic noise and smelled sulfur. It was from a gun. His eyes opened wide to find the muzzle of a rifle at his nose.

"What the hell are you doing, Jack?" It was Charles. But he wasn't the one holding the gun. Jack looked up the gun barrel to its owner, John Henry. A very angry John Henry.

Underneath his arm, Jack felt a soft cotton-clad body move. He blinked, his mind sluggish. Releasing his hold on the woman near him, he focused on who he had been caught with in a compromising situation.

He suddenly knew before looking. Caroline. He jumped out of the bed, astonished when he saw her lying next to him, clad only in her undergarments, corset and petticoats. She was on top of the blanket, he underneath. What on God's green Earth had happened?

"Get dressed, Mr. Fontaine." The order snapped Jack's attention back to her father. The man still aimed the rifle at him.

Jack's clothing was thrust at him before his fuzzy mind cleared enough to register he was standing there shirtless, his drawers slightly unbuttoned and barely holding up over his hips.

"Daddy?" Caroline squeaked, her head tipped up to stare at her father. Jack noted she didn't seem worried about being exposed, although her father, her brother and Billy stood around them.

"Caroline, cover yourself," her father ordered, throwing

the bedsheet over her. At least she blushed at the sound of his cold voice.

As Jack buttoned his trousers and shrugged into his shirt, his muddled mind searched for memories of the previous night. How the hell did he end up in bed, Caroline's bed? But his head pounded fiercely, and he couldn't figure it out. Frankly, he thought he was going to lose the contents of his stomach. He closed his eyes, his fingers pushing against his temple.

"But daddy, it isn't what you think," she argued, her shrill voice piercing Jack's brain like a dagger.

"Caroline, shut up." It was Billy. Jack peered through slitted eyes at the man. He was glowering, his voice furious. He wasn't her father, why was he so mad?

Holding the sheet around her, she scrambled out of bed shaking, her eyes flooding. "Daddy, please..."

"Tilly!"

The slave appeared instantly. "Yes, massa?"

"Take your mistress and get her cleaned up. She's got a wedding to go to."

"No, no..." Caroline wailed as Tilly pulled her out of the room.

John Henry glared at Jack, his rifle no longer pointed at him, but Jack saw he kept his hand over the trigger.

"So, you be thinkin' to take a memory of my daughter with ya', huh?" the family's patriarch bellowed. "How dare you touch her, with your filthy Yankee-loving hands?!"

"No sir," Jack said, searching his fuzzy memories of the previous night. Whiskey and Emma and Caroline and, and, nothing. "I wasn't trying to do any such thing..."

Billy spat the chewing tobacco at Jack's bare feet, barely missing them. Jack's ears started to buzz and his stomach flipped.

John Henry's eyes burned holes into Jack, and he felt their heat. "Charles, get him ready. Samson's getting the preacher."

Jack shook his head. He couldn't stay here. There's a war and he needed to get back to Washington. He wobbled, the room swaying before him. Jesus, how much whiskey did he drink? With a deep breath, he struggled to steady himself and felt a hand under his elbow, helping him. Charles.

"Sir, nothing happened." But was he sure? He thought he had been with Emma. His breath hitched. Emma. Oh, dear Lord...

"Mr. Fontaine, I've welcomed you into my house, as a son, and in return, you seduced my daughter," the man stated angrily. "You will pay for such an offense in the only honorable way."

"Still think we should shoot him," Billy seethed.

Jack's eyebrows furrowed as he stared at him. Billy seemed overly hostile about this....

"Billy, father," Charles interrupted. "Let me get Jack cleaned up."

John Henry eyed Jack from head to foot and back again. "Get him ready. I expect the reverend to be here shortly. Billy, come with me." And they left the room.

Jack slumped to the bed as Charles looked at him incredulously.

"Jack, what the hell were you thinking?"

Caroline allowed Tilly to drag her out the door and down the hall, but at the door to the bathing chamber, she planted her feet firmly on the floor.

"Enough," she stated, yanking her arm free of the slave's grasp.

"But massa Henry says to get..." Tilly flustered.

"I know what my father said." Why did that little darkie call her father Henry? Caroline huffed. No respect from these people! "I can bathe myself. Get my blue dress ready." She smiled. "We haven't much time."

The slave nodded frantically and hurried away. Not so stupid after all, she laughed, walking into the bathing room.

Her plan had worked so well. She was rather pleased with herself. Oh, she had worried she might not succeed because it took so much whiskey to get Jack inebriated and direct him to her room instead of his own. Using Emma's name to lure Jack, she had brought him to her room. He leaned on her most of the way, mumbling something incoherently, her sister's name on his lips, which thoroughly disgusted her. But she drove on and barely got him to her bed when he passed out.

Part of her, some dim voice inside, whispered she'd gone too far, but the reason was clear. She'd had her hat set for him since his first visit. And she knew he was attracted to her—she even had correspondence from him that proved it. Well, he never mentioned marriage or love, but she was sure that would come until this silly war had interfered. Another reason why she refused to help run the house was because she needed to avoid marring her beauty with manual labor and fretting about meals and so forth. She needed to be gay and pretty for her husband. She smiled.

But he wanted Emma.

She snorted as she poured water into the washbowl. Everyone knew Emma was too young for him, too immature and what he needed was a real woman. He needed Caroline. Soon, he'd realize how wonderful they'd be together.

She dampened the wash cloth and ran it over her nude

body as she stood in the sitz tub. Her nipples puckered under her hand, and a bolt of desire shot through her body, imagining Jack Fontaine's mouth on her breasts, his shaft between her thighs. She moaned, feeling herself moisten at the thought. Tonight, he'd be hers.

And poor Emma. Caroline knew most of the men were going to enlist. A wicked smile crossed her face. Emma would do fine in any case. She could have Billy now.

Billy. Caroline's breath hitched. She'd miss him, but she had to admit, he was beginning to bore her. Things changed between them after he began to demand she answer his notes. That'd never work because she was the one in control. Perhaps, if he didn't get himself killed, she might play with him again in the future, but not now. She was going to marry Jack and live in luxury because his family was rich.

She finished her bath and dried off. Donning her blue silk gown, Caroline waited impatiently, stomping her feet as Tilly tried to quickly dress her hair. The minister should be here, and she wanted the vows said right away...before Jack realized she had manipulated him into marrying her.

"Oh, enough!" She stood, grabbed her fan and left for the parlor.

As she headed for the staircase, she heard muffled sobs and Billy's muted voice. She suddenly stopped and strained to listen.

"Emma, Emma," Billy murmured. "Don't cry. He isn't worth it."

"Oh, Billy," her garbled voice said. "He lied to me."

Caroline's lips twitched. She wished she could see them. But she sighed and went down the stairs. She'd see Emma soon enough. They quieted at the sound of her footfalls on the steps. She pretended she didn't know they were there, standing off to the side in the hallway. The infamous hallway, Caroline smiled. The one where she had begun to seduce Jack. She'd remember it fondly, always.

Caroline rounded the doorway to the parlor and came face to face with Rev. Jameson talking to her father. Out of the corner of her eye, she saw Jack, looking somewhat greenish. Despite his sickly hue, he was still handsome in his navy blue uniform. The yellow piping down the outer seam of his pants stood out against the dark blue. He clutched his hat, the large black-feathered plume dancing against his sleeve. He was nervous. How divine. The two silver bars on his collar shined in the sunlight. She recalled he was an officer—captain was it? In the cavalry, like Charles. Oh yes, she liked that—the thought of being an officer's wife.

"Why, Miss Caroline, do come here," Rev. Jameson drawled, stretching out his hand to her.

With a shy smile, she walked over to him.

"Let's get on with this," her father growled.

Rev. Jameson gave John Henry a stern look but nodded.

"Come, my child," he told her, placing her in front of him. She heard her father's bellowing voice call all the rest in.

Jack stood next to her, rigid and tense. She glanced at his face as Rev. Jameson began to drone about the sanctity of marriage. Jack's face was stony; he never gazed at her or anyone else. Just stared ahead, his eyes unblinking.

"Do you Jacques Baptiste Christopher Paul Fontaine take Caroline Ann Silvers to be your lawfully wedded wife? To have and to hold, from this day forward?"

Heavens, how many names did the man have again? She gulped.

"I do." His voice was flat, unemotional, his jaw tight.

"And do you, Caroline Ann Silvers, take Jacques Baptiste

Christopher Paul Fontaine as your husband, to have and obey, till death do you part?"

Obey? Seriously? "I do," she answered, smiling broadly.

"Then by the powers invested by St. Paul's Church and the Commonwealth of Virginia, I announce you man and wife," the preacher stated. "You may kiss your wife."

Jack glared at the man for a second before his stony face returned. He bent, and she lifted on her toes to meet him. His lips barely touched her lips before he released her hands.

Her lips thinned, then one side curved upward. He was angry. Well, she'd show him later how good it would be.

Behind her, she heard another muffled sound, and her smile widened.

———— ✦ ————

Jack knew he was damned. He barely heard the preacher, his mind still trying to recall memories from the fog of the previous night. Nothing. All he remembered was Emma. And her sweet laugh, how she smelled of strawberries and the honey of her lips. He still felt the taste of her nectar in his mouth.

He saw her before the ceremony, as Charles was still trying to talk to him. She looked devastated. When their eyes met, scorn filled hers, sending daggers his way. He felt them stab him when he uttered the damning words "I do." And at the end, he heard her moan through her closed mouth. It sliced deep into his heart, destroying it.

His wife was smiling at him. He remembered thinking at one time that she was pretty. Now, she was his responsibility. The one thing he hadn't wanted, not this way. Their forced marriage was for honor, family name, tradition—everything he had abhorred and run from before now stared him in the face.

"Get your bags. We leave now," he said gruffly. He saw her flinch and, inwardly, that pleased him. For some reason, he couldn't shake the thought that he might have seduced her while under the influence of abundant alcohol. Then again, she might have done so to him. The cloud in his mind didn't help, and he was tired of trying to figure it out.

"But I thought..."

"Caroline, I have to return to Washington. You are my wife and will do as I tell you."

"You don't have to be rude," she countered stiffly and turned, storming off.

He groaned inwardly. He was being an ass. With a sigh, he reached in his pocket and felt the rough edges of the handkerchief inside. Emma's. He should return it. But he couldn't. A wave of sorrow washed over him, and he glanced up, finding its source standing ten feet from him.

Emma stood tense, her hands clenching the shawl around her shoulders. Her eyes were bloodshot and puffy. Billy was by her side, his stare at Jack still full of anger.

Jack walked over to her. She stiffened, and Billy stepped to intercept him, but she touched his shoulder. With a shake of her head, he grudgingly moved away.

"Emma, I'm so—"

"No, Jack, don't." Her voice was brittle, breaking.

"I want to apologize," he pleaded softly.

"For what? That I was too good to seduce, unlike my sister? If you had to get strapped with one of us, why not the prettier one?"

What the hell? "Emma, you have it all wrong."

Her shoulders straightened and her mouth thinned. "No, I don't believe so, Mr. Fontaine."

Her eyes betrayed her and she knew he caught it. "Emma..." he wanted to reach out to her, to touch her, but he couldn't. He was married, dammit. "If you need anything. Ever. Write to me."

She laughed. It was a hollow, almost vindictive laugh. "Jack, get out of my house. Now. And don't ever come here again." She turned on her heel and walked away from him. Out of his life. Forever.

"All we ask is to be left alone."
~ Jefferson Davis, 1861

CHAPTER TEN

Washington, D.C., June 1861

Jack pushed Goliath faster the last couple of miles to reach Washington before sunset. Turning down the path into the city, he pulled up on the reins, slowing his mount. Even from a distance, he could see the town was crowded with the Army and more civilians.

"Whoa, boy," he murmured to the black thoroughbred, patting the side of its neck as the horse slowed to a walk. Jack slackened his grip on the reins and sat up, thinking about recent events.

After his hurried wedding and his failed attempt to apologize to Emma, he had gathered his wife, her slave Tilly and a wagon full of trunks and bags to take to the James River. They hardly spoke to each other after arguing over Caroline bringing the slave. He didn't want anybody in bondage serving in his house. He wasn't exactly an abolitionist, but he just couldn't tolerate being among that particular institution's standard bearers. Not after what had happened years ago because of his father. And after being at the Point, he had grown even more against slavery. But he had given into his wife just to quiet her rants and because of his need to leave. So he bought her passage to Washington

and abruptly left her standing on the dock, complaining
that he was deserting her, the words echoing in his head for
miles. He hadn't deserted her. He had to get to Washington
and report in. Her luggage was way too cumbersome to
transport by land. Plus, he needed the distance from her.

At first, he rode hard through the countryside, searching
his thoughts for what had happened. The first night, he
dreamt of Emma, of how she felt in his arms, how her skin
tasted, but in the midst of those pleasurable memories came
her parting words —*leave and never return.*

He woke, battered and torn emotionally. On the second
day of hard riding, he finally pieced the fragmented scenes
together and found his answer. Caroline had poured him
way too many drinks and was always at his side, refilling his
glass after every toast. She later lured him into her room
with the promise of helping him with Emma. Oh, yes, she
had helped him all right. Right into her bed. But there was
no memory of actually coupling with her. He must have
passed out, but just being in her bed had damned him.

By the third day of riding, it became obvious that the
lands around him were devolving into war. More people
were on the roads, some moving further inland, others
leaving. Groups of men, both militia and armed civilians,
marched. They gave him room to pass, probably because he
was riding fast and hard and looked so haggard.

At least he was back in Washington, a temporary home
until he learned the location of his unit.

Oh, and then there was Caroline.

He jerked in the saddle, bringing Goliath's head
up, breathing hard as the animal sidestepped. Damn,
just thinking about her could unseat him. He tried to
remember when her ship was docking. Maybe today, or
was it tomorrow? With a heavy sigh, he realized she might

be in his home even now, waiting for him.

He adjusted himself, the saddle leather creaking beneath him. Checking in with high command had been difficult to endure. The officer he reported to eyed him as though he was the enemy. In fact he asked Jack, because he was from the South, whether he too planned to resign as so many other southern soldiers had. Jack said he had no such plans, but the man's look didn't change, although he said nothing more other than to give Jack his assignment under George McClellan. Jack inwardly cringed. He remembered George B. McClellan. A graduate of West Point long before Jack, he was a member of the 2nd Cavalry and Jack had met him once. The man's attitude annoyed Jack. He was a pompous ass. But a strong recommendation from his previous commander, along with his high marks at the Point had been why Jack was assigned to McClellan's command.

Arriving home, Jack reined in Goliath at the front of the house and dismounted. Straightening his jacket, he looped the reins around the hitching post and strode toward the door.

Virginia

Smack.

The dough hit the tabletop again. Stretching the gooey piece out and flipping it half over, Emma pounded it again. She kneaded the dough for a moment and began peeling it off the wood when a pair of black hands stopped her.

"Miss Em, I be thinkin' it's ready," Sally said gently. Taking the dough from Emma, she rolled it and stuck it in the baking pan.

Emma ran her flour-covered hands down her apron and,

with an anguished sigh, paced the kitchen. Baking was her latest attempt to fill the hours of the day. Her skills were improving, but she was far from good. She didn't have to be in here at all with Sally and the kitchen slaves, but she needed something to keep busy so her mind didn't wander back to that night.

"Sally, what else do you have that I can do?" She sounded desperate. And she was. Another tremble went through her. Exhaustion, she heard Sally whisper to her father. Maybe. She avoided sleep. Sleep brought dreams, dreams about one particular night and the following day, when she went from being in Jack's arms to witnessing his marriage to her sister. The dreams made her scream out loud. She woke the whole house and yard. So, she stayed up.

"Child," the elder slave said, shoving a biscuit and cup of cider into her hands. "You need to get some food inside you and sleep."

Emma stared at the flaky biscuit. She wasn't hungry. And when she tried to eat, it made her want to retch. But Sally, who helped raise her, knew her well and wouldn't let Emma leave without eating. She took a bite of the bread and slowly chewed, trying hard not to spit it out.

Sally shook her head. It bothered Emma that the woman felt sympathy for the poor rich white girl who was in love with her sister's husband. The thought twisted her stomach, and she put the biscuit down.

"Honey," Sally said, caressing Emma's cheek. "I'm sorry for ya', but it's time to be getting this place ready for the summer. You've a whole lotta folk dependin' on ya'. And a daddy that's besides himself worryin' about ya' too. Be thinkin' about that."

Emma gave her a small nod and a wan smile. Inhaling, she straightened her shoulders and stood tall.

"Emma?"

She turned at the deep male voice behind her and saw Billy standing there, holding the reins to Angel and his horse. He smiled, raising his hand with the leather straps, asking her to come for a ride.

With a smile, she gazed at him. He'd been coming every day, trying to coax her out, even if it was only to the porch to talk to her. In his hands usually was the newspaper, and they'd read it together. She appreciated that he was trying to get her to laugh again. But the hole in her heart was too big. She now felt nothing. A mere void was safer. She could live with that as long as the memories stayed away.

What could it hurt to ride Angel again? Maybe a change of scenery would help. Besides, she doubted Sally'd let her do anything more in the cook house.

But she wasn't dressed for company. Her floured and greasy work dress and aprons made her look poor. *Yes, but the poor had their mates.* She blew a hair out of her face and resolved to join Billy.

"Billy, I'll go with you but need time to dress appropriately."

He gave her an exaggerated bow as she left to change. Halfway to her room, she glanced over her shoulder and found him smiling at her. He, too, hadn't smiled much since Caroline had left. Why, Emma had no clue but figured it wasn't her place to ask. They were friends, and that was all she needed now. She hoped.

<hr/>

Jack heard Caroline's shrill tongue before he reached the door. Then came the crash of glass. He breathed deeply and had to stop himself from doing an about face to head back to command and request a change in assignment, closer to the enemy. His personal enemy was here in the form of his wife.

Wife.

It was time to atone for his misdeed, he solemnly thought. As he got to the door, it swung open.

"Sir," the black servant greeted him. Jack smothered a chuckle at the man's lined, tense face. "Glad to see you're home."

More noise came from the back of the house. The sound of a table falling.

Jack raised his eyebrows. He turned to his servant, "George?"

George gave a short shake to his head. "You didn't send word you'd be bringing a wife home, sir."

Jack actually laughed. He slapped George on the shoulder. "Didn't mean to pick one up." He shrugged.

George glared at him. The man had been Jack's slave throughout his life. He'd left George and most of his belongings back in Louisiana, but his mother had sent George here with strict instructions to obey his master and report to her anything out of the ordinary. That last command got Jack's attention. "George, we'll just keep this piece of news to ourselves, you hear me?"

"Yes, sir."

Jack walked back to the bedroom and found Caroline and Tilly unpacking.

"Finding everything you need?" he asked.

With her scowl turning into a smile, accompanied by softening eyes, Caroline cried "Jack! Oh Jack, I'm ever so glad you are here." She looped her arm through his arm and stretched up to kiss his lips, but he turned his head, leaving her access only to his cheek.

"I need you to help me and Tilly unpack. That house slave of yours is worthless, I might add."

"George is my servant and he's fine. I just arrived, and I'm tired and hungry. We'll discuss your things later."

She frowned at him but didn't hold it long. "All right. It's been a long trip for both of us. So we'll eat and get some sleep."

He grimaced at her reference to sleeping. In the days it had taken him to get here, he couldn't remember having bedded her that fateful night. Holding her when the gun barrel was shoved at him, yes, he remembered that. But nothing else.

She led him to the dining table which was set with a linen tablecloth, candles, china and dinner—steak, potatoes, bread, wine and cheese. A meal fit for a king. Tucking Caroline's chair in under the table, he sat down himself and poured their wine.

Caroline smiled at him. The silence between them hung heavy. He hated being with her. He tried to recall why he used to think she was so pretty and dainty. Looking at her, he could see she still was. But it didn't matter either way because she was his wife now.

She prattled on about her voyage, but he barely listened. He wanted to drink her away. When George came to remove the plates, Jack ordered a bath for Caroline.

"A bath?" she asked.

"I thought you might want one after your journey."

She smiled. "Of course."

"Good," he stood, picking up the bottle and his glass. "I'll be in shortly." He strode to the front parlor and dropped into the stuffed wing-back chair near the window. Pouring more wine, he downed the glass in one swallow. Tomorrow, he was off to war. Off to Ohio or wherever McClellan was.

He didn't care, just as long as it was away from here. His eyes closed, and he felt himself drifting to sleep.

"Sir."

A nudge at his shoulder awakened Jack to find George staring at him. Jack blinked heavily, feeling sluggish, lethargic.

"Massa," the servant said again.

"What, George?" He tried sitting up straight and cursed. He had dropped the wine glass, and the floor reeked of alcohol.

"She's been calling for you."

"Who?" His brain was foggy. Thankfully, he had not slept deeply enough to dream. He was tired of bad dreams, especially about the woman he couldn't have.

"Your wife, sir," the elder black man answered.

Jack stood, pulling his waistcoat down. "Night, George." And walked toward the bedroom.

Inside the door, he stopped. Caroline sat on their bed, a sheet pulled across her lap. She wore a sheer, voluminous gown, giving him a hint of her body beneath it. Her long blonde hair hung loosely around her shoulders. She looked edible. And she was his. He had to remember that.

She patted the space next to her.

With a frown, he unbuttoned his waistcoat. "Caroline, tell me the truth. Did we actually..." He needed to know.

She blushed. He wondered whether she could do that at will. No, of course not.

Grinning, she responded, "We were together and drink overtook us."

He sat next to her and caressed her cheek with his hand. "Well, I still seemed the culprit in compromising you." He touched her hair, which was soft and silky. "Perhaps, this time, we'll get it right, huh?"

She smiled shyly.

He bent closer and kissed her. His tongue played at the corner of her mouth, trying to get her to part her lips. She did and his tongue plowed into her mouth, exploring, playing, tasting. It was nice. But not the same. Oh, his body responded as expected. He tightened, his scrotum contracted and his member hardened. He leaned her back on the mattress.

She responded to his kiss, playing with his tongue, tracing the inside of his mouth. When he caressed Caroline, he felt her body beneath the sheer fabric. He cupped her breast, and his thumb rubbed her nipple, making it harden. He sucked in his breath. His mouth left hers and traveled down her neck, his tongue leaving a wet path as he kissed where her neck and shoulder met.

"Caroline," he whispered against her skin and was pleased when she shivered beneath him. His hand lowered to pull the gown up over her head and bare her body. Her nipples were tight coral nubs and he suckled them. She mewled with pleasure.

She yanked his shirt out of his trousers and lifted it. He released her and threw off his shirt. He unbuttoned his fly and the drawers beneath. Free of clothing, his shaft sprung forth. Caroline's hand closed around it, stroking it. He groaned. For a virgin, she held him just right, exerting enough pressure to increase his desire.

He put his hand between her legs, running his fingers along the folds of her flesh. Her nether lips were swollen and wet. As he inserted one finger, it was doused in her juices, and he heard her groan. Another finger joined the first and pumped into her. She was wet and writhing under his hand. She was ready for him.

He rose above her, placing his manhood at her opening,

but before he entered, he looked into her eyes. She was panting.

"It'll hurt," he warned her. "But only once, then I'll make the pain go away."

She nodded impatiently. He felt her opening wider for him. He slowly entered her, being careful. He'd taken only one virgin in his life, and it had been a disastrous affair. He remembered her screams and the painful entry because she hadn't been ready—wasn't allowed to be. But Caroline was ready and more than willing.

A small warning went off in his head, but he ignored it.

She grasped his hips. He entered further. She was velvet soft inside. Before he pushed again, her hands reached back to his buttocks and pulled him to her. His erection went in to the hilt. She moaned, arching her back as he thrust into her.

Another warning, a voice in the back of his head, but again, he refused to acknowledge it.

He moved rhythmically in and out of her slick canal. She moaned loudly, almost screaming. It drove him over the edge—the sounds she made, the way her hips rose to meet him, her hands grabbing onto his buttocks. Faster and faster he thrusted, deeper and deeper, her body accommodating every move. He lost control, and when he felt her tighten around his shaft, shattering beneath him, he spilled his seed against her womb and collapsed on top of her.

It took a moment before his mind began working again and his breathing slowed. Something seemed wrong. He pushed up from Caroline and found her smiling at him, looking thoroughly sated. Would a virgin feel that way?

Getting off her, he went to the washstand and threw the water from the basin onto his face. He didn't like how he was feeling. His skin prickled. Looking into the mirror, he caught her staring at the sheets with a cup in her hand. A cup?

He spun around. "What are you doing?

She froze. He went back to the bed as she tried to place the cup on the nightstand. His arm shot out and he grabbed the cup.

"Jack," she started. She sounded scared.

He glanced into the cup. Red liquid that looked thicker than wine. Jack dipped his finger into it. It was thicker than wine. When he withdrew his finger, he realized it was coated with blood.

"Caroline," his voice hardened dangerously. "You were a virgin, weren't you?"

"Darlin', please," she wheedled.

He threw the cup and it shattered on the floor.

"You were going to put that on the sheets to prove to me you were." She flinched before his accusation, and his anger flared. "I thought I compromised you and did the honorable thing. But I'm not the guilty party, am I?"

"Jack, be reasonable."

His eyebrows shot up. "Madame, I do believe I'm being very reasonable." *Christ*, he had lost everything, and now she was no longer a virgin. He was overcome with heartache. Anger followed. Deep, penetrating, settling on him.

"You know, I may just divorce you."

He saw her panic as she scrambled to sit up. "Jack."

He laughed. "For the love of God, we may not even be married. Confederacy laws probably aren't even recognized legally, not even for weddings."

She gasped. "You wouldn't do that to me."

Jack ran his fingers through his hair, his mind racing. He picked up his clothes, grabbed a pillow and blanket and headed to the door, where he stopped.

"I won't divorce you, not now." He didn't wait for her response. Instead, he walked out the door to the couch.

Falling onto the cushions, he beat the pillow. "Dammit!"

Vaguely, he heard her sniffling, but it did not soften him. Tomorrow he'd leave to go fight. And he could hardly wait.

Virginia

Emma sat at the desk, staring blankly at the pages before her—the accounts for the estate. Her father had been acting strange lately. He had been avoiding her since Caroline's departure. Perhaps he felt he had acted rashly because she knew he missed her sister. And he would be missing Charles soon enough.

She dropped the quill and sat back in the chair, resting her head against it. She pinched the bridge of her nose. Everyone was leaving her. Soon she'd be all alone. On this big estate, full of slaves. How would she control them? She didn't know. Her father did, but unless he started to participate in life again, it'd be up to her.

"Knock, knock."

She glanced up and smiled. Billy leaned in the doorway, dressed in his militia grays.

"Don't you look dapper?" she commented.

He gave her a crooked grin. "I was wonderin' if I could get you to go on a walk with me."

Standing up, she walked around the desk. "Yes, I think that'd be marvelous." Looping her arm in the crook of his, she followed him outside.

Billy had finally broken through her screaming fits, her rage and remorse. He comforted her without saying anything; he just hugged her and listened to her rants. It had been soothing at a time when she needed the support.

But this was the first time he had appeared in uniform. And she felt him tense under her hand.

"Billy, what's the matter?" she asked as they rounded the side of the house and went toward one of the rose bushes the estate was named for.

"You know, the militia's been trainin'."

She laughed. "Yes."

He cleared his throat. "There's been a call to gather forces in Petersburg. They think there's a fight coming."

"But it shouldn't be much," she argued. "I've seen the reports in the newspapers. Both us and the Yankees sayin' it'll be over by Christmas."

Billy stopped and turned to face her. "Hopefully." His bare hand rubbed the inside of her arm languidly. It mesmerized her. "Emma, I'm leaving to go defend our right to live as we want, against any Yankee invaders."

She nodded. She didn't like the sound of this.

"And there was something I wanted to ask you."

"Anything, Billy."

He held her hand as his other hand went behind his back and he knelt. "Emma Silvers, I want to have a reason to look forward to coming home. I want to come home to you. So, I'm askin' you—will you do me the favor of marrying me?"

Emma's mouth dropped open. *Marriage?*

**"It is called the Army of the Potomac
but it is only McClellan's bodyguard...If
McClellan is not using the Army, I should
like to borrow it for a while."**
~ Abraham Lincoln, 1862

———∿∿∿———

CHAPTER ELEVEN

Rich Mountain, Virginia
July 11, 1861

Cannons and gunfire roared not far away while Jack
sat on Goliath, waiting with Major General William
S. Rosecrans and other officers as the ground before them
erupted between the two opposing forces. Rosecrans sat
atop his mount, aiming his looking glass toward the troops.

"Where the hell are my reinforcements?" Rosecrans
snapped, closing the telescope.

No one uttered a word. Union troops had forced
Confederates into battle in western Randolph County,
Virginia at Rich Mountain. Jack knew if he could see
through the sulfurous smoke, he'd find the enemy's
commander, Lieutenant Colonel John Pegram, standing
with his officers, assessing the damage or victory, as
determined by the men still alive on the field. But visibility
was difficult at the moment.

The sound of a horse, ridden hard and fast, came barreling
toward them, the horse skidding to a stop behind Jack's

group. Jack heard the creak of leather as the rider leapt off the animal to get to Rosecrans.

"Sir," the rider said, reaching the commander's side. Rosecrans bent in his saddle, lowering his head to better see the man. He snatched the note offered and unfolded it. "Hell and damnation, I tell you!"

"What does the general say, sir?" Jack asked.

Rosecrans wadded the note. "That pompous Ohioan's holding his troops in case the numbers against us increase. So he'll have fresh troops while mine are slaughtered." He spat. His bitterness sounded louder than the guns below.

Jack shifted in the saddle. It wasn't the first time he'd heard of McClellan's maneuverings. The man organized the Army in Ohio well, recruiting and training first the Ohio militia, then expanding into the armed forces of the West after he re-entered federal service. It had been quite a jump in rank for the West Point graduate when he made major general due to the influence of Treasury Secretary and former Ohio governor and senator, Salmon Chase. He outranked everyone except Lieutenant General Winfield Scott, head of the Army and an old veteran of the War of 1812. Perhaps it was too big a jump for the railroad president. One thing was for certain, Jack felt the same as many officers—the man's ambition rankled all of them.

McClellan's drive reminded him of his wife's. Caroline's machinations to make herself his wife were well done. Jack blotted out the obvious setup he'd allowed himself to get caught in. Caroline's plan had worked, and he was stuck with her. After reciting their vows and consummating their marriage, and after his anger about being betrayed had subsided, he packed his bags and left for the Army again. The long trip west gave him time to see clearly how she'd coerced him into marriage. A marriage made in hell.

A cannon exploded near Rosecrans' entourage, momentarily dispelling Jack's self-loathing and forcing him to focus on the battlefield. As the smoke cleared, he heard his commander and several others scream "Huzzah!" as Pegram's forces retreated.

Jack wished he could get Caroline to retreat as well.

***

"You may kiss your bride."

Emma heard the preacher's words, meant for her and Billy. Had she really said the vows? Had he? Was she truly married? The thought caused her to shudder just as Billy's lips touched hers.

Her mind was a whirlwind after the past couple of weeks. So much to do, and none of it seemed real. Ever since the attack on Fort Sumter and Virginia's alliance with the Confederacy, war fever had gripped Rose Hill. Her father's raising of a local militia gave him something to concentrate on, coaxing him out of his widower's grief. It also meant that Billy was at the house daily, as he was the ranking captain of the group per John Henry's appointment. Billy made sure to see Emma and whittled away her resistance until she had accepted his marriage proposal.

She wished Charles were home. He had left not long after Virginia's secession—not long after Jack had left for the North. Charles' military experience placed him within the new Confederate Army, and he had written her of his role drilling men. Her fingers had traced the lines of his writing, noticing the flourish and his excitement. What she wouldn't have given for his presence now. Had she made the right choice regarding Billy?

Billy claimed he loved her. Of course, she told him she loved him, but did she? Did she love him anymore than as the childhood friend he had always been? Even now, as his mouth pressed against hers, did she feel any of the spark, any of the fireworks that Jack Fontaine had caused?

The clapping around her and Billy brought her mind back to the present. This was her wedding. Unlike her sister's quick ceremony with only her, Charles and their father as guests, Emma's included the neighbors, Billy's parents and even the house slaves. They stood applauding the joyous occasion. Billy smiled at her. Their kiss had been a public display of her commitment to him. She only wished her heart felt as committed.

"Congratulations, my beautiful girl," her father murmured as he bent and kissed her cheek. "And you, boy, you best take care of her." He slapped Billy on the shoulder.

As the crowd surrounded them, Emma felt trapped, suffocated as everyone wished them the best. Many of the men nudged Billy. Oh yes, she noticed. Her gut twisted.

"My missy Emma, now all grown up," Sally cried as she stood in front of her. The head house slave, the woman who was a second mother to her, could not embrace her. It wasn't proper for her to hug Emma with all the others around. That particular rule of the peculiar institution of slavery made Emma sad. She so needed a hug, but not from her husband. That thought made her skin prickle with aversion.

"Thank you, Sally," she muttered, finally finding her voice.

The black-skinned woman chuckled, her plump body quivering. "Now, don't you be worried none. We'll get this all cleaned for ya'." She winked.

Billy slid his hand under her elbow. "Come, sweetheart. Everyone's expecting us to go start eating so they can." He pulled her chair out and seated her before taking his own seat.

The slaves served dinner, and she had to squelch a nauseous feeling upon seeing the abundance of food. As the new mistress of the Silvers home, she had spent the last two weeks figuring out the upcoming months, how much they could sell, how much they should keep to get them through the winter, and it was a stretch. Particularly with her father feeding his troops from her store of grain and greens. And now this. They had a selection of beef and three different fowl, multiple salads, breads and fruits. Plus cases of wine, opened and served freely throughout the meal. Her head hurt considering their dwindling supplies.

Better to brood over that instead of what lie ahead. The newlyweds had only tonight. Tomorrow, Billy and his unit were to report to Richmond. News was about of a Yankee invasion. War hawks circled the Confederate capital. The Yankee aggressors were coming.

She barely ate. During the speeches for future happiness, she sipped her wine but found it hard to swallow. Billy glanced at her often, smiling. He was happy. She wished she was. He should have been Jack, as she had hoped and desired. That was before Jack found her wanting and took her sister instead. Although the screaming in her sleep had stopped, her dreams, despite the exhaustion from running the house, still found Jack lurking there.

Billy embraced her as they danced on the parquet flooring, which had been moved outside for the occasion. His hold was strong and steady. She tried to smile. He was a good man, and she needed to thank God that Billy at least wanted her.

The party goers were in high spirits, fueled by the celebration and alcohol when, in the middle of a dance,

Billy stopped. Emma's thoughts, which had been working at maintaining an illusion of happiness, came to a halt when she heard him whisper in her ear, "Come, my beautiful wife."

She gasped when he locked his arm under her knees and lifted her. The dwindling crowd clapped, hooted and hollered as he took her into the house. Embarrassment flooded her, and she buried her face in his shoulder.

"Sweetheart, they mean well," he said softly as he stepped across the threshold and headed for the stairs.

With each step, Emma's heart thudded. This was her wedding night. The night she was to become a woman. Anxiety snaked down her spine but not because of the act necessarily. No, it was because her husband was Billy and not Jack. Caroline had succumbed to Jack and he to her, and Emma's heart broke as a result.

The scent of roses filtered through the air, filling Emma's nose with their essence. She looked up. She and Billy were in the guest bedroom. Billy lowered her to her feet. "I wanted to make this special for you," he said softly. Did she hear fear in his voice? Or was that only her?

Emma swallowed and gazed about the room. It held several vases of roses, on the dresser, nightstands, table, windowsills and along the floor. And bright red petals were sprinkled across the bed.

He came up behind her and encircled her waist with his arms. He kissed her neck as his hands reached back and untied her bodice lacings.

She bit her bottom lip, fighting the tears pooling in her eyes. He turned her to face him and covered her mouth with his. Her stomach clenched.

"Oh, my darling," he murmured as he pulled down her bodice. With a flick of his fingers, her skirt came

undone, and he reached underneath and pulled the
strings to her petticoats and cage crinoline. As her gown
and undergarments pooled around her feet, a small voice
inside wondered at how quickly he was undressing her.
Her corset came loose, and he unhooked its busk. It fell
onto the heap at her feet. Considering she had never seen
him with another girl besides Caroline, she was amazed he
knew what he was doing.

Emma saw his eyes darken as he reached for the hem of
her chemise and raised it over her head. Her nude body
shivered as his eyes devoured her. He growled and picked
her up to place her on the rose petal-covered mattress. He
shrugged off his shirt and discarded his boots and pants to
climb in next to her. "Oh, Emma," he whispered against
her mouth.

His kisses were warm. Not hot, but she could get used
to them. Slowly, her hand circled his neck, bringing him
a touch closer. She felt him hum in her mouth. With
resignation, she breathed the rose-scented air deeply. Billy
was her husband, and this was his right. And maybe he
would help her forget Jack. She pressed her body against
his.

Billy moaned as his arms encircled Emma tightly. Still
kissing her, his tongue invaded her mouth as his hands
lowered onto her buttocks, lifting them and pulling her
closer. She felt the pressure of his arousal next to her pelvis.
It was hot and hard, but the tip of it was smooth against her
skin. When his hand reached between her legs, his fingers
tracing the folds closer to the front, she trembled. Fear
raced through her. Not from excitement as Jack's touch
had caused but from intimidation.

"Emma, relax," he murmured as his lips trailed down her
neck, down her chest and to a nipple. He brought the tip

into his mouth and suckled. Tingles blossomed, sending a warmth through to her core. She felt the sensation flood her lower abdomen. And when his wandering fingers skimmed the slit between her legs, she felt the wetness there. Next, Billy slid one finger inside her. She clenched at first, feeling invaded before her body welcomed it and released more of her juices.

"Oh, Emma," he rasped, removing his hand, "open your legs."

When she did, his member fell to her slit. He reached between them and placed the head of it at the opening where his finger had been. Fear swept over her as he kissed her neck. His member slid inside her as he murmured her name.

It was wrong. She cringed as he started to move inside her. It shouldn't be him. She wanted to tell him to get out when she heard him moan and felt him thrust deep inside her. She gasped at the pain, biting her cheek to avoid screaming as he entered her, feeling herself stretch to accommodate him. He stopped moving, looking into her face.

"Oh, Emma, please don't," he said, his hand wiping the tears from her face. "It only hurts once."

Her body opened to him, but she felt sick. He continued to move inside her, withdrawing and re-entering, and her body met his, answering his thrusts. She bit her bottom lip when he rose above her, moaning as his actions increased, her hips keeping time with his. Deep inside her now, Billy went faster, and her slick canal tightened around him, squeezing harder.

"Oh, Emma! Yes!" Billy roared at the last plunge, lifting her hips off the mattress as he filled her with his seed.

She turned her head, weeping, her heart torn. *Jack.*

As Jack got closer to the front door of his house, he couldn't help but feel something was wrong. His insides clenched. Surely Caroline was home, although she was the last person he wanted to see. But he was tired and had nowhere else to go.

It had taken three days of hard riding back to Washington after the Union victory at Rich Mountain. The story about Pegram's troops being turned away was repeated in every paper he saw on his return trip. The victory was credited to McClellan. Jack himself saw the small grin cross the officer's face as he read the telegram from Washington, calling on him to lead the Union forces to even greater victories.

McClellan had taken a train to the capital, but Jack rode his horse. He needed the ride. What he had seen and heard on the battlefield haunted his dreams—the moaning of the wounded, the blood, the legs, arms and abdomens ripped to shreds by metal projectiles. Riding hard, wearing both himself and his horse out, brought exhaustion and much-needed sleep. Sleep where dreams had no place. Well, most of the time.

At the door, he stopped. He heard muffled noise from inside, as though Caroline had company. Great, he thought. The last thing he wanted was company. As he turned the knob, he wondered where George was. He walked in, the servant's name upon his tongue when Caroline's laughter rang out, followed by several male voices.

He frowned. Dropping his saddlebags at the door, he strode to the drawing room.

Caroline was entertaining four young men—two in dark suits, the other two in navy wool uniforms. Officers.

Everyone was laughing and holding glasses of what Jack guessed to be his brandy.

No one had heard him come in.

"Good afternoon, gentlemen," he stated as coolly as he could, tamping down his rising anger. With a nod to Caroline, he added, "my dear."

Her eyes widened, and he caught a flicker of something. Surprise, perhaps? She schooled her features and smiled as she stood. With a step, she was at his side, on her toes to kiss his cheek.

"Darling, I'm so glad you're home," she greeted. "You should have sent word." She tried to kiss his mouth. When her lips touched his, he didn't respond, his eyes fixed on the men.

Her mouth twitched. "Let me introduce Senator Wilmington of Indiana, his aid, Mr. Cassidy and Lt. Wilcox and Capt. Carter."

Carter grinned at him, like a child whose best friend had been caught stealing a toy. Jack bristled. What the hell was going on, he wanted to yell at her, but gritted his teeth instead.

"Gentlemen, to what do I owe this honor?" He managed to control his tone though it took all the strength he had.

Cassidy stood, his round body quivering as he laughed. "Came to see your lovely wife on an investigative tour," he stated, his tone that of a politician's. It grated on Jack's nerves. "You have quite the lady here, Captain."

He eyed them speculatively. "Yes, well, gentlemen, I've just returned from the West. If I could ask you all to leave." It wasn't a question but a command. He wanted the lechers out. Even Carter.

"Of course," Cassidy replied. Turning to Caroline, he

took her hand and kissed the back of it. "Thank you for your kind hospitality."

She smiled. The others also thanked her and left.

With a vicious glare, she turned to him. "How dare you? Of all the rude..."

"What the hell are you doing entertaining men while I'm gone?" he demanded.

She looked at him with shock. "How vulgar war is making you," she commented flatly. "As to those gentlemen, what else am I to do? I was bored waiting for your return."

His temper flared still more. "You will not entertain any man in my absence, do you understand me?"

"What does it matter to you who I keep company with?"

"You are my wife. You will do what you are told," he ordered. "You vowed to obey me. And to honor me. You will be respectful of me and your position here."

"Position," she scoffed.

He stormed out of the room but stopped and turned to her. "And you will sleep with no one but me. Am I making myself clear?"

She laughed. "You. Yes, just like before you left for war? You left me in our bed alone."

He bristled. "And you lied to me, implying you were a virgin."

Her head fell back in laughter. When she looked at him, her haughty spoiled-daughter face was in place. "I was. One past indiscretion, when I was taken advantage of, and you'll hold it against me?"

His gaze narrowed. "Darlin', I doubt anything has ever been taken from you without you asking for it." He left the room, but instead of heading toward the bedroom, he went to the front door.

"Where do you think you're going?" she shrilly demanded.

"I've work to do." He slammed the door behind him as she screamed his name.

Jack swallowed more of the smooth dark amber brandy, welcoming the scorch as it slid down his throat. He sighed and ran his fingers through his hair. Damn, she was beautiful, he thought to himself.

She took the glass from his hand and reached up to kiss his lips. "Jack, let me help you forget," her soft, seductive voice cooed. His body tightened at her suggestion.

"Leslie," he replied. "I'm so glad you're here."

She laughed. "All you had to do was ask."

After he left Caroline, he went to The Eagle saloon on First Street and found his long lost lover lounging at the bar, listening to some distraught politician rant about the new president. It took him but a second to suggest the man find another ear. She'd laughed at his arrival, claiming she came to Washington for new clients, and with the War, her income had grown.

He bought her for a week. He refused to go home. Instead, he put Leslie up in her own suite at the Carlton Hotel and made his home in her bed. Not that he needed her for sex, though that was obviously on the agenda. No, what he needed was her comfort. The very least he had thought Caroline could give him, but as far as he was concerned, she had betrayed him both in bed and in their marriage.

With Leslie, everything was simple. He paid for her company—no responsibility on his part after he bought her time. It was her duty to attend to his every need, every desire, even if it meant doing nothing. No marriage vows, no attachments. She was beautiful, alluring and for hire, not his legal obligation. After that night, so many years ago at home, he wanted no duty to family.

Despite all he had drunk, Jack's member hardened and he rolled over onto her. When she giggled, he impaled her with it. Her lips and hands roved over him as he entered her. She murmured his name and moaned with insistence, but he heard none of it. Instead, his mind transformed her ebony hair to auburn, her porcelain white face to a sun-kissed one, with freckles sprinkled across her nose.

"Jack," the vision called. Emma's voice.

With a groan of frustration, he withdrew and fell to Leslie's side. "I'm sorry," he muttered without looking at her.

He knew she'd say nothing. It wasn't her place. As her hand stroked his hair, he succumbed to the blackness and freedom of sleep.

August 1861

Emma tried to thread her needle again. The late afternoon sun poured into the drawing room, making it terribly hot. No breeze came through the open windows. Sally had Mary's son Titus fanning Emma with some tweed stretched across a square frame at the end of a long pole—a pole longer than the boy was tall. He hadn't complained, actually didn't speak even once, but she pitied him as she sweltered in the heat. Finally, in an act of Christianity, or maybe frustration as he almost dropped the device on her, she sent him away. But as perspiration ran down her neck, beneath her dress and past the chemise and corset lacings, she wished she'd kept him there.

When the white thread missed the needle's eye on her third attempt, she threw it down, along with the cotton shirt she had been sewing. Her fingers ached from clutching the material so tightly, and her back ached. She had finished four shirts already for her father's militia boys, the Charles City Knights. Sipping her lemonade, she glanced out the window at some noise. It sounded like a carriage and team.

She walked out the front door, straining to see through the cloud of dust in the lane, wondering who'd come calling.

A carriage pulled by four bay horses thundered into the drive and stopped at the porch. She watched warily as her slave opened the door and dropped the step from the vehicle. Inside, there was the sound of silk rustling. The passenger leaned out the door to take a step, and Emma's mouth fell open in utter surprise.

Caroline.

Cautiously, Caroline stepped out of the carriage and onto the ground before she looked up at Emma. She smiled as only Caroline could, in a show of bravado at returning home. Emma waited, watching the carriage. Tilly emerged and began to arrange Caroline's skirts. But no Jack.

Emma's upper teeth tugged at her bottom lip. But when she noticed Caroline's smile falter as she started to swoon, Tilly caught her and Emma sprang forward.

"Hello, Emma," her sister said.

"Caroline, are you all right? Where's your husband?" Emma feared he'd be there soon. Could she handle seeing him again? A flash of hatred and fear twisted her stomach. She hoped he'd stay away after he had betrayed her.

The two helped Caroline inside and to the settee in the front parlor.

Sally appeared instantly. "Oh, Miss Caroline. Tilly, go get her some lemonade."

Emma's brows furrowed, confused. "Caroline, the trip here couldn't have been easy. Why did you come?"

Caroline's smile wavered. "Jack decided it would be better if I came home to rest."

"Rest? Caroline, are you ill?" Fear coiled inside Emma. With the war effort and the raising of troops, getting a doctor would be nearly impossible.

"No, Emma," she said softly, her hand resting on her stomach. "I'm with child."

Emma's gaze fell to her sister's stomach, which still looked flat. She blinked. Buzzing filled her ears, so much that she couldn't hear Sally coddling Caroline or anything else for that matter. The edges of her vision blurred, and she heard herself moan as the blackness came and her knees buckled.

> "The time for compromise has passed, and the South is determined to maintain her position, and make all who oppose her smell Southern powder and feel Southern steel."
>
> ~ Jefferson Davis at his inaugural speech, February 16, 1861

CHAPTER TWELVE

Rose Hill, Winter 1861

God must hate her. Emma stifled a groan as Caroline's voice echoed throughout the house, calling for Tilly. Poor slave. Emma pulled her shawl closer around her shoulders. This winter was cold, harsher than any she could recall. She watched the flames flicker in the fireplace and closed her eyes. She had never felt so alone as she did now.

Caroline waddled into the parlor, her hand on her lower back, supporting it because of the baby growing inside her. "Have you seen my Tilly?"

Emma wanted to tell her that if she'd stop slapping the girl, she'd probably come when called, but she bit her tongue. Nothing got through to Caroline. The woman was a grouch and had only gotten worse as the weeks went by. Sally warned Emma that her sister'd probably have a rough confinement simply because she had never been restricted from anything before. Her condition kept her housebound, and at almost six months along, her mobility was slowing. According to Sally, she'd spend the last three months in bed. Emma feared the demands Caroline's increasing confinement would bring.

"No, sister. Why don't you go sit and I'll see if I can get her." Emma rose to leave when she heard a groan behind her. Caroline had slumped onto the settee, her face swollen like her stomach. Emma's eyes narrowed. "You did tell Jack you were expecting, didn't you?"

Caroline glared, her jaw tightening. "Of course. Who do you think sent me back here?" she snapped.

Emma left the room, and a troubling thought occurred to her. If he knew she was in the family way, why hadn't he written to find out how she was? Emma took the mail every time there was a delivery, but nothing came from him. Somehow, that seemed strange, considering her sister raved about how wonderful he was to her and their grand life in the Union capital. But when pressed as to why she was home, the woman grimaced, saying he was going to war and felt it better for her to be home with loved ones. *Posh!*

Glancing into the drawing room, she didn't find Tilly. So she walked down the hallway to the back of the house. Tilly no doubt was hiding. She'd hide too if she had to answer to Miss High-and-Mighty. She bit her lower lip. It wasn't Miss but Missus. Just like she was. Mrs. William Bealke. But unlike her sister, she remained barren. Granted, they had only the one night together, and he left before dawn with her father to gather their unit and march to Richmond. Emma fought the urge to cry, clenching her hands at her sides. Not even a child to look forward to. The notion upset her when she saw her sister's bulging belly. Jack's baby.

As she walked farther down the hall, she heard the

rattling of metal and leather. The way it sounded on a wagon. She heard a man say very clearly, "Whoa," and the hooves stopped. There was a commotion outside and she frowned. What was happening?

Boots thudded to the back door. "Emma! Emma!"

"I'm here," she replied. Her mouth fell agape, and she froze.

Billy was home! So was her father! But they looked dismal. Billy was supporting her father. John Henry's head was wrapped in bandages, very dirty-looking bandages. His eyes were sunken, his face thin, and he stared ahead with a pain-filled gaze.

"Daddy," she cried, racing toward them.

"Oh, my darlin' Emma," the man said softly, his hand reaching for her face as she approached him. He trembled under her touch.

"He was standing too close to the artillery," Billy interjected. When Emma reached to touch John Henry's cheek, Billy added, "He got stung by the blast, Emma. Too close, and when it exploded, he was thrown." He released his grip on his father-in-law as the slaves came under Sally's direction and moved John Henry toward the stairs.

Emma watched her father, and her heart faltered. He looked almost dead. She trembled. War, this dreaded war. Wasn't it to be over by now? It was close to the holidays, and both sides had boasted it'd be finished by then. Tell that to the troops she'd had to run off two days hence. Troops looking for supplies and food, and she had none to spare.

"Emma, I'm sorry," Billy said, pulling her into his arms. "I tried to get him to leave long before the fighting, but he wouldn't listen to reason."

She shuddered. It was all too much. Her sister pregnant. Her father injured. All her household responsibilities.

Unless...she looked up at her husband. His face showed all the signs of fatigue. Lines creased his eyes, his face gaunt and dirty. Once tawny-colored hair had turned dark, matted with mud and sweat. The arm around her shoulders was thick, his chest hard and lean. It was as though he was another man. She twisted free of his grip.

"How are you doing?" she asked, her eyes roving over him, seeing his butternut-colored short coat and pants stained with hard work and war.

He grinned wryly. "I'm okay. Can stay a couple of days if you'd like."

"Of course," she replied coolly. "I have Caroline home as well."

She caught a flicker in his eyes at the news. "Home? What's wrong? That Yankee dead?"

Emma chewed her bottom lip. He sounded harsh, not like the sweet man she had wed. "She's with child. He sent her home so we could care for her. He's with the Union army."

"Child?" he muttered. His jaw tightened. Emma noticed and was going to ask about it when he released her and smiled. "Tom here," he motioned to the wagon driver "and I could use some food, and I need a bath."

Caroline huffed a disgruntled breath as she tried to push her ungainly body off the cushions. The babe kicked at her, and she fell backwards, her hand to the bulge protruding from her. Another kick. She figured she'd be black and blue by bedtime at this rate. Three more months. She was so uncomfortable. This child wouldn't let her sleep, always making her get up to relieve herself, plus she couldn't bend over and see her feet. She felt miserable, as though this nightmare would never end.

Tilly came scurrying in, her bare feet silent against the wood and carpeted flooring, but as usual, she knocked the table, sending the vase of flowers teetering. "Miss Caroline."

She glared at the slave. Insolent creature, that one was. She'd slap her hard for making her wait. "When I call for you, I 'spect you to be here."

The slave knelt before her, close enough for Caroline to reach. As she pulled her hand back, the girl closed her eyes. Caroline swung hard, slapping her cheek. It reddened even under the dark skin. Slightly mollified, she pulled the girl's chin up. "You go get me some tea. And be quick."

Tilly nodded and jumped to her feet, leaving the room as fast as she could.

Caroline grimaced. Good help was getting so difficult to find, she thought, rubbing her belly. Another kick. *Heavens...*

"Caroline?"

She looked up and smiled. Her Billy was home. "Billy," she exclaimed, excited. Quickly she tried to get up, but the creature inside her made a simple move nigh on impossible to do.

"Let me," he said, coming to her and taking her hand. He pulled and supported her weight at the same time, getting her to her feet. Heavens, she felt fat. And as his eyes roamed over her, she grimaced.

"I've put on some weight," she said, self-conscious. He was bound to find her ugly, even disgusting, carrying another man's child.

He held her chin up. "Is the child mine?"

Caroline saw the hope in his eye and felt a moment of sadness threaten to overwhelm her. Her breath caught in her throat. She couldn't answer and shook her head instead.

He gave her a tight nod and looked away. She felt his pain and cursed Jack for putting her in this condition.

When Billy's eyes returned to her, his lips curved at one corner. "You look good."

She saw the tick in his cheek. "I'm told you married my sister. See, aren't you glad I taught you?" She gave him a weak smile.

"Caroline," he whispered. "I've missed you."

She closed her eyes. Heaven. "I've missed you, too."

He laughed. "But you managed to stay busy I see."

His vulgarity about her condition irked her. How dare he make fun of her? But when she looked into his beautiful grey eyes, they regarded her warmly. Her precious Jack had dismissed her so coldly, she felt lost. Billy had always been there for her, even if he did marry her sister. But Billy still seemed to feel something for her. Did he love her?

"How long are you home?" she asked, her heart fluttering—and the baby kicked as well. Little tyrant.

"A week, maybe," he replied. "I brought your father home. He isn't well. Hurt on the field by cannons."

Her breath hitched. "Daddy's hurt? Oh, heavens..." She was so frustrated as she padded across the floor.

"Yes, darlin'," he whispered, taking her arm and returning her to the settee. "Relax, I'm sure he'll recover physically."

She looked at him, puzzled. "Billy, what's wrong with my father?"

She watched him swallow hard. A memory of him swallowing her flooded her mind.

"Caroline, I'm sorry. Your father's injury hurt his brain."

<hr />

That night, Emma stared at the canopy above her bed, counting the folds in the fabric. Billy lay next to her, his arm thrown across her stomach. His heavy, even breaths on her neck assured her he was asleep. Something she needed herself but doubted it'd come to her tonight.

Arranging for her father's room, redoing the menu for the added company, ordering a bath for Billy and his man, having their soiled uniforms laundered and dealing with Caroline's demands had just about done her in. Sleep should've come easily. Billy attempted to make love to her, trying to fill her with his seed in hopes she'd become a mother, but he had failed. He couldn't maintain his erection, and she was no help. What a miserable end to her day. God really must hate her.

Her eyes blurred and she sniffled. Billy reacted by pulling her against him, and he snuggled his face in her hair. She tried to relax and enjoy his embrace but melancholy prevented it. He didn't love her. He loved Caroline. She'd seen his face at dinner and noticed her sister's lightened, jovial mood. Emma tried to deny it to herself, but it was right there in front of her. Billy and Caroline had been involved with each other. When or how, she wasn't certain, but she refused to spend any more time thinking about it.

Once again, her sister had won. She had married the man Emma loved with her whole heart but apparently had a liaison of some type with Billy too. A lone tear fell. Yes, God hated her.

March 1862

Emma sat, knitting another blanket for Caroline's baby. From the corner of her eye, she saw Caroline lying on the settee, her bare feet resting on the pillowed arm. Emma grimaced at her sister's swollen ankles and feet. The woman hadn't worn shoes for the last week, waddling barefoot on the wooden floors of the main house. Happily, the spring air was warm, but Caroline complained of the heat and Emma just shook her head.

The heat wasn't the only thing Caroline complained about. Anything was fair game. The slaves stayed out of her way. Well, all of them but Sally. Sally just scolded her and laughed, a rich, deep laugh that seemed to placate Caroline and soothe Emma's nerves.

"Just be thankful you're not going through this," Caroline told Emma.

Emma bit her lip. It made Emma sad to hear her sister so unhappy about approaching motherhood. Emma simply couldn't understand her sister's attitude when her own womb remained empty. Unfortunately, Billy's brief return had done nothing to change that.

"The war, Emma," he told her. "It mars a man. Let me get through this and then..."

Let him get through the war? The war that was to have ended last Christmastide? The war that continued even now? Stealing every man from every home? She shook her head again as Caroline continued to rant about her condition. The woman never ceased. Instead of staying in bed as the doctor had told her to do, she roamed the halls, refusing to be "trapped" in her room. It was enough to drive everyone mad.

Except their father. Emma heard the chimes from the grandfather clock and looked up. One o'clock. Time to get daddy to eat. That is, if he was still in the library where she had left him this morning. She didn't understand it. He seemed so alert, so rational, only to suddenly forget the present and dwell in the past, when she and Caroline were children and their mother alive. At those times, he also became short tempered, violent in his language and actions.

"Caroline, I need to get father," she stated, putting her knitting down and rising.

"You can't just leave me like this."

Oh, yes I can. The evil thought flashed through her mind and she came close to saying it but dampened her anger. It did no good to express it. "Here, give me your hand," she said, holding out her arm.

Caroline grasped it and with her other hand pushing behind her, she managed to stand. "Thank you."

Emma nodded and headed to the hall.

"Oh! Emma, wait!" Caroline's panicked voice rose.

Quickly, Emma turned and found Caroline doubled over, clutching her stomach. She uttered a pain-filled sob. From underneath her skirts, liquid spread across the wooden flooring.

"Sally!" Emma cried. "Hurry! I think Caroline's having her baby!"

Caroline cried out, loud enough to be heard as far as the fields. Sally entered the room calmly. "Come, Miss Emma, help me get her to her bed."

With both of them holding Caroline's elbows, they steered her to the staircase, taking one step at a time. Jemmy raced into the hallway, and Sally told him to start boiling water.

"What about Doc Hemmings?" Emma asked.

"Child, we don't need no doctor," Sally reassured her. "I done helped ten childrens come into this world. We'll be good."

It took no time to guide Caroline into her room and onto her bed. She screamed, clutching the bed linens in her hand as another contraction came.

"Emma." She grasped her sister's hand after the pain passed.

Pain seared Emma's arm as Caroline tugged her closer. They were alone. "Yes, Caroline, I'm here." She wished her sister'd release her wrist.

"I. Need. You to tell Jack," she grunted and her mouth twisted. "Tell Jack…"

"What do you want me to tell him?" She'd probably retch if it was to tell him his wife loved him.

"Tell him," Caroline gulped. Her eyes were bloodshot, their pupils shrinking. A sheen covered her skin. "Tell him the babe is his…"

"Of course," Emma interrupted.

"No, promise me! Promise me you'll tell him."

Emma frowned. It seemed like a ridiculous request, but she nodded. "Yes, Caroline, I'll tell him."

A fleeting smile came to Caroline's face before it contorted and she screamed.

**"Will you pardon me for asking
what the horses of your army have done
since the battle of Antietam that fatigues
anything."**

~ Abraham Lincoln's directed remark to
George B. McClellan, who had excused his lack
of action in the fall of 1862 due to tired horses.

CHAPTER THIRTEEN

*The Peninsular Campaign
Virginia, May 1862*

Jack stared down the line of his troops. They stood tense, straight, a couple of them shook, but they had their Springfield rifles loaded and ready. The air was filled with black powder, fire and smoke. Screams from men and horses fought to be heard above the noise of cannon fire and gunshots and a hint of drums and bugles in the distance. This cacophony had been continuous for the last few hours with little change. Advance, withdraw, only to advance again. War.

Jack inhaled the sulfur-laced air. "Ready!"

The order went down the line.

"Aim!" He heard the sound of rifles being raised. "Fire!"

Gunfire sounded behind him as smoke from numerous firearms engulfed them. In the distance, more moans and screams filled the air, only to be drowned out by the return volley. Jack heard the shriek of bullets. One grazed his right temple. He felt its heat. But he didn't move. This was what he had trained for, why he was here. Surprisingly, fear shot straight down his spine, but a strange indifference kept control of him.

If he died, it didn't matter. That thought stayed with him throughout the day.

The heat and mugginess of late May hung in the air, made worse by a layer of gunsmoke as suffocating as a blanket. His wool uniform weighed heavily, sodden with sweat and water from the Chickahominy River, which they had crossed two days ago. And his skin crawled with lice. The price of being a soldier, he thought.

After spending the winter under McClellan's command training troops for this elephant of war, Jack began to think what he had witnessed at Rich Mountain was all the war he'd see. Well, perhaps not the only. Battles with his wife had raged as well. Caroline had unleashed her fury at him the few times he stepped inside his own house. Her demands that he stay, to be her real husband, only drove him back to Leslie. He continued to live at the hotel, with Leslie as his mistress. She was the only comfort he had. He couldn't divorce Caroline. The Army did not approve of officers who couldn't handle their personal affairs. Dissolving a marriage was not acceptable.

Caroline had given him the out he so desperately wanted. George had remained at the house under Jack's direct order to make sure she didn't destroy it. He was also to report on any more male company she might have. Jack couldn't trust her. She claimed she had been assaulted long ago, but because of the way she had responded to his lovemaking, he concluded she had to have had a lover or two herself.

But she would not have one while she shared his last name, by God.

Two weeks after he moved into the hotel, George reported that Caroline was ill. Jack grimaced. Half of Washington was sick. Too many people, too little room. Illness spread through the Army and spilled over to civilians. But when his servant said she wasn't improving, he grudgingly returned home, made her pack and sent her and Tilly back to Virginia. Everyone knew the sick got better when taken care of by loved ones in a familiar environment. Let her father deal with her.

Unfortunately, that meant Emma would have to deal with her, too.

Caroline climbed aboard the buggy, peaked and nauseous, too sick to complain. Tilly gave him a sorrowful look as she sat across from her mistress. *Damn!*

A volley came screeching across the field at them. Confederate General James Longstreet's men held their ground between the Union troops and Richmond. Jack often ruminated on the makeup of commanders in this war. Both sides touted West Point graduates. Men who knew the art of war. The common belief this'd be over by the previous Christmas was, sadly, not the case. Neither side would quit, Jack surmised, until one side's soldiers were all dead.

His thoughts scattered when he heard cannon fire in their direction.

"Drop!" he ordered down the line. His men scrambled to the ground, some faltering over the shoulder-to-shoulder line. Soldiers to Jack's right barely had time to react when a mass of metal struck the group. Blood splattered in the air, and one man screamed. His leg was ripped from his body and flung back among the men behind him. Several yelled in pain as cannon ball fragments lodged in them.

Jack stood stunned, absently wiping his face, his hand covered in blood. The dismembered soldier lay dying, blood pumping out of the wound where his leg was once attached.

War is hell.

In the distance, Jack heard the gunfire ceasing, and he prayed silent thanks to God.

"Sir," the private said, handing Jack a piece of paper. He frowned as he looked at his messenger. When had this soldier arrived? Jack's ears were ringing—had been from the first firing of the guns—but the soldier's sudden appearance unnerved him. He shoved the paper at his corporal. "Read it." His voice sounded angry.

Corporal Rawlings tore open the note. "It's an order to retreat, Captain."

The wide field they'd been aiming at had quieted. It was a cease fire of some sort. Jack just nodded and motioned with his head to get the men back.

Jack marched alongside them as they stumbled toward camp, some five miles in the Virginia forest line.

"We'll take them secesh tomorrow!"

"Bastards! Thinkin' they're better 'en us."

Jack didn't hear the voices as numbness enveloped him. His own troops were quiet, only the clanking of metal and leather and the crushing of leaves under boots created any noise. As they walked into the midst of the Union camp, Jack turned down the officer's lane and barely made it to his tent before collapsing on his cot.

"Jack, what a fight today. Old Mac could've had them." The male voice laughed. "If he'd actually tried harder."

Jack opened his eyes and sighed. A sting of pain that

hadn't been there minutes ago shot up his right arm. Sitting up, he looked at the man as he stepped into the tent and slumped onto the only chair. Eric looked too neat and clean after a day full of bloodshed.

"So, did you win?"

Eric looked at him, his mouth dropping open until he burst out in laughter. "Yessir, got me a new pony."

Jack glared at him. "You bastard."

"Now Jacko, what can I say? You know Mac ain't going to put it all in. No, gots to save some for when those rebs come out of the woods." No matter what the reconnaissance report, McClellan remained convinced his fighting force would be overwhelmed by the number of rebels. That had delayed any trip south until the President removed some of the man's power and gave him only the Army of the Potomac to command.

A move that had placed Jack back in Virginia. And close to Rose Hill.

"Jack," Eric said, his voice flat. "You better get that looked at." He pointed at Jack's left arm.

Jack ignored him. He moved to get up from the cot, but as he pushed off, pain seared his arm. He started to fall when he glanced at his coat. It was covered in blood.

May 31, 1862

The skies opened up the following day. Fighting lulled as storms roared through, drenching everything in their path. The next morning, the swollen Chickahominy separated the Army of the Potomac, dividing McClellan's larger force into smaller contingents. Bugles sounded and drums rolled in Confederate General Joseph Johnston's camp. They would engage the Yankees at Fair Oaks. A battle that would seriously wound the general.

It was also another defeat for the Union. The troops sat close to Richmond, but McClellan did not complete the sweep. Instead, orders came down the line to retreat to north of the river to join the rest and wait for General McDowell's reinforcements.

"Can you believe this?" Eric threw the paper down to Jack.

Jack put his pencil down on his report and sat back in his chair.

"Now Eric, why should this surprise you? You were there, back at Yorktown, and saw him fall right into Confederate hands."

"Are we goin' to retreat all the way to Washington, Jack?"

Jack blinked and tried to focus. Eric had said something. "What? No, no, I don't think so." As his friend continued, Jack's mind returned to his plan.

They were maybe ten miles from Rose Hill. He felt compelled to go there. After all, his wife was there. And Emma. He'd be a fool not to acknowledge part of him wanted to see her. He figured he'd take a detail, to reconnoiter the area a little east of where the army sat across the Chickahominy. No detail was needed, but it would provide a good ruse for his commanders and for Emma if she was still angry with him.

Still angry...how could she not be?

But fear had seeped into his bones. The fighting was way too close to the Silvers' property. Perhaps it had even entered their lands. He couldn't help but worry. Thus, he'd spent all the last evening planning his mission. And given McClellan's fear of numbers, Jack had a perfect opportunity.

Standing up, he grabbed his coat and hat. He gritted his

teeth against the pain as he shrugged on his coat. Regardless of how his arm felt, he was leaving.

"Jack, where you going?"

"Got a detail to do. You know, search out the enemy's position and numbers." He dismissed it, as though it was just part of the daily routine. He had done the same thing while in the cavalry, so why not use the same excuse now?

He had to get to Emma.

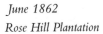

June 1862
Rose Hill Plantation

Jack's supposed desire to search the area had worked. McClellan believed Johnston's men outnumbered his own. He granted Jack a detail of ten soldiers and sent him on his way. At first, Jack took the men into the fields to search, hoping none of them mentioned he was going around in circles. Circles that tightened near the river-edged property of Rose Hill.

It was twilight as Jack marched toward the big white house. It appeared to be in good condition, unlike the rest of the property. The fields had not been destroyed by war activities, but they looked shoddy. The land was obviously untended. Where were the slaves?

Puzzled, he drew closer to the house. When he was within feet of the porch, the front door opened and Emma stepped out, armed with a rifle.

His eyebrows rose as he gestured to his men to stop. They halted. His gaze devoured her like a starving man would consume a meal. She wore a brown work dress, her hair pulled tight off her face. She stood rigid. He watched her eyes, those beautiful brown eyes, blaze.

"I want you off my land." Her voice was cold.

He took a step, meaning to say something, when she raised the weapon and pointed its muzzle at them. The gun's length equaled her height.

Click.

The sound of a hammer being cocked reverberated and reminded Jack of another time. God knew, he was familiar with that noise. He took another step. She aimed at him.

"Now, ma'am," he stated calmly.

Her eyes narrowed. Then, he saw a miniscule drop of the muzzle and barely contained his smile. The weapon was too heavy for her. Behind her, a slave, just a boy, moved into place with his own weapon aimed at them.

Jack gawked. Arming a Negro? His fear escalated. It had become clear the Silvers weren't safe here. He swallowed the knot in his throat. She had to listen to him. He'd make her believe him when he told her he was there to help.

"Please, Emma," he said softly.

He saw the flicker in her eye and her arms tense. If she pulled the trigger, the recoil would hurt her severely, sending her backwards several feet, especially at her light weight. He reached for Emma and she squeezed the trigger. He was at point blank range so he dipped his shoulder and raised her arm, pushing up the muzzle. The bullet pierced the porch's roof as Jack wrapped his arms around her, pushing her down.

He landed on top of her, his hands shielding her back from hitting the wooden floor hard. He felt her heaving body through the metal stays of her corset. Finally, she was in his arms again. Damn, she felt so good! His stared into her eyes and her gaze warmed, but a moment later, it hardened. He didn't move. Didn't want to move.

From inside the house, a baby wailed. She stiffened in his grasp. Her face became stony, and hatred flared in her eyes.

"Get off me, Jack."

"By some strange operation of magic I seem to have become the power of the land."

~ George McClellan's self-appraisal shortly after he assumed command of the Union forces around Washington, 1861

CHAPTER FOURTEEN

Rose Hill, 1862

She couldn't breathe. Yankees at her door. Jack. Everything happened at once, and she ended up in his arms. Wide eyed, she refused to blink, afraid he'd be gone, that it was a dream or maybe a nightmare. No, his emerald green eyes stared into hers, and his mouth was so close. The heat from him warmed her. His arms were so inviting and his fingers squeezed her back, making heat pool in her stomach.

Behind them, she heard the baby cry, and a woman shrieked. Reality slammed into her, almost like Jack had, but, it wasn't anywhere near as desirable. A crash of furniture finally caught her attention, and she stiffened. Yankees. Yankees had invaded her home while she lay here in Jack's arms. A glance at his shoulders made anger flare inside her again. He was wearing blue. Yankee blue.

"Get off me, Jack."

The warmth of his breath brushed across her as he let go of her and moved to get up, but his hand remained on her back. Granted, he had kept her from hitting the floor, but he was too close. She was burning from his embrace. Once he got her back on her feet, she pushed him away. Quickly, she bent to retrieve her rifle, but he beat her to it.

"I don't think you'll be needing this right now," he stated, grabbing the gunstock and moving a step away.

Furious, she stormed into the house. Chaos reigned. Tilly was screaming, her hands over her ears. Jeremiah stood to the side, his weapon also gone from his hands. If those Yankees took another gun, she'd use her father's sword on them.

"Emma." Jack called from behind her.

"You're in charge of these vermin," she seethed, hearing another door bang up upstairs. "Why are they searching my home, Lieutenant..."

He ignored her.

"Sergeant Foley," he called, standing at the foot of the grand stairs.

"Yes, sir."

"Get the men back down here," he ordered.

Emma cringed. They sounded like a herd of cattle thumping down the stairs. She wanted them out of her house. She fought every bit of desire to have Jack stay. She must be going mad.

"Miss Emma." It was Sally behind her. Emma turned. The elder slave was holding Caroline's baby in her arms. The child's crying had distracted Emma on the porch. Despite the puffy cheeks and red-rimmed eyes, the baby had quieted. Stroking the downy head of the three-month-old calmed her.

"I sees Massa Jack returned," the slave murmured. "I's done tole you he'd be back."

Sally was the only one there who remembered those dark days a year ago. Emma's world had been turned upside down to find the man she loved marrying her sister because he had compromised her. The slave had held her many nights when she couldn't sleep without waking, screaming until her lungs hurt. And despite the glimmer of hope in Sally's eyes, Emma refused to fall under his deceitful spell again.

Emma watched the soldiers march out her door, only to find Jack standing next to her. She searched his face as he watched her, taking little notice of the child. Her eyebrows creased. Like everyone else along the James River, she'd heard the fighting, constantly fretting over whether they should board up the house or hide in the smokehouse. The slaves, the handful she had left after the long winter, had hidden the remaining horses, chickens and grain from raiding armies' quartermasters. Both sides had appeared at her door, Confederates last fall and Yankees two weeks ago, looking for supplies. Paid in Confederate and Union dollars, Emma knew she'd never get back the value of what they stole. And now Jack was there. She'd yank that gun from his grasp and hit him with it if he tried to take anything more.

"Massa Jack," Sally said. Her voice broke the eye contact between Emma and Jack.

He gazed in her direction, a crooked smile coming to his lips. "Sally, with a baby," he said, the smile faltering as he glanced at Emma.

She waved the slave away and then walked to the parlor. Outside the window, dark had descended. Federal men stood on guard. Her blood boiled.

"Is that necessary?"

He leaned against the doorframe. "There're fields full of soldiers not far from here. Fight hasn't gone out of their blood. It's safer if you have some practiced men handling the weapons."

"I know how to shoot," she stated flatly. "Billy..."

Jack was next to her now. "Billy? Frankly, I'm a bit surprised he isn't here."

She scoffed. "He's off killing Yankees."

His head cocked. "How Christian of you."

She turned her head away, but her heart fluttered at the sound of his voice. "What do you want, Jack?"

～～

Silence hung between them, thick as wool. Jack felt her hostility rising—hate and fear mixed.

Where was her father? Where was Caroline? Hiding? And a baby. Emma had a baby. His gut twisted. Thinking of her being held by another man ripped through him, his mind going black at the thought. Yet he had no right to feel that way. He was married to another.

Something was amiss. He swallowed the knot of apprehension in his throat. She looked too thin to have had a baby that young. In fact, her dress, a simple frock of faded calico, hung from her frame. She didn't have the cage crinoline on, and from what he could tell, not many petticoats, as the skirt lay flat over her hips and buttocks. He glanced at her left hand and saw the narrow silver metal on her ring finger, what looked like a wedding band. He wasn't totally sure as she noticed his gaze and hid her hand in the folds of her apron.

"Emma, Emma, why is Nathan crying? Oh, Jack," John Henry started, as he walked into the entry way from the library. The worried look evaporated from his eyes and he smiled. "Jack, what do you think of your son?"

Jack's brows furrowed. His son?

"Daddy, please," Emma said, sweeping past Jack to take her father's arm. "Why don't you go back and lay down." As she turned her father, she looked over her shoulder at Jack, shaking her head tightly.

"Not until you tell me why the boy is so upset. I heard him crying."

"He's just hungry. Sally's feeding him now." She prodded him along.

Jack stood still, trying to figure things out. John Henry had aged considerably since he'd seen him only a year ago. The man's hair was tousled, as if he hadn't combed it in days. His chin was whiskered from lack of shaving, his shirt slightly askew. And he had appeared in only his shirtsleeves, a rare occurrence for the master of the house. What had happened to him? Had he seen a scar on the man's temple? Perhaps that's why he hadn't thrown Jack out. His animosity could not have ended so soon, especially if Caroline had told him that Jack had virtually abandoned her, threatening divorce.

Where was Caroline?

He started for the stairs as Emma came back, her face drawn. He reached out and took her hands, pulling her close to him.

"Emma, your father..." he started, his arms wrapped around her. Just to hold her again, to comfort her, and she seemed to relax, but it didn't last. He felt the sharp line of her shoulders stiffen under his embrace. He didn't recall her feeling so thin before. His hand traced up her neck, his fingers weaving into her tightly wound bun, and he held the back of her head to look into her eyes.

"What has happened? Was your father injured? Who did you marry?" His mouth twisted as he asked, "Where is Caroline?"

Her eyes reflected a myriad of emotions. Her bitter laugh surprised him as she broke away.

"So she lied to me. Not for the first time, but how pathetic." Her eyes blazed. "Nathan is your son."

Jack was stunned. It was the effect she wanted, had strived for and yet, it brought her no satisfaction. She longed to be in his arms again, to be embraced in his warmth. Her gaze rolled down his body and back to his face. He had become lean, and when he held her, his chest, shoulders and arms were hard, the line of muscles rippling with his movements. Those green eyes remained the same, vibrant above high cheekbones, a straight nose and a sharp jawline. His jaw twitched as minutes passed and the news settled.

He'd hate her before she was through, although she had pined for him when he left her. God still hated her. He'd make Jack desert her–again.

Her gut clenched. Those thoughts were evil. What about her husband?

"Where is my wife?" The words were hard and cold. What else had she expected?

She swallowed hard, fearful of his reaction. "She's dead, Jack, died in the birthing bed."

He blinked. Color faded from his face. Puzzlement crossed his eyes. "She wasn't carrying when I sent her home."

Emma nodded slowly.

His expression turned cold. She felt chilled by it.

"That is not my child."

Memories of Caroline's last few hours, rocking in labor pains, came back to Emma. Her sister's plea to tell Jack the babe was his echoed in her ears. What had Caroline done to make her fear that her husband would deny being a father?

"Jack, she swore..."

He laughed and walked away. "Emma, after all this time, you believed her?" He snorted. "You don't understand. There is no way that child is mine. None."

"Of all the people to say that," she said, her nerves bristling. "She was your wife."

He faced her, anger etched into his face. "Yes, she was. And I know perfectly well what she was."

Tilly snuck up next to her, tugging at her arm. "Miss Emma."

Emma stared at his snarling face, not understanding. He had betrayed her to be with beautiful Caroline. He had married her. How could he deny his own child? It wouldn't take long for him to figure out he was Nathan's father, just by counting back the months. Granted, she hadn't told him when the child was born, but his disbelief made her withhold that information.

How dare he deny Nathan? She'd give anything to have had him herself. Her heart wept. Not for Caroline but for the babe whose father denied him. With utter disgust, she turned and followed Tilly.

Jack steamed at the idea. Caroline swore the child was his. Of course, otherwise, the babe would be considered a bastard. Jack had been foolish for tolerating that woman, knowing she entertained men while he was at war. He had no doubt she had continued after he moved out. He spat in disgust, marring the wood floor, but he didn't care.

Staring at nothing, he gradually felt the slave's presence. Sally was shaking her head at him. He snorted. She could berate him all she wanted. It was strange. He never really grew accustomed to being married, and now, he didn't know how to act as a widower. A thought came to him that he was free, but a crushing feeling hit him. Emma wasn't free. Who had she married?

"Massa Jack."

He gave up ignoring the slave. "What?"

The plump woman waddled up to him, still holding the babe. He sucked on the cloth over her shoulder. Jack shook his head. There was no resemblance in that child to him. Couldn't be his...but a thought struggled for acknowledgement. They had consummated their marriage fully. His eyes closed tight. *No, no...*

The rustling of Sally's skirt and apron stopped, and he opened his eyes. She was standing in front of him. "I know Miss Caroline, helped raise her as well as Miss Emma and Massa Charles," the woman's soft voice said. She adjusted her hold on the infant. "But, I's believe Miss Caroline. This here child is yours."

"Sally..."

"Now, I know she done you wrong with Miss Emma. Cain't help that now. But don't you be takin' out on Miss Emma any troubles you had. That poor chile was bad then and has more than enough on her plate now witout you yellin' at her." She kissed the babe's head and glanced at Jack with a smile. "He looks jus' like you."

He gritted his teeth but did look. The babe had a fuzz of light brown hair on his head, and his eyes were sky blue. Hell, Jack didn't have a clue what he himself looked like as a babe, and his brother was too close to his age to remember. He shook his head.

"I don't see any resemblance."

She chuckled. "Of course, you be looking the wrong way. But I see you in him. Don't you be worrying none about his eyes. All white babes be born with blue. I'm bettin' they'll change right directly."

Jack was about to argue the point when he heard the roar of cannon in the distance. It was faint but distinct. He swallowed. The War. They had to leave.

"Sally, despite how I feel, I have to go."

She nodded. He started toward the door when she spoke. "Ya know, Massa Jack, Miss Emma shed plenty a tear over you. Used to scream something fierce at night in her sleep after you took Miss Caroline. I 'spect she'll be screamin' again now you done return."

"But I haven't returned," he countered. "I just had to make sure she, I mean all of you, were all right."

"Uh huh," she murmured. "So you came back only to leave her agin?"

"I can't stay and protect her! She has a husband, for God's sake." He ran his fingers through his hair. He had a son he needed to protect. Damn. "Where's the bastard anyway?"

"Massa Billy? He be off fightin'."

Hell and damnation! She married Billy? Jealousy enveloped him.

"Sir, we gotta rider lookin' for us," the sergeant interjected at the door.

With a snarl, Jack grabbed his hat and headed toward the door, only to stop and look again at the boy. The infant was curled fast asleep on the slave's shoulder. A son. Christ.

"Tell her, tell her..." he was lost. That he would return?

Would he? Could he? "I will be back. I promise." And he stormed out the door.

Emma stood behind the stairs, listening to Jack trying to deny Nathan was his, and her heart twisted for the babe. It skipped a beat when she heard Sally bring up those dark days. She was afraid the slave was right and she'd have no sleep tonight for fear of the screaming.

And when Jack swore before he marched out of her life again that he'd be back, her heart shattered because she knew it was a promise he wouldn't keep.

"It was not war – it was murder."
~ Confederate General D.H. Hill, describing
their defeat at the Battle of Malvern Hill

CHAPTER FIFTEEN

Virginia, July 1862

Damn! They retreated again. Jack spat on the ground as orders came down the line. The hasty defensive maneuver against the onslaught of Robert E. Lee's army fell apart quickly. Jack inhaled deeply, the gunsmoke-filled air foul but familiar, almost calming, a strange effect and one he'd contemplate later. Turning on his heel, he ordered his troops to cease fire as they retreated further down the peninsula toward York. McClellan was an ass, having left his command to make it to the James River and aboard the *USS Galena*. It was a horrible example for the men who'd follow him to hell and back, Jack thought.

The ground the Union retreated from was Malvern Hill. Jack knew the area. It was the site of Billy Bealke's family home. He wondered about Billy's strong attachment to the Silvers sisters. The man had always been around their home, was always so attentive to them. And he had married Emma.

A bullet whizzed past his ears, snapping Jack back to the present. Since leaving Emma two weeks ago, he'd been plagued by thoughts of her and her son. No, his son.

And his dead wife's. Had he caused her death by sending her home when she was carrying his child? Did he feel remorse for what happened to her? With the roar of gunfire and cannons everywhere, it was difficult to feel much of anything other than numbness.

"Sir."

Jack looked at the soldier and took the note he held out. More orders, to take position with McCall's division as Union forces encircled Malvern Hill. He crumpled the paper. The men voiced their concern. Where was their general? What stupidity, to leave his troops as the Confederates advanced. Jack glanced at his timepiece. Three in the afternoon.

Confederate forces had been under attack by Union guns, situated well on the hillside, but now, General Armistead's forces attacked the Federal line and were soon to be reinforced by Magruder's men. Excitement raced through his veins. He ordered his men to aim and fire, watching the impact their firepower had on the enemy. Groans and screams competed with the sound of rifles and cannon fire. He witnessed some of his troops fall to the ground, some crying out in pain from their injuries, others silent forever. Once again, Jack didn't move. He had no concern about his own health. If he was to die there, so be it. He was ready.

He is yours.

Jack thought he heard Emma's voice in his ears and shook his head. But he could see her now, in his mind, despite focusing on the fight before him. Issuing orders to reload, he fought the distraction of memories of Emma.

As the sun set, its glorious colors muted by a thick layer of smoke enveloping the land, the secesh troops stopped at about 200 yards before reaching and breaking the Union middle. The wounded force retreated, and Union guns fell silent as night descended on the field. Jack swallowed hard, trying to wet his dry throat. His mouth tasted like it had cotton in it, and his nostrils burned from the gunsmoke hanging in the air. His eyes were dry and gritty. Standing firm on the sodden ground, he struggled to focus and keep his balance. With his ears still plugged from the noise of artillery and rifle fire, he turned to inspect his men.

An hour later, Jack sat at the table near his tent, paper before him. A report on injuries, supplies and performance on the field had to be written, but he just stared at the paper, numbness spreading through him, stealing his ability to think clearly. He heard some men talking quietly around the camp, more of them resting after days of strenuous activity. Tension was thick. They were in Confederate territory, the enemy only yards away. And their commander was...

Thwack.

The table wobbled from the weight of saddlebags that had been dropped on it. The rattling broke through Jack's thoughts, and he looked up at the tall, lanky officer standing before him. Rathborne Sinclair, caked in dirt, sweat rolling off his temples, his blue eyes bloodshot, grinned broadly.

"Done with your report, huh?" The man laughed, yanking his hat off to wipe his forehead.

Rathborne, Captain of Company C, was an old friend from their days in Texas. The Ohioan hadn't been like many of the other Northerners of the 2nd Cavalry who had held his Southern slave-holding family against him. Resentment among the ranks toward Southerners in the Union Army was barely concealed, and Jack was well aware of it. It didn't help that his southern drawl occasionally seeped into his speech.

"Jack, were you hit or what?"

Jack blinked. He apparently hadn't been listening to Rathborne's account of his ventures on the field.

"Sorry, deep in thought, I guess" he replied.

Rathborne leaned across the table, his voice dropped, "Just what did you find on the reconnaissance? You haven't been the same since you returned."

"Nothing." He denied even to himself that things were different. But it hadn't gone unnoticed by others.

"Bullshit," Rathborne spat. "Jack, I've heard some of the men talk. You're not sleeping, you ramble to no one, and that drawl of yours has gotten thick at times. Mind you, I know you well enough, but others..." he sighed. "Others could cause you problems."

Jack closed his eyes, shutting the world out. *Caroline, why? A babe. Why had she never told him? It was a responsibility he didn't want. Hell, he never even wanted a wife. Never.* Visions of his father loomed large, the reprimanding patriarch of the Fontaine family. The forced lessons of tradition, honor, family name and justification for ignoring the rights of others. Especially the slaves. The tears on his mother's face. He shuddered again at the memories.

"Jack!" Rathborne's voice penetrated through the fog inside his head. He opened his eyes, not realizing that his hands had closed into fists.

"I," he glanced up, his voice gravelly. "I went to see my wife."

"Good God, man, have you lost your wits?"

"The fighting was close to her family's home. I couldn't not go." He bit his tongue to keep from saying more. Admitting it was his wife's sister that drew him there would not endear him to his friend.

Rathborne stared at him, silent. Inhaling deeply, he finally said, "I gather it wasn't an opportune visit."

"Caroline and I had had an unfriendly discussion before she left. And now, she's dead." His breath hitched when saying the words. Once again, a wave of sadness hit him, then relief, the tension dissipating. Guilt quickly followed that. It was wrong not to grieve for your wife—especially when she had died giving birth to a son...his son. Knowing Caroline, however, Jack's doubts remained. She had manipulated him into marrying her, only to entertain other men when he returned to duty. Despite Sally's words, he still didn't believe the child was his, but that didn't eliminate his obligation to raise the child as though he was.

"Oh, Jack, I'm sorry," Rathborne's soft words interrupted Jack's thoughts again.

Jack snorted. "Yes, and she left me with a brawling brat." Abruptly, he stood, knocking the table, the inkpot tipping and spilling across the paper.

Rathborne righted the bottle and stared at his friend. Jack paced. He knew his friend's eyes were on him. He couldn't tell the Ohioan about his wife's presumed infidelities. His masculine pride wouldn't allow it.

"You could ask for leave, Jack. Surely McLaw..."

"To hell with McLaw..." he snarled. "I'm better off here. At least here, I can kill the enemy and not get arrested for murder." Odd thoughts invaded his mind. Yes, he could vent all his pent-up frustration there, on the battlefield. Escape his own fate, the fate he'd sworn to avoid. And now, the only woman he wanted, once again, he couldn't have. She had married someone else. He remembered her touch. That memory never left him. Perhaps that's why his marriage was a disaster and why he could find no release now with Leslie.

Rathborne's eyes still bore into him. "I suppose that's true. Look, I've a report to write. So do you. Daylight'll be here sooner than we think. Hear Mac's taking us north. Word is, he'll be stripped of commanding the whole army for not pushing Richmond." The man shrugged. "I be thinkin' he knows Lee. Scared of him."

"Naw," Jack gave his friend a half-hearted grin. "He be thinkin' Lee's got more men. Been on his staff in Washington. Always wantin' more men himself. The President, I think, is tired of waiting."

Rathborne snorted and pulled a flask from his saddlebag. "I'll leave this for you. I think you need it more than I do right now." He placed it on the table as he stood and grabbed his bags. "Write your damn report. And get some rest."

"Right," Jack muttered, watching the man amble off. He sat back down, crumpling the top page on the stack of paper and picking up the pen again. With a weary sigh, he pulled the wadded lace handkerchief from the inner pocket of his uniform jacket. Emma's handkerchief. It was worn and dirty, the lace hanging on by only a few threads. But it gave him solace. Holding it kept his personal demons at bay better than whiskey did. Dipping the quill in the inkwell, he wrote his report, handkerchief wrapped inside his other hand, and tried to forget what he'd lost and lose himself in blood and war.

The change in military command of the Union Army kept Jack occupied for several weeks. McClellan's decision to retreat rather than pursue and take Richmond made Lincoln place Henry Halleck general in chief of the Army and place General John Pope in command of the newly formed Army of Virginia. Both men had served well in the West, and Lincoln's hopes for continued success brought them back East. Jack, along with many other commanders, bristled under Pope's arrogant command. A few, like John C. Fremont, actually refused to serve under him, making Pope bring in General Franz Siegel from the West. The German had a grasp of military tactics, but stories abounded of his failure at Wilsons' Creek in Missouri, of his withdrawal, leaving Union troops vulnerable.

But Pope's presumed success in the East failed to materialize. Jack, along with the rest of McClellan's Army of the Potomac, marched north toward Manassas Junction, Virginia to reinforce Pope's forces. When they arrived, however, Stonewall Jackson's troops bombarded Pope's troops, confusing and worrying the general after Jackson's forces also destroyed the federal supply depot at Manassas. Pope lashed out, hoping to overcome Jackson before General James Longstreet's troops arrived.

Jack understood the scene evolving before him late on August 28 as he led his men once more into the mouth of hell. His ears fell deaf to anything other than the roar of cannons and rifles, the moaning of the wounded and the sound of bugles and drums signaling down the line. He had his men retreat and then try again. The ground sucked his boots into a mire of blood and water. At times, his men didn't respond fast enough. They were sluggish in the mud, some having to dig their brogans out of it before they could move at all.

That night, Jack ate with the other officers. Rathborne brought another full flask with him, and they split the contents, absorbing information as it came in. Longstreet's men, thirty thousand strong, give or take ten thousand depending on the officer who heard it, was spotted only a night's march away.

Gulping the last of the smooth Kentucky whiskey—

where Rathborne got it, Jack didn't ask—he noticed the tension in Pope's voice.

"Pack up, Jack," Rathborne grumbled. "Bet you five, we'll be gone tomorrow."

Jack shook his head. "We'll be here forever. Maybe we should just let them go."

His friend asked "You'd give up your chance to return home?"

With a loud laugh, one that made half the men around him turn, Jack's face became hard. "I left home over ten years ago. I will not return. Not under the current circumstances and probably not afterward." The venom in his voice came from his soul. He caught Rathborne's look of surprise and saw out of the corner of his eye the men around him speaking in lowered voices. He didn't care. Jean Baptist Fontaine could rot in hell for all Jack cared. And even that wasn't enough punishment. Not for the dictating tyrant he had been and still was.

September 17, 1862
Sharpsburg, Maryland

Jack looked down his line of infantrymen, all poised and ready to be called on. Tugging his pistol out of its holster, Jack snapped the barrel out, re-loaded and shut it.

He'd been ready for days, perhaps weeks by that time. It all ran together in his head because sleep or any real rest had constantly eluded him. It was either look forward to the fight, for the chance to kill, or succumb to nightmares. Every night, when he lay his head down and closed his eyes, Emma, the child, his father and Caroline spoke. Well, perhaps Emma was silent, but her eyes told him the truth.

The child was his. And despite his own denial, he had a responsibility he couldn't ignore.

McClellan resumed command of the combined northern armies as the Army of the Potomac after Pope's disaster in August along Bull Run Creek, near Manassas Junction. As Pope retreated to Washington with his troops, Lincoln had switched back to Little Mac, and the men welcomed his return. But it didn't slow their return to Union lines because scouts informed the general that Lee was heading north, presumably to take Washington. The route took them through occupied Maryland. Regardless of why Lee moved above the Mason Dixon Line, McClellan remained cautious.

The snail's pace of the Union Army rattled the nerves of soldiers like Jack. The quiet was Jack's greatest enemy. Too much free time allowed his mind to wander. He wrote numerous reports, drilled his men to excess, played every game in camp that'd take bets from an officer and avoided everyone at mail call because no one wrote him. His misery was complete.

Emma was south, caring for his son. Virginia was a battleground and would be till this war ended because the secesh capital sat in Richmond. Rose Hill was less than a day's ride from there, sitting on the James River. Prime land for an attack. For occupation. For death. He had to get them out of there, and his need grew daily. But the army was not granting leaves, particularly to officers who wanted to enter enemy territory to rescue their families.

Four days earlier, Jack had led a reconnaissance patrol into an area just outside Frederick, Maryland where the Rebs had camped the night before. While scouring the site for any clues as to their direction, one of his men came up to him.

"Sir," the corporal said, handing Jack three cigars wrapped in a piece of paper.

Jack took the cigars and pulled the paper off them, but as he peeled the wrapping back, he found writing on the inside. He stared blankly at the page. The handwriting was familiar from his days at the Point–the writing of Robert E. Lee. Commands for the next line of movement. He dropped the cigars and jumped onto Goliath's back, racing to McClellan.

The general read the orders and his lips curved upward. "Here is a paper with which, if I cannot whip Bobbie Lee, I will be willing to go home."

Excitement spread throughout the camp, even igniting Jack. He ordered his men to be ready to move. A move that didn't happen for another sixteen hours.

"What the hell!" Rathborne threw his knapsack down after another patrol. "Those Rebs gotta know they've lost their orders. They'll switch what they're doing when we could've moved and had them by now!"

Jack snorted. "You know Mac. He won't move till he's damn good and ready. Hear he's waiting for the rest of the army to get up here. Hedging his bets not on us beating Lee but just finding him."

And the forces did arrive. Lining Antietam Creek, the Union Army found Lee's across the water. The landscape turned blue within a day. But it wouldn't be until the 17th that Major General Joseph Hooker led the first attack. "Fighting Joe" was his nickname, and Hooker definitely lived up to it, swearing loudly as troops marched across a cornfield. After the first line of gunfire, the Rebs returned fire. It took only a short time for the devastation to unfold. Jack stood witness as gunfire downed over half of the 12th Massachusetts alone in only minutes.

Orders came down the line. Jack inhaled. With his revolver drawn, he shouted, "Forward!"

They fell in with the rest of the advancing troops. Hooker's front line was near a little white church on a knoll. As they drew closer, grey Confederate uniforms broke, scurrying into the woods as Hooker swore violently, almost demonically, firing his own weapon.

But the tables were turned. Jack saw the other army coming toward them like mad men, guns blazing into the Union line. He halted his men. The first volley from the Rebel line looked like a scythe in a field of corn, cutting down the lead troops within minutes.

"Front to the left!" Jack ordered, spinning toward the woods. His men quickly followed as the Rebel army burst onto the field with a bloodcurdling yell, scaring men out of their wits.

Battle raged across the cornfield, back and forth, under the noonday sun. The Confederate center became part of a sunken dirt road that separated the farms during peacetime. It served as a trench the Rebs used to annihilate advancing Yankee troops by simply rising from it to fire and then drop down again for protection. Unit after unit fell back under the onslaught of Southern fire until a New York unit found a spot where they could fire down into the lane. As they did so, the sunken road became a slaughter pen, the Rebs unable to move out fast enough to evade Yankee gunfire. Their bullets came fast and furious in retaliation for the destruction of their own.

Jack withdrew his men from the attack on the sunken road to aid General Burnside's brigade as it struggled to cross Antietam Creek by a bridge. The larger force of twelve thousand, though, was easy pickings for the Confederates on the bluff above.

"Sir, 12th reporting," Jack said, reaching Burnside.

The general was grizzled and dirty. Stroking his long sideburns, he looked at the bluff and shook his head. Jack turned in time to see a group of flamboyantly clothed Zouaves from New York charge up the hill, screaming at the top of their lungs, only to be quickly repulsed.

"Three hours. Three hours, I tell you," the commander muttered.

"Sir," Jack tried to get his attention. "We outnumber them. They won't have enough men or firepower to last."

Burnside turned and stared at him. Wide-eyed, almost frantic, he seemed startled by Jack's voice. He shoved the telescope into Jack's hands. "Really, Captain? What is it, Captain?"

"Fontaine, sir."

"Captain Fontaine," the officer stated, his lips a cruel grin. "Do you see them leaving? Do you?"

Jack extended the scope and looked. At first, it appeared they were retreating, but then, he saw a grey cloud behind them. One that grew bigger every moment. Reinforcements.

"Sir, they've got reinforcements."

"What?" Burnside yanked back the scope and looked. "Fire and damnation!" He stormed to his portable desk and scribbled a message and handed it to his aid. "Take this to the General."

Jack frowned and pulled at his collar, standing with Burnside. The soldiers tried to get off the bridge on the other side but succumbed to gunfire. Jack refused to send his men to their death without a direct order.

The aid rushed back into camp and gave Burnside the response he awaited. He opened it and uttered a curse. "It would not be prudent." He threw the paper to the desk.

"The bastard refuses to send me reinforcements. Damn him!"

The carnage continued till sunset, when all firing stopped. Jack heard the wounded on the field and went with others to carry them away. It was a waking nightmare. With each injured man removed, numerous dead remained. Jack knew the same degree of destruction could easily happen wherever the armies collided for as long as the war continued. And Virginia was ripe for similar carnage.

Emma and his son could easily become victims.

The thought ate at him, and his stomach twisted.

He couldn't let that happen and prayed they were still safe. He had to believe they were. But as he stood there, in the blood-soaked field with its harvest of dead, he knew he had to take them away from Rose Hill, away from Virginia. But where? He'd sworn he'd never return to his own family. It was the last place he wanted to go—ever. But, Jean Baptiste Fontaine was a wealthy man with connections in Europe as well as the North. He could protect them and would, especially when he learned Nathan was his grandson.

Swallowing the bile rising in his throat, Jack made a decision.

At first light, the Union Army discovered Lee had retreated to Virginia. And so had Jack Fontaine.

"If you don't have my army supplied, and keep it supplied, we'll eat your mules up, sir."

~ William T. Sherman, to an army quartermaster before moving his army from Chattanooga toward Atlanta

CHAPTER SIXTEEN

Rose Hill, Virginia, Fall 1862

Emma heard him coming. She sat rocking the baby, cooing softly, trying to get him to sleep. Nathan stared into her eyes, determined to stay awake. His little body was tense, but when she hummed a melody, it relaxed him. And his vibrant green eyes would close. Her humming hitched as she looked into Nathan's eyes. Jack's eyes. How could he deny this child?

The even step and click of wood, a rhythm of sorts, grew louder. It stopped in the doorway behind her. Still gazing out over the veranda railing, she ceased humming but not rocking.

"Billy, you shouldn't be up," she scolded.

A tight laugh echoed behind her. "You tell me that every day. If I don't get up and practice, how will I ever be able to dance with you again?"

Emma closed her eyes. Dance. Billy would never dance again, not with only one leg and crutches. She could hear his rasping breath. He was braver than any man she knew, not giving up despite having lost a leg. It had to have been devastating to awaken in the field hospital with only one leg.

Billy hopped over to the chair next to her rocker and fell onto the seat. His crutches crashed to the floor. She glared at him, still rocking, hoping the movement would keep the little one asleep.

"Sorry," he murmured.

Silence filled the air. The affectionate companionship they'd shared prior to the war was slipping away with each day.

She rocked for a few more minutes, feeling the babe grow heavy in her arms. At close to eight months, he was no longer just a squalling bundle of hungry, sleepy flesh. Emma realized the little boy was getting under her skin and into her heart. He was hard to resist despite the fear that he might not make it to his first birthday. With Caroline gone, he had no one but her to mother him. Especially since his father had abandoned him. Little Nathan was the closest Emma would ever come to having her own child...

"Miss Emma, let me take that boy," Sally said, holding out her arms.

Emma rose slowly, trying not to jostle the sleeping babe. Nathan cooed in her arms, his little lips pursing in his sleep. She smiled and bent to kiss his forehead before she handed him over to the slave.

"Thank God for Sally," Billy said. "At least she's still here."

Emma went to the railing and looked out at the fields. The barren fields.

"How many are gone?" he asked.

She sighed. "Last report, ten more. Field hands, mostly." The price of war. With Billy having returned maimed, he couldn't be of much help. Her father was sinking more and more into dementia. And Charles was still gone. Everything had fallen into her lap, and she hated the burden. "I'm not sure how we'll get through the winter, especially if we get another visit from either side."

The chair behind her scraped the wood floor. She should look at him at least. He had not inflicted the injury on himself, nor the pain and suffering it caused. It hurt her to see him trying so hard to stand again, to feel like a man again. She was a coward for not looking.

Billy struggled to get up. The damn crutches hurt his armpits, no matter how much wrapping Sally put on them. The pain in the stump of his right thigh ricocheted through him at every movement. It speared into his hip and back. Morphine helped, but it was harder to come by, and he knew it could make matters worse in the long run.

He saw his wife wince whenever he hobbled around, the look gnawing at his gut more and more each day. Last winter, after escorting her father home, he'd left again as an able-bodied man. A skirmish with Yankees not far from Winchester got him in a mess, with a gunshot to his calf. The butcher of the 5th Virginia had dug too deeply into his leg, searching for the bullet, despite Billy's protest that the man was only pushing the lead further in. He could feel it tearing the inside of his limb. Blood splattered everywhere. Lightheaded and sick, Billy was overwhelmed by darkness as the man shoved the metal probe deeper still.

Two days later, he awoke to a searing pain in his leg. When he tried to move it, nothing happened. He looked down to find it was missing from below the middle of his thigh, which was wrapped in bandages. That had almost done him in. An amputee. He had returned home an invalid. He remembered Emma's face when she glanced into the buckboard to find him prostrate and in pain. It had paled even in the heat of July's sun.

That first month home, he'd lost himself in all the alcohol he could drink—with Sammy's aid. The old slave had kept him supplied, but why, Billy didn't know. Bedridden and drunk, he snapped at Emma every time she came to change his dressings and feed him. Even now, he had to bite his tongue to keep from yelling at her, wanting her to hit him or scream or something.

She had taken on the responsibility of the house, the remaining slaves, her father, her nephew and now her husband. She had no choice. He saw the wear and tear it had on her day after day. The only joy she had was Nathan, but there was sadness even in that.

"I see you're walking better," she finally said. She turned to him and gave him a fleeting half smile. "Before long, you'll be using only a cane."

It was a lie, but if it made her feel better, he wouldn't argue the point.

He leaned harder on the right crutch, freeing his left hand to caress her face. "Oh, Emma, I'm so sorry."

He saw the sheen of tears in her eyes as she shook her head and placed her fingers on his lips. "Shh," she said.

"I did wrong to you," he finally stammered. Guilt invaded his soul. "God's punishing me. I can only beg your forgiveness."

She nodded. "It's all right..."

"No, no it's not." Self-anger and hatred spurred him on. She had done nothing to deserve this. "I should have stopped her. I knew what she was up to..."

"Billy, don't," she whispered.

"Emma, I know you loved Jack. She took him from you, and I'm sorry." He saw her shudder.

"Billy, stop, please." A tear trailed down her cheek.

"You know I love you. I loved Caroline too. Perhaps, I loved her too much. I gave into her," his voice graveled. "Because I took her, I can't really have you." He faltered as her face fell, and his stomach pained him almost as badly as his wound. But he deserved it. And her hatred.

Her hand flew to her mouth, deadening a sob.

"Emma, I love you, but you deserve so much better than me," he ground out. "And I'll never be able to give you a child. Please," he begged, "forgive me."

———⁓⁓———

In the pre-dawn hours after the battle at Antietam Creek, Jack slipped out of camp, taking his bedroll, revolver and Goliath. Taking the horse was a gamble, but Jack didn't care. Rathborne would know he'd left for Virginia, but he trusted the Ohioan to remain quiet. Why, he wasn't sure. The man could turn him in and reveal where he'd gone, but something deep inside Jack told him Rathborne wouldn't.

It was quiet where Confederates had been camped. Lee had also left under the cloak of darkness. In a fit of self-loathing, Jack asked himself what other man would desert his own son and leave the woman he loved vulnerable to the enemy. He had to get them to safety.

Leading Goliath out of camp had been relatively easy. Sentries were alert but scattered. After what had been a day full of death, even the bravest lads couldn't stay awake. But Jack felt every inch of him alive and alert as he moved slowly through the woods, trying to hide himself and the large black beast.

Sun rose on a cool fall morning. He had stopped to

survey the ground ahead and let the animal graze. If he could shadow Lee's army, he'd have cover to escape the Union. But, when the Confederates found him, he had to be able to walk away a free man. He pulled off his black felt officer's hat, feeling chilled with his scalp exposed to the breeze. The hat's brim rose on the sides, anchored by a brass eagle on one side, a dark plume on the other. He yanked off the bird as well as the plume. The sky-blue cord, the color of the infantry, around the crown was next, followed by the brass bugle ornament of the foot soldier and the number twelve, which indicated his unit. The now unadorned hat still had the army form, so he grabbed the brim and forced it to curl under.

He pulled off the U.S. emblem from Goliath's chest strap, and flipping the saddle blanket hid its U.S. marking. He couldn't remove the brass medallions from the bridle without destroying the piece and reluctantly left them in place.

"You were stolen," he said to the horse, patting his withers. "Remember that if they ask."

The animal raised his head, still munching on grass, and snorted as though in agreement. Jack chuckled.

His clothing was next. It would be risky to ride into Virginia dressed as a Yankee soldier. He then rode into Morgantown, which straddled the borders of Virginia and Pennsylvania. Shoving his frock into his saddlebag and throwing his overcoat underneath the bedroll, he looked for someone to exchange clothes with. The appearance of the town square indicated the village had been ravaged by the war.

Goliath's hooves created a small cloud of dust as they plodded along the street. Jack scanned the storefronts, hotels and saloon, but all was quiet. Except for the pattering of feet behind him, he would have thought the town deserted. With a slow smile, he turned in the saddle and saw two young boys, back far enough to prevent being kicked, their eyes riveted on Jack.

"Whoa," he said, flicking the reins and leaning back in the saddle. He concentrated for a moment before saying anything. He'd been up North for so long, he knew he didn't sound as Southern as he needed to now without working on it. The boys were about ten or twelve. Their clothing was too small to be of use to him, but... "Good morning, gentlemen."

They stopped but didn't run and stood staring at him as though he was the devil delivered. He guessed he probably was.

Their ragged and dirty clothing was promising, though. He hoped someone bigger would happily exchange their equally shoddy wear for a finely tailored wool suit, especially with winter coming.

"Perhaps you boys can help me," he continued, slipping back into his Louisiana drawl. "Is your daddy around?"

***

Emma lay on the mattress, her eyes wide open, unable to sleep. It was before dawn, still dark outside. She heard the grandfather clock in the hall chime four and quietly sighed. So close to the time to rise...

It had turned a bit chilly in the early morning hours. She shivered, wanting to edge back into Billy's embrace, but she didn't. He had insisted they sleep together again. That his injury was better, but she saw him fighting the pain. His stump still looked inflamed. But he remained stoic, pulling her into his arms every night, claiming he could keep her warm. That was true, as even his breath on her back helped.

She shut her eyes and shuddered. A week had passed since he'd confessed to her. He appeared much relieved afterward, but she hadn't been. She sometimes still enjoyed his company. But the fact that he'd slept with Caroline had been salt in her wounds.

Why had his revelation surprised her? Caroline had taken everything that Emma had or hoped for. Everything. Even as a child she had been greedy. First taking Emma's dolls, clothes, ribbons and schoolbooks, then taking men from her. She didn't doubt Caroline would have stolen Angel, too, except the mare didn't like Caroline and bit her on any occasion when she got too close. What a smart horse Angel had been... Then the Yankees showed up and found her in the woods where Emma had hidden her.

Caroline took Jack. And then, she learned Caroline had taken Billy, too. The news had almost destroyed Emma. What did she have left? Nothing but a house to run and maintain, her brother's fate unknown, her father's mental stability waning, slaves leaving...and Caroline's baby. A baby God had granted Caroline and Jack but not Emma and Billy. Billy had tried to make love to her since he returned from the war. But he couldn't last because pain from his leg intensified as his excitement grew.

Frustrated, she threw off the blanket and got up. Nathan slept through the night now. Tilly took care of him when Sally was busy and slept in the same room with him, freeing Emma to leave the house. She put on her chemise and corset, knowing her weight loss would make it necessary to adjust them soon. Shrugging on a simple work dress of brown and cream plaid, she eased her way down the stairs and out the back door.

Even the armies remained quiet at pre-dawn. Emma hadn't heard of any more battles nearby, but fighting men passed through on their way north. The patrols that rode through the area, to "protect" the families of soldiers and prevent any mischief were troublemakers themselves. But they, too, slept now.

At that hour of the day, she could spend some rare time alone, with no one fretting over her health or coming to her with their problems. It was a slice of Heaven.

She moved silently to the barn. The two remaining cows needed to be milked–a chore she disliked but one that had to be done. Tilly was worthless at it and Sally too old. Emma needed Jemmy and Jeremiah and the remaining hands for fieldwork. Frankly, she always dreaded the morning. Reports, of another hand leaving, more food being taken, a chicken missing, seemed to occur daily. Money was scarce, and goods to buy were dwindling. Winter was going to be hard.

The barn door needed repair, too, because it had become hard to open. Emma slammed her shoulder into it with all her might, and it slowly gave way.

"Morning, ladies." She hung her lantern on the peg. Glancing at the dim light, she realized she should have left the lamp and made her way in the dark because their supply of oil was low. Grabbing the stool and bucket, she stepped to the first stall.

"Why, hello there, my pretty."

Emma froze. The male voice came from a dark corner of the barn. It had startled her. She didn't recognize the voice. Fear snaked down her spine, and her hold on the bucket tightened. She swallowed the knot in her throat and slowly turned.

The speaker revealed himself and went toward her.

"Who are you?" she demanded, taking a step back.

He was young, close to her age but slovenly looking.

Wearing torn clothing, he reeked of sweat, blood and whiskey. He grinned at her, his dry, cracked lips parting to show her yellowed, broken teeth.

She took another step back as he came closer, and she met the wall of the barn.

"Oh, pretty, it's been too long," he drawled slowly, his knuckles caressing her cheek.

Her breath was ragged as she gulped huge breaths. His greasy black hair fell in disarray around his whiskered and weathered face.

"You better leave me be," she warned, but her heart thudded so loudly that she couldn't hear her own voice.

"Why? Me and you could have a good time." He was excited knowing he had her cornered. His fingers trailed down her neck and into her bodice, yanking it down and splitting the material. "Ah, ain't they ripe for the pickin'," his voice was husky as he grabbed her right breast and squeezed it out of the corset.

She opened her mouth to scream when his other hand covered it. "No, I'm thinkin' you should be quiet. All I'm wantin' is some of you. If you scream, I'll have to shoot your husband, the cripple." He let go of her breast but not her mouth. She wished he hadn't. When he brought his hand back up, it held a knife.

"See?" he said, using the knife to slice down the front of her dress and petticoat.

Emma closed her eyes. Then she opened her mouth to bite his hand when she heard the click of a gun at the door.

"Boy, get off her." The voice was angry, demanding. It was Jack's. She blinked. No, it couldn't be Jack.

The vermin holding her didn't even flinch but shouted over his shoulder, "You can have her after I am done with her."

In a split second, the man released her as an explosion sounded in the barn. Sulfur and gunpowder filled the air as the man fell into a heap on the floor, blood pouring from him.

"Emma."

She couldn't hear well after the shot.

"Jack?"

The sun hadn't yet reached the horizon, but Jack figured he was close to Rose Hill. He was so tired, he slouched over Goliath's neck. The animal plodded along slowly, but Jack wouldn't stop.

At the top of the rise, he glanced down and saw the house.

"Boy, we made it," he whispered to the horse, patting his neck. With a second wind fortifying him, Jack sat up and nudged his ride faster. "Almost done, boy, then you can rest."

They crossed the creek and entered the pastures surrounding the barn. Jack saw a woman leave the house, carrying a lantern to the barn. She was thin, with a regular work dress on in some dark color, and her hair was pulled back in a knot on her head. He wanted to call to her, but he'd have to yell for her to hear him, and at this time of the morning, it probably would scare her to death.

She walked into the barn before he got there. He smiled. Milking cows. Funny how war could change a person, in this case from privileged young lady to hardworking farmhand. Not that Emma had been as spoiled as his wife, but he'd bet his horse she'd never expected to milk a cow in her life. He chuckled.

As they made it to the barn, Goliath sidestepped, snorting

and shaking his head. Something felt wrong. Jack slid off the horse and pulled out his revolver.

The door wasn't closed, and he slipped through it. In the dim light, a vagrant was holding a knife to Emma, whose clothing was torn. Cocking his weapon, Jack spoke.

"Boy, get off her," he demanded, his military-trained voice loud and clear.

The dirty scum laughed and refused to step back, muttering something Jack couldn't hear. Emma's face was pale with fear. Jack took aim, bent on killing the bastard. Without another thought, he squeezed the trigger.

The man fell to the floor as Jack raced to Emma and grabbed her arms. She was shaking badly.

"Emma," he said. "Emma?"

"Jack?" She said and screamed, just as the back of his head exploded. Pain engulfed him, and his world turned black.

"Strange as it may seem to you, but the more men I saw killed the more reckless I became."

~ Union solider Franklin H. Bailey in a letter to his parents

CHAPTER SEVENTEEN

Rose Hill

A low hum of voices slowly became more distinct as Jack fought the blackness that enveloped him. With effort, he forced open his eyes and immediately regretted it. The bright light burned, and he closed his eyes again, turning his head away. Severe pain stabbed the back of his skull, and a moan escaped him.

"Why, look who's up," a male voice said.

Jack grimaced. He knew that voice, but the pounding in his head clouded his thinking. Suddenly, relief arrived in the form of a cool cloth gently placed across his brow. He opened his eyes again. Everything was blurry. He blinked and focused. Emma. He relaxed. She looked all right. He'd stopped that man in time.

"Thank you," she whispered, smiling slightly before backing away.

He tried to reach for her, but his movements were sluggish, as though he was swimming in mud. "Emma," he called, but his voice had no strength.

"What are you doing here, Jack?" The gravelly voice asked.

Jack lifted himself from the mattress, fighting a wave of blackness that threatened to overwhelm him. He concentrated on the form sitting across the room, and his eyes finally focused. It was Billy. He thought the man was off fighting, or that's what he recalled from a couple of months ago.

"I came back to check on Emma and..."

"My wife?" Billy's voice sounded hard.

"Billy," Emma intervened, her voice soothing Jack's frayed nerves. She helped him sip some water from a cup. The sweet liquid trickled down his parched throat, and he gulped, wanting more.

"Miss Emma," Sally called from the doorway.

Emma smiled, taking the cup from Jack's lips. She pushed an errant strand of hair from his face before she stood up. Her touch had reached inside him, to that place he had locked closed long ago. As she stepped away, he almost begged her to come back until he saw her husband glaring at him. Emma glanced from Jack to Billy. "You two be mindful, you hear me?"

Billy's glare disappeared when he looked at her. "Of course, darlin', ole Jack and I just have some business to discuss. Hurry on."

She snorted and sailed out the door with Sally.

Jack sat up, swinging his legs off the bed to the floor. Bile rose in his throat, and he swallowed the bitter taste. He stared at Billy. The man was haggard looking and almost gaunt. He wore civilian clothes, his long hair tied back. He looked like a veteran, prematurely aged by war. It seemed the battlefield could have that effect overnight. By the end of this fight, there'd be no young people left in the country, Jack mused.

"You married her?"

"Yes," the curt reply. Obviously, Jack's arrival did not sit well with the Confederate.

With extreme effort, Jack rose unsteadily to his feet, but at least he was standing. His head throbbed.

"You realize you killed that bastard, don't you?"

"That was my aim," Jack stated. He'd have done anything to save Emma. "Where the hell were you?"

Billy sat like a statue, anger in his eyes. "So, you deserted the Union? You're a man without a home?"

Jack flinched. That's what it must have looked like with him showing up in civilian clothes. To them, he was a traitor to the South, and now, it appeared he had deserted the North. "I came to take my son to safety..."

"Oh, so now you accept him as yours?" Billy guffawed.

Emma stood at the door, the baby in her arms. Jack grabbed the bedpost, suddenly weak from the pain in his head, but his eyes locked onto her. She walked slowly toward him, the babe's eyes open and wandering around the room. As they got closer, Jack saw the child's eyes were green, like his, and the tuft of hair on his head dark brown, almost black. The color of Jack's.

Emma noticed Jack's reaction to the baby's coloring, his unspoken acknowledgement that the child was, in fact, his. "Your son," she said softly.

Jack was amazed. Nathan had grown so much in the last three months. His eyes and hair were so similar to Jack's own that he could never deny the boy again. He reached out to touch the baby's small hand that had fisted on Emma's bodice. When Jack's finger traced the tiny hand, the baby squealed and grabbed it, wrapping his own tiny fingers around his father's.

A slave boy ran into the room, up to Billy. Jack was vaguely aware of the boy's frantic panting as he spilled the news to his master.

"Well, well, well." Billy slammed his walking stick to the ground. "Seems our good ole Yankee-loving Jack here's brought attention to more than just us."

Jack pulled his hand back and turned.

Emma held the baby tighter. "What'd Jemmy say?"

"Word of Jack killin' that bastard got back to his men. We got patrols, Jack, vigilante groups to keep the peace and such, with the other men gone to fight for our freedom," Billy replied. "You done killed one of Wilcox's men. They had one of their own watching, saw you ride in. Jack, they're coming, and they'll kill you if they find you here. And once these groups get started, if they find you, they'll kill the rest of us for 'aiding and abettin'."

Jack heard Emma gasp. He'd put them all at risk if he stayed. But he wasn't leaving without them.

"I'll go. Wasn't planning on staying, but I'm taking my son with me."

"You can't be serious," Emma stated, her eyes shifting wildly. "Where do you think you can go? I'm not letting you take the baby!"

"I'm taking him to my parents. You're too close to Richmond here. The fight will return here and soon. They want Richmond and will wipe out anything in their way. I won't leave him here."

"No!" She hugged the baby tighter, enough so that he wailed.

"Emma," he started as Sally raced into the room.

"Enough!" Billy roared. His deep voice boomed off the

walls, quieting everyone, including Nathan. They waited
for him to continue. "Emma, take Nathan away. Jack and
I'll discuss this."

"Billy, please..."

"Emma, go," he said calmly.

She patted Nathan's little back, glaring at Jack as she and
Sally left.

Jack let out the breath he'd been holding, watching her
walk down the hall, his son peering over her shoulder at
him. "Guess I should have figured she'd be attached to the
little one."

The throb in the back of his head returned. He massaged
his temples, trying to stop the pain. It didn't work.
Frustrated, he turned.

"You need to persuade her to come with me," he stated,
hesitating before adding, "And you, too, of course."

Billy frowned, his eyes fixed on the door beyond Jack.
"Did you love her?" he asked quietly.

Jack's brows rose. It seemed a strange question to ask
under the circumstances, and he wondered for a moment
who Billy meant. "I beg your pardon."

Billy's sad eyes turned back to Jack. "Caroline. Did you
love her?"

Jack's mouth twitched. It was a fair question. "I cared
about her, more than she knew," he answered carefully.

Jack noted Billy's look of regret. "Why do you ask?"

Billy shook his head grimly. "Caroline was," he paused.
"Lovely, difficult, but a jewel," he whispered.

Jack snorted. He was correct about her being difficult,
that was for sure. "She never told me she was with child,"
he added. Would he have kept her with him had he known?
He knew the answer–no, because he'd never believe the
child was his. The look on Billy's face made him keep

that to himself. What Jack saw in the man's eyes told him everything. Billy had loved Caroline.

Billy laughed hollowly. "She had a difficult time, I was told. Blamed you for everything, that was, till the end."

His skin prickled at the tone of Billy's voice. "You loved her." At his nod, Jack continued, "Why did you marry Emma?"

The grief-stricken face of the tormented man made Jack's head throb even more.

"I love her, always have. She's my friend, my companion," he said and inhaled deeply, schooling his features. "She needed me when you threw her away. And I needed her. But..."

"Then take her away from here," Jack pleaded. "Come with me."

Billy snorted. "No, I can't leave. But I want you to take her."

"Are you mad? She hates me. And she won't leave you." He had noticed the man had remained seated the entire time Jack had been awake. "Billy, why are you here? She told me you were off killing Yankees."

Billy's mouth twisted in a maniacal smile. "I got me a few. But not enough." He put his cane down and struggled upright. The right leg of his pants hung loosely below the knee.

Jack fought to keep his mouth shut.

"Lost it last winter," Billy stated, finding his balance with the cane. "I'm not the man she deserves. Been thinkin' for a while I never was. I'll never be a real man again." He hobbled toward Jack. "I can't walk so I can't plow or plant or do much of anything." He sighed. "I can't give her a child either. What good am I?"

With a deep frown, Jack shook his head. "Surely she knows all that. But, after time, you'll improve..."

"I'm dying," Billy said point blank. The pain of his exertion was clear in his eyes as his jaw tightened. He chuckled drily. "The butcher who hacked my leg away was a crackpot. Doc Brown says the man messed up and I've an infection festering. He claims I need to submit to the knife again. I won't do it."

"Emma won't leave you." It was one thing Jack new without question. She would adamantly refuse.

"If you're sure about that child, you'll need her to care for him." He grabbed Jack's arm. "You can give her a child."

No, she couldn't have Nathan. Then the meaning of the man's words became clear. "I can't. She's married to you."

"She loves you," the man said stoically. "Always has. I need you to take her, make her happy, give her children."

Billy had to be mad, Jack decided. But the pain was so clear in his eyes and his grip on Jack's arm so desperate. Jack helped him back to the chair, with Billy breathing hard, his face tense. He reached for the cup on the table but missed.

Jack picked up the cup and handed it to him, wrapping the man's hand around it. He could smell the laudanum and started to say something as Billy downed the entire contents in one gulp.

Wiping his mouth with the back of his hand, Billy sputtered, "I can't make it without this poison, and supplies are harder to get." His eyes fell for a moment. "I love... loved...both of them, but Emma has never really been mine, nor me hers I'm figurin'. And she knows it, what with Caroline being home and me..." His voice slurred a bit before it faded. He swallowed hard and gazed at Jack. "So I'm begging you."

Jack felt his stomach turn.

Jemmy ran into the room. "Massa Bill, Toby says he's hearing there be men riding on the road here," he panted.

Billy became desperate. "They're coming for you. Take your son and Emma. You'll need to take John Henry too. I'll hold them off as long as I can."

"No, let me help."

He smiled at Jack. "By taking care of Emma, you are helping. Go."

Jack backed out of the room as Billy started issuing orders to Jemmy.

Emma was to finally be his.

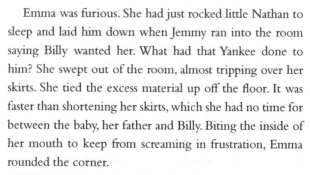

Emma was furious. She had just rocked little Nathan to sleep and laid him down when Jemmy ran into the room saying Billy wanted her. What had that Yankee done to him? She swept out of the room, almost tripping over her skirts. She tied the excess material up off the floor. It was faster than shortening her skirts, which she had no time for between the baby, her father and Billy. Biting the inside of her mouth to keep from screaming in frustration, Emma rounded the corner.

"What...," her voice faltered. Billy sat in the chair, looking out the window. The laudanum haze in his eyes as he glanced at her made her heart drop. Her darling husband was in so much pain, and there was nothing she could do to help him.

"Come here, my lovely Emma," he said in his drug-induced voice.

She straightened her skirts as well as she could, put her shoulders back and held her head up. He was up to something. She knew it. And where was Jack?

Then she spotted him standing in a corner of the room.

She felt the heat of his gaze on her. Ignore him, she told herself, and she went to Billy, grabbing his outstretched hand.

"Darlin'..."

He pulled her closer, wrapping his arms around her. "Emma, my darling Emma," he murmured into her stomach. He glanced up to her. "You know I love you."

Her brows furrowed. He didn't sound good. She had a distinct feeling she wasn't going to like what he was about to say. "Yes, dear, I know."

Billy snorted, giving her a half smile. "Good, now I only want what's good for you. And for that reason, I need you to pack for Nathan and you. Jack'll take you out of harm's—"

"What!" Did she hear him correctly? Anger flared throughout her body. "What are you talking about?"

"Jack's right," he said dryly. "The Yankee scum will be back. They want Richmond, my dear. By taking the capital and all that, they win." He hugged her tightly. "Rose Hill is too close to Petersburg, our railroad hub, and too close to the capital. To take them both will be the aim of those bastards. I can't risk losing you, too."

Her heart screamed. Tears rolled down her face. They'd talked about this once, a long time ago, when the Union Army was at their doorstep. She ran her hand through Billy's hair. "All right, let me have Sally gather your things—"

"I'm not going," he interrupted her.

"Of course you are."

"No." His answer was quiet but firm.

Emma probed his eyes, hoping for a way to reach him, but Billy wasn't giving anything away. She turned her head toward Jack. He stood silently. She broke Billy's hold on her and stormed over to the green-eyed rake. "You put him up to this," she said, shaking with anger.

He looked at her and slowly shook his head.

"Damn you!" She flayed her fists at his chest. "I will not leave my husband." Jack grabbed her wrists to stop her pummeling him.

"Emma, it's for your own good," he said, his voice low. "I am taking my son. I need you to help me get him to safety."

She yanked her hands away and turned back to Billy. Her husband held his hand out again for her, and she went to him, dropping to her knees to bury her head against his chest. She heard his heart beating fast, but his heat soothed her. The clicking of boots on the hardwood floor grew faint as Jack left them alone.

"Emma, my darling Emma," he said softly, pulling her face up toward him. He reached down and brushed her lips. "I've been a fool for years over you and Caroline. My own weaknesses have ruined us. And the judgment for my betrayal came from the War."

"You're talking nonsense," she said, touching his cheek with her hand.

"No, darling, you know I'm telling the truth," he smiled sadly. "My leg is infected, the poison will kill me," he paused when she gasped. "You've known I'll never be whole again. I can't even give you a child."

"That's not important," she argued.

"Yes, it is very important. I want you to be happy. And I know I've never really had your heart. You gave it to Jack years ago," he stroked her hair as she shook her head in denial. "Emma, go with Jack. He loves you. He can give you children."

She gulped, her heart racing. What was he thinking? She wasn't a brood mare to be bartered and traded. "No, my place is with you."

"Emma, they're coming. You know what those men will

do. Now, they won't hurt me, not an invalid, but you," he shuddered. "I can't let them hurt you, and this is the only way."

Tears hit her hands. She hadn't noticed till now that she was crying. She inhaled deeply but couldn't breathe. Her vision blurred, she focused on Billy's eyes. She knew it hurt him to shove her away like this, to another man. But he wanted her to leave.

"Go with him. I'll hold them off," he pleaded. "Then I'll catch up to you. I promise."

They were the words she wanted to hear, although she didn't believe them. She would never see him again. But his expression begged her to agree. Slowly, she nodded.

"Good," Billy said, sounding relieved. His resigned tone bothered her, but she had no time to question him as he gently pushed her away. "Go get the babe packed. And always remember, Emma, that I love you."

She stopped at the doorway, sobbing because his words touched a deep wound inside her. A lump in her throat made speech impossible. Swallowing hard, she nodded once, acknowledging she had heard him.

Emma was running away with Jack, the man she had loved so long ago. After all this time, she finally could be with him, encouraged by her own husband. Oh, how she had grown to hate Jack Fontaine!

> "The great fact which we asserted from the first is now placed beyond reach of controversy. We said the North could never subdue the South, and the North has now proclaimed the same conclusion."
>
> ~ The Times (London), September 14, 1864

CHAPTER EIGHTEEN

Virginia, Fall 1862

Jack rode Goliath to the back of the house. The horse pranced in reaction to his rider's agitation and the people surrounding the buckboard. It took every bit of energy to keep his mount under rein. And none of it helped Jack's head. Jemmy had aimed the butt of his rifle to knock out the man assaulting his mistress. As God was his witness, Jack'd never let that slave get behind him again. He grunted as he slid off the saddle and his boots hit the ground.

The few house slaves who had managed to pull the wagon around back were loading it with whatever supplies they could muster after Jack had told them to get the buckboard and not the carriage. A nicer vehicle traveling across the war-torn South would raise too many questions. It was important for him and his charges to be as inconspicuous as possible.

Sammy rounded the corner of the barn with a large unfamiliar horse. Goliath snorted loudly, throwing his nose in the air and neighing to it. Jack looped the reins over the wagon's wheel and went to the slave.

"Where's Miss Emma's horse?"

"Sir, the Yankees done took 'er," the man replied, plodding slowly.

Jack took the large chestnut's lead. "This one looks about twenty if not older." He lifted a hoof. It was caked with mud and manure but was well shod. He hoped that spoke well for the entire animal. An older horse could be steadier but might lack the necessary energy for the trip and be stressed by cannon fire and troops.

"Is this horse the only one available?"

Sammy patted the white-striped muzzle. "Petey is a good boy. He'll get you where you be takin' Miss Emma and the baby. He ain't nev'r left us down."

Wonderful. Jack closed his eyes, his fingers squeezing the bridge of his nose. So many miles to cover with winter edging closer. The crisp autumn air and rustling leaves only added to his raging headache. What he needed to know was where the armies were.

A loud snort and dancing hooves immediately got Jack's attention. It was Goliath. Jack spun and found John Henry almost at the horse's head. The stallion stared wild eyed, his head up, ears alert and hooves stomping as the older man approached.

"John," Jack began. But he stopped when he saw how the man's soothing tone quieted the beast. Of course, the apple in his hand helped. Goliath loved apples.

John Henry turned his head and after a second, he grinned. "Jack, I knew you'd be back."

Jack raised an eyebrow. There was something not right with John Henry. The man had had impeccable style as a rich planter but now looked slovenly. He stood there only in shirtsleeves, with no necktie, his tan trousers dirty, his salt and pepper hair long and mussed and whiskers on his face. As he petted Goliath's neck, the horse happily munched on the apple he had given him, John Henry behaved as though it was just another lazy summer afternoon on the estate. Slaves bustled around him, loading food, blankets and trunks in the bed of the wagon. And yet, John Henry didn't seem to notice or care.

Sally stepped out the back door with a jacket in her arms.

"Massa John," she said as she stepped behind him, opening the jacket.

"Why thank you, Sally," he said, sticking his arms into the coat. "Has Sammy gotten those tools fixed?"

"Yessir, he's done that last week," she answered warmly.

"Good, good. Go tell Caroline her husband's here."

Jack flinched. Sally glanced at him before she answered. "Yessir."

She walked up to Jack, her voice lowered. "Massa John done been injured. His mind ain't workin' right." She shrugged and walked back into the house.

Tilly emerged, carrying Nathan. The baby, wrapped in swaddling, was awake, his eyes roving and him responding to all the sights and sounds. Jack watched, fascinated. He hadn't expected a baby would move him so. He held out his arms without realizing it, and the slave slipped the child into them. Nathan's green eyes locked onto his, and he felt a pull at his heart. The little body shifted and Jack adjusted his grip, mesmerized. That was, until the babe opened his little mouth and wailed loudly.

"Let me take him."

Jack heard her voice and turned. Emma. Dressed in a chintz dress, a crinoline underneath, a bonnet on her head and a shawl around her shoulders, she looked beautiful. She had swept her hair up, leaving a few tendrils hanging about her face and neck. He couldn't move.

She took the child from his arms and began to hum in Nathan's ear, rocking slightly. The child quieted.

The two most important people in his life stood within feet of him. His responsibility was to get them out of there. Suddenly, his necktie seemed to tighten around his throat, suffocating him. He tugged at his neckline.

She was his. He should feel elated. Her husband had given her to him. His stomach twisted. But this was all wrong.

"Massa Jack, Massa Jack!" Jemmy yelled, skidding to a halt before him.

"Slow down, boy," Jack said with a chuckle. The boy panted, gulping huge amounts of air as his body shook. "What did you see?"

"Riders, sur," the slave sputtered. "Comin' this way fast. On the lane from the rails, sur."

Jack looked up and beyond the boy. They needed to get out of there fast. "Go tell your master what you told me. Go, boy."

Emma stood next to him. He turned to her. "We need to leave now."

"Daddy, Tilly," she called.

John Henry already sat in the driver's seat of the wagon. Tilly leapt into the wagon bed, taking the baby from Emma's hands. Jack helped her up to the seat.

"Can he drive?" Jack lowered his voice so John Henry wouldn't hear him.

She nodded. "He has his moments when he's fine. Driving is easy. He hasn't yet forgotten how to do that."

He wasn't sure whether that was good or not, but he nodded and went to Goliath. With his foot in the stirrup, he swung into the saddle, adjusting his weight as the animal sidestepped.

"Let's go." He led them from behind the house and through the fields.

Jack hoped Billy could hold off the Yankee soldiers long enough to get Emma and the others away in time. His nerves tingled with anxiety. He had two women, a baby and another man who apparently wasn't right in the head. It was going to be a long trip.

***

Billy sat on the veranda, the Enfield rifle in his right hand. He watched the wagon and rider head out from the backside of the house toward the vacant fields. They were exposed and that vexed him with Wilcox's patrol heading his way, but Jack's was the shorter route southwest, and it avoided the road vigilantes would take.

He swallowed the knot in his throat as he watched Emma leave. His heart hurt, worse than he thought it would. How could he stand to lose her? He had loved her since he was a boy, and, as a man, he'd helped her through the tears she'd shed after Caroline stole Jack from her. But ultimately, Billy had betrayed Emma. When Caroline returned carrying that bastard's child, it tore him apart. It ate at him so much that he finally told Emma he had loved Caroline, too. His confession had hurt her even more than Jack had. He saw it in her eyes every day.

He grabbed the cup next to him and drank, feeling the whiskey burn his throat and belly. The fire momentarily took his mind off the stabbing pain in his leg. He'd kept it a secret from Emma, but he could smell the rotting flesh now and knew she would have insisted he return to the surgeon. Fortunately, though, God had shown him how to redeem himself with her, and he had seized the opportunity. He had given her a chance at happiness with the man she truly loved.

And he planned to stop Wilcox and the others from pursuing them. He hoped, in the melee, he'd be put out of his misery forever. But before being killed, he needed to make sure Emma and the others had enough time to get away from the posse headed in his direction.

Art Wilcox and his mangy men turned toward the house. Billy knew Wilcox well enough—trash through and through, unfit for any sort of military service. Billy himself had denied Wilcox's enlistment in the Charles City militia. Wilcox could barely read, and his brother, also in the patrol, could hardly speak the English language let alone read or write it. The other three were barely old enough to shoot a gun with any effect. While the Confederacy might take them for fighting, Billy hoped it wouldn't come to that. However, they made excellent targets from his seat on the second-story porch.

Billy lifted the cup again and felt the cool porcelain against his lips. His thinking was a bit muddled because of the combination of laudanum and alcohol. As Wilcox brought his horse to a stop and dismounted, Billy's mind cleared and hatred flowed fast through his veins. He downed the rest of the contents, set the cup aside and raised the rifle to his lap, his fingers playing against the hammer and percussion cap.

"Good afternoon, gentlemen," he called, his voice from above catching them by surprise. "To what do I owe this unexpected and unwanted visit?"

Wilcox looked up at him, moving the brim of his hat back to see, and lowered his revolver.

"Good day, Billy," the man responded with insincere

politeness. "We're lookin' for a traitor to the cause, the man who shot one of my men. Shot him dead in yer own barn."

Billy was silent. The pain in his leg was deadening, along with his ability to think quickly. The last sip of John Henry's finest was working, and he wanted to enjoy the moment free of agony. It wouldn't hurt Wilcox to wait.

"That bastard of yours was here. Tried to rape my wife. He deserved to die," he stated coldly.

Wilcox's men raised and aimed their arms at him. Billy smiled when he heard them cock the rifles. Wilcox himself stood there, his head cocked to the side, and he shook his head and laughed.

"Phil could be a bit forthright with the ladies, but he ain't ever got a complaint from them."

Billy's anger threatened to overtake him, but he fought it. It wasn't time yet. Billy feared Jack hadn't made it far enough away. "Ladies of the night will take money, even from trash like you and your men, without complaining about the stink you leave behind."

Offended, Wilcox took a step forward, revolver in hand. "So, you be hidin' this killin' son-of-a-bitch, huh, Bealke? God knows, my men knew t'wasn't you who went into that there barn, gun raisin'."

Billy put his hand under the muzzle of the weapon and his fingers on the trigger, ready to strike. "Get off my land, you bastard. I don't have anything here for you."

Wilcox let out an evil laugh. "No, you ain't, ya' damn cripple. Maybe while we're here, I'll go enjoy the missus. Bettin' she be missin' a man inside her."

Temper now out of control, Billy raised his rifle, cocked and aimed. "You bastard. Go to hell!"

Wilcox's grin turned into a snarl as he aimed his revolver at Billy. "Afta you..."

Simultaneously, six guns exploded.

———✦———

The wagon moved slowly. No one said a word. Even the baby had settled in Tilly's arms, asleep. They could no longer see the house or its outbuildings, which he secretly was grateful for. He led them just southwest of the property, close to the James River. He needed to get them far away from Rose Hill. Silently, he prayed that God would grant him enough distance before all hell broke loose, especially before it got any more personal for Emma.

The air was still. It was peaceful, quiet, surrounded only by nature, yet fear gripped the travelers he led, threatening to explode.

Behind them, gunfire sounded. Jack recognized the faint short pops readily enough. Back at the house. He turned in the saddle to gauge the distance they'd covered and to check on Emma. Goliath snorted, his hind legs sidestepping as he picked up on the danger.

Emma reached over and pulled the reins from her father's hands, yanking them back, trying to halt Petey. The stallion balked. John Henry took back the tack, uttering "Whoa."

"Emma," Jack said loudly, guiding Goliath toward the wagon. But he was too late. Despite her skirt, petticoats and crinoline, she leapt from the buckboard to the ground.

"Billy!" she cried, picking up her skirts with both hands and running back to Rose Hill.

Another round of gunfire roared through the air. She screamed and ran faster. Jack fully understood why Billy had made sure they all left. He knew the man's pain was killing him and that Billy wanted to make this sacrifice to save Emma. But if she returned, it would be bad for her. Even if the patrol had left, she'd find Billy dead. That thought and fear for her safety drove Jack to urge Goliath into a gallop, quickly covering the short distance she had traveled. He could see her breathing hard, her face red from exertion. Her tight corset reduced her air intake and her ability to move fast.

"Emma!" He pulled the reins and jumped off the horse. Within two steps, he had her in his arms.

"No! Let me go!" she railed. "We have to help Billy!"

Jack bit his tongue as he pulled her close to him. "Emma, my dearest Emma," he ground out, remorse filling his soul. "It's too late."

She stilled. He felt a tremor go through her. A sob escaped Emma, and his shirt became damp as she cried, her face muffled against his chest. He ran his hand up and down her back as he held her, falling to his knees when she crumbled in his arms. Nothing else existed for him but her. He wanted to absorb her pain, her guilt for leaving her husband. And he wanted to continue holding her in his arms.

He rocked her back and forth, murmuring softly that everything would be fine, though he knew better. Her crying slowed, her gasps for air lessened. He eased his hold on her when her spine began to straighten. She turned stiff in his arms, and he dreaded what he knew was coming. He deserved it but still hoped against it.

Emma looked up at him, her face red and wet, her eyes bloodshot. Her lips thinned, colorless under the noontime sun.

"Damn you," she said tightly. "You planned this. You wanted to make me a widow." Her voice held a venom that made Jack's blood turn cold. "I hate you, Jack Fontaine."

"I cannot spare this man. He fights!"
~ Abraham Lincoln, when asked to remove
Grant from command

CHAPTER NINETEEN

Virginia, Winter 1862

The skies turned gray as thick storm clouds moved into Virginia. Riding ahead of the wagon, Jack grimaced, mentally cursing the weather. Rain. For those on an open buckboard, it was not good. He had spent the previous afternoon rigging his canvas tent on tree limbs bound upright to the wagon sides and had stretched the canvas over the wagon as cover. All he had was his dog-tent, a square piece of material used as a last resort by enlisted men and big enough for two soldiers to occupy. His wall tent was in the Union army's supply train. So his makeshift cover had no sides and left the wagon driver exposed. He prayed Emma would take cover when the skies opened.

They'd been traveling for a week at a snail's pace. Not because of the horses or the baby, though Nathan did slow them down. Jack never realized the amount of energy and care such a tiny being needed. Tilly was his wet nurse, which rather surprised him. Unfamiliar with how that worked, he had no idea how the timid slave fed his son. The only answer his questioning looks got him was that

Sally bid her do it. Emma offered no explanation so he dropped the subject.

Next was laundry. Not for their clothes but for the little one. Diapers. Had to be done daily. At first, Jack insisted they stop for that only every other day, but all it took was one skipped afternoon and the stink that came with it before he reconsidered. Thank heavens women took care of babies, he mused, because men would be utterly lost.

The other problem with their trek was the James River. The banks were too soft on the direct route for the heavy buckboard to navigate it. Jack had to take them closer to Richmond, beyond Petersburg. Forever thanking the good Lord, Jack had counted on dry weather continuing so the water level remained low. His prayer was granted, and, finally, at a solid bank, they had crossed easily.

Once across, though, Emma became almost catatonic. She hadn't spoken a word since that fateful afternoon they'd escaped Rose Hill. The day she became a widow. She said little to her father and Tilly and nothing to Jack. She refused to even look at him if she could. She ate sparsely. Jack knew she didn't sleep. He himself slept lightly, his loaded gun in his grasp, and he often walked the area around them, looking for signs of mischief. She was usually awake. And he discovered that even at two o'clock in the morning, she refused to acknowledge him. She blamed him for Billy's death. There was no point in trying to explain that Billy's sacrifice had saved her, or that setting himself up as he did had relieved him of dying slowly and painfully from the infection following his surgery. Jack's worry over her increased daily as she seemed to be losing herself and nothing he did could change it.

The only saving grace for her was Nathan. She played with the lad, rocked him to sleep murmuring sweet nothings to him. Jack actually caught her smiling at the boy.

John Henry walked up behind him and slapped him on the shoulder. "Give her time, my boy. She's in mourning and deserves that right."

He shook his head but answered stoically, "Yes, of course. I'm just worried."

"So am I, so am I," the elder Silvers muttered.

Jack stared at the man as he went over to Petey, producing a piece of carrot for him. The man's thinking bewildered Jack. Times like that, he seemed lucid, knowing what was happening, only to change without notice. Sometimes he was like the man he'd met as a West Point cadet years ago. John Henry often referred to Jack as Charles or Billy and said that Emma or Caroline was his wife. But there was also a negative to his changing personality. John Henry, if the mood hit, became violent. His language turned rude and outright hateful, including cursing, until he switched back to behavior and speech of the refined planter, the gentleman he had been. Jack wanted to ask Emma about it. How it had happened and how long had he been ill, what the cure was and length of the illness, but anytime he got close to her, she flitted away, beyond his reach. He ran his fingers through his hair as frustration settled in. How was he going to get them across four states, avoiding the War and authorities, without her cooperation? *Damn.*

Jack knew the bulk of the Union Army, McClellan's command, had been up in Maryland back in September. The damage from that day on the field in Sharpsburg, near Antietam Creek, had been hell for both sides. Those images still haunted him. The ghosts hovered and the guns echoed in his sleep, another reason why he rarely slept for long. Who could with those horrific scenes playing again and again and again? Even now, when he heard a snap in the woods, he flinched. He thought he was numb to it but discovered that wasn't so.

But as to where the fighting raged now, he was lost. He needed to find out. The group he led headed into southwest Virginia. Who would they find? He had no doubts both armies would hinder them. Both would want him to either fill their ranks or be shot as a traitor. Pulling his frock coat tighter around him, he kept his Union regalia–his greatcoat and officer's frock coat–in his saddlebags. The fact that he'd have to pretend in order to protect everyone worked on his nerves, but too many lives were at stake.

The clouds thundered.

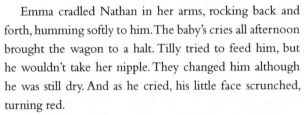

Emma cradled Nathan in her arms, rocking back and forth, humming softly to him. The baby's cries all afternoon brought the wagon to a halt. Tilly tried to feed him, but he wouldn't take her nipple. They changed him although he was still dry. And as he cried, his little face scrunched, turning red.

Neither her father nor Jack were worth a penny in help. Men never knew how to handle babies, but because Emma hadn't given birth, nor really been around babies, she had no idea what Nathan wanted either.

"Here, Miss Emma, try this."

Emma stopped staring at the child and bounced him lightly as she looked at Tilly. The slave handed her a wadded piece of cloth that was wet.

"What am I to do with this?" She frowned, confused.

The slave sighed loudly and took the next step. When the baby's mouth opened for another wail, she shoved the wetted knot into it. The child's eyes opened wide, amazed

at the piece in his mouth and quickly started to suckle on
it.

"Cloth?"

Tilly beamed. "Wetted with sugar water," she replied.
"He be startin' to teethe."

Jack walked up. "He's sucking a rag? That's all it took to
make him quiet?"

Emma's lips curved in a smile as she watched Nathan's
mouth work on the rag. She glanced up at Jack. "He's
teething."

Jack nodded. He looked so handsome, ruggedly so,
out here in the wild. The slight warm breeze blew at his
shirtsleeves. He had left his frock coat on the wagon when
he went to get firewood. His brown waistcoat and tan
trousers were dirty from days in the saddle. A lock of his
dark hair, now longer than usual, fell across his forehead.
The late afternoon sunlight highlighted his angular jaw,
high cheekbones and nose. That once straight aristocratic
nose now angled slightly. She wondered when it had been
broken. Knowing his rakish past, some man probably
broke it because Jack seduced his attacker's woman. Those
emerald eyes sparkling in the sun tugged at her.

Jack's luscious mouth, those lips she remembered
touching hers, ravishing hers, curled slowly in a smile. Oh,
how she wanted to taste them again.

Nathan spit the rag out and wailed, breaking the spell
Jack had on her.

"Shush, my little one," she cooed, placing the rag back in
his tiny mouth and rocking him. She'd been a fool to fall
back under Jack's magic. He had made her a widow. She
had to remember that. Heavens, she was barely two weeks
into mourning for Billy. Jack was a traitor to all. But, a small
voice in the back of her mind interrupted, could she ignore

the man and the blatant fact that Billy had more or less given her to him? Fury washed over her at her thoughts. She gritted her teeth and forced her desires away.

For her own best interests and everyone else's, if the opportunity presented itself, she should turn him in as the killer he was. But her heart screamed no.

———∞———

Jack saw it. The flicker in her eyes, the one that showed him the beauty of Emma. Her anger and hostility had vanished, only for a moment, but he'd take that moment and her quick smile. Hope danced inside him but quickly died when her eyes turned cold again and her smile disappeared. He groaned in utter frustration but should have known better. It was the first time in two weeks that she actually talked to him, even looked at him. That alone was a triumph. His heart raced at that second.

She walked away, singing some lullaby to his son. He glanced up. Twilight was settling across the Virginia countryside. They'd stay there tonight, but he needed to move them faster. They had the mountains to tackle before the first snow. And before that, they needed supplies. Game would be hard to find in the winter, and with armies foraging across the land, it would be even worse.

Tilly walked past him, carrying a bag over her shoulder. "Massa," she greeted, heading to the wagon.

He grimaced. He'd lived the past six or more years without needing to own a servant. He'd heard the abolitionists' rants but never considered himself one. Life could be lived without holding a person in bondage to serve him. When Emma brought Tilly with them, it rubbed him wrong, but he didn't have time to argue.

In the long run, and as much as he disliked it, that slave

was feeding his son. She shouldn't be burdening herself with all the chores, particularly if their food supplies dwindled. He knew that starving cows barely produced milk. Human women had to be the same, regardless of their status.

Tilly fascinated him. She had cowered under his wife's rule, but now, she wasn't so afraid. As she hung clean wet diapers on the side of the wagon near the fire, he saw her confidence building. Maybe being a wet nurse made her feel important.

He gathered more firewood and returned to camp as Emma walked up to Tilly with Nathan. As he got closer, he heard them speaking but couldn't distinguish the words. Emma handed the boy to the slave. Tilly sat, unbuttoning her bodice, and Jack spun away. It'd been way too long, but for the love of all that's holy, this wasn't the time to think about any of that.

Dropping the firewood near the wagon, he stormed off to get Goliath.

"Where are you going?"

Jack's foot faltered. John Henry stood in the shadow of the trees near his horse.

"John," Jack said, bringing his breathing under control. "Don't stand back there."

The older man chuckled. "Site of her titty got you going? Don't deny it. I'm rather enjoying it myself."

Not the conversation he wanted to have right now. "Sir, if you'll excuse…"

"Surprised you haven't bedded her yet. Hate to see you so hard up, son," the older man stated. "Emma's got a year and a day of mourning 'fore she can wed you. That's a long time. Not sayin' for you to take my girl down the wrong path, but you can definitely use…"

"Sir," Jack buckled the girth and swung up in the saddle.

He would not have this conversation with the man. He wasn't about to take the slave. A shudder passed through him as a vision of the past reared its ugly head. Of another slave girl being forced to service him and his brother. He shook his head. "I'm scouting the area. It's too quiet. Makes me nervous." He squeezed his knees and Goliath bolted.

———✂———

Emma stirred the pot again. Cooking wasn't one of her virtues, but neither was it Tilly's. Oh, she had no doubt the slave knew more than she claimed, and Emma was beginning to think the woman was using Nathan's nursing as an excuse to get out of a lot, but she had no recourse. Emma couldn't nurse the baby. Resentment coursed through her veins. She'd a husband who wanted her sister and Jack who gave Caroline his child, and there she was, stooped over a low fire out in the fields of some godforsaken part of the state, mixing vegetables and rabbit in broth.

The fire kept her warm as a chill settled in with the night. She wondered how she could possibly sleep in the cold. The fire wouldn't last all night. In fact, Jack had made them extinguish the flames early last night, claiming it was a beacon to everyone else. With no heat from the fire, it was too cold. They had wrapped Nathan tightly inside a wool blanket, and he slept between her and Tilly in the wagon bed. His little body stayed warm, but she froze. The cool air seeped into the space despite her own wool blanket and being fully dressed underneath it.

With a sigh, she remembered having had Billy to keep her warm when it was cold. She vanquished the thought. When had he been there when it was this cold? Never. And when he came home last spring, his pain and thrashing made it necessary for her to sleep on the edge of the bed. No, he had offered no comfort.

But Jack could keep her warm. She closed her eyes, letting the thought swirl in her head for a moment. Of his tall, muscular frame holding her close...then pain shot up her hand and she yelled, dropping her spoon into the pot. She brought her hand to her mouth, sucking on the inside ridge that had hit the side of the heated cast iron pot as she stirred. Pain radiated from the burn as she tried to soothe it with saliva. She deserved it for allowing that lustful image to come to mind, betraying her husband's memory.

"Are you all right?" His deep masculine voice asked.

She looked up. Of all the people to come to her, she must be damned. "I'm fine," she answered brusquely. She hoped he'd leave.

Instead, he took her hand and looked at the red mark on the tender flesh. She could tell he was fighting a smile. "That's what you get for dreaming when you cook."

She withdrew her hand, despite the pain in doing so. "I wasn't dreaming."

He looked at her, a wicked smile on his lips. "Of course, that's why I saw you stirring with your eyes closed."

Emma felt the heat of her blush on her cheeks. "I got something in my eye."

"Uh huh," he murmured but backed away to go see his son.

Blasted man. As she brought the bowls closer to fill them, she ignored the pain but remembered his warm eyes and his tender, warm sensual lips. A flutter came to her, and a memory of that summer's kiss reverberated in her mind.

"Good evening." Another male voice came from the

path Jack had just left. Along with the voice was the sound of horses and leather.

Soldiers.

———✧———

Jack heard them too late. He cursed softly as he stepped away from his son and moved closer to the riders, counting three in the firelight. Confederate soldiers from the make of their uniforms. Unfortunately, the Confederate soldier's rank insignia wasn't discernible and he knew he had to tread carefully. They might just be bushwhackers willing to fight whoever they encountered.

His hand went to his side, reaching for his revolver, only to find it wasn't there. A shiver of fear snaked down his spine. He stood there weaponless, having tossed the gun aside when he had unsaddled Goliath.

"How can I help you?" He squared his shoulders and looked at the leader.

The man shifted in his saddle. "We're scouting the area for Yankees and supplies. Saw your fire. Mind if we join you?"

Jack didn't like the sound of their voices. If he refused, they'd take their supplies. If he agreed, they could still take them. *Damn.*

"May we have the honor of knowing whom we're addressing?" John Henry's strong voice asked as he walked into the group. His patriarchal tone, power and authority resonating, caused the officer to turn directly to him.

"Sir, we are of Virginia State Line Division, General Marshall's brigade. Lt. Sebastian Winston," the man said, bowing in his saddle.

"Good southern boys," John Henry said, his tone approving but still in charge.

"Yes, sir," Winston said. "We're looking for supplies and deserters."

Jack felt the man's gaze settle on him with that last word. He didn't move, wouldn't allow them to see him flinch.

"I see, well, you won't find much here, lads," John Henry said. "We're simply moving to my cousin's in Louisiana since those damn Yankees burned our home."

Winston's eyes narrowed as his two soldiers muttered in the background. "I can see you don't have much, that's true. But we did see a magnificent horse a ways back."

Jack couldn't stop himself. He took a step forward, angry. They would not take his horse. They needed the beast for this trek, not to give to a damn secesh. A hand gripped his arm, stopping him from going forward. He turned, surprised. Emma.

Winston gazed on Jack, his mouth twisted. "Tell me, sir, how you have such a strong beast still? And why aren't you fighting?"

John Henry stepped up, quickly answering, "My son-in-law is on leave from the Charles City militia to escort his wife and child to safety. Surely, you understand."

Jack fought every nerve not to react to John Henry's cover. Or was it? Would his mind switch again and turn him over to them? He also heard Emma's quiet gasp and her hand became rigid, her grip tense. This was a test for them, he decided. She could easily turn him in as a traitor to the cause, an accusation that could get him pressed into service or shot, probably the latter. A quick glance showed him her lips had thinned but she said nothing.

Winston frowned.

Jack pulled Emma closer, wrapping his arm around her waist, claiming her. Through the corset stays, he squeezed her, willing her to relax or their scheme might be revealed. Her body molded against his, as though she understood the situation. She fit so right next to him and he caught a whiff of her scent, sweet like roses, mixed with firewood and the smell of dinner. He wanted to devour her. It took every ounce of strength not to kiss her, take her in his arms, but he had no control over his lower body. His member hardened instantly and Jack used Emma's full skirts to hide his reaction from the Rebs.

Off to the side, held by Tilly, the baby woke with a cry, shattering the tension.

"Well, you be careful out here," Winston stated, backing his horse away. "We got Yankees in the area and raiders." He tipped his hat and rode off.

No one moved other than Tilly with the baby.

"Very good," John Henry said, giving Jack and Emma a wink. "What's for supper?"

Emma turned toward Jack. She bit her lower lip, one of the things about her he loved. Yet, her eyes were cold.

"Touch me again and I'll turn you in," she hissed and left his side.

Emma went back to the pot, stirring again but watchful. Her nerves were frayed. Away from Jack, she was cold. She had felt his arousal against her hip, his warm arm around her, marking her as his. That embrace had been comfortable and seductive. His scent of the outdoors, horse and leather had invaded her nose. All of it made one thing perfectly clear to her. She desired him and wanted him. The man who was a traitor to his country, had stolen her sister and killed her husband.

Yes, God still hated her.

"Any man who is in favor of a further prosecution of this war is a fit subject for a lunatic asylum, and ought to be sent there immediately."
~ Nathan Bedford Forrest, May 1865

CHAPTER TWENTY

The temperature dipped during the mid-November nights. Frost hadn't formed yet but it was coming. Goliath and Petey turned fuzzy as their coats grew thicker for winter. The nights sleeping without a fire, in an attempt to remain undetected, came to an end at Emma's insistence. She claimed Nathan was too young for colder weather. Jack cursed silently but agreed. He stayed up, feeding the flames until the late evening when exhaustion took over.

Emma wrapped Nathan in a wool blanket placed on top of another blanket and curled around the babe as they slept with the warmth of the fire. John Henry pulled Tilly next to him, spooning behind the slave, their combined body heat keeping them warmer, similar to her with Nathan. They slept on the other side of the fire. Jack stood watch. At first, he stayed awake easily, his senses on alert for any intrusion. He also relied on the beasts because he knew they'd detect an intrusion faster than he could.

Eventually, his attention returned to Emma. She looked so peaceful, serene, cuddling his son. That thought still took some adjusting to. If the lad didn't look like him, he'd swear

Caroline gave birth to another man's brat. He never knew of her condition and his anger over her secrecy hadn't abated. Granted, a small voice inside reminded him that his wife might've failed to tell him because of his actions toward her, sending her home without him. They'd only slept together once and he got her with child? The irony was appalling.

He knew Emma was supposed to be in mourning, but he couldn't allow her the privilege of appearing so, not dressed in widow's weeds and staying inside. No, this trip could not be delayed. The war was escalating. He'd seen that back in Virginia and Maryland. Her period of grieving would have to wait. He had no way to make it up to her. In her eyes, nothing Jack did could make up for it. Another dagger in his heart.

He stoked the fire, reviving the flames and went to sit behind her. He looked over her side and saw his son, swaddled so only his face showed. An angelic face, so unlike his parents. His little nest of hair rested against Emma. She only had a cotton blanket over herself, using her wool one for the child. Her front would be warm but her back would chill. He got up and dug through his saddlebag to pull out his wool greatcoat. As gently as he could, he draped it over her. She whimpered, her hand reaching behind her, open, trying to find someone. No doubt Billy, he snarled to himself. Her face contorted, as if in panic. He feared she'd startle and wake Nathan.

When he saw her body shiver, he realized the coat didn't work as well as he'd hoped. He stepped closer and lowered himself behind her. She was taller than Caroline but still small to him. It would be so easy to snuggle up behind her, make her warm. He longed to do so, but she'd be furious at him, that he was "taking advantage of her." She trembled again. With a snort, he threw caution to the wind and laid down behind her, rearranging the coat to cover both of them.

She'd left her hair down to cover her neck and for that, he was grateful. He nuzzled into it, so soft and silky despite them having been traveling and living outside for a month. She smelled of firewood and herself. He inhaled and inched closer. The heat of her body thawed his and he snaked his arm around her middle, settling in close behind her. He sighed. She fit perfectly in his arms.

This was how it was meant to be. How could he convince her of it? He'd figure it out later. The comfort was too much for him and he fell asleep in the arms of bliss.

Emma grabbed the cotton blanket by the corners and pulled them together, fashioning a bag to haul the dirty diapers for washing. She needed the walk and gladly left Tilly with the baby and her father to go to the creek. Her mind jumbled with thoughts and emotions, all conflicting.

The last couple of nights, Jack gave in to her demands and left the fire going because it was better to keep his son from freezing during the night. Thankfully, the child slept and that alone put her at ease. It was the other thing that disturbed her. The fact that she slept. And how she had rested in the cold made her worry.

During the night, Jack had lain next to her, holding her in his embrace. She fluttered once in her sleep and felt his hard body behind her, warm, right against her back and legs, his arm around her middle. And she allowed herself to enjoy his heat, his comfort, knowing it was wrong but she didn't fight it. As dawn came and Nathan squirmed in her arms, she discovered she was alone. She wasn't sure he had been there except for the faint whiff of him on the Yankee coat that covered her. Fury swept through her, as though he'd taken advantage of her, violated her even though he'd done nothing other than keep her warm. She should yell at him to leave her be. Inside, that little voice said no, and she admitted only to herself that she hoped he'd do it again. That desire made her a slattern to her way of thinking. Her husband dead, maybe a month now. It was too early to be with another man. Except, her logical mind argued, if it was only for heat, then it was okay.

He can give you a child.

She blanched, her foot hitting a rock. Furious at herself, she kicked the errant stone away, continuing to the creek.

As she reached the bank, the water was like her stream back home. A wave of melancholy washed over her and she closed her eyes, willing the feeling to pass. The bundle in her hands became miserably heavy and it reeked. Diapers. Dropping the laundry, she grimaced. It was slave work, but her slave was watching Nathan. She reproached herself. She'd taken the soiled diapers to get away for some quiet time alone. Away from her father, from Tilly's quirky laughter at Nathan's play and the baby's crying. And away from Jack, though she had no idea where he was. After getting wood for the fire at breakfast, he jumped on his horse and muttered something about shelter and a train before the horse took off.

She wiped her brow with the back of her hand, surprised at the perspiration there. It had turned very warm, especially odd after the previous night's cold. She felt grimy and probably smelled. Oh, how she longed for a bath, to sink into warm water and wash her body and hair. Her weary gaze stretched across the water before her and she toyed with the idea of bathing. The water'd be cold, though. Still, she did have to get close to it to wash the cloths.

She smiled tightly. She could always walk into the water, and if it splashed her, well she'd use it. With her mind set, she glanced down at her gown and grimaced. She wore the crinoline and undergarments. A curse formed but she repressed it. Instead, she undid her bodice, tugging her arms out of the sleeves. The upper portion of the dress fell back and she reached under her waistband to untie the crinoline and petticoats. Granted, it was an extravagant item to have worn on such a trip, but she'd no idea how long they'd be on the road or what the conditions would be like. Now, it was too big and intimate an item not to wear and leave in the wagon instead.

Pushing the dress, crinoline and petticoats to the stone-cold ground she stood on, she stepped out and threw everything up onto the boulder behind her. She untied the strings to her corset and then nimbly unhooked the busk, adding it to the pile. Next off were her low-heeled boots and stockings. Standing there in her chemise and pantalets, she moaned softly, curling her bare toes as she rocked back on her heels. So decadent, she thought.

She grabbed the blanket, unraveled its knot, pulled out the bucket of lye soap, flipped the fabric closer to the water's edge, and spilled the diapers. With a deep sigh, she knelt and took the first diaper, plunging it beneath the water. The stream lapped at her and had a chill to it. Goosebumps spread up her arms, and she fought the desire to flee. By subjecting herself to the coldness, it could act as a penance and absolve her sins. Well, that or at least expel thoughts of Jack and his wicked green eyes.

He can give you a child.

Billy's voice sounded again. *No*, she wanted to yell back at the ghost voice. Instead, she yanked another diaper and sank it into the water, scrubbing it against the rock below.

The heat of the sun warmed her bare skin above the chemise and her arms and feet. She took a step into the water. The shallow end had warmed in the afternoon and covered her up to her calves without a chill.

As she shoved another diaper below the water's surface, her mind wandered. She saw Billy's face, his sad look as he told her he loved her. A drop of water hit her neckline, just at the slope to her breasts. Then another. It wasn't rain nor the washing splashing up and hitting her. No, it was her tears.

She sobbed now, freeing the tears she had held back because she had a house to run, a baby to care for, slaves to attend and a father going senile. Plus her brother Charles— she didn't know whether he was alive or dead. Tears for the child she'd never have. And the men she'd loved who forsook her for her pretty sister. Her throat turned raw. Her heart twisted. Alone. She was alone. The pain was unbearable, and she doubled over, gripping her stomach, the diaper slipping away on the water. Her knees buckled and she sank onto them in the water, crying. This war, this awful war, was slowly killing her.

***

Jack stopped Goliath on the grassy knoll and sighed. What he wouldn't give for a battle. To feel the adrenaline coursing through his veins, the smell of sulfur, the sound of cannons and guns roaring. A chance to actually fire a weapon and see the bullet tear into another man's flesh. He closed his eyes. Damn, he was going to hell for such thoughts. But they were safer than the ones he had all night. Of Emma, her warmth, her touch, of burying himself inside her. Those wicked thoughts ran through his mind all night, his blood racing as she nestled in her sleep into the crook of his body.

The fact that he got any sleep at all amazed him. He woke just as the night sky started to leave. She was flush next to him, breathing softly. He wanted to kiss her neck, her cheek, to bend over and catch her lips. Stifling a groan was difficult but moving away was worse as his hardened member nudged her buttocks, craving to pierce the folds of her sex. That last thought got him up fast and into the tree line for firewood.

After breakfast, he'd needed to get away from her. He could still smell her sweet scent. Could still remember the feel of her silken hair against his cheek. Quickly, he saddled his horse and muttered he needed to find out whether they'd have company and to look for shelter. With a swift squeeze, he got his horse to gallop away.

It wasn't a wasted morning. He found the Virginia Tennessee Railroad, one of the few east-west lines still operating. But he also found evidence of troop movement in the area. No clues were left as to which side. The numbers were low, perhaps fifty. Fifty, though, could do incredible damage.

Running his hand through his hair, he felt it was damp with sweat and grimy with dirt. He'd run the animal all morning, trying to burn off his desire and find shelter. He couldn't continue sleeping next to her. Plus, despite the day's heat, it was winter. They needed to move.

Clucking to his horse, he switched his weight in the saddle with pressure from one leg to steer Goliath in the right direction. His stomach growled. It must be noontime. The sun beat down as he rode back to camp. He recognized the copse of trees ahead and knew Emma was on the other side. His lips curved in a lopsided grin as he imagined her cooking. Her long glorious brown hair highlighted in gold from the sun, tied back in a braid that had a tendency to unravel.

He felt his body tightening and hardening. Frustration filled him. He could not ride back into camp aroused. With a glance at the water, he smiled. No doubt he stank of horse, leather and dirty wool. He slid off the animal, dropping the reins. He rapidly undressed as his horse munched on the grass, looking for green blades.

Totally naked, he walked into the water. The bank water was warm, but further in, it was cold. Good, he needed the cold to kill his stiffness. He dove in.

Emma gulped for air as her tears stopped trickling down her face. One hand clenched a diaper. With her other hand, she wiped her cheeks, blinking the remaining tears away. Her legs felt chilled and she looked down. While crying, she had wandered into the water. Her pantalets were soaked, as was the lower part of her chemise. She sighed. The tears that she'd added to the stream had been pent up inside her for the last eleven months. Longer even. Never allowing herself the time to grieve, her bottled-up emotions had finally been released and she thanked God she was alone.

It was then that she saw the ripple in the water's surface. Surprised, she didn't move. The ripples got bigger and fear seeped into her veins. What animal would cause that?

Suddenly, the water parted and a man's head and torso emerged. A naked man. He sputtered water out of his mouth and his hand wiped up his face, clearing his eyes of water and his hand went up to push his hair back.

Emerald green eyes fell on her. Jack. She watched the water sluice off his body, down the well-honed planes of his muscled chest and abdomen. His arms rippled in definition. Jack Fontaine was lean, his body muscular, like a Greek god. She simply stared.

His lips curved in a wicked smile.

She knew she should leave but her body refused to listen.

He walked right up to her. His hands cupped her cheeks as his lips touched hers. Startled, she gazed at him. She wanted this. With his mouth on hers, her lips parted and his tongue traced them. His touch was gentle but insistent as his tongue invaded her mouth, dancing with her tongue. She couldn't help herself and leaned into him. He growled into her mouth as his hand slipped around her neck and held the back of her head.

He tasted sweet, like lemon and Jack. This was what she had craved. Him kissing her, desiring her. Heat flowed from him into her and pooled deep inside her, coiling. Fire burned in her, one only he could put out. She felt his hardness. Only the thin layer of her chemise acted as a barrier—one that could easily be removed.

That thought and her own burning for him to be deep inside her crashed in on her. Instantly, reality slammed home. She struggled and broke free.

"What are you doing?" She screeched.

A flicker in his eye, a flash of disappointment at her tone, caught her attention. He gave her another crooked grin.

"I was taking a quick swim. I didn't know you were here."

She uttered a sound of disbelief and turned back to the bank, picking up a wayward diaper. Her undergarments clung to her, wet and revealing. She felt the heat of his gaze on her hips and buttocks. The water splashed and she knew he was following her. Of course, he would. They were alone here, she partially undressed and him totally naked.

She felt his desire and feared it matched her own. He could ravish her and her body would welcome him. In fact, her body craved him. She had never "craved" Billy. No, once it had been solely Jack, until he discarded her that night for Caroline. Caroline's manipulation of him and Billy struck her hard. Anger filled her bones. Always Caroline over her– always.

Disgust filled her and she swung around, facing him. "This is what you wanted, wasn't it? Just to take me and me beg for you."

His brows furrowed. "Whatever are you talking about?"

"This is why you killed my husband, isn't it? To finally take the other sister?" Emma knew she sounded irrational. Jack never truly wanted her, just Caroline. Only now, there was no more Caroline, but Emma stood there, hungry for a kiss from this man in the creek in the middle of nowhere. Her inner fear again, that Caroline had been his preference, twisted inside her and before she knew it, she lashed out at Jack, despite the meek protesting voice inside her.

He hissed. "Are you calling me a killer?"

She glared at him. *No!* But she silenced that inner voice, refusing to listen.

Goliath trotted to him. His clothes were tied to the saddle.

She so wanted revenge for everything she'd been denied because Caroline had come before her in everything, mostly men, even now from the grave. "Didn't you kill that man in the barn?"

His eyes narrowed. "He was going to rape you."

"But you killed him," she flung at him, her voice angry. *What was she doing?*

Jack took a step toward her again, still naked but no longer aroused. Within two steps, he was in her face. "He had a knife, Emma. I didn't have any choice but to kill him. I had to save you. And yes, I'd do it again."

She inhaled deeply but said nothing. Memories of that horrid man, of his hands on her, his knife at her throat, burned deep. He could have raped her. Killed her. Jack had saved her. Her skin crawled. He had been so close. Jack's aim was deadly, practiced.

But he did stop the man. Kept her from being violated. The inner feud raged and she realized it must be hysteria.

His eyes widened as he stood still, feet firmly planted on the ground. She could see the tension in his shoulders and chest and he crossed his arms.

"I've killed more than I remember. It's war, Emma." He pivoted on his heel, went to his saddle and yanked off his bundle of clothes. Stepping into and buttoning his drawers, he glared at her. "You think that's what your brother and I learned at The Point?"

"Well..." she faltered, angry at him and herself. How dissolute was he? Could she ever trust him again?

Shrugging his shirt on, he looked at her one last time, his eyes cold and hard, like his voice. "Emma, if I were you, I'd be scared. Who knows, I may kill *you* next." He swung himself up into the saddle and yelled to his mount. The horse leaped and took off at a sprint.

Emma sank to the ground. What had she done? Her world crashed down as Jack raced back to camp. Leaving her alone. Always alone. The worst was that she had asked for it. Her vision blurred again.

∼∾∼

What the hell! Jack rode through the trees, only half dressed and gripping the reins tightly. Goliath was skittish, sidestepping through the foliage. Thoroughly disgusted,

Jack leaped from the saddle, uttering another curse.

She had called him a killer.

He spat and decided to walk back to camp. But Goliath wouldn't move. Jack tried to relax and school his thoughts, realizing the horse was responding to his own black mood, and sighed. *Damn flighty animal.*

The scene at the stream replayed in his head. He'd jumped into the water, seeking relief from the heat and to wash off sweat and grime, only to surface and find the angel of his dreams, all clad in white. It appeared she had been waiting for him. Well, that was the way he chose to see it.

He'd never before seen her in that state of dishabille. The simple scoop-necked, cap-sleeved chemise fell to her shins, the leggings of her pantalets underneath were cuffed in lace at her calves. Her copper-colored hair was in disarray around her shoulders, falling free of her braid. Her undergarments were wet from the middle of her thighs down, the fine cotton clinging to her body. Wind had blown the front of her chemise against her, and he saw her pearled nipples outlined in the fabric. She was beautiful, and he drank in the sight, wanting to store it forever. He began hardening as he had stepped closer.

Her amber eyes sparkled in the water's reflection. He saw the tear-stained cheeks. Those coral lips, slightly opened, called to him. Before he knew it, his mouth was on hers. His tongue traced the seam of her lips and devoured her when she opened to him. He tasted the salt of her tears, mingled with peppermint, arousing him even more.

It was so wrong and so right. And she wanted him. He knew it. The way she responded to him was perfect, inviting and delicious.

Then she stopped him. Her accusations hit him like a bullet–hard, fast and brutal.

Yes, Jack knew he was a murderer. What soldier wasn't? But those men he had killed, even that white trash who had attacked her, would haunt him forever.

The carnage at Sharpsburg was the hardest memory to bury. The sunken lane, filled with the dead, the Reaper having come to collect them all. Even now, they beckoned him to join them...

He stopped abruptly, Goliath within a breath of his back. Jack closed his eyes, wishing away the spirits. When he gazed ahead, he saw John Henry holding Nathan, saying something in low tones to the child. Jack actually enjoyed a moment of peace while gazing at his son. Someone untouched by the madness.

He ran right into Tilly. The slave rolled her eyes up to his, a slow smile coming to her.

"Massa Jack," her fingers rolled up his chest. "Le'me help you."

She took his hand and placed it on her breast, squeezing it. It was heavy in his hand. She rolled his thumb over her hard nipple.

He stood, gazing down at her, not expecting what was happening. His mind clouded. Tilly was a young, pleasant-looking slave. No doubt she was used to laying with men. But the vision of her changed to Fanny, her laughter echoing in his ears. And then her screams as his father bellowed instructions to become a man...

Bile rose in his throat as he pulled his hand away from Tilly. Even though she offered herself, he couldn't. With a hard swallow he walked briskly over to John Henry.

Emma's father looked at him with a sly eye. "You're a strange one, boy," John Henry began. "Emma's gotta mourn. Leave her be. You've got another way. Use her to slake your lust."

Without responding, Jack picked up Nathan and twirled him in the air. As the baby squealed, he knew they had to leave; two days there had been too long. He'd go insane with another.

———◆◆◆———

Over the next few days, Jack tried to stay away from Emma. She'd be better without him. But he couldn't. He was like a moth to the flame. A smile came to him. Her cheeks were pink from the sun and the touch of color made her look more angelic than before. He wanted her. God, how he wanted her. He was damned.

In the distance, drums and bugles played. Advancing troops. The War reared its ugly head again.

"The dead covered more than five acres...about as thickly as they could be laid."

~ A veteran Confederate soldier, describing the carnage after the Battle of Cold Harbor

CHAPTER TWENTY-ONE

Border of Virginia and Tennessee

After a week of self-loathing isolation from Emma, Jack found himself awake in the middle of the night because his son's scream pierced the air. Everyone was up. The babe was burning with fever. Tilly swore they needed willow's bark to reduce it, so Emma sent Jack to find a willow tree in the direction the slave pointed. In the predawn light, Jack pulled on Goliath's reins, halting him. What the hell was he thinking? For the love of all that was holy, he couldn't tell a damn thing other than that there were trees all around him and none "drooped" like a willow.

Damn!

He sat still and heard a noise in the distance getting louder. His gaze narrowed as he tried to find the source. Off to his left, he saw movement and flickering lights. He slid off Goliath, dropping the lead. In the slowly fading night, he crouched and saw rows of white canvas tents, and the dying lights of a fire or two left for the guards. One tent after another, the flag hanging at the lane of larger tents, officers' row. It must be a Federal camp, Buell's Division.

Jack rocked back on his heels, weighing his options. As dawn approached, he could keep looking for a willow tree or find what he needed in the surgeon's tent. He glanced down at his clothes. He wore his navy trousers without the gold piping on the outer seam and a white cotton shirt. No waistcoat or jacket. Damn, he'd just jumped on his horse and left. The cool night air kept him alert and awake. Going into camp was a risk. He had left McClellan's army after Sharpsburg, no notice given, just left. They could arrest him for desertion. He stood messing his hair; his morning whiskers would work for the scene he had to present. Hooking his thumbs in his suspenders, Jack exhaled the breath he'd been holding and went to find help for his son.

Two sentries walked the perimeter of the camp methodically, neither looking around, just taking step after step. Jack waited until they passed and then sauntered into camp as though he belonged there. The smell of campfire and burned beef hung in the air, along with horse manure. The scent of the meat made his empty stomach growl.

He had gauged the layout of the camp previously and figured the hospital tent was to the right of his current location. At the next row of tents, he pivoted down the lane to the large wall tent at the end. So far, so good, no one had seen him. Dawn threatened at any moment and his time was running out.

In his path was an empty whiskey bottle that had been cast aside. Jack picked it up, tilting the dark amber bottle in the twilight, praying it still had a dreg left but he couldn't tell. He took a gamble and turned it upside down so any drops hit his lower lip and chin. The moist contents fell, cascading onto his shirt, the pungent smell of cheap alcohol enveloping him. Tossing the bottle aside, Jack continued to the medical tent.

"Soldier."

Jack didn't stop.

The cock of a weapon filled the air. "Stop."

The gun and voice came from his left. He stopped and stifled a curse.

The crunch of frost-covered grass combined with the sound of leather and metal hitting cloth grew louder as the patrol got closer. Jack closed his eyes. Nathan was sick. He needed to get help for his son. Concentrating hard, he dropped his shoulders and let his hip fall slightly, to give the appearance of a man far gone in his cups.

The soldier walked to his front, his rifle pointed at Jack's chest. The private was a boy, pale faced and young, as though he had been recruited after taking his pa's wagon to market. Jack cringed. Boys sent to fight a man's war. Youth scared easily. He had to use that knowledge. Especially when the lad's eyes narrowed, trying to discern who Jack was.

"Identify yourself."

Jack's lips twitched. "Ah, private, ya' know me." He forced a hiccup. "Lieutenant... Lieutenant Masentof," he slurred.

The boy pulled back a step at the smell of whiskey and his brow knitted. "I don't..."

"Shhhhh," Jack stuttered, putting his finger to the boy's lips. "Can't have commander findin' me," he forced a laugh. "Least not now."

"Sir, you best be layin' down then."

Jack nodded. "Good advice." He made himself stumble. From the corner of his eye, he watched the soldier shake his head before returning to his post.

Ahead was the surgeon's tent. He bent beneath the tent flap and entered the world of noxious medicines and tools.

Butchers, the whole lot of them. Jack knew some of the Army's medical doctors were good, but lack of supplies and the hundreds requiring immediate aid after a battle could frazzle anyone's nerves.

He scanned the supplies but didn't find anything he could use. Malingerers, those cowards who wouldn't fight, claiming illness of some degree, lay on the cots lining the tent. He shook his head. The surgeon for this unit must keep his medicines with him instead of within reach of those men. He stepped out and went into the next tent. It was an officer's tent, and it had the scent of the medicine tent. The frock lying across the chair next to the portable desk had the green shoulder insignia with the designated medical corps emblem. The jacket's owner still slept to the side.

Jack crept up to the man and pulled his revolver out of his waistband. Cocking the trigger, he aimed at the man's temple as his hand covered his mouth. The man woke up, startled.

"Shhh," he hissed. "Get up, nice and slow. Do not make a noise."

The surgeon gave a quick nod and quietly sat up, blinking, trying to focus on Jack.

Jack kept aim on the man but figured he wouldn't put up much resistance. He was a medical doctor, not a soldier. The man wasn't young, though. Older than Jack, closer to John Henry's age, with the sparse hair on his head graying and his face wrinkling. But his eyes looked clear and bright, like a younger man. Jack snorted. Battlefields were hell and apparently quickly aged medical staff, who were under constant pressure.

"Doctor?"

"I'm Dr. Spencer," he said calmly. "And who might I be talkin' to, with such a drawl as you've got?"

Jack bit his tongue. His Louisiana dialect had reasserted itself because of being around fellow Southerners. He searched his word usage carefully. It would not help to come off as the enemy. "I need your help."

Spencer inhaled. "Yes, I believe you do. But enough so to wake me?"

Jack shook his head. "It's my son..."

"Sir, who are you?" The man's gaze roved over Jack and found his trousers the same cloth as the doctor's.

"Jack Fontaine," he muttered. "My son is very ill. I need a doctor so you're going with me." He brought the weapon closer.

"Mr. Fontaine, you're stinking drunk, which can be the only explanation for you to roam a Union camp for services that your town could..."

"I'm not from town. On the road to a new one, and he came down with this last night. You're the closest help I've got." He gestured with the hand holding the gun.

Spencer rose slowly, his eyes barely leaving Jack. "Fontaine, Jack Fontaine," he mulled quietly. He grabbed his pants and slid them on, easing his arms into the suspenders. "I know the Fontaines. Just north of New Orleans."

Jack tensed, uneasy. He needed for them to get a move on, not talk.

"There's also a Fontaine I've read about on the deserter reports," the doctor added.

Jack flinched.

The man snorted. He'd seen Jack's reaction. "Oh, yes, surgeons get those reports. Amazing who we might find in our wards, alive or dead."

Jack didn't move, his mind searching for a way to convince the doctor this was more important than to haul him in for desertion. He'd swear to turn himself in if they would just move on now.

"Sir, we've gotta get going," he urged as the doctor went to one of his chests.

"What's wrong with the boy?"

Relief flooded through him as the man dropped the lists. Jack flicked a glance toward the closed tent flap. "Fever."

"I see." Spencer opened a black satchel, rummaging through its contents and adding more to it. "How old?"

"A babe sir," Jack stated. The patrol passed the area he'd just come through. Two minutes tops was all they had.

Picking up his coat, Spencer shrugged it on and grabbed his bag. "Let's get going. I need to be back soon."

They edged out under the early dawn sky. Jack pulled one of the horses from the line of tethered mounts and glanced back at the surgeon who stood silently. The man didn't look like the type of rider to go without a saddle, Jack surmised. Quickly, he saddled the horse, cursing every second that passed as their chance for making an easy departure grew smaller. With the bit in the horse's mouth, Jack eased the bridle over its ears when he heard another weapon being cocked.

"Whoa, soldier. Where do you think you're going?"

They were never going to get out of there. He swallowed the acid in his mouth as he turned. The man pointing the weapon stood before him. The doctor had vanished. *Hell!*

"I do believe we got us a man thinkin' of leaving this fine army," the soldier said, his voice laced with sarcasm.

Jack's gun was tucked in his waistband again, but if he went for it, the soldier could fire before Jack could free it. Fear snaked down his spine. He had been caught. He'd never get his son the aid he so desperately needed. And Emma was out there, alone, with a slave and her father. His mind worked frantically, looking for an escape.

"Private Wilson."

"Yes sir." The soldier promptly came to attention, lowering his rifle.

The surgeon appeared, his voice commanding authority. "Soldier, we've heard of a family not far, needing attention. Now, what type of example will we show if we can't help our fellow countrymen?"

Wilson's eyes flicked. "Sir, orders..."

"Private, I'm countering those orders. Do not question me." Spencer walked over to the horse, handing Jack his bag.

"No, sir," Wilson answered.

Jack pulled up into the saddle behind the surgeon. As the soldier backed off, they rode out of camp.

"And you, sir," Spencer shot over his shoulder. "I do remember you, Captain Fontaine."

<hr />

Emma teetered near exhaustion. Worry and fear filled her as Nathan's temperature seemed to climb and Jack had not returned. She paced within yards of the fire but not too close as the bundle in her arms had enough heat to warm them both. His crying had stopped and he remained asleep as long as she kept moving. Tilly took him sometimes and they both bathed him in tepid water, hoping it would cool him down, but Emma feared it wouldn't help.

Where was Jack?

Her father was still asleep, thankfully. It took both her and Tilly to calm him down when he started yelling for her mother and Sally. The last thing Emma needed right now was for him to have one of his fits. He was getting harder and harder to deal with daily. She watched confusion settle over him, and he lashed out about common things, but she discovered if she talked of old times, before the war, peace came to him.

Dawn was fast approaching. And still no Jack. Fear gnawed at her belly. She'd heard those drumbeats last night, faint but there. Soldiers were not far away. What if he had been caught? Killed? And the baby?

No, she wouldn't allow herself to think such things. She looked down at the angelic face resting in the crook of her arm. His face was still flush, his little lips pursed and quivering. God couldn't hate her that much to take this child from her, she prayed fervently.

It was then she heard the hooves pounding close. She fought to remain calm for fear of waking her sleeping angel. Swallowing the knot in her throat, she glanced in their direction. Jack's dark bay stallion, his mane wild, caught her attention first. Jack was back.

The horses flew through the fields and stopped within feet of her.

Jack jumped from Goliath and raced to her. He leaned down and kissed her quickly as his fingers touched his son's head. Horror filled his eyes as he looked at her.

"He's burning up."

She gave him a weak nod, her eyes blurring.

"And what do we have here?" The other man stood before her, his big rough hand touching the child's head.

"Emma, this is Dr. Spencer," Jack hastily introduced.

She eyed the doctor's clothes. "A Yankee doctor?"

The older man laughed. "I've been a doctor for many years, dear. Doesn't matter what I'm wearing."

She gave Jack a questioning glare. He shrugged. "Stole him from Buell's army."

The doctor took the child from her arms before she could protest. Nathan woke with a cry of fury. The man's soft tones calmed the babe down. He inspected his patient, and Emma heard him cooing to Nathan every so often.

"Stole him, Jack?" she muttered, never taking her eyes off the child.

"It was far easier than trying to find a goddamn willow tree in the dark," came the stiff reply.

"You'll have the whole federal army here, Jack. What will we do then?" She threw the accusation at him and stormed off. Had to get out of his reach when all she truly wanted was to be held safely in his arms.

"Emma," he said softly, pulling her into his arms. "Please."

She was so tired, the fight had been drained from her. She fell into his arms and leaned into him. The smell of horse, leather and wool mingled with Jack's deep masculine essence. It invaded her nose and she welcomed it. If she could ever just have the time to be with him, she'd happily drown herself in him.

The doctor was in front of them, handing the child to Tilly. "Fevers like this will come and go as he grows. You two being new parents are bound to fear quickly and sometimes, that fear is good, but he'll break it soon. Here," he rummaged through his bag and pulled out a miniature brown glass bottle. "Willow bark. It can be bitter. Put it in some water and give it to him. It'll help. Just a pinch, though." He looked at Emma. "You, my dear, need to rest. You tell this husband of yours that your health is just as important as your child's or it'll be up to him to care for the changing and whatnot." He winked.

Emma felt the warmth of a blush rush up her cheeks

as she nodded. The man thought Nathan hers and
Jack was her husband. A dream that she wished but felt
uncomfortable hearing. Apparently so did Jack as he
released her immediately. Her knees nearly buckled as relief
swept through her, knowing Nathan'd be all right.

The doctor turned sternly to Jack. "I can see why you
left, Captain. I don't normally help deserters, but I see your
reason. You planning on returning?"

"But of course," Jack promptly replied.

He answered a little too quickly for Emma's taste. He'd
take her and his son to his parents and leave her again. But
of course, why would he not? Everyone else had abandoned
her. She thought she'd scream but refused to give in to the
urge because she wanted to take care of Nathan.

The doctor leaned in. "There's a house just across the
border into Tennessee. Less than two days' ride under
normal conditions. The Parkers live there. Large house.
They've got a brood of young'uns. Go there. Tell them I
sent you. Get your son well and your wife rested before
you go further."

"Yessir," Jack answered. "And thank you, sir."

"Yes, thank you," Emma joined in.

The doctor chuckled. "I'll find my way back. But don't
stay here. I'll have a report to do for General Morgan." He
got on his horse and rode away.

They watched him go. She wanted to say something to
Jack. Hoped he'd say something to her about the doctor's
assumptions but instead, he turned away from her.

"You heard the doctor," he said to her quietly, over his
shoulder. "We need to pack up and leave."

Her heart missed a beat. Nothing. He'd already left her.

Crossing the border wouldn't be easy. Jack looked down the slope. Below them was the town of Stickleyville and it was swarming with bluecoats. It was early December, and cold winds whipped through the hills, freezing his breath and stifling his curses. He'd hoped to take the Virginia and East Tennessee Railroad line into Tennessee. Train passage would cut their travel time, allow Nathan and Emma to rest and give him an opportunity to settle down and think. He had come close to being arrested. Repayment of his debt to Dr. Spencer, though, had to wait until after his family was safe.

Safe. Safe from what? Yankees? His father? Himself?

But the scene below him made it clear that boarding a train would be impossible. Hell!

He reached into his pocket and pulled out the slip of paper with the Parker's address on it. With a last rueful glance, he reined Goliath to the left and returned to the wagon.

John Henry wasn't allowed to drive the buckboard now. They were too close to the federals, and his violent behavior, along with his mood changes and memory lapses, made him untrustworthy. Emma held the reins. She was so brave. His gaze drank her in. She smiled faintly at him as he approached, making his heart skip a beat.

He reproached himself for his wayward thoughts, the better to keep from saying or doing something foolish. The War was a demanding mistress, one he couldn't escape or ignore. He had no doubt he'd be pulled back into her wicked embrace, and he, like the rest of the soldiers, had a good chance of not surviving. He didn't want to take Emma as his wife, only to make her a widow again. He resigned himself to the fact that he needed to get his son— and her—to the safety of his family's home and then leave.

There was no other choice. Besides, she said she hated him. He was a killer, after all.

"We can't take the train," he told her. "Too many federals down there. We'll have to ride around them."

Emma nodded. With a glance back at her father and Tilly, she said, "We'd better get going. Nathan's asleep. The roll of the wagon wheels calmed him to slumber. No doubt we'll regret it tonight, but..." she shrugged as she bit her bottom lip.

Lust slammed into him. Oh, how wanted to soothe that lip. To roll his tongue over it, caressing her pain away. He hardened and shifted in his saddle, trying to alleviate his desire. His mouth went dry.

A cry came from the back. She broke her gaze from him to turn, and he was thankful she had looked away. If he had stared into her eyes any longer, he'd forget about the child and simply take her away.

"He's teething," she said.

"I beg your pardon?" He pushed his lustful thoughts aside. Babies. He groaned inwardly.

"Your son's teeth are cutting. It's painful."

"What about giving him more of that medicine?"

She scowled. "He's not sick. Teething is normal. Wish I had a teething ring for him, though. Didn't think to bring the one from home." He heard her voice quiver. Home. The home she grew up in. The one her husband died in to give them the chance to live.

Jack's mind raced. He had to get her mind off home. He so wanted to erase the pained look in her eyes. Then a thought struck him. He couldn't eliminate her pain yet—he'd work on that—but he had something else in mind. Reaching into his saddlebag, he felt the contents and then pulled out one of the items.

"Here, try this," he said, handing her a baked square of flour that felt like a stone.

"What is this?" She turned it, testing its hardness in her fingers, her brows knitting together.

"Army-issued hardtack," he replied. "All soldiers receive a ration of it. It's hard as nails and not easy eating, but it may be good for the boy to gnaw on."

Somewhat reluctantly, she turned and gave the hardtack to Tilly. They watched her rub it along the baby's lips, and he stopped wailing as his mouth clamped onto a corner. They laughed.

Jack's gaze slid back to Emma. She nodded her gratitude. Hardtack. He snorted. He wanted to give her so much more.

"Come on," Jack whispered softly in Emma's ear in the morning. "If we get moving, we should be at the Parker's by afternoon."

Throughout the day, the cold air nipped at her ears, but she was almost numb to it. Her father's mind had been drifting for days. He remained mostly silent but periodically rambled about Rose Hill and the field hands or her brother, who he sometimes called Jack Charles. At times, she was Caroline to him.

On the other hand, offering hardtack to Nathan had been a brilliant way to reduce his discomfort and give all of them some peace. Although he gnawed on it for hours at a time, it barely showed any signs of wear.

Around them, fields and homes had been destroyed for as far as the eye could see. Jack shoved his hat further down on his head. At first, Emma thought it was to block the wind until she realized he was trying to conceal his face better. The land was crawling with federals. Their small party didn't linger or stop, and he didn't talk except to urge them forward.

The skies finally opened, raining sleet on the weary travelers. The ice pellets felt like pinpricks on her face and she shuddered. Behind her, Tilly set Nathan down and hauled out the canvas flap to raise it above their heads, though because the sleet fell at a slant, the flap didn't shield them much.

"There," Jack yelled above the wind, pointing down a muddied lane.

She turned. A large two-storied house sat perched on a hill. Smoke came from the chimney. She smiled at him.

As they drew closer, Jack glanced at her and then darted to the house. She watched him knock on the door. It had to be the Parker residence. Heavens, she was freezing, the chill reaching inside her bones. No one behind her had uttered a sound. The last time she had looked, Tilly was sitting on her father's lap, with Nathan in her arms and a big wool blanket wrapped around them.

Standing on the porch, Jack talked to the man who had answered his knock.

She snapped the reins on Petey's back and the older stallion picked up his hooves, moving at a faster pace.

When Emma reached the house, Jack helped her from the seat just as the sleet began changing to snow.

"Darling," he said smoothly, kissing her cheek. "Come meet the Parkers."

His greeting startled her. The endearment and kiss were unexpected, but the look in his eyes silently bid her to play along. After she took Nathan from Tilly, Jack slipped his arm around her waist and escorted her to the porch.

"Mrs. Fontaine, so glad you are here. Dr. Spencer is an old family friend. We're more than happy to have you stay here and rest." The older woman who greeted her, Mrs. Parker, led Emma by the arm. "I'm Patricia Parker. Do come inside."

Emma could have melted when she walked into the house. Warmth from the fireplace permeated the home. She smelled the burning wood and the stew cooking over the flames, and her stomach growled.

Patricia chuckled. "I bet you're hungry. And the little one?"

Nathan gurgled as Patricia took him from Emma. "I daresay, he does look like you. What pretty green eyes. Just like your husband's."

Emma swallowed the knot in her throat and pasted a smile on her face. "Yes, just like Jack's." Oh dear, he must have told them they were married. It was the only logical assumption but a lie nonetheless. And what would her father say about that? Would he play along? She strongly doubted it. These people needed to know the truth before they were deceived any further. Just as she opened her mouth, a male voice sounded over her shoulder.

"Why yes, they're as green as mine," Jack replied.

They laughed, which eased the tension, but it sounded hollow to Emma's ears.

"Well, we're glad to have you," Franklin Parker stated, carrying in a small trunk. "Here, follow me."

Franklin took them to the first room on the right upstairs. Setting down the trunk, he stated, "This is your room. Your father will have the one next door. I'll put your slave with ours. After everyone gets settled, we'll all eat." He left them.

Emma glanced around the room. It was small, with only a double bed, a single table, and one set of drawers, but even that small amount of furniture made the room seem crowded. The bed loomed big before her.

"I had to tell them we're married," Jack stated blandly. "They don't have room to spread us out, nor did they think they'd have to, travelling as we are."

Her eyes fixated on the bed. "We, we can't." To sleep against him while outside, fighting the cold, fully dressed and around everyone else had been safe. There, the two of them would be alone in a bed, and that was not safe. Her stomach flipped. "I'm in mourning. I can't do this."

She watched his eyes, those beautiful green eyes, turn cold. Colder than the ice outside. "There is no choice. I'd rather sleep with the horses but can't; therefore, you'll have to put up with me." He threw on his jacket again, saying "In fact, I need to take care of them so we can leave tomorrow. Or you could tell them I'm a deserter and your widowed brother-in-law, not your husband, in which case, we'd have to leave tonight."

He stood there, glaring at her. She shook her head and with a snort, he left the room.

She collapsed on the floor, fighting tears of frustration and anger. Why had he said that? Had he lied to the Parkers just so he could bed her? Billy's words echoed in her head— that Jack could get her with child. Was that why Jack was escorting them to his parents' home? Only to bed her and leave her? She wanted more than that from him, had always wanted more until Caroline had stolen Jack from her.

Now she could have what she had always dreamed of, to be with Jack. But would she be happy after all? She raised her head and silently screamed in frustration.

"**Eventual victory must be yours, as far as man can judge. But at how terrible a cost? Look this well in the face! That of extermination...Let the South go.**"
~ Archer Gurney, Paris, France, in a May 24, 1861, letter to the editor, New York Times

CHAPTER TWENTY-TWO

East Tennessee, December 1862

Dinner at the Parker residence, consisting of beef stew and bread, was more than she'd eaten in a long time. And there was ample laughter, a simple delight that had been in short supply as well.

Her father actually acted like the gentleman she'd always known. Conversation flowed with no mishaps and no mistaken names. It helped that many of the subjects were about years long before the bloodshed, before lives were lost and homes destroyed.

Emma enjoyed herself for the first time in ages. They had baths prepared for her and Nathan and she assumed for her father and Jack, given their appearance at the table. A bath... it was a luxury she would never take for granted again.

Another sip of wine, though, and she'd be asleep at the table. *What scandal!* She giggled at the thought. Travelling the countryside with an unrelated man, a slave and her senile father was enough to raise eyebrows in itself. But their hosts were unaware of the impropriety because Jack had told them a tale about his marriage to Emma and about their son. She was seized by the thought that what he said was the way it should have been, before Caroline changed everything.

Yet, she should not forget Billy, who had made the ultimate sacrifice to save her. She put down the wine glass as her thoughts strayed, causing her to miss the last part of the ongoing conversation.

Jack stared at her with his emerald eyes. Had they deepened in color because of the wine or because of his desire for her? She prayed it was the first reason, but because she didn't have a friendly relationship with God, she feared it was the latter.

"My lovely wife and I thank you for your hospitality," Jack said, rising from his chair and coming around to her. Easing her chair back, he cupped her elbow. "We've had a long trip, with much more ahead of us, so we bid you good night."

She blinked, feeling slightly lightheaded and was glad for his support. With a smile, she added, "Lovely meal. Thank you."

"But of course, my dear," Patricia replied warmly. "You look tired. Go get some rest."

"We will." Jack directed her to the stairs. "John Henry?"

Her father chuckled. She thought he sounded better, more like his old self, and she was thankful for that.

"I do think I'll be up shortly, my boy."

On the first step, Emma lost her balance. Jack caught her, scooping her up, and her head fell against his chest. She heard a low rumble and knew he was laughing at her. She wanted to protest but didn't have the strength. How much wine had she drunk? Wrapped in his warm arms, she dismissed the question and allowed herself to relax.

Closing the door behind them, Jack walked to the bed and set her down near it. She stumbled and giggled as he caught her again. She gazed at him from hooded eyes. He was so handsome. Her hand reached up to touch his cheek.

He gave her a low chuckle and drew her hand down. "Let's get you into bed."

She tilted her head. "What if..."

"Shhh," he whispered.

With a frown, she was going to try asking again but then felt his nimble fingers undoing the buttons on her bodice. She felt the pull of the placket as he skimmed down to her waist and reached to undo her cuffs.

At the ties to her crinoline, he paused. "Why did you bring this contraption?"

"A proper lady wouldn't leave home without it," she murmured as he plucked the tie free, as well as the ties for the over and under petticoats.

With the ease of a practiced rake, he pushed her bodice off her shoulders and arms to let the dress and undergarments fall to the floor. "Well, it should be left here."

She bent her head to look down at herself. Standing before him in only her chemise, corset, pantalets and stockings, instead of being chilled, she felt warmth spread through her. Her blood raced as the thudding of her heart grew faster. Desire pooled inside her, coiling in her lower stomach.

He reached for the tie on her corset lacings and yanked them free. Placing his hands on her waist, he pushed in and the busk hooks unsnapped. With a grin of accomplishment, he peeled the garment away from her.

Feet frozen to the floor, she felt fully exposed even though she still wore her chemise and pantalets. When his hands reached under her pantalets, releasing the garters and rolling down her stockings, she plopped back onto the mattress.

The fire of his fingers on her bare calves had given her chills. Her toes curled. As he stood up from kneeling before her, she bit her bottom lip, embarrassed. He watched her mouth. She wished she could stop biting her lip, but it took a long time for the commands from her wine-sodden brain to register.

He gently placed her bare feet on top of the mattress. It was soft and warm from the fire, but she was bereft without him. She whimpered when he went to put her clothes across the tabletop.

"Jack," she called.

His brows furrowed as he shook his head and pointed to the dresser drawer sitting on the floor. It was Nathan's makeshift bed. She blinked, trying hard to focus through the wine haze. The babe was deep asleep on the soft sheeting. It must have felt so much better than the wool he'd slept on for the past month or so.

"Be quiet, sweetling," he whispered. "Let the babe sleep."

He returned to her side but remained standing.

"And you? Will you sleep?"

A faint smile crossed his face.

"Sleep, Emma," he murmured softly, close to her ear, and he kissed her forehead. Tucking the comforter around her, he turned away.

"Jack." She reached for him. "Please don't leave me," she pleaded. She wanted him next to her, to hold her.

He looked at her, not moving, deep in thought. He'd held her every night for the past week after it had turned cold. And he'd told the Parkers they were married, so they now shared a room. Surely, he wouldn't reject her now.

Fear and embarrassment collided within her, the heaviness of his denial growing with each second that passed. The room wobbled before her as she tried to remain awake.

Suddenly, she heard his reply. It was a heavy sigh, resignation or regret, she didn't know which. She struggled to focus as he pulled his shirt over his head and stepped out of his trousers after removing his boots and stockings. The only thing remaining was his drawers. He padded to the opposite side of the bed. It dipped as he slid beneath the covers. He drew her close and spooned against her back as they'd done when sleeping outside.

"Now it's time to sleep, Emma," he murmured into her ear, his voice vibrating against her bare neck. Relaxing completely, she slipped into oblivion.

———⚬⚬⚬———

It had been a bad idea, a very bad idea. When Emma nestled next to him, Jack thought his body would explode. Clad only in her chemise and pantalets, she molded her body to his. He could feel her softness and the growing heat inside himself. She snuggled within his embrace, her buttocks against his hardened shaft, and he bit the inside of his cheek to keep from groaning. With his arm around her waist, he pulled her closer still, brushing her breast with his hand.

He would have sworn she moaned in her sleep as he touched her. He was a damned jackass for doing it, but he wanted her badly. It had been way too long since he'd been with a woman. But he desired Emma alone. Only she could quench the fire that burned inside him. It'd be so easy to just lift her chemise and hips, to enter her through the split in her pantalets.

That thought made him release her from his tight

embrace. It was utter madness. He wouldn't take her, not like that. What was he thinking, what had he become? When she sighed and shivered, it sent another bolt of desire through him. Memories of her in the stream, wearing little more than what she was now wearing, returned full force. The taste of her mouth, the feel of her soft skin. He wanted it again and more. Fire raged through him, coiling down his chest to his belly and tightening hard below. Damn!

He wanted to get up but didn't. Where would he go? Nowhere. Desperately he tried to distract himself by thinking about the war, the men he'd left behind. He even tried to conjure images of the blood and hell of the battlefield.

It was going to be a long night.

He shut his eyes, and sleep finally came.

Drifting through the haze of slumber, he found himself on a battlefield. Where it was, he didn't know. Did it really matter?

Amid the smoke of gunpowder, he heard the orders. Advance. He sent the command down the line and heard the clanking of metal and leather as weapons were hoisted and positioned, ready to fire as the enemy came forward. The air filled with the streaking sound of cannonballs and grapeshot. Bullets whizzed between men, a few hitting their mark in flesh, unleashing howls of pain from the victims. The screeching and the reek of sulfur, burnt wood, fouled bodies and death was terrible to hear and smell.

He focused on the line before him, not knowing or caring whose it was. Across the field were other men, following their commanders to their deaths, like him and his troops. For what reasons, it didn't matter. Just move forward, aim, shoot, reload, go forward again. Half the men before his command dropped like flies at the next onslaught, and as his troops stepped over their bleeding bodies, he noted they all looked like Rathborne. Odd, really...

"Ready. Aim. Fire!" he yelled. They all followed his command, and as he turned to see the results, Charles Silvers stood there, his gun pointed at Jack just as a Union bullet hit between his eyes...blood, blood everywhere...

"Jack!"

He was shaking. Shaking hard. No, he was being shaken. The scene in his head dissipated. Charles' bloody body scattered with the smoke.

"Jack!"

A woman's voice. On the battlefield?

Someone was hitting his arm. He could hear her voice. Emma. Emma? His eyes flew open.

"Emma? What? What's wrong?" He blinked, trying to clear the haze. Around him was a room, dimly lit by the weak flames in the fireplace. He was not on the battlefield. This wasn't a hospital. Relief washed through him. The Parker's.

"You were yelling, Jack," Emma said, trying to keep her voice low. She ran her hands over his forehead and cheeks. "You're perspiring."

"Sweat, Emma, it's sweat," he muttered. "Only women would refer to it as perspiring. I dreamt I was on the battlefield, all the blood..." A shudder passed through him.

"There's no war here," she said soothingly, wrapping her arms around him and kissing his cheek. "No blood." She kissed the corner of his mouth.

Lust returned to him as her lips touched his skin and her breasts smashed against his shoulder and arm. With a savage moan, he turned to her, pressing his lips against hers, his tongue tracing the seam between her lips. She parted them and he invaded her mouth, seeking, taking possession. Her tongue danced with his and sought to enter his mouth, exploring.

He eased her back down, caressing her neck with his lips, then cupping her breast. Squeezing lightly, he scraped his thumbnail across her hardened nipple. She moaned into his mouth, almost unraveling him. He needed to touch her skin, not the fabric covering it. He fisted the chemise up and slipped his fingers beneath and fondled her again.

"Emma," he groaned, nibbling her neck.

Her hand threaded through his hair, not tightly, but she didn't let go either as his mouth travelled to the nipple he had flicked. His lips surrounded it, devouring the nub and he suckled, tugging on the tip till she arched her shoulders, pushing herself to him. He released her and his tongue blazed a trail to her other breast. She quivered beneath him and he smiled as his tongue swirled around the hard pearl before he pulled it in, his teeth scraping it. At her mewl, he laved the sting away.

"Jack," she whispered, her hand on his shoulder, squeezing it tightly.

His hand wandered over her flat stomach and he vaguely noticed the gap at the waistband to the pantalets. She was too thin. His fingers traced between the split in her leggings, over her curls to her nether lips. He heard her gulp for air as he fingered between the folds of her wet and swollen flesh. He suckled harder as he slipped a finger inside her. She was soaking, ready for him. His manhood throbbed when he put a second finger in and withdrew it, only to slide it back in again.

She groaned, her back arched and her thighs parted more. He released her breast and kissed the valley between them as he positioned himself between her legs. With a glance up, he saw her eyes darken as her lips parted and she licked her bottom lip before tugging at it with her teeth. He watched her eyes as his fingers entered her slickness again, and her lids lowered as a moan escaped her.

He wanted her. She wanted him. It would be so easy. His shaft was at her weeping lower lips, and his body thrummed. He raised his hips to descend and enter her when everything stopped as the baby wailed.

It had the same effect on him as artillery fire. They briefly froze in place before he rolled off her. She leaped off the bed, pushing her chemise down to pad over to his son.

"Oh, sweetheart," she murmured, lifting the squalling child into her arms.

Jack fell back onto the bed. He needed to have a talk with that boy.

Emma cooed to the baby, changed him, rocked him, giving him all the attention Jack wanted and needed. Frustrated, he washed in the water basin and dressed.

"Jack," she said.

He sighed when he saw she'd covered herself with the blanket. So much for seeing her naked again. "Yes, my dear."

She gave him a half smile, her cheeks reddening. "Go see if you can get us some milk, or get Tilly."

He nodded and left the room.

When he descended the stairs, he saw the lower floor was washed in dawn's light. The snow had stopped, which was good. He peered out the window. It didn't look too deep. Water dripped off the overhang, so the snow was melting already. It meant a sloppy road, but at least it would be passable.

He walked to the dining room, intending to go out back and find a cow or Tilly. From the corner of his eye, he noticed someone and his step faltered. A man sat in the wing-back armchair near the table.

"Mr. Parker, sir, good morning," Jack greeted. "You startled me. Didn't think anyone else'd be up yet."

The man's face was hard and cold, so unlike last night. It made Jack's nerves jump. Fear snaked up his spine, and he wished he had his revolver.

"Mr. Fontaine," his voice cool. "What's your wife's name again? I can't seem to recall."

Jack squinted, feeling as though he was on an iced-over pond with the sun melting the edges.

"Emma."

"Emma, yes, I remember now." Franklin Parker stood. He was a good-sized man, about Jack's height, give or take an inch. And he was holding a revolver. "Nice chat I had with your father-in-law. He kept referring to her as Caroline."

Jack froze. His eyes narrowed as he gauged the man. Thoughts scrambling, Jack considered possible responses, none of which were especially good. His main concern was whether he could get everyone out of there alive, including himself

"Caroline was his older daughter," he answered. His mouth was dry as he swallowed the fear knotting in his throat. "And she was my first wife."

"And Emma?" Franklin took a step, aiming the gun at him.

"She's my current wife." He prayed fervently to a God who hadn't seemed to hear him before now. He gave Franklin a tight smile. "You'll have to forgive John Henry. He was in charge of our militia and too close to a cannon when it was fired." Jack touched his temple and gave a nod.

Franklin's eyes widened for a second, but he didn't lower the gun. "Your drawl sounds N'Orleans style."

"I grew up not far from there, about thirty miles upriver, in Avoyelles Parish."

"So, you a coward, boy, or a traitor?" The man's eyes were like iron, his jaw ticked.

Jack's mouth thinned. "I'm afraid, sir, I don't understand what you're implyin'."

"Most of our boys are gone from around these parts, off fightin'. Why ain't you?"

Jack tensed. He remembered news through the ranks of one of the Union's victories, Admiral Farragut capturing New Orleans in April, before McClellan's ships left for Virginia. The Confederacy's largest port was under Union occupation, but not the entire state. He could use this information to his advantage, but he wanted to know first what John Henry had blathered about besides Caroline.

"My father-in-law's home was burned by the Yankees," he claimed. "I've a wife and son to care for, so I'm taking them to my parent's home. Need to see them safe 'fore I can fight more."

Franklin frowned as he considered Jack's explanation. It was obvious he couldn't decide whether to believe it or not.

"Seems unsafe to be travelling there. But I'm taking a leap of faith, boy, in believing you. Could be you're a Yankee anyhow, and I don't take kindly to being duped," the man said, but he lowered his weapon. "Snow isn't deep. Sun's to shine it 'pears. Federals are all around here, though. Our son's already at the war. We lost one for the cause as it is. I won't have them bluebellies on my land lookin' for the likes of you. I want you out of here."

Jack nodded. He went to get Tilly and took her to Emma. As the slave girl held Nathan and parted her bodice for him to drink, Jack motioned to Emma.

"We've got to go. Franklin says there're federals all around here. It's not safe for us."

Color drained from her face. "I'll get us packed."

"I'll ready the wagon. Make sure your father is up and dressed." He turned to leave, but she touched his arm. The embers of what almost happened earlier stirred his blood, and it took all his strength to dampen them.

"Jack, about..."

"Emma." He knew what she was going to say, and he couldn't bring himself to listen. He wasn't good enough for her. He never had been, truth be told. And he couldn't offer her his name so it was just as well they'd been interrupted. He needed to stay away from her. "Sorry about this morning. I won't let it happen again."

He left the room quickly, not wanting to see the relief in her face, and vowed to stay far away from her. His heart, held only by a fragile thread, broke.

**"Then write to my mother and father
that I tried to do my duty."**

~ 16 year-old Private James Sullivan,
Company K, 21ˢᵗ Massachusetts, after a surgeon
told his sergeant, "He can't last five minutes."

CHAPTER TWENTY-THREE

Tennessee, December 1862

Emma stood there, her mouth drawn. Her insides twisted and shattered after what Jack said. He had denied wanting her. Tears blurred her vision. She had given him her heart only to have him break it—again. Last time, she had hidden her pain and married Billy. Memories of that time had yet to fade–her relationship with her husband had been tarnished by his love for Caroline and hers for Jack. But now, considering Jack was a widower and she a widow, and that Nathan needed a mother, Emma thought she and Jack would marry, whether he wanted her not. But apparently, Jack didn't share that vision.

Vaguely, she heard Tilly humming to Nathan, and her pain came to a sudden halt. She had no time to wallow over the wound in her heart. Inhaling a deep, ragged breath, she rubbed her eyes and swallowed hard. Her charge needed her. With her shoulders straight and her head high, she opened the small trunk to dig out a clean dress for the babe.

"Finish up and get him dressed," she ordered Tilly. She

bit her tongue and looked at the slave. Nathan was at Tilly's shoulder, and she patted his back to make him burp as she sashayed to the bed. She grabbed the dress, never looking at Emma.

Furious at herself, at Jack, at the world, Emma quickly left the room to get her father ready. She really had no one to blame but herself for allowing Jack to do what he did. She had behaved like a slattern.

But the self-accusation did not make her feel any better. In fact, it made her angry, on the verge of actually cussing— how unbecoming that would be. Even now, she could hear her mother scolding her for even thinking about doing it.

"Daddy, it's time for us to move on," she stated, walking into his room as if it was another day at Rose Hill.

He gasped as she threw the curtain back from the lone window and the sun poured into the room, reflecting brightly off the snow.

"Dear girl, it can't be that late," he protested, struggling to sit.

"No, it's early but federals are on the move. The Parkers want us out as we won't be safe here." She threw his clothes onto the bed.

"Did you get Caroline and the babe up?"

She rolled her eyes as she put his belongings into the satchel. "Yes, Daddy. Tilly's fixin' to get Nathan dressed as we speak."

"Good, good," he mumbled, moving his legs off the bed.

"Five minutes, daddy, five minutes. Don't be takin' any longer, you hear me?" She didn't wait for him to answer and left the room.

Tilly had Nathan ready and the trunk packed by the time she returned. Franklin took the piece down the stairs and they followed him. John Henry was last, lugging his satchel. Though dressed, he still looked lost. Emma sighed. He looked lost most days now.

"Honey, I'm so sorry," Patricia said softly as they followed her husband out the door and into the crisp December morning. She patted Emma's arm. Her sympathy made Emma bite her lip as tears threatened again. She was being exiled with the man who wanted nothing to do with her except to act as a mother–for the time being–to his son. And her reward? Nothing.

"I understand," she murmured and gave the worried woman a weak smile.

Patricia nodded. An unspoken thought passed between them, men interfering where there was no reason for it. "I packed a barrel of flour, some salt and sugar along with a side of pork," she added. "There're also a couple of loaves of bread and an apple pie in there as well." She glanced quickly at her husband. "It's Franklin's favorite. Thinkin' it's the least we can do, considerin'."

Emma swallowed. "Thank you."

The woman shoved a bag into her hands. "These are some clothes for your son. They're from our boys and long outgrown. Nathan's growin' fast. And there are a few items for him to play with. You take care of that babe."

Emma nodded. The tears rimming her eyes would fall, and she refused to look Patricia in the face. Instead, she took her father's hand and climbed aboard the wagon. She was the last to settle.

Jack nudged Goliath on, and they left that cold December morning heading west.

The next couple of days rolled along without incident. Driving the wagon had become taxing, and Emma's strength was always drained by the end of the day. Despite the long hours and continuous motion of the horses plodding and the wheels turning, they never seemed to make it far. Jack rode ahead, scouting the area for signs of either Union or Confederate troops and ways to avoid them.

Emma watched her father slip further away mentally. He stared into the campfire each night, at times with a grieved expression, otherwise his face was blank. He called her Caroline sometimes and referred to Jack as Charles or Billy. Tilly remained Tilly and Nathan–the child was lost on him at times.

Emma thought of Charles. She hadn't heard from her brother in months. Where was he? Was he alive? Had he written only to have his letter undelivered? Between her father's condition and her brother's absence, she became fearful. But her responsibilities had grown too much for her to succumb to the fear.

Soon, nighttime came earlier and darker, and silence fell upon the group. Nathan's gibberish was about the only sound from any of them. Emma was too exhausted even for talk.

Jack didn't sit with them for long. He spent the majority of his time with the horses or scouring the perimeter of their camp. He rarely glanced at Emma, and when she caught him looking her way, his pained expression nearly undid her. Regret was what she saw and it filled her with remorse.

Although Indian summer-like weather came much later than usual, it dispelled the nighttime chill. And Jack's embrace was gone as well.

———— ∿ ————

Jack rode ahead of the wagon, angry with himself and circumstances beyond his control. On that bleak December morning, he stopped Goliath and considered another possible path through the Cumberland Mountains. He'd led the wagon around Knoxville after glimpsing a rebel army in the area, but he didn't know whether they were totally clear of the threat. Mentally, he cursed. They'd need supplies before long. What the Parkers had provided might sustain them through the next three days, but maybe not. His son was eating grain faster than Jack could have imagined. But he noticed Emma rarely ate, which also concerned him.

At supper, he sat by himself. Madness threatened to engulf him when he looked at her. He wanted her, craved her, needed her and yet, denied himself. He felt unworthy of her attentions. Oh, he knew she'd give her body to him, but what of her heart? He'd ruined that possibility when he married Caroline. Anger washed through him at the thought of his deceased wife. She had manipulated most situations in her favor and he'd become one of her victims. And, because of that, he had lost the woman he loved.

At the Parkers', he had wanted to reclaim Emma, finally make her his. But it wouldn't have been right. Although he didn't deserve her love after what had happened with Caroline, his seed might offer some redemption. He had already fathered a child, something Emma desperately wanted. And her dying husband's request was that Jack give her one. Trying to save his son and the woman he loved while war raged around them was dangerous enough. To father another child now would be madness—and another responsibility he didn't want.

So, as night fell, he guarded the camp and got little sleep as usual. It was the price he had to pay for being a traitor and a deserter, both as a soldier and as a man.

In the morning, a light wind blew, skirting across the field. It was cool, a prelude to colder weather ahead. They had to clear the mountains and get more supplies before winter arrived in full force. Jack pulled the collar of his jacket tighter around his neck and rode on.

"There." Jack pointed to a nook in the mountainside. "The mountain will shelter us from the wind tonight."

Without a word, her mouth grim, Emma pulled on the reins to turn the wagon. Evergreens flanked the opening, helping to break the wind and conceal them as well. When the horse stopped, she dropped the reins and breathed a sigh of relief.

She gathered her skirts and leaped off the seat. The days of gentlemen assisting her onto or off a wagon seemed like a lifetime ago.

"Here, hand him to me." She opened her arms to take Nathan from Tilly. "Come here, mister," she teased him and he giggled in return. She smiled. He was the joy of her otherwise dismal life, and she needed that small pleasure before making dinner.

"I'll go get us something to eat," Jack announced, walking away, rifle in hand.

John Henry began to follow him.

"Daddy," she called him. He didn't stop. With a deep sigh, she tried again. Nothing. "John Henry Silvers."

He slowed.

"I need firewood, daddy."

He nodded and turned toward the trees.

She prayed he wouldn't go far nor forget what he was about. She sat the baby on the blanket Tilly had laid out and got his bag of toys.

The slave started a small fire with the kindling she had stacked and waited for her master to return. Before long, he brought her wood, and together they built a reasonably good fire for cooking. Emma sat a pot on it and heated water, removing some of it for a mash for Nathan as Tilly undid her bodice. She lifted the baby and settled with him in her lap as he suckled from her nipple.

Emma watched, her envy growing every time she did. Inside, she ached, wanting to feed her own child, but Jack never even came close to her now. It was a sin, she was sure, to bear a child out of wedlock, but as time passed, she fought her yearning daily. Jack swore he wouldn't touch her again, and she feared he'd keep his word. Her tears had dried after that rejection, but the pain lingered, deep and hard.

She refocused and found the young Negress staring at her before Emma bent her head, biting her lower lip. Heavens, did her pain show? From the look on Tilly's face, it did.

Jack returned, his kill hanging from a rope.

"My o' my, whatever did you kill?" she asked. Of all the things to say. Her ladylike behavior had almost completely deserted her.

He grinned. It was the first one of those she'd seen in days. He had dimples when he smiled like that. Her heart skipped a beat. He was devilishly handsome, his face rugged, whiskered and still tan from the summer. Oh, why didn't he want her?

Standing before her, Jack dropped the turkey. Her eyes widened. It was huge.

"I'll pluck him and cut him up." Jack pulled the knife out of the sheath tied to his leg. "He'll cook faster in small amounts."

"Jack," she said. He waited. "We're running low on supplies."

He nodded.

Supper had been simple. Turkey and biscuits. Jack had told them to sleep while he finished cooking the rest of the bird. Nathan fell deeply asleep, and John Henry and Tilly did so not long after. Emma, though, couldn't fall asleep, her thoughts too at odds to allow her to rest.

"Are you cold?"

His deep voice caught her off guard. Emotions wrestled within her. She envied her father having someone to keep him warm on such a chilly night. She grabbed the extra quilt the Parkers had given them and reached to take the babe from Tilly's arms when Jack grasped her arm.

"Emma," he said softly. "It's Christmas Eve."

Was it? She had no calendar, no invitations to festive galas, nothing to note the time other than dark, dreary and cold days.

"Emma, please," he begged, pulling her close. "Come with me."

"Jack," she shook her head. She'd refused to let him get close again.

"I need a word with you, and I don't want to wake them."

She clamped her eyes shut. Why was she so weak around him? His touch, what she'd been craving, burned her through her clothing. Why was he doing this? After an eternity of ignoring her, what could he possibly have to say now? Could he break her heart anymore?

But she followed him as he led her away from the others, closer to the trees.

Away from everyone else.

<hr/>

After they were far enough away in Emma's mind, she

wouldn't continue. He turned to find her wide eyed and her face pale.

With more of a jerk than he intended, Jack drew her into his arms. When she finally realized it, she fought him, thrashing at his chest.

"Let me go!"

"Emma, keep..."

"Get your hands off me!"

He released her but held onto her fingertips. "Emma, please. This is important."

"You going to kill me now?" Her voice was frantic, and he felt her tremble.

"What?" *Oh dear Lord!* "Emma, for God's sake, please, no. I would never harm you."

He let go of her fingertips, and she fell to the ground in fear.

With a sigh, he bent down. "Emma, darlin', I need to tell you something. I've got to leave."

She blinked rapidly. "What?"

He stood and held out his hand to her. Slowly she placed her hand in it and he helped her stand. She wasn't trembling now, and he relaxed a bit.

"Wherever did that thought come from? I'd never hurt you, you know that."

Her eyes watered as she shook her head. "But you did."

He closed his eyes. "Emma, I wish I could change everything." He ran his hand through his hair, frustration combined with lack of sleep battling for control. "Look, we need supplies. We're not too far from Murfreesboro, I think. A day's ride there and back. It'd be faster if I go alone. We're pretty secluded here, if you think you can hold on." He continued holding her hand, needing to feel its warmth. "That bird should keep you until I return."

She gulped and he watched the motion of her throat. Her neck was long and perfect, the type that begged for kisses. He wanted to be the one to kiss it, as he wanted to do on the nights when he had curled around her to keep both of them warm. Nights when he thought she'd reject him, as would have been her right, for being so forward.

"You can't leave me, I mean us," she sputtered. "What if the Yankees come? What if..."

"Emma," he interrupted. "There's movement around here. I think it's the Federals. Maybe Rebs. I'm not sure, but I'd rather know who it is before continuing with you and my son." He brought her closer. "Please don't fight me on this. I promise I'll be back." He gave her a lopsided grin and tried to lighten his voice. "It'll be my Christmas present to you."

With a deep breath, she allowed herself to relax into him. He was rock solid, a contoured wall of strength. Heat radiated from him, warming her, and desire unfurled deep within her. When he lightly caressed her cheek on his last words, she dreamed about what she really wanted for Christmas.

He was leaving them to get them food, to find where the armies were, to protect them. War still reigned in the land. Despite his promise to return, he might not.

It was almost too bold to think of, and even harder to say, but it might be the only chance she ever got. "I want that and more for Christmas," she whispered.

His brows furrowed.

There, she had said it. She rolled her bottom lip under her teeth, fearing his rejection again.

"Oh, Emma," he replied, "you don't want..."

She placed her fingers on his lips, silencing him. "Yes, I do."

His eyes flickered before turning dark, and his arms momentarily tensed. Her mouth felt dry and she couldn't breathe. He devoured her with his gaze. She wetted her lips as nerves began to overtake her. He would reject her again, she was sure, whether it was because he had preferred her sister or for some other reason.

He growled, interrupting her thoughts as his lips claimed hers. She gasped in surprise, and he took her reaction as an invitation to plunder her mouth. He tightened his embrace. She encircled his neck and met his lips with a force of her own. He ran a hand down her back, heat from it penetrating her clothing as it continued over her hip and buttocks, cupping her against his arousal.

She shivered with delight. He wanted her. The unexpected joy of it caused her to sigh deeply as he kissed her neck, nipping as he went. His other hand sank into her hair, which she'd hastily arranged that morning, and pulled out the pins holding it up. Her long tresses fell loose and cascaded down her back, like a waterfall caressing his skin.

She moaned aloud. Inside, she burned with desire, want and need pooling in her lower stomach.

"Oh, my love," he rasped, taking her earlobe between his teeth and gently tugging it. His tongue skittered down her neck again to her collar. With a groan, he began unclasping the pin at the top of her bodice. He undid the buttons with the expertise of a man who was familiar with the design of ladies clothing. When his hand slipped into the opening, it burned against her skin despite the cold air threatening to chill her.

He kissed her along the swell of her breasts, searing her with his lips, tingles branching down and through her. He pulled the ribbon at the top of her corset and opened the clasps on the busk, freeing her breasts from the boning. With a growl, he lowered her scoop-necked chemise, giving him full access to one of them. His tongued blazed a trail to her pearled tip, engulfing it and he suckled, his tongue teasing the taut bud.

Desire blossomed within her. She threaded her fingers through his hair, enjoying the feel of his silken locks. His mouth covered her other nipple, teeth lightly grazing the hard nub, making the flames within burn brighter, and she groaned.

Without releasing Emma, Jack slowly backed her against a boulder. She felt the hard cool rock behind her, but because of the fire he stoked in her, it could have been made of ice and she wouldn't have complained. Its uneven surface cut into her back as he raised her, but she barely noticed as his lips reclaimed hers. Her hard nipples were abraded by being rubbed against his wool vest, making her tingle even more and moan louder still.

"Shh, darlin'," he warned as he lifted her skirts and petticoats.

She inhaled sharply as the cool air hit her below.

With her skirts bunched at her waist, held there by his body, he reached down to her thigh at the opening in her drawers. She parted her legs as his fingers got closer to the apex. She was panting, but she realized and accepted that and wanted more. His fingertips skimmed the folds to her core. Her lower lips swelled and became heavy. As his finger slid into her, she gripped his shoulders and parted her legs a tiny bit more.

He inserted two more fingers inside her. "You're so wet for me," he growled, as he withdrew them and then plunged them back inside her. She moaned and curled one of her legs around his hip. It almost undid her when she heard the sound of her juices laving his fingers as he stroked her insides.

"Jack, please," she whimpered. She worked a hand between them and down the length of his clothed erection.

———

Jack so wanted her, to be buried deep inside her, and he knew she was ready for him. When she stroked his arousal through his wool pants, the heat from her hand and the pressure of the buttons on his fly against his sensitive organ made him hiss.

He'd already decided to pleasure only her, knowing later she'd regret it if he took her fully. As his fingers pumped harder, he felt her slickened sheath clenching at them. When she began undoing the buttons on his pants, his started losing his resolve to avoid taking her completely. If she actually touched his skin, he'd lose the battle entirely. She clamped a hand onto his shoulder, digging into it, and kissed him hard.

He wanted her, needed to claim her, make her his. His carnal need, primal, began to surface as she clumsily worked at the buttons on his drawers. With a low growl, he pulled his fingers out of her and finished the unbuttoning himself. She gasped when he withdrew his hand, and he knew she had been on the verge of climaxing. After taking her to that plateau, he couldn't leave her unfulfilled.

"Emma," he muttered, his arousal resting against her curls as he smashed her into the rock. "You don't want me like this." There, he'd said it and put his own fears out on the table.

———

She didn't listen. Her hand wound around his hardness. The skin itself was so soft. She felt the large vein along the organ vibrating rapidly. Smiling to herself, she stroked the heavy sacks below—something she'd never done to her husband. Of course, the times she had been intimate with Billy could have been counted on one hand. Wiping that thought from her mind, Emma fingered the head of Jack's manhood, tracing the ridge. She heard him swallow hard, a low rumble coming from his chest. She touched the opening with her fingertip and was surprised to find it wet.

"Oh my God, Emma," he rasped.

She looked into his darkened eyes. She, too, ached with need, and it would be so easy...She gripped his shaft and brought it against her soaking entrance, placing the head inside her wet folds.

That was his undoing.

He plunged into her as his mouth captured hers again. She gasped as he filled her. He was so big, and, for a moment, she burned as he buried all the way in. Within an instant, though, her body accommodated him. He withdrew almost completely, and she whimpered. Again, he filled her, her back and bare shoulders getting scraped as he lifted her against the boulder. Over and over, he delved deep inside, filling her. She braced herself between Jack and the rock as she wrapped her legs around his hips.

He groaned against her neck and she panted wildly, gasping for air as he took her higher and higher. She clung to him as she approached the precipice of something she hadn't experienced before. He plunged into her again, and she lifted her hips to meet his thrust. With Jack's next thrust, her world shattered. With her eyes shut, she saw the stars explode into a million pieces.

Jack thrusted one more time, moaning at his own release.

And as his seed filled her, he buried his teeth in her bared shoulder. As he showered her womb, the exquisite pain from his bite made her climax again.

Together they slid down the rock to the hard ground, Emma on top of Jack. He wrapped his arms around her and her skirts covered them. She'd never felt so sated. She was exhausted, happy, warm, in love. Her head fell to his shoulder as a sigh escaped her.

What the hell had he just done?

He had acted like a complete scoundrel, no better than his father. He had taken what wasn't his. Hard. Against a rough stone, exposing them both to the cold and possible discovery. He'd simply lifted her skirts and claimed her, although she wasn't his to claim.

He would go to hell for it. And the troops ahead of them would gladly escort him to the gates.

His heart slowed from its frantic pace. He felt her body draped over his and knew he had satisfied her, but no true gentleman would have done what he did. He had treated her no better than a slave...he cringed at the memory of that night long ago.

The sweet smell of Emma's hair and her self invaded his senses. Like roses. Somehow she still carried that scent, now mixed with the scent of their arousal. He was still inside her but softening, depleted.

He closed his eyes, trying to shut out the fear threatening to overwhelm him. She felt so warm covering him after he'd caught her as they slid to the cold ground. She shivered as he held her, startling him. She was halfway undressed because of him. She could catch cold and die!

"Emma, Emma," he prodded, sitting up with her still in his arms.

"Hum?" she murmured sensually.

He began to harden again. *No!* In one swift move, he lifted her off him as he scrambled to his feet. Her skirts fell into place as she found her footing and he released her to shove himself back into his drawers, buttoning them and his pants shut.

She looked confused and blushed slightly at the sight of her exposed breasts.

With more expertise than he cared to reveal, he gently tucked them back inside her chemise, rehooked her corset and began buttoning her bodice.

"I can get that," she said languidly, pushing his fingers away.

He watched her, running his hand through his hair. He hoped the bruise on her shoulder would fade soon. Deep in the throes of passion, he'd been powerless to stop himself from biting her. As Emma finished dressing, he wanted to run his fingers through her loosened hair.

"Let me take you back to the others. I hope they're asleep," he muttered, praying they hadn't heard him or Emma scream in ecstasy. That was a memory he wouldn't forget.

Smiling shyly at him, she nodded.

Back at the camp, he picked up Nathan and placed him in the curve of Emma's body as she laid down. He covered them with the quilt and blanket he'd used for the past two weeks. Carefully, he snuggled around her backside, kissing her lips quickly before settling down.

"Merry Christmas, Jack," she whispered.

"Merry Christmas," he murmured against her ear. He saw her smile and close her eyes.

He waited for her to fall asleep, which didn't take long. Quietly, he got up, wrapped the coverings around her and the babe and walked away.

Saddling Goliath, he patted the horse's neck and mounted him. With one parting look at his son and Emma, he rode off, knowing the army ahead of them, Major General William S. Rosecrans' Army of the Cumberland, waited.

And the Union Army waited for his return.

> **"My paramount object in this struggle is to save the Union...if I could save the Union without freeing any slave, I would do it; and if I could save it by freeing all the slaves, I would do it;and if I could save it by freeing some and leaving others alone, I would also do that..."**
>
> ~ Abraham Lincoln, in a letter to Horace Greeley, 1862

CHAPTER TWENTY-FOUR

Tennessee, December 25

Emma woke slowly to the sounds of Nathan chirping on the ground next to her. She refused to open her eyes. It was cold, and she huddled further under the blankets. The child let out a wild yip but began baby talking again. She finally peeked out at the early sun, which was barely above the horizon. She felt stiff and sore. Her hips ached, as did the insides of her thighs, and her back felt as though it had been lashed or scraped. She eased herself up onto an elbow and winced at the pain in her shoulder. She tried to figure out why she felt so miserable until the events of the previous night hurtled back into memory.

Jack had made love to her standing upright, propping her against a rock. And he'd actually bitten her on the shoulder.

A warm and comfortable wave washed through her. That was the way it was supposed to be between them...

She smiled. *Jack.* She reached behind for him, but all she found was bare ground. She looked around, but there was no Jack. He'd left her again. She felt abandoned but tamped down the emotion. He promised he'd be back, and this time, she believed him.

Looking at Nathan, she found the baby fascinated with a new toy—a carved wooden horse. Jack must have left it as a Christmas gift for his son.

It took effort for Emma to rise, but she finally did, motivated by Nathan's giggles as he played with his new toy. She changed Nathan and set him on the blanket as she began cooking porridge and making biscuits. But the ghost of abandonment, betrayal and fear threatened again to seize her. Her heart thudded faster, and her breathing shortened. She closed her eyes, teetering on unsteady feet, feeling both alone and at total union with Jack. She argued with herself—he had made love to her, she still felt his tender touch, deep but vibrant.

He left them to get supplies and would return. She believed him. She had to. When he took her the previous night, it was clear he truly wanted her, that he didn't just need her for Nathan's sake. Steeling herself against feelings that threatened to spoil her newfound happiness, she inhaled deeply, resolving to fight them.

The smell of burning biscuits suddenly invaded her nostrils, and she jumped to the cast iron pan, quickly removing the food from its hot surface. She had barely saved the biscuits from being ruined.

Knowing Jack wanted and needed her was clear. But nothing was clear about whether or not he loved her. Once, she had thought he did, until he married Caroline.

She had survived that painful time, but now, was his want
and need enough for her?

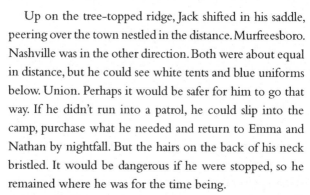

Up on the tree-topped ridge, Jack shifted in his saddle,
peering over the town nestled in the distance. Murfreesboro.
Nashville was in the other direction. Both were about equal
in distance, but he could see white tents and blue uniforms
below. Union. Perhaps it would be safer for him to go that
way. If he didn't run into a patrol, he could slip into the
camp, purchase what he needed and return to Emma and
Nathan by nightfall. But the hairs on the back of his neck
bristled. It would be dangerous if he were stopped, so he
remained where he was for the time being.

Emma had been on his mind all night. He could still hear
her moans, her panting as he entered her. The feel of her
legs wrapped around him, her mewling as he slammed her
against the rock wall, plunging into her over and over again.
He'd behaved as though she was a whore. He never meant
to take her the way he had, but when she placed the head
of his swollen arousal in the folds of her wetness, his resolve
had crumbled. Even just the memory of what they'd shared
had begun to excite him again. *Damn!*

Jack was so distracted by his thoughts that he'd lost his
focus. It returned with lightning speed at the sound of rifles
being cocked on either side of him.

From among the trees, another horseman appeared,
dressed in federal blue.

"My, oh my, what do we have here?" the rider asked as
he got closer. "A Rebel?" His eyes moved from Jack to his
horse, and Jack saw them widen. "On a Union mount, I see.
Stolen, no doubt," he sneered.

Jack tightened his grip on the reins. He'd forgotten about

the damn U.S. insignia on the bridal. His mind raced, trying to figure out his odds as he stared at the man who shared Jack's rank.

"I see our secesh thief here's tongue got tied." He laughed as did the two cavalrymen aiming at Jack. "Mind telling me your name, boy?"

Jack's eyes narrowed. "Captain Jack Fontaine, Army of the Potomac."

The man raised his eyebrows as he continued to grin. "Really? Here in Tennessee?" He chuckled. "Are you lost, soldier?"

"And you are, Captain...?" To hell with protocol, Jack thought.

The man sat straighter in his saddle, but the smirk didn't leave his face. "Captain Wright, under Major General McCook, Brigadier General Sheridan's command."

Sheridan, West Point class of '53, had graduated before Jack. He remembered the man well. Sheridan had been an aggressive little bastard, letting nothing get in his way. He was the type to do well in the military, and, considering his rank, apparently he had. Or, Jack mused, perhaps Lincoln had simply become desperate for officers. Oh yes, Jack well remembered Sheridan's hot temper after losing a horseracing contest to him. Jack's old mount, Windswept, had beaten Sheridan's nag fair and square. But Sheridan had protested to the commandant, claiming the race had been rigged.

McCook also was a former Pointer, two years older, but Jack had no specific memory of him. Hell, half the armies in the war were commanded by West Point graduates. The question was, what would Wright do with Jack?

"So, *Captain*, care to explain what the hell you're doing out here in the west, if not joining the Rebs? Hearing how deep that secesh accent of yours is, you figure you're close enough to home to desert?"

While weighing the predicament he was in, Jack regarded Wright. The man next to Jack spat on the ground, his gun never wavering in its aim. They were spoiling for a fight, but at three to one, Jack wasn't fool enough to give it to them.

"I'm on special assignment from the Secretary of War, scouting the area." Damn, that sounded foolish even to his own ears. But under the circumstances, it still might work.

Wright's jaw ticked. "You're dressed like a secesh."

Jack guffawed. "Can't be riding through here as a Union officer, alone, and not get shot. You know these Rebs."

At length, the officer replied, "Fine, but we're takin' you in to let command figure what to do with you." He turned his mount and started back to camp with Jack and the two soldiers following.

Phil Sheridan sat at the table outside his wall tent with his commanding officers. It was Christmas morning in Tennessee. He'd rather be anywhere else than here. All the major fighting was back East, but to get there, he'd have to do well at his current location first. The West was filled with low-lying Rebs that slithered about, claiming the land was theirs. His anger flared anew. Time to run the bastards to ground.

"Sir." A courier stood before him, holding out a folded missive.

Sheridan, or "Little Phil," a nickname that irked him because he was short, bit back the anger bubbling up. The soldier looked terrified. Sheridan enjoyed the moment and then nodded to his lieutenant, who took the note.

"McCook's ordering us to get ready to move."

The other men around the table mumbled as Sheridan smiled. He loved war, really embraced the beast, anxious to fire into its beady eyes. The next day, they would descend on that stinking secesh town along Stone's River and crush the bastards...

Led by Captain Wright, men and horses headed toward his tent, redirecting his attention to them. Although Wright followed orders to the letter, Sheridan hated him. But he couldn't find a good excuse for getting rid of the man, other than to use him in the infantry during a fight. Arms crossed, Sheridan leaned back in his chair.

"General Sheridan, sir," Wright saluted.

Behind him, two soldiers stood with their weapons trained on someone Sheridan couldn't see. "What've ya' got today, Captain?" Wright was a wheedling little bastard and made Sheridan's skin crawl, but at times, he had been invaluable.

"A Reb, sir. Claiming to be one of ours."

Instantly, Sheridan's interest was piqued. He motioned for Wright to move. The man they had been discussing stood there erect, his shoulders back and head high. His civilian clothing was torn but not smelly, unlike the rags many of the Southerners wore. Sheridan frowned. The man looked familiar.

"Who the hell are you?"

The man looked straight ahead. "Captain Jack Fontaine, sir."

"Claims he's from..." Wright started to say until Sheridan waved at him to be quiet.

Silence. Sheridan's eyebrows raised in an unspoken question.

The green eyes flashed as Jack looked straight ahead. Those eyes...

"Captain Jack Fontaine, sir, U.S. Army."

Fontaine. Oh, yes, now he remembered. "Class of...?"

Smiling, Jack quickly glanced at Sheridan, his green eyes sparkling with pride. "'54, sir."

Sheridan laughed, "I remember you." His raked the man with his gaze. "You look like a stinking Reb, Fontaine."

"Yes, sir," the quick reply.

"Explain yourself."

"On a mission for Stanton, sir, to check on Rebel numbers."

Sheridan snorted. "You're obviously with McClellan's cavalry. An officer."

Jack shuffled a little, and Sheridan noticed his jaw clench. "Sir, I'm here on a personal matter also." His voice was low.

Sheridan didn't like the sound of that. Command never let personal issues interfere. Ever. "Yes?"

Jack inhaled, hoping his story would pass muster. Sheridan apparently didn't like Little Mac and his pretentious need for reinforcements. However, Jack knew "Little Phil" to be hotheaded and aggressive, so he had to be careful.

"My wife and child, sir. Got Stanton's approval to take them to family, using that as a way to sort out Confederate numbers."

Sheridan stood, his hands clasped behind his back. "Sounds a little off to me, Captain."

Jack shrugged. "Seen General Bragg's army, sir, marching south of here."

Sheridan's face was unreadable, but his eyes bore into Jack's. "You realize, sir, I don't believe you."

Jack had no choice but to stand his ground. He looked straight ahead, but, from the corner of his eye, he saw Sheridan apparently debating with himself.

"If what you say is true, I'll have you go to Murfreesboro and check the numbers there. Your damnable southern tongue oughta get you in as a secesh." He spat on the ground, disgust on his face.

"Yes, sir."

"Captain Wright'll go with you." When Jack nodded and turned to go, Sheridan added, "And Captain, I'll give you to noontime but no longer. If you're not back here by then, I'll shoot you myself for desertion."

<hr />

Jack rode into Murfreesboro unarmed and alone. Wright hovered in the tree line above the town proper. The bastard was armed with a Spencer repeating rifle, and the heat of the man's gaze burned Jack, the awareness of the loaded weapon aimed at him. He tried to ignore the growing fear that Wright would shoot him just because he could get away with it. Instead, he fought to concentrate on his mission, which was to find supplies for Emma and Nathan while pretending to scout out Rebels.

Confederate soldiers loitered about, watching Jack warily, but he saw few civilians. He knew the Rebs were as cautious of him as he was of them. The air was heavy with tension; it even made Goliath skittish.

Jack stopped in front of the general store, throwing his reins over the hitching post. Murmuring in Goliath's ear, he eyed the soldiers, looking for sudden movement. They obviously admired his mount. As fighting continued, good horses were becoming more rare in both armies. Jack knew they'd try to take the horse, but he'd trained Goliath to his commands. The horse had a wild streak in him, which made him hard to handle by anyone but Jack. Comforted by that knowledge, Jack took his saddlebags and strode into the store.

Standing at the counter, the balding storekeeper, head glistening with sweat, nervously wiped his apron. "Can I help you, mister?"

Jack smiled easily. "Yes, sir. I'm in need of some supplies."

The man's eyes darted to the front door. "I'll see what I have if you've a list..."

Jack tried hard to look relaxed. "No, sir, I just came for a few items. I need a sack of flour, salt, some meat and sugar."

The man looked at him. "I may have some of what you need, if you have real money."

Jack fished out a wad of paper money from his pocket, dumping it on the countertop. The storekeeper's eyes widened.

"That'd be Union money."

Jack nodded. "Didn't think you'd be wantin' Confed."

The man greedily took the cash. "I'll get your stuff. Ya' be needin' anything else?"

Jack spied a bar of French-milled soap on a ledge against the wall. He picked it up and sniffed. It smelled like roses. He closed his eyes and was reminded of Emma. He put the soap on the counter, along with a metal teething ring. "Add these too."

The man nodded and left for the back room.

Jack glanced out the store windows and snorted. Two lads were trying to untie Goliath.

The storekeeper returned with Jack's items, placing them on the counter.

"Thanks," he said, opening his saddlebags to put them inside.

"Mister, you be careful. If they find you got Union money or you ain't conscripted..." his voice trailed away.

Jack nodded and thought, if the man only knew... Slinging the bags over his shoulder, Jack walked out to find Goliath gone. He shook his head and pursed his lips, whistling loudly.

Down the street, behind another building, he heard a ruckus of men swearing, boxes falling and hooves clattering. Around the corner came his bay stallion, reins flying and the saddle askew.

"Whoa," he ordered and Goliath halted in front of him, nostrils flaring. Jack patted his neck. "Good boy," he whispered softly. He squared the saddle and adjusted the straps, throwing the saddlebags across Goliath's flanks and securing them.

"Mighty fine horseflesh you got there, boy."

Jack nodded in agreement and put his foot in a stirrup.

"Ain't seen too many Yankee horses 'round here much." The man spat his tobacco juice within an inch of Jack's foot.

Jack silently cursed. The Union saddle, with its oblong air hole designed to reduce a horse's sweating and increase its stamina, stood out plain as day. *Damn!*

The man and his companions, Confederate soldiers all, stepped closer. "I don't see you in uniform, boy." The older man obviously was the leader, but Jack couldn't determine his rank because his uniform had no markings.

"No, sur," Jack drawled. "Ain't involved till I get my wife and son to my folks in Lou's'ana."

The older man spat again, his face scrunching as he thought about what Jack had said. His weathered skin made him appear old and wise, but the glint in his eye bespoke pure evil.

"You ain't one of them parolees?"

Jack stood up straight. "No, sir. I ain't takin' no oaths." Some captured Confederates were released if they swore not to fight anymore against the Union. Knowing the southern mentality, though, Jack wagered that many broke their oaths the minute they got away safely.

But Jack knew he was no better than them. After proudly swearing to fight for the Union, he had not only deserted the North but was a traitor to the South as well.

"Where's your woman?"

"Waitin' for me to return. Good day." He pulled himself up onto the saddle and backed Goliath away from the reach of the men and galloped out of town.

"I counted a company, maybe," Jack reported to Sheridan upon returning with Wright.

The general chewed a piece of straw. "Captain Wright, you have anything to add?"

"Just that this man's a traitor," Wright snarled.

Jack's hands clenched.

"Explain yourself," Sheridan demanded.

"Saw this stinkin' bastard talking to secesh, bold as brass," he spat.

"What do you have to say about that, Captain Fontaine?"

Jack seethed. "Yes sir, I did talk to them" Sheridan continued to glare at him. "The man in charge asked me about my horse. Saw he had a Union saddle on him. Told him I stole it."

Sheridan laughed, but it was brief and humorless. "You say you counted a company, huh? We'll see." His went to his table, pulled a sheet of paper to him and grabbed his pen. "Fontaine, I'm having a tough time believin' your claims.

Till I hear otherwise, I'm assigning you to my command. We'll see how good you are at scouting when we march out of here tomorrow." He finished writing and signed his name with a flourish. "I'm placing you in the ranks. Wright, get Captain Fontaine quarters..."

Jack's gut twisted. "Sir, I have supplies and food that I need to get to my wife."

Sheridan eyed him. "And you left her alone in the woods to get them?"

"Had no choice, sir." He'd say whatever it took for him to get the items to her, anything. "She lost her family's home last fall because of the war. I'm taking her and my infant son to my folks. Then I'll gladly return."

Sheridan laughed out loud. "Captain, if I gave into half the sad stories my men told me, we'd have no army. No, I won't let you go. Lieutenant Rhinehart, find someone to take these goods to Mrs. Fontaine and then report back here. We're moving in the morning."

"Yes, sir."

Jack ground his teeth, swallowing hard. He had become a captive of the Union Army. His stomach twisted and the pain in his chest grew as his heart sank. He'd left them alone, in the wilderness, with only a rifle and nothing else. More and more, John Henry was slipping away mentally. Nathan was only a baby. Tilly was a slave, trained to submit to white people. And Emma, his darling Emma. What had he done? They'd all starve or be killed–or worse. He had to get out, somehow, some way, without being killed himself.

One thing was for certain. If Emma survived, she'd hate him forever.

"The South must be made to feel full respect for the power and honor of the North."

~ New York Times, June 26, 1861

CHAPTER TWENTY-FIVE

Jack adjusted the cartridge box on his belt, sliding it to the familiar spot. He sighed with resignation. This war would never end. Neither would the one raging in his soul.

Sheridan's man had found a sack coat for him to wear because he'd left his officer's frock and greatcoat with Emma. His navy blue pants with the matching sack coat showed obvious rank. Regulars wore sky blue pants with navy jackets. Officers wore navy all around and fitted frocks. Goliath snorted, his hooves dancing in readiness as the order came to move. A light but icy cold rain began to fall. Jack felt its sting against his face and hands. The physical pain matched the pain in his heart. He prayed that the soldier charged with delivering the supplies and food had made it to Emma and that she had heeded his message to continue to his boyhood home without him.

He'd promised to return to her, but when he spoke the words, he knew it was unlikely he'd be able to fulfill the promise. Having a wife and child—something he'd found himself thinking about a lot recently—was against his better judgment, especially in war time. Forced to return to the fight, Jack prayed for only one thing—that the Almighty would protect Emma and his son.

Thoughts of her warmed him inside—how she smelled, how she felt, how she tasted. Remembering the look on her face as she climaxed while he was buried deep inside her made him twitch in the saddle. It was a beautiful memory, one that would sustain him through whatever was to come. And then a thought suddenly brought him back to the present. He'd spilled his seed inside her. She could be carrying his child now, but he prayed fervently that she wasn't. *Damn!*

Jack shook the thought from his mind and looked at his troops. He'd been given roughly half of Company A, Wright the other half. The Army of the Cumberland had been drilled repeatedly by Rosecrans, and the men ached to be put to the test—or that's what Jack had heard. The battle ahead would be fierce, more deadly than Sharpsburg or any of the other battles Jack had been in.

Despite the responsibility Jack had been given, he wasn't trusted. Wright rode only a few feet away from him, watching him closely, preventing any attempt at escape. Wright's hand stayed close to the revolver sticking out of his belt, and he itched to use it. Jack had to watch his front as well as his back. Perhaps he would die in battle, ending his misery, but he probably wouldn't be that lucky.

Rosecrans split his army into three columns and assigned a different route to each to meet the growing number of Confederates at Murfreesboro. Jack's column marched south out of Nashville to take the Nolensville Turnpike to Triune, then head eastward to meet the others and attack. Approximately half of the force of eighty-two thousand that Rosecrans commanded at Nashville now rode along the same stretch Jack had traveled alone only two days earlier.

The rebel cavalry under Brigadier General Joseph Wheeler constantly harassed the Union troops, racing in, striking a blow and disappearing into the Tennessee wilderness. Their latest attack had been that morning, just as the line began moving, before the rain picked up. Jack actually enjoyed the diversion. He relished any means to expend his pent-up anger, although what he really wanted was to sink a bullet between Wright's bushy eyebrows. Unfortunately for the Union, Wheeler's horsemen knew the territory, and their riding skills far surpassed the futile defensive maneuvers of the enemy. They struck with the speed and deadliness of lightning. And at no time was Wright positioned so that an "errant" bullet might hit him. But then again, Jack wasn't an easy target for the lanky Yankee either.

"I'll shoot you if you help those damn secesh," Wright threatened after the last raid.

"Go ahead, try. But God help you if you miss," Jack retorted.

Even then, Wright rode slightly to the side and back, waiting and watching.

Emma waited and fretted. An entire day had passed and still no Jack. And no additional food or supplies.

It'd taken her an hour to find her father, who had wandered off into a stand of trees, calling for her mother. When he saw Emma, he looked bewildered. She knew he slipped away a little more each day.

Tilly, thankfully, was still with her. She feared the slave might disappear, especially with Jack gone. So many slaves had simply left after the Yankees invaded. But Tilly remained. She had become attached to Nathan, and Emma could only hope that he'd hold her there longer.

A cool sprinkle brought her back to the present. Glancing upward, she grimaced. Grey clouds filled the sky, and a brisk wind swept through their small encampment. She shuddered, pulling Jack's greatcoat tighter around her. Trudging to the wagon, Emma grabbed the canvas flap and rope.

"Tilly, put Nathan down and come help me."

Struggling with the rope, they pulled the cover taunt for shelter. It was a simple task that allowed her mind to wander. She wanted Jack back. Why had he left her, them, there, promising to return? At first, she feared he'd been taken by one of the armies or even killed. But now she believed he'd simply gone off. Willingly abandoned her. He'd taken her that night, ravished her like a man driven to stake a claim. He had even marked her skin. He'd stroked her, kissed her, devoured her, but all of it had been for naught. Now, he was gone for good. She had to accept that he'd never come back.

But a small voice struggled to be heard, deep from within her heart. It entreated her to believe what Jack had said. He'd promised before he'd return for her and his son, and he had. This time was no different.

And yet, it was in so many ways. Uttering a frustrated, strangled noise, she pulled the fabric taught, lacing the rope through the copper eyelets.

The sprinkle turned to a steady, cold rain. If it fell any harder, they'd have to spend a cold and wet night without the comfort of a fire. Intent on feeding the current feeble flames with wood that had been stored under the wagon to keep it dry, she almost missed the sound of leaves crunching beneath a horse's hooves. She glanced up to see a horse walking toward them, its rider dressed in blue. Jack!

"Jack," she greeted, taking a step toward the man, until it hit her that the horse wasn't bay but black and the rider was dressed in full Yankee uniform. He was just a boy, really, his brown eyes sorrowful.

"Mrs. Fontaine?"

She gulped as her heart sank.

December 29, 1862

Murfreesboro sat near Stone's River, in a valley of rich soil. The townspeople were sentimental to the Confederate cause and warmly embraced General Braxton Bragg's army. A flat, open area, it was not a defensible position but one Bragg simply refused to leave. No land in Tennessee was to become Union controlled. Areas close to the Nashville Pike and the Nashville and Chattanooga Railroad had dense cedar forests, virtually impenetrable to infantry. Small outcroppings of limestone, like teeth scattered throughout the area, also slowed the movement of artillery and wagons.

Not only was the land spiteful in its makeup, but scouts reported Confederate forces in the area equaled those of Rosecrans. In some cases, they numbered more than the federal army, with the cavalries of Nathan Bedford Forrest and John Hunt Morgan in the vicinity. Wheeler's riders still attacked Union lines, and Southern horsemen danced around them, making Rosecrans uncomfortable.

Jack removed his hat and swiped his brow. Sweat still formed despite the cold. It had taken three days to make it there, three days of Wheeler's incursions, three days of watching Wright and his itchy trigger finger. Three days of worrying about Emma and his son.

His thoughts were interrupted by yelling, gunfire and the pounding of hooves. Jack turned to look at the end of his command and found Confederate cavalry racing into their lines. They set fire to a couple of supply wagons, whooping and hollering as they hijacked another one loaded with boxes of ammunition.

Jack steered Goliath toward the rear, digging in his heels to make the horse fly into the attack. But by the time he arrived, it was over.

"Where are they?" he demanded from a mounted officer at the scene.

The horse was snorting and sweating hard from exertion as the officer gasped for air, pulling back on the reins. Blood on his thigh was quickly spreading. "Rebs. Came out of nowhere. Got three wagons, one full of ammunition, and" his breath skipping "even captured some of our men."

Jack frowned. "Get to the surgeons."

The officer nodded and left. Wright rode up next to Jack.

"Planned that well, didn't you, you liar?" he snarled. "Wished I was here a moment ago. Would'a taken you off our list of concerns."

"Wished you could've made it sooner. I've a bullet with your name on the side." Jack spat without breaking eye contact with the bastard.

"Enough, gentlemen," barked Sheridan. "Let's assess the damage. Get patrols out and send the rest to bed. Tomorrow'll be here soon, and those Rebs'll be expecting a call."

Jack watched as the general rode off, ignoring Wright. The man leaned forward in his saddle, staring at him.

"Yeah, we'll see what tomorrow brings, all right. Gotta watch them bullets, secesh lover, one of them might stray too far, you hear me?" Wright laughed as he rode away.

Jack's gaze narrowed. Tomorrow might bring all sorts of bullets looking to make his chest their target, and he welcomed them.

It took the next day to form the attack line. Rather a ridiculous effort, Jack thought. Displaying one's troops to the other side, as if in a show of strength. Rosecrans' men made a line two miles northwest of town. The Union line was four miles long and planted parallel to Bragg's. Sheridan's troops, including Jack and his co-commander, were in the middle, facing Major General Patrick Cleburne's division. Near a copse of trees, Jack assessed the situation and didn't like what he saw. Confederate numbers looked equal to the Union's. But at least Rosecrans did not exaggerate the number of rebels the way McClellan always did. Perhaps that's why his reputation was building in the West and why command in the East had floundered, unlike Lee's.

The day lingered on, with tension building on both sides. Jack felt as though he was under constant watch. When Wright was called away, another seemed to take his place, eyes glued on Jack. His shoulders became tight because of all that scrutiny. He scanned the area but could not find a way out. Not yet. Stationed in the center of the line, he had little freedom of movement. He gritted his teeth, frustration and worry gnawing at his gut.

He found paper and pen. Quickly, he jotted down his will, giving everything to Nathan and for Nathan to be under Emma's care. What he had in assets would see to their safety. Blowing the ink dry, he folded the paper and sealed it.

"Hackman," he called to the first private he saw. The

man responded quickly. "Give this to that butcher in the hospital tent. What's his name? Worth?"

The private nodded. "Yes, sir." He took the paper and bolted.

Jack sighed. At least before he left for hell, he'd make sure his son and the woman he loved were taken care of. Sleep, though, remained elusive.

The following morning, in the predawn light, gunfire exploded over Major General John McCown's division. Confederate General William J. Hardee's men rushed into McCown's lines during breakfast, wreaking havoc and mayhem in the first wave of attack. Many of McCown's left flank scattered behind Brigadier General Jefferson C. Davis' brigade.

The attack triggered a chain of events down the line. Within hours, Hardee's men drove Jack's forces back three miles to the railroad. Rosecrans raced across the field, redirecting troops from attacking the Confederate right to defending his own right. Jack, along with many others, saw that the general was covered in the blood of his chief of staff and friend, Colonel Julius Garesche, who had been beheaded by a cannonball.

Emma hadn't slept since a soldier had arrived two days previously with supplies from Jack. She'd feared he'd died, but the man claimed he hadn't. At first, she was furious at Jack for deserting her, but soon, after a fit of hysteria over the idea of her "deserter" deserting her, she searched the bag. Relief flooded through her. Food.

Reaching in further, she found the soap with her name penciled on the wrapping. Rose-scented soap. She inhaled the smell, closing her eyes. It made her think of home and simpler times. Before the war. Before death and longing had become her constant companions.

The teething ring for Nathan was a godsend. The child had happily chewed on hardtack, but it wasn't made to withstand his gnawing forever. The rounded metal ring worked well, once she'd warmed it in her hands. Typical of everything given him, Nathan promptly stuck it in his mouth. She smiled as he gurgled happily.

It was the last item in the bag that stopped her—a piece of paper with Jack's father's name and address scrawled on it. Her insides twisted. He didn't think he'd return. She sank to the damp ground at the impact of yet another loss.

Although only a couple of days had passed, it seemed like an eternity to her. She couldn't decide what to do. It was an eerie time. Often, she felt her father's eyes on her. He never said a word to her, offering only short answers to whatever she asked. The man's eyes were vacant except when Nathan was awake. She caught her father calling the boy Charles sometimes, but she didn't correct him. It hadn't worked when she had. He appeared to forget recent things easily, as though they had never happened. But if she asked him about his youth or his marriage to her mother or even about her own childhood, he became animated, telling tales she'd long forgotten.

He appeared to be happiest reminiscing about the past, and Emma wished she could join him there. It certainly had been more pleasant than the present.

She stirred the oatmeal in the pot over the flames. A chill wind swept past her, managing to blow up under her skirt and petticoats, surprising her and making her shiver. It was so quiet. A cloak of despair descended on her, causing her to gasp aloud.

"Miss Emma?" Tilly called softly.

"I'm okay, Tilly." She must have been loud. The girl was nursing Nathan, whose periodic gurgles were the only sounds to be heard.

Suddenly, there was a loud clap like thunder. Emma frowned because a cloudless day was dawning. Then she realized the noise had come from far away. She heard it again and again. Cannons. Smoke began filling the air, darkening it. Cautiously, she stepped toward the trees, the copse blocking her view of the battle. She was away from the protection of the wagon, a few yards from the trees, when she saw movement among them. She squinted, ignoring her rising fear, curiosity and hope overshadowing it. Maybe Jack was there, returning to them. She took another step, and with it another crack came, this time close by. The trees shook and a gust of smoke billowed through them, along with the screams of the men hiding there. Her mouth fell agape as several men dressed in grey fell. Being only a short distance from them, she saw they were soaked in blood.

In shock, she fell to her knees and then saw a soldier in blue riding through the mayhem with two others, guns blazing. They shot the wounded grey before turning their horses around and riding back toward the slaughter.

Slaughter. The word caught in her mind. Jack. Fear gripped her. Jack was hurt, she knew it, felt it deep within her. He could be lying on the ground, bleeding, like the men now dead before her. She needed to go to him.

"Tilly," she called.

The girl came with Nathan propped against her shoulder as she patted his back. He burped loudly, and Emma smiled and took the baby from Tilly. He gave Emma a big grin, his lips stained with milk. She kissed his forehead before handing him back to the slave.

"Tilly, I've got to go. Jack needs me." She sounded like a lunatic, but she didn't care. "Look after him and my father. I'll be back soon."

Jack reloaded his revolver. Looking down the row of his soldiers, he saw they stood ready. A few were trembling. The first time in battle and facing the enemy head on like they were, scared most men half to death. It was a normal reaction. To be casual about it or to welcome death would be insane. But Jack felt insane right now.

The first wave of the attack caused Union forces to retreat. The second wave by Generals Jones Withers and Benjamin Cheatham struck hard and fast. Jack's men and the rest of Sheridan's command were the only defensive forces. The general had gotten them up at four to prepare for the day. The Confederate onslaught was repulsed and repulsed by the Union. But the cost had been high. Sheridan's three division leaders had been killed, and about a third of the men lay wounded or dead from the three-hour ordeal. As the Confederates pulled back from Sheridan's forces, the carnage around Jack reminded him of Sharpsburg and that valley of death, with the moans of the injured and the stench of sulfur, gunpowder and rot.

"Ah, gloating over the dead, you bastard," hissed the voice behind him. Wright. He'd wondered where the man had gone during the battle. Hoped he was one of the many lying on the ground.

"Missed your chance," Jack stated flatly.

Wright's eyes flared as he leveled his revolver at Jack. "Guns are still firing." He cocked his. "You are a deserter, a secesh, and a traitor, and I'm going to send you straight to hell."

A gun went off. Jack blinked, expecting to feel pain, but numbness remained. In front of him, Wright sank to the ground. There was a bullet hole between his bushy eyebrows, a look of shock frozen on his face.

Jack looked at the gun in his hand. His thumb was on the lever, but he hadn't fired. How had the bastard gotten shot? He turned to look behind him when he felt a thud against his shoulder. A searing pain shot through him as he glanced down to the left side of his chest. His navy jacket still looked navy, but there was a hole in it, just below his shoulder. He tried to lift his left arm, but it wouldn't move. Couldn't move. His shirt was sticking to his body as blood poured from the wound. His ears rang.

Slowly, his knees buckled, and he sank onto the hard winter ground, unable to stop himself from crashing onto the blood-soaked land. As he slid into oblivion, he thought of only one thing. Emma.

"You will keep constantly before the
public view in Great Britain, the tyranny of
the Lincoln Government, its utter disregard
of the personal rights of its citizens, and its
other notorious violations of law."
~ Robert M.T. Hunter to Henry Hotze,
November 11, 1861

CHAPTER TWENTY-SIX

Murfreesboro, December 31, 1862

Emma rode Petey toward the sound of battle, dread
filling her each minute as she got closer. The air was
thick with gunpowder and the sound of artillery, accented
with the tattoo of rifle fire and voices, muddled but audible.
She slowed the horse to a walk as they went through the
trees on a hill and stopped at the top. Hell's gates opened
before her.

She'd never seen such destruction and chaos in her life.
Men ran or galloped on horseback in all directions. Rifles
cracked and cannons boomed. Bodies were strewn across
the fields. And somewhere, in the midst of it all, was Jack.
Was he alive? Wounded? Dead? She remained frozen in
place, watching as the wrath of God descended below and
not a thing she could do to stop it. Fear gripped her.

She slid off Petey's back and dropped the reins, knowing
he'd stay put until she returned. Purposely but slowly she

walked forward, hugging the tree line, shrubs and rock outcroppings, clutching Jack's greatcoat tightly around her.

Horsemen galloped past her, intent on robbing the foot soldiers running ahead of them, or worse. They wore gray coats and rode pellmell into the line of navy, guns blazing, heading toward the wagons. Wagons filled with boxes. One of the men noticed her and stopped, staring down at her from his tall mount. She glared up at him, unable to move. His lips twitched.

"You best be leavin', missy," he drawled.

She shook her head. "I can't." She couldn't tell Jack's enemy that she was there to find a Yankee, which would have put both of them at risk.

He cocked his head, looking at her quizzically. Her Virginia accent had caught his attention, and he added, "This ain't no place for a lady."

But she refused to move.

"Ain't you got a gun?"

She patted the coat but didn't expect to find anything, and she didn't.

His lips thinned and he pulled a revolver out of his belt. He opened the cartridge cylinder and snapped it closed. Bending down, he offered her the gun. "Take it. You won't leave, and I can't leave ya' here with nothin'."

She grabbed the handle gingerly. "Thank you."

He nodded, tipped his plumed hat and sped off to join his men.

Emma gripped the handle, feeling the weight of the weapon. She'd learned how to fire a rifle back at Rose Hill but hadn't tried firing a revolver. Shoving the piece into her coat pocket, she prayed she wouldn't have to use it.

Emma continued searching for Jack, her skirt rustling along the ground, stirring up dead grass and leaves and other litter. Her toe caught on something, tripping her, and she barely stopped herself from falling. Lifting her skirts, she looked down and froze, horrified. She had tripped over a hand and forearm torn from someone's body. The mangled mess of blood, bone and tissue made her nauseous, and she covered her mouth to keep down the rising bile.

Shocked by the grisly discovery, Emma didn't see the man coming toward her, nor did he see her. When he bumped into her, she lost her footing and began to fall into the mess at her feet, but the man uttered a curse, dropped what he had been carrying and grabbed her around the waist.

"What the hell?" He pulled her upright, his face red with anger. "You can't just stand there, staring like a billy goat."

She blinked rapidly. The young man, dressed like a Yankee, spewed numerous curses as he bent to pick up his stuff. It took her a moment to realize he hadn't questioned her presence.

"Please, help me," she started. "I need to find..."

"Honey, we all need to find them, but they ain't here," he interrupted, his voice laced with heavy sarcasm. "The wounded be out there. Now, be a good girl and leave. Ain't got time to be messin' with you."

Her brows knitted as she watched him pick up small bottles, strips of cloth and metal objects and stick them back into his leather-wrapped box. She noticed the green diagonal stripe on his coat sleeve with a symbol stitched in the center. The insignia of the medical soldiers. Quickly she bent and picked up a long metal stick, its ends rounded with white porcelain caps.

"Doctor, I..."

He laughed absently. "Ain't no doc, missy. Just as you ain't no nurse. Who the hell are you?" He grabbed her wrist.

She clenched her jaw. His fingers dug into her wrist, hurting her as she thought about how to answer him. "I'm Mrs. Jack Fontaine. I came to find my husband."

The man's brows tipped upwards. "Fontaine? No, no, not familiar with that name, but then, I don't know many. Look, we've got wounded all over the place here. Not safe for you." He spat on the ground. "Since you're still not movin', get out of my way." He let go of her wrist and wiped his right hand on his soiled jacket before extending it to her.

His rudeness only made her stubborn. "I'm not leaving, but to get 'out of your way,' where would you suggest I go?"

The man's face contorted. "You are wasting my time." He stood glaring at her. The silence between them grew, and he turned his head as though scanning the sea of bodies.

Emma gritted her teeth, planting her feet firmly on the ground. She wasn't leaving, no matter how much he complained. But as he stood there, eyeing the bodies, she noticed a twitch in his cheek. He was pale, and she wondered what inner demons he was battling as he gripped the medical bag tighter. She looked past him at the dead and dying.

What if Jack was among them? She couldn't leave until she knew.

"Ain't goin', then help me," the medical man finally stated, as though he had read her mind. "Too damn many for me to get to on my own. Any aid I get will move me faster and maybe, just maybe, your man'll turn up as we head on."

She sighed with relief and nodded.

"Hospital Steward Brad Judd."

Gingerly she placed her hand in his. "Emma Fontaine."

He gave her a tight smile. "Not the best place to meet, but glad you're here. We be needing all the help we can get." With that, he was off. "Come on, then. And shove that hat low on your head. Watch where you step. God only knows what we'll find out here."

She pulled the brim lower and followed him. He led her through a rugged plain pocked by mini craters from artillery blasts and horses' hooves. In the twilight hours, they heard gunfire less frequently, but the moans and screams of the wounded prevailed. Occasionally, Judd pushed her down, covering her body with his. Only seconds later, the ground shook violently with nearby explosions. When the debris settled, he jumped up, swore, yanked her upright and apologized for his language.

When she looked across the battlefield, the dead bodies didn't seem real to her. But at the first body where Judd stopped, she once again thought she'd retch. It lay twisted, the soldier's mouth agape, eyes wide with horror. The upper part of his head had been ripped apart, and remnants of blood vessels and brains were splattered on his face and coat. The next two also were dead—one by a bullet to the chest, its effect mercifully swift. The other man's face was buried in the muck and one of his legs was hanging by a tendon, the bottom half twisted backwards.

Judd made a few notes over each body and searched their jackets for any papers identifying them. The three men all had papers showing name, rank and unit, but only two papers were legible. The third man's blood had soaked through the wool, to the paper, covering the penciled information.

Like a trained dog, Emma followed Judd, not making a noise or complaining. She lifted her skirts to step over puddles of blood and various body parts. After the third victim they'd found, she had lost the contents of her belly, heaving till everything was gone. She turned numb and was losing hope of finding Jack alive.

Judd was looking at her and saying something, but she couldn't hear him. The buzzing in her ears was too loud. She was in shock.

"Mrs. Fontaine," he tried harder and shook her shoulders.

She swallowed, blinking. Her eyes were red and her cheeks wet from tears she didn't know she had cried. The ache in her heart grew.

"Ma'am," Judd tried again as he sat her on a rock outcropping. Pulling out a flask, he yanked the cork free with his teeth and pressed the flask to her lips. Obediently, she opened her mouth and he poured the liquor into her.

It spilled down her throat, the fire reaching all the way to her stomach. Its burn stirred her senses. Sputtering, she stayed his hand and leaned away.

"Sorry," he muttered. "It's like you're in a trance. Rest now. Where I'm going is rough. Sheridan's men were stalled there. Command's calling it a slaughter pen. Let me see how bad it is. I may need your help, but, right now, I'm ordering you to rest, you hear me?"

Her gaze never left his. If she looked away, she'd see the hell behind him again. She could smell it—sulfur, the coppery scent of blood, and excrement from horses and men. Slowly she nodded.

"Good," he said. "I'll be right back. If you need me before, holler."

As though yelling would have done any good. All the men lying on the ground had hollered, but no one had heeded or helped them.

The sun was setting, coloring the battle's aftermath in the grey-pink of winter. Vacantly, she scanned the still bodies, but nobody looked like Jack. She feared she'd missed him as he lay dying in the field, alone, in pain. Her hands clenched as she fought the desire to scream when, from the corner of her eye, she saw one body move. She turned her head toward a man who was fighting to breathe. He moaned. Or had he actually talked? She went closer.

He lay face down in the mire, a pool of blood beneath him. As he raised his head feebly, he moaned again, "Help."

She froze. The voice sounded like Jack's. Within a second, her strength returned full force, and she raced the few feet to the soldier in blue.

"Jack?" She turned him over as he bellowed in pain. His chest was bathed in crimson. Pushing his mud-caked hair off his face, she wanted him to open his eyes. He looked so like Jack but was filthy. "Jack?"

His eyes flashed open. Those emeralds were wracked with pain. It was Jack!

"Mister Judd!" she cried. "Mister Judd!"

She heard him clomping toward her, his medical box rattling.

"Let's see what'cha got." The steward pushed her hands off the man and felt his cheeks. "He's cool but not cold yet." He grabbed Jack's collar, ripping it apart, yanking downward. At Jack's vest, he pulled harder, the brass eagle buttons flying into the mess around them. The shirt underneath was red, plastered to his chest and Jack flinched as Judd ripped it off.

Emma gasped. The wound looked like a gorge. Shreds of his shirt and jacket stuck to the jagged edges of his flesh. Black gunpowder residue clung to his skin. When Judd twisted Jack's shoulder to see his back, blood spurted from the bullet hole. Jack didn't utter a sound, but his face paled under the waning sunlight.

"I can't see that it exited." The steward reached for his box, throwing the lid open. "I can't tell if it's a bullet or shrapnel or what," he stated angrily, rummaging through the box.

"We need to get him under better light," Emma finally stuttered, her voice returning. "You can't do anything to him in the dark."

Judd looked at her and saw the battle raging in his eyes.

"Hell," he muttered, looking around him. "You two, over there," he called to two men searching another area nearby. She could barely see them as evening set in.

They ambled over, shovels in hand. Gravediggers. She shuddered.

"Grab him and follow me." Judd closed his box and stood.

The two plain-dressed soldiers grumbled but dropped their tools and scooped Jack up in their arms. Jack groaned as they jarred his body, their walk unsteady because of the rough ground. Emma followed, her eyes never leaving him.

They headed to the Union camp. Emma's nerves became more frayed as they walked into the Yankees' tented grounds, her skin crawling. They were there to kill Southerners, to prove they were the masters of the land. They'd killed her husband, the way she figured it, and maybe her brother, too. And now, they could take the man she loved from her. Oh, how she hated them. Still, she would not leave without Jack, so she swallowed her pride and anger and proceeded to the hospital tent.

Inside the tent was another world. Oil lamps and candles lit the area, reflecting off the white canvas and illuminating the nightmare around her. At the far end, where there were tables made from simple wood slats and rails, was the surgeon's ward. Cots filled with the wounded and dying covered the rest of the area. The smell of kerosene, beeswax and alcohol filled the air. Moans and screams punctuated the stillness of the morbid scene and ricocheted throughout the tent.

Judd motioned to an attendant to clear the cot in the far corner and waved to the grave diggers, who dumped Jack onto it and retreated. Emma was at his side immediately. Judd shoved a pan of water and a sponge into her hands. He gave her the flask as well.

"Clean that blood off so I can take a better look."

She nodded and he left.

The sponge emitted an odd odor, and she wrinkled her nose in disgust. Putting the sponge down, she reached underneath her gown and ripped off a section of her petticoat. The sponge would be more absorbent, but she refused to use it because of the way it smelled. Plunging the piece of petticoat into the water, she washed the blood and gunpowder from Jack.

Jack opened his eyes and stared at her. "Emma," he whispered.

She gave him a weak smile. "Shush now." But he had passed out again.

Judd returned, a pained look on his face as he ran his fingers through his hair. "Surgeon's too damn busy."

"Can't you fix him?" she asked, desperation creeping into her voice.

He shook his head. "I'm not a fully trained doctor..."

"Do you know what will happen if he isn't seen soon?"

"Yes," he muttered. "Same thing if they see him now. They'll take his arm."

She gasped. "His wound's in the shoulder."

He gave her a hard look, but then it softened. "They'll

take it all up through the shoulder blade unless the bullet can be found."

"Then find it," she demanded.

"They'd probably still amputate to make sure there's no gangrene."

Emma's mind whirled, remembering Billy and the pain he had endured after his leg was amputated. He was so miserable that he'd gladly sacrificed himself for his family. For her. Anger and anguish fought for control. Her fists clenched at her sides, and she felt the weight of the revolver in the coat pocket. A loaded revolver.

"Then he can't stay here," she said, her voice tight.

"And where would you take him?"

Her mind raced. The trip back to the camp was too far. Being jostled on horseback would hurt Jack further, if he even survived the trip.

Judd eyed her speculatively, lowering his gaze to the bulge in her pocket. A mixture of emotions played across his face, wavering between refusal and resignation. With a tired sigh, he muttered, "There is a house, a shack really, just beyond camp. I know the officer using it. Ain't seen him in a while but reckon' maybe I could convince him to give it up for a, uh, nurse."

"He'd do that? For a 'nurse' who cares for only one man?" She didn't believe him. She stroked the gun, not wanting to use it, but...

Judd snorted. In a voice so low only she could hear it, he stated, "Where d'you think I get my 'medicinal' whiskey from?"

She suddenly understood and nodded. She'd do anything to save Jack.

Judd persuaded a couple of wary musicians to move Jack. Neither questioned why one officer should be moved to private quarters when no one else of his rank had been. Judd led the way, his bag in hand, and they put Jack on the cot in the shack as Emma lit the lamps. The shack wasn't much bigger than her bedroom at Rose Hill. It had a fireplace, a tiny table and two chairs, a cot and one window. Though bleak, it was perfect for Jack.

Judd and Emma pried the uniform jacket, vest, suspenders and shirt off Jack. He moaned as they twisted his body to take off all the soiled clothes. His wound started to bleed again.

She placed her hand on his forehead. "He's going to burn with fever soon if we don't get that out."

Judd paced the room, running his hand nervously through his blond hair. "I'll never get anyone here fast enough."

"At least look for the bullet," she begged. She hoped if he could find it, he could remove it. She'd grovel if she had to.

His eyes narrowed, his jaw ticked. Swiftly, he went to his box and removed a metal wand, the one with the porcelain tips that she'd picked up earlier. "Where's that flask? I ain't got no water here."

Emma pulled it out of her coat pocket and then placed the coat on the chair. The cabin was cool and Judd stoked the embers but claimed the cool air would help Jack, slow his bleeding. She'd try to remember that as she shivered, holding the lamp above the wound as the steward splashed whiskey on the wand.

"Hold that back," he ordered. When she withdrew the lamp, he poured whiskey onto the wound. Jack shot upright and yelled, his eyes wide open in pain as the alcohol burned into his shoulder. And just as promptly, he fell back into oblivion.

Judd motioned for the light and gingerly stuck the probe
into the hole. Emma watched him. The man's hand shook,
and a fine sweat formed on his upper lip and forehead as he
paled, moving the rod around till he struck something. He
withdrew it and looked at the white end that was no longer
white. It was gray. He smiled.

"Found it." He stood up and stepped back.

"Then take it out."

He shook his head adamantly. Fear had come over him.
Emma frowned.

"You have to."

"I can't," he argued. "Not trained to."

"He needs your help," she implored.

"No!" He walked away and came right back. "They
won't let me do things like that."

Frustration took control of her. Reaching for the coat,
she yanked the revolver from the pocket and pulled the
hammer back as she pointed the muzzle at his chest. "Yes,
you will."

Raising his hands, he looked at her. "I can't." His hands
shook violently and all the color had drained from his face.
He was terrified.

It suddenly dawned on her. The man's flask wasn't for
medicinal use. He was a drunkard.

She released the hammer and lowered the weapon,
devastated. Putting the gun down, she looked at Judd's tools
and saw a long pair of tongs. "Teach me."

He flinched at her determination but nodded. They
went back to the cot. He poured a bit of whiskey on the
instrument and handed it to her.

"Carefully search for the bullet again. It's down to the
left. Don't push it. We don't want it to go deeper. Then,
insert the tongs, closed, till you get to the cartridge." He

swallowed hard. "I'll hold him down. It'll hurt him, but if he's going to live, we gotta get that out."

She nodded and, with the utmost care, followed his instructions. Jack jerked when she placed the bullet extractor into his flesh, and the steward barely had enough strength to hold him down. She grasped the bullet and Jack moaned as she withdrew it. The bloody, misshapen lead came out and she dropped it on the floor.

"Give me your petticoat," Judd ordered, pressing the wound shut as it bled.

She turned away from him and reached underneath her skirt to unbutton her petticoat. It fell to the floor and she stepped out of it to hand it to him. He wadded up the garment up and pressed it against Jack's shoulder.

The realization of what she had done to Jack struck her, and she began to tremble. Judd grabbed her hand, dragging her to his side of the bed and placing the hand where his was. "Press hard. I'll need to stitch it up."

She nodded, only vaguely aware of what he was doing. She was too focused on Jack.

Judd pried off her hand and used the curved needle and black silk thread to stitch the hole closed with three easy loops. "You'll have to take him."

She looked at him. "Where? Why can't we stay here?"

"If command finds out I've helped you with this, I'll be in trouble and your husband placed under the surgeon's care. Regardless of whether he lives or not with what we did, it won't matter to them. I'm not qualified to practice, and they'd never take you as being a whit of good. They'd decide amputation was still better and saw his arm off anyway."

"But is it safe for him to travel? Look at him!" She

panicked. It was late, freezing out, and she'd no idea where her horse was, let alone Jack's.

The steward laughed nervously. "Ain't no choice. Look, rest for now. Somehow, I'll find his horse or a horse and blankets and some pain killers for you to take. The surgeons will be busy for a while yet, but the rest gotta sleep. This fight ain't over yet. We're still here and so are they, so guns'll be firing tomorrow too. You need to leave tonight."

Her bottom lip trembled although she fought to control it. All she could do was give him a quick nod.

He smiled at her and touched her arm. "You're a brave woman. Because of you, he still has an arm and possibly a chance to live. Next thirty-six hours will be the hardest. Fever'll set in. If his arm turns black, then he's a goner. Gangrene. Nasty way to go." He shook his head in disgust. "He looks strong and going with you, his chances are better than if you stayed here." He walked to the door. "Don't be lettin' no one else in. I'll be back before long." And he slipped out the door.

Jack moved restlessly on the bed. She went to him. "Oh, Jack," she cried, tears falling freely down her cheeks. He felt warm, his face flush. He murmured incoherently and she shuddered.

How on God's green earth was she ever going to get him out of here? She looked upward, and her heart cried out, praying to a God who had tormented her for loving the wrong man.

"Our condition is horrible...Troops
utterly disorganized and demoralized.
Road almost impassable. No provisions
and no forage."
~ General Braxton Bragg, April 8, 1862

CHAPTER TWENTY-SEVEN

Pain. Sharp, deep, unrelenting pain. If he remained still, it pulsed only in his left shoulder, but if he moved, it radiated throughout his body. He moved as little as possible but sometimes had no choice. Periodically, his mouth was forced open and a bitter, biting liquid was poured down his throat. He'd cough it up if he could, but he lacked the strength.

The sounds of violence became faint and the air grew still. He sometimes thought he was dead until movement sent a godawful anguish through his nerves and muscles. But the "poison" had begun to lull his pain as it muddled his already foggy mind. Despite the hard cradle he occupied, he slipped into merciful oblivion and darkness.

When Jack eventually woke, eyes wide, he didn't move. He was physically drained. The rope bed cut into his back and buttocks. He felt damp and uncomfortable. The bedclothes were soaked, as though he'd had a fever that recently broke. He propped up on his elbows, but the shock of pain from his shoulder caused him to collapse in agony. Regaining his breath, he swung his legs over the side of the bed and pushed himself to a sitting position and felt slightly cooler. His gaze swept the room.

A wood slat ceiling, logged walls, two doors and a window. He saw a chest and a table with two chairs. And in one of the chairs sat John Henry, a stern look on his face, a revolver in his hand. The muzzle was pointed at Jack.

What the hell had happened?

The door opened and Emma walked in with a pot and an armful of linen.

"Jack," she murmured, a concerned look on her face.

His angel. She hadn't left him. He glanced back at her father.

She followed his eyes and put down what she had been carrying.

"Daddy, please," she pleaded, taking the revolver by the barrel, as though it was just candy and he a child.

"Caroline, don't..."

"I'm Emma, daddy." She sighed deeply, aggravated about having to correct him so often. She steered him toward the doorway. "Why don't you get me some more firewood from the next room, near the fireplace there?"

With a turn, she was at Jack's side, her palm on his forehead. "How are you feeling?"

That touch, oh yes, he remembered her light touch. "Weak. My arm hurts."

She grinned. "Yes, well, you were shot." She felt his bindings, her fingers working the knot.

He grasped her wrist. "I don't understand. I was on the battlefield. What happened?"

Her lips quivered. "Why don't we see about getting some clothes on you?"

He couldn't move. The pain reached behind his eyes. His mind was clouded with memories of people, sharp instruments, a painful trip here and Emma caring for him. She must have undressed him. Was she the angel who wrapped her body around his to warm him?

He frowned and focused on her. She looked tired. Ragged, really. Her hair fell down her back in a waterfall of curls with only a few hairpins holding the sides back. Her day dress was a drab brown plaid, the collar stained with perspiration. She was pale and gaunt.

"How'd you get me back here? Where are we?" His questions made her tense. "You shouldn't be here. I sent my father's address..."

"Yes, and how was I to find it in all this mess?" Her eyes flared, her cheeks flushed with irritation. Her hands fisted on her hips as her anger grew.

He sighed. "Emma, you told me I was shot. Fell on the battlefield. I didn't ride back here myself. And where are we, anyway?"

She looked away and dipped a rag in the pot of water. Squeezing the excess out, she wiped off the sweat from his face. "I got your message, the other message you sent. You know, the soap? I figured you gave me the address, expecting I'd use it and leave but also, with that soap, hoped I wouldn't." She refused to meet his eyes. "Then, we heard the sounds of the battle. I had to find you."

He felt her hand quiver as she wiped his neck. It hurt to raise his left hand, but, by God, he had to touch her. His fingers encircled her wrist as he pushed himself off the cot with his right hand. For a moment, he felt lightheaded but struggled to stay upright.

"You were insane to go there. You might have been killed, taken prisoner, any number of things," he responded in a hard voice. "What about Nathan then? Hum?"

She pulled her hand away. "I got a weapon."

He gazed beyond her to the table with the revolver. His brows inched higher. "A LeMat? Where did you get that?" It was an expensive piece. A Confederate-made weapon out of New Orleans. One neither he nor John Henry owned.

"What does it matter how I got it?" She turned away.

He looked down. When he stood, the blanket fell off him, and he was naked as the day he was born. *Damn.*

A thud sounded on the mattress. His clothes—uniform navy pants, suspenders and a plaid shirt. No drawers. His nose wrinkled at the thought of the woolen pants against his naked flesh. It was a small price to pay, he figured, reaching for the pile.

"When I learned you were going to be taken to those butchers," she said, "I convinced the medical steward to remove the bullet himself and let us go." She pulled the sheet off the mattress. "He even found your horse for me. Found Petey, too, in the woods where I'd left him."

"Emma..."

"No one'd take him. He's too old, not quick enough for your line of work." She reached over and pulled up his right suspender. Nodding toward the left side, she said, "Best be leavin' that one down for a while."

He snorted as he sank into a chair. "Yes."

"Daddy and Tilly found this shack deserted. Needed to get you out of the weather anyway."

"How long?"

"Almost a month."

Without a sound, he repeated the words to himself. With a groan, he rested his left arm on the table. The pain had dulled during the time he'd spent in bed, but he wasn't ready to use the arm much.

"We gotta go," he mumbled, rising to his feet.

"Here," she said, throwing the pillow at his left side. He

reached to catch it, but pain shot through to his shoulder. "Uh. Not yet, we ain't leavin' till you can use that arm better. Heavens, you'd never be able to hold Goliath now."

As she bustled about the room, adding additional logs to the fireplace, he stared out the window. The woman had risked too much for him, and he didn't deserve it.

Another week passed. It was the middle of February now, and they still waited for Jack's arm to recover. Each new day, he felt the muscles mending and the pain lessen. At first, he moved it gently. Now, he was lifting things, starting with his shirt, a lightweight item, increasing the weight as time continued, and he convinced himself he was stronger, despite the stabbing pain. But he needed the arm to be as good as it had been, so he could ride, hold a rifle... embrace Emma and make love to her. His body needed time to heal, but his patience wore thin.

"Come here," he called after his son as the toddler crawled away, giggling.

"Don't encourage him," Emma scolded him. "He'll be harder for me to watch if you keep that up."

"He's a boy," he replied smugly. "Boy's gotta grow strong and be curious so he can fill his role in Society." At her grunt, he smiled. The significance of his words struck him. "Role in Society" sounded like something his father would say. The door to his past threatened to open, and he mentally slammed it shut. He abruptly stood and headed for the door—stepping away from the familial setting and the responsibilities it implied.

Outside, warmer temperatures had melted the previous week's snow, turning it to mud. But the brisk breeze made it clear that winter was far from over. He inhaled and knew conditions would deteriorate.

Tilly must have realized it as well. She and John Henry carried more wood to the shack.

"Massa Jack," she said as they came closer, "You be lookin' like yous be ready to ride."

He chuckled. "Soon, Tilly, soon."

She smiled shyly at him, but Emma's father scowled. John Henry seemed more himself. His memory lapses hadn't gotten any worse, and he wasn't as quiet as he had been. But one thing had changed—he detested Jack. Waking up to find the old man pointing a gun at him wasn't exactly new to Jack. He'd done the same when he found Jack in bed with Caroline. Now, though, Jack figured John Henry saw him as a traitor to the South. Or perhaps, the cause of Caroline's death. It didn't matter. Emma and Tilly kept John Henry occupied with chores and Nathan, leaving him little time to spend around Jack.

One thing they did was keep the guns away from Emma's father. Given his obvious dislike of Jack, he couldn't be trusted, not to mention they had no ammunition to spare. All Jack had were ten rounds for his and Emma's rifles. The Le Mat was fully loaded except for one cartridge. He didn't want to know how the first cartridge had been used.

Jack picked up a grimy rock with his left hand and threw it. The motion unleashed a fury of pain in his shoulder although the rock fell only eight feet away. Rubbing his wounded flesh, Jack worried. They needed to go and soon, before the ground thawed and fighting resumed.

Emma was near her wit's end after spending more than

a month in the little shack, with Jack and yet, without him. She wanted to scream.

The long ride back to the camp after Jack's injury had nearly finished both of them. At first, she rode behind him and tried to keep him from falling, but he was too tall and weighed too much for her. Eventually, she strapped him into the saddle and walked on the right side so she could drop back and support him if he slid. Frustrated and exhausted as she was by the effort, his moaning and groaning tore at her soul.

Fear of exposing Jack to the elements had also heightened Emma's anxiety, and she was greatly relieved when they reached camp and her father, in a lucid moment, told her about the abandoned shack. It took a full day to clean out the shack, but it proved to be a lifesaver when winter hit hard in the Tennessee Valley.

Emma stayed with Jack night and day, cleaning his wound with melted snow, which took the place of rainwater, or "sweet" water as the surgeons called it. The wound oozed pus and though Judd had told her pus was good and showed the wound was mending, Tilly adamantly claimed it didn't. They also used a combination of boiling water and the rest of the whiskey Judd had reluctantly given to Emma to clean the wound, but Jack put up a fierce fight because of the pain. Yet she had to take care of her man as well as she could, however much he fought her.

Of course, Jack wasn't hers. If he belonged to anyone, it was the Union Army. And she had stolen him from them. If caught, he could pay with his life, for he'd surely be tried as a deserter. Jack had deserted his post to get her and Nathan out of Virginia, and then she took him to save his life from those butchers they called surgeons. She saw what they had done to Billy and refused to lose Jack too.

Although she'd kept Jack's wound clean, he developed a fever. Emma wiped his face, trying to cool him. He shivered so badly that she'd covered him with most of the few blankets they had, but then he acted as though he was drowning. The only thing left to comfort him was her body. It had worked. He had relaxed when she slid into the bed with him, trying to cover Jack without touching his inflamed torso and arm. But she had hardly slept.

Emma's father was livid because of what she'd done. After Jack's fever broke and she found her father pointing the gun at him again, she realized she'd gone too far.

Now, she avoided Jack but continued to worry about his wound. Her heart twisted when he didn't seem to want her, but she realized he was in too much pain for physical desire. And when her menses came, it reminded her again that she was still barren.

Emma loved Jack. She wanted him. She had assumed the role of mother to his son. The ties between her and Jack were there. To survive, they had pretended more than once to be married. Much as she loved Nathan and knew he needed her, she desperately wanted Jack to give her a child of her own.

"Ouch," Emma cried when the needle jammed into her finger as her vision blurred. She sucked on the tiny wound, fighting to stop the tears from falling.

"Miss Emma, the light be fadin'," Tilly softly said. "Cain't see to be fixin' that piece, donna think?"

Emma bit her bottom lip and nodded. She could finish repairing the tear in Jack's shirt the next day and put it down. Tilly wasn't a bad girl, not at all, despite how much Caroline had complained about her. The slave's help with Nathan and her father had been invaluable.

She looked at Tilly as she hummed, swaying her hips,

rocking Nathan who suckled at her breast. Envy pricked at Emma, but she ignored it.

Tilly burped Nathan and put him in the open chest drawer that served as his bed.

"Good nigh', missy." Tilly climbed into the bed with Emma's father, whose snoring she briefly interrupted.

Emma nodded and turned. The only other bed was Jack's. She could barely make herself go there. Every night, she waited for Jack to fall asleep before climbing in and turning away from him, even though she didn't want to.

She went into the other room. The flames were low and would be nothing but embers by morning. When sharing Jack's warmth, Emma could sleep. Quietly, she removed her dress and corset to slide in behind him. A sob escaped her before she could stop it.

He turned toward her. "Emma," he whispered, caressing her cheek with his hand.

She couldn't move. He must have been dreaming. Had to be. He was using his left hand.

Jack's emerald eyes stared at her. They grew darker as the moments passed. He brushed her lips with his, then pressed harder. She closed her eyes. If it was a dream, she was the one dreaming.

His tongue traced the seam of her lips, pushing at them for access. How could she deny what she so badly wanted? Her lips parted and he invaded her mouth, searching, exploring, his tongue dancing with hers. He hummed in her mouth and she relaxed.

Jack held her in his bare arms, and, under the cover, his skin rubbed against her petticoat. His hand skimmed down her neck to her chest. He cradled her breast in the palm, pinching the nipple with his fingers. She groaned in his mouth, arching her back toward him and felt his smile against her lips.

He grasped her petticoat and pulled it up. She shrugged, and he freed her of it. "Oh, Emma," he sighed as his lips traced down her neck to her breast. His tongue swirled around her pearled nub. Lips engulfing it, he suckled, his teeth grazing the nub before he nipped it. She inhaled sharply as her excitement grew. He laved the tender nub with his tongue and nipped it again.

Desire pooled between Emma's legs as his hardened arousal pressed against her stomach. Her split pantalets became damp.

Jack laid her on her back and lifted himself above her, his hips between her thighs.

"Your arm..."

"Is fine," he murmured against her stomach before kissing it. His tongue dipped into her navel and then went to the waist of her undergarment. Jack glanced up at her, a wicked gleam in his eye as his hands reached around to her back, releasing the button. Rocking back on his knees, he pulled the pantalets off and tossed them onto the floor. Her stockings went next.

Jack looked at Emma with a lazy smile, his gaze roving over her nude body.

She bit her lip, embarrassed, but it didn't last long. On his knees before her, he was like a Greek statue, muscles defined and sculpted. And his member was thick, hardened with arousal.

Lowering himself between Emma's legs, Jack kissed the inside of her thigh, and she nearly leapt off the bed. He chuckled as his left hand splayed over her stomach, holding her down. He kissed her other thigh on the inside. The apex of her thighs turned to liquid, her lower lips heavy.

Jack kissed them and she shivered at the feel. When his tongue slipped between them, her hips lowered instinctively. Slowly, he licked, up to the nub at the top and back again. Then he suckled her mound until her hips swayed. Finally his tongue delved deep inside her core.

It was the most intense feeling she had experienced since he had been inside her. Her excitement grew as Jack inserted a finger, then two. They slid in and out as he suckled again. Emma gasped for breath. Her mouth went dry. Her hips rose and spread. When he fingered her again, she felt the sky explode into a million pieces. Wave after wave washed through her, intensifying as his mouth replaced his fingers and he lapped at her. Slowly Jack brought Emma back down, but she still panted uncontrollably beneath him.

He rose up, smiling deviously.

"You are wicked," she managed to gasp.

He grinned as he kissed her lips and slid his hardness into her soaking sheath.

She gasped again as he lifted his head to look at her. Eyes locked on hers, he withdrew and plunged back in. She clung to him, her hips meeting his thrusts. She reached to kiss him but he shook his head.

"I want to see your eyes when you climax," he whispered.

She tried to swallow but couldn't. Every time he entered her, she felt him nudging at her womb. She wanted him to go even deeper. She wrapped her legs around his hips, meeting and withdrawing in rhythm with him. Her body hummed, the pressure building again. She saw Jack clench his jaw, his eyes narrow and darken, his lips thin as he plunged faster and faster.

Emma writhed beneath him as the stars exploded again. She groaned and felt Jack thrust harder, lifting her hips as a strangled moan escaped him and his seed filled her. Then he collapsed onto her. Sated, Emma felt a wave of happiness settle over her, the heat of their lovemaking and his body protecting her from the cool air.

The click of a gun's hammer jerked them back to the real world.

"Get off her, you son of a bitch."

> **"We** have been grossly cheated by the
> North and I would rather that every soul
> of us would be exterminated than we
> should be allied to her again."
> ~ South Carolina Secessionist T.H. Spann,
> Letter to Annie Spann, January 27, 1861

CHAPTER TWENTY-EIGHT

Jack tensed. Still inside Emma, he shielded her nudity after hearing the familiar sound of a gun being cocked. He shut his eyes. It was John Henry, and he had the Le Mat. How had he gotten hold of it after all they'd done to keep him away from the firearms? One day, maybe today, the man would kill him.

Jack's wound ached. Slowly he turned and got off the bed, pulling up the blanket to cover Emma.

"John Henry..."

"How dare you? You're married! To her sister!" Enraged, the man sputtered like lava from an erupting volcano. His eyes bore holes into Jack as he raised the revolver level with Jack's chest.

Emma leapt up, holding the blanket in front of her. "Daddy, stop!"

"Get dressed," her father ordered her, never taking his eyes from Jack. "You Yankee-loving scalawag. She's not even done mourning, but you couldn't keep your filthy hands off her. I oughta send you straight to the Devil."

Jack carefully reached for his trousers and put them on. His arm stiffened with pain. The old man would have been justified in killing him. "Sir, I know this doesn't look good..."

"Damn right it don't!"

"Daddy, please," Emma interjected again.

"If she carries your bastard..."

A whirlwind of thoughts raced through Jack's mind. Emma. His son. He had to protect them, get them out of the war zone. If John Henry finally fulfilled his threat and shot Jack dead, they'd be even worse off than before. Jack said the only thing he could think of to save them–even if it meant losing Emma. *Damn!*

"Then it would be Billy's son," he said flatly.

───≈≈≈───

Emma's heart sank. Jack had just made love to her. Surely, he didn't mean what he'd just said.

"You're damn right, I won't have no stinkin' Fed in our family, no sir," John Henry spat. "Bad enough you seduced my darling Caroline, who was easily persuaded. But my Emma's too smart for that. I'm figuring you must have promised her something..."

"No sir, I didn't."

Emma's eyes blurred, and she clenched the blanket tight to stop from trembling. Caroline easily persuaded? She'd laugh out loud if her father hadn't just stated that she, Emma, was too smart to fall for such a thing. Too smart or too plain to be seduced–was that what he really meant? Once again, even from the grave, Caroline had come out ahead.

No matter now. The pain in Emma's heart was because Jack had denied promising her anything. And the truth was, he hadn't. Not marriage, not love, nothing. But many men would have married again to help raise a child, and Nathan was motherless. In Jack's absence, Emma had replaced Caroline as Nathan's mother–a responsibility she had accepted without hesitation because she loved the boy. She also loved his father. Yet Jack still had no intention of marrying her apparently.

She wanted to retch, but anger and pride kept her from doing so.

"No, daddy, he's right," she said, tamping down her emotions. "He's promised me nothing. A Yankee, through and through. Nothing but to get us safely to his folks, remember?" She wrapped the blanket tighter around her and padded barefoot to her father, holding out her hand to him. "Caroline's no longer with us, daddy. She's gone to heaven. But there's the baby, little Nathan," she lowered her voice, focusing on John Henry and refusing to look at Jack.

"Baby?" Her father asked.

She smiled weakly at him, fighting the tears that threatened to fall. He looked lost and scared. It was exactly how Emma felt. She bit hard on the swollen flesh of her bottom lip, the lip that was swollen from Jack's kisses.

"We have to leave, to get to Jack's father's before the Yankees find us."

Her father scowled. "Yes, but he's one of them."

Her lips trembled, losing the battle to keep smiling. "But he's the only one who can get us there. Then he'll leave."

John Henry looked beyond her. She had no idea what Jack was doing, and she swore to herself that she didn't care. Her father finally gave her the gun.

Tilly was at the doorway, and, at Emma's nod, the slave went to her father. She took his arm. "Massa, you be needin' to come wit me." Turning, they left the room.

Silence prevailed. She heard Jack dressing behind her as she hugged the weapon to her breasts. Despite her desperate attempt to steel herself against this Union deserter, her heart wept.

"I'll go," he said softly, leaving her in the room. Alone.

Bereft, she sank to the floor and stared at nothing.

———✦✦✦———

Nature's hint of an early spring had disappeared quickly by morning. Icy air and clouds had moved in and frost covered the ground. The cold seeped through the clapboards, matching the cold in Emma's heart. She'd remained on the floor, tears streaming down her face, for what seemed like hours. She had only the blanket wrapped around her naked body and could feel her own dampness mixed with Jack's as she rocked on the floor, her world in shambles.

Emma had repeatedly given Jack her heart only to have him throw it away time and again. She was glad she had never said she loved him, although he must have known how she felt. Why else would she have risked everything to save him from the battlefield? Or to brazenly tell him that night in the field that she wanted him? She had given herself to him, but now her skin crawled where he had touched her. He had betrayed her again.

Jack hadn't returned to the cabin that night, but she doubted he'd left them. After all, he had his son to consider. Her loving nephew needed a mother. That would be Emma's job until Jack remarried.

Emma vaguely realized Tilly was there. The slave had said nothing but helped her to her feet. She gently wiped Emma's body with a wet cloth, as though she knew Emma wanted to be cleansed of Jack. Without a word, she helped

Emma dress and brushed out her tangled hair as she huddled before the fireplace.

A cry from Nathan interrupted the peace that had finally settled on Emma under Tilly's aid. Her own little world might have stopped, but life went on and the baby was hungry. Tilly left to take care of him. Emma swallowed her wounded pride and stood, shoulders back. She had family to care for and chores to tend. She erased Jack from her mind and, she hoped, from her heart as well.

Jack cursed again when his boot slipped on the slick frost. He was cold and his shoulder hurt to high heaven, but he deserved it. After leaving Emma the previous night, he had joined the horses under the eaves of the shanty. Wearing his wool pants and jacket and covered with saddle blankets, he had sat there sleepless, damning himself for hurting Emma again.

He had dismissed her on purpose and taken no responsibility for his actions. He had convinced himself she still mourned the man she had married and maybe even loved. But he had never been able to fight his attraction to her. And after she'd saved him from certain death at the hands of the field surgeons...Ensuring her safety, telling her he loved her and marrying her were what he should have done instead of taking her in the same small cabin where her unpredictable and sometimes violent father stayed.

Damn. Once more, it hit him hard–he was no good for her.

The smell of coffee and pork fat frying, a rare treat, wafted his way, making his stomach grumble and interrupting his self-loathing. If he could smell those things, anyone else nearby could, too, but he simply sat there, savoring it instead. Not that he'd get any of it anyway. He hadn't the strength to face Emma. God knew he deserved her wrath, and he'd leave her if it wasn't for Nathan.

The cabin door opened and Tilly came out with his tin Army plate, covered with a rag, and a cup of steaming coffee. Surprised, he stood and went to meet her.

"Massa Jack." She handed him the plate.

He took it but asked, "How's she doing?" *Damn*, his voice sounded shaky.

The slave shrugged. "She be doin'." She turned away but came back. Her voice dropped though no one else was close enough to hear her. "Massa, I's can make her some tonic ta make sure there ain't no babe, if'n you want."

He stood there, breathless, barely aware of the heat from the tin plate in his hand. He wasn't especially surprised by what Tilly had said. The slave community on his father's land had many recipes, probably including one for aborting a child.

A wife and children were things he hadn't wanted until he'd met Emma. But then he spoiled his chance with her as he fell into Caroline's trap. Nathan's birth had resulted in a responsibility he could not ignore.

With a war raging, however, it would be foolish to marry again and to have more children. But Emma wanted a child. Billy had asked him to give her one. He strongly doubted she'd want to bear his child now, but he couldn't bring himself to accept Tilly's offer. He just stared at her.

Emma watched through the window as Tilly took food to Jack. She wanted to wipe the smile from his face as he took the plate. The slave said something to him, and she watched him bend his head to hear her better. When they finished talking, Tilly nodded and turned with a spring in her step.

What had she said? Did he want Tilly too? The thought of Jack caressing another woman, holding her, kissing her, sliding into her, made Emma cringe. In fact, she thought she would be ill.

"Emma, honey, are you all right?"

She blinked rapidly, willing her mind to rid it of thoughts of Jack as she pasted a smile on her face. "Of course, daddy."

John Henry sat at the small table and frowned, assessing her.

Nathan. That sweet happy boy played on the floor with his blocks, chirping quietly.

"Well, get yourself something to eat."

She swallowed the bile that rose in her throat at the mention of food. "Later." Her voice was on the verge of cracking. John Henry nodded.

Later never came.

Emma woke with a start the next day. Despite the dirt on the window, weak morning sun poured into the room, but something else had awakened her. She sat up and yawned. As her eyes focused, she saw there was a strong fire thanks to a sturdy stack of wood. It should have dwindled during the night. Her brows knitted. Jack. He must have been there.

Swallowing the knot in her throat, she straightened up. With her heart still in tatters, somehow she had to rise and see about Nathan. She heard the child's giggle through the door, and anxiety gripped her. What if Jack was still there? How should she act?

As she went into the other room, she found Jack on the floor, playing with his son.

He looked up and gave her a lopsided grin. "Good morning."

Her gaze devoured him like a starving dog devoured its dinner. His emerald eyes sparkled, reflecting the flames in the fireplace. Dressed in his navy wool pants and white shirtsleeves, his long legs were stretched out before him. He balanced Nathan's feet on his thighs as he held the child upright. The babe gurgled, a drooling smile stretched across his face.

"Oh, my, let me take him," she said, grabbing the linen piece off the table and scooping up the boy to blot his mouth.

Jack studied her as he stood. The grin was gone, leaving him looking pensive, as though he was unsure of himself. But it disappeared so quickly, Emma wasn't sure she'd really seen it. He grabbed his sack coat off the chair, his eyes never leaving her.

Tilly stopped stirring the pot that hung above the flames and wiped her hands on her skirt. "Here, missy," she said softly, holding out her arms.

Emma felt her face heating. The boy was her defense against Jack and she hated to give him to Tilly, but the child began to fidget in her arms. He was hungry. She handed him to the slave. Tilly took Nathan, cooing at him as she unbuttoned her bodice. Emma heard her talking to the babe, but she kept her eyes on Jack.

"I'll go get more wood and something more substantial for breakfast," he said, picking up the rifle and shoving the revolver into his waistband. "John Henry, I could use some help."

Her father glanced up at hearing his name. For the most

part, he had remained quiet, lost in his own little world, except for the momentary breaks in his melancholy. Moments when he remembered everything that had happened more than five years ago, even though he couldn't recall what he'd eaten for breakfast only hours earlier. Unfortunately, sometimes when the melancholy left him, anger took its place. No cause or reason could be determined. But now, he was more congenial and picked up his jacket to follow Jack.

Absently, Emma watched them walk into the woods and disappear among the trees. She shuddered as a chill swept through her. Something felt wrong but what it was, she didn't know.

***

Jack crunched through the snow as he and John Henry scouted for prey. He had encouraged the old man to accompany him because he wanted to see how bad John Henry's feelings were for him. Jack was wary about fighting in the area, so they didn't go far. He wanted to remain close to the cabin in case of trouble. Heavens only knew who might find them. The longer they remained there, the stronger his fears became. When the snow and ice melted, he would have to get them back on the road to Louisiana. Spring's arrival was coming and with it, more fighting. He had no doubt both sides were preparing for the next battle. Tennessee was ripe for the picking, as he'd seen in Nashville and Murfreesboro. Frankly, he was edgy because he'd seen no signs of either army recently. Idle armies could be bad.

John Henry had a lucid moment and began asking Jack what their chances were of safely getting to the Fontaine's when Jack spotted a rabbit and killed it with one shot. Breakfast. It also ended the conversation.

On the way back to the cabin, the hair on the back of Jack's neck bristled and he stopped. John Henry ran right into him. "Shush," Jack warned, pointing ahead.

Three saddled ponies were tethered to the post before the front door of the cabin. The animals showed nothing to indicate their origin—that is, fed or secesh—but to Jack, both were bad. The riders obviously were inside the cabin.

Shoving the dead rabbit into John Henry's arms, Jack leaped over some downed trees, slipping on the snow, but he didn't fall. His son was in there, and Emma. Closer to the cabin, Jack heard Nathan's cry and Emma's soothing tones virtually drowned out by a man's roar.

He pulled out the revolver, cocking it as he stole to the door. It wasn't fully shut, and, with a nudge, he opened it further. Before him was a hellish scene.

Emma stood to the side, hugging Nathan to her. Her face was pale, arms wrapped tightly around the little boy who screamed, aware of the escalating tension.

Two men stood there dressed in filthy, tattered clothes that reeked of sweat, dirt and horse manure. Their oily, matted hair fell below their shoulders. Jack noticed their bloodshot eyes, weathered skin and, as they laughed, their broken yellowed teeth. Some of the country's finest, paying a call to the neighbors.

"She'll like it. They all do, dirty whores," one of them snarled, throwing Tilly across the small tabletop. In a lightning swift move, he tossed her skirt up.

Tilly screamed, trying to get away, but a third man came out of the other room, his handgun pointed at Emma. He laughed.

"Don't," Emma whispered.

"We don't hurt white women," the man stated flatly.

Jack's temper flared. Violating slaves apparently was

accepted. As the girl lay there, unable to move because of the way she was spread on the table, Jack's demons came out. For a brief time, everything seemed as raw and violent as it had been thirteen years ago. *Another cabin, another slave girl, his childhood friend, sprawled nude and just as vulnerable. Held down by two other men and her owner, demanding Jack take her...*

As quickly as the memory came to him, Jack buried it again. All it took was a wail from Nathan to get his attention again. He raced in and elbowed the man in his ribs with such force that he could hear bone break. The other man holding Tilly's arms above her head released them to grab his gun. Tilly rolled off the table as Jack raised his gun and fired, hitting the man in the shoulder.

"Drop your weapon or she gets it," the third man ordered, cocking the gun he had pointed at Emma. But Jack kept his own weapon cocked and waited. Each man eyed the other, assessing. Jack knew he could kill the bastard, but what if he pulled the trigger when Jack's bullet hit him? His momentary indecision made the man snort. "Yellow bellied bastard, I'm..."

Emma stared at Jack, her eyes wide with fear. Fear and a clear message. She wanted him to shoot the man. Her hand braced the back of Nathan's head as she nodded her head slightly. In that split second, she turned away, shielding the child with her body. Outraged, the man moved to shoot her and Jack pulled his trigger. The bullet whizzed through the air, hitting the intruder between the eyes. As his body thudded to the ground, the other two men ran outside.

Jack stood there, his revolver smoking from the blast. Nothing mattered more than the two people in front of him—his son and Emma. Nathan cried, angry and upset by all the commotion. He squirmed in Emma's embrace.

Vaguely, Jack saw Tilly hurry over to the babe, her clothes righted. She took Nathan. Emma's eyes were unblinking as she stared at him, her lips paling as blood drained from her face. Just as he reached her, she collapsed in his arms.

"I cannot comprehend the madness of the times. Southern men are theoretically crazy. Extreme northern men are practical fools, the latter are really quite as bad as the former. Treason is in the air around us every where and goes by the name of Patriotism."

~ Thomas Corwin to Abraham Lincoln
January16, 1861

CHAPTER TWENTY-NINE

Jack carried Emma to her bed, laying her gently across the mattress. She laid there limp, barely breathing. His own heart thudded wildly.

"Massa Jack," Tilly whispered behind him. Placing his son on the floor with his wooden horse, she dampened a rag and pushed Jack out of the way to place it on Emma's head.

Jack backed out of the room, his eyes never leaving Emma. He prayed that God had heard him and would make her all right. But once out of the room, he knew he had to go after the two men.

Stepping outside the cabin, he found only one horse remained. John Henry stared at him from the trees, still holding the dead rabbit.

"Jack?"

He shook his head and went back inside, collected the

body of the man he had shot and carried it outside and into the woods. The ground was too frozen to dig a grave, so he gathered tree limbs and other foliage to cover the body.

They needed to leave, before the man's friends returned. He sighed, wiping the sweat from his brow. He didn't want to move Emma until she woke up. His shoulder twinged, pain streaking down his arm and into his chest. *Damn!* He needed to rest himself, because if they ran into trouble on the road, he doubted he could control Goliath and shoot with only one good arm.

On his way back to the cabin, he saw Emma dash out the door and go to the side. She hugged her stomach and bent over, retching and heaving. She groaned, and, pale and trembling, wiped her mouth when done.

Jack became alarmed. Why had she been sick? He quickened his steps but stopped as Tilly walked to her, holding a tin cup. Emma took it and drank. The contents must have tasted awful because she shuddered when she finished. Handing Tilly the empty cup, Emma went back inside.

Jack's temper flared. What the hell had that slave done? He stormed up to her. Grabbing her wrist, he twisted it, making her drop the cup.

"I told you not to give her that poison," he snarled.

The girl cowed before him. "But she ain't well, massa..."

"If you've harmed her or made her loose..." He couldn't say the words. If the concoction made Emma abort a child, he'd kill the girl.

Tilly shook her head frantically. "No, sur, afte' ever'thing, she's a mite jittery."

"What the hell are you saying?" He released her wrist.

She rubbed the reddened skin, looking at the ground. "She ain't slept much nor ate hardly a thin', massa."

He closed his eyes, banking his anger. No, of course not, she'd been too upset to do either. He had hurt her anew, soon followed by witnessing the attack on Tilly and the threat to her own life. It was no wonder Emma couldn't keep anything down, and it was all because of him. *Hell and damnation!*

"She's not with?"

She shook her head. "Nots that I's can see."

He nodded. Sending Tilly back inside, he returned to his father-in-law and the dead rabbit. They'd eat and let Emma rest some more. If they didn't leave soon, though, they'd have more "visitors." Union troops. Confederate troops. Or more "patrols" like the white trash who wandered the area, claiming to be the law while their betters were fighting. The dregs of society, with loaded guns and no one to stop them from ransacking or anything else, all in the name of the law. He flexed his shoulder and winced.

<hr/>

Emma held her hand on Nathan's forehead and could feel the heat radiating from it. It wasn't as bad as it had been, but still, the baby was cranky. Fortunately, Tilly's bout with the same illness had passed, but she feared the slave's inability to feed him enough milk wasn't just due to her illness. He was nearly a year old, had been crawling around the cabin and had begun pulling himself by using furniture for support. He'd be walking in no time.

Emma rocked back on her heels, pressing her fingers to her temple. The light headedness and weakness that threatened was beginning to take control.

Her tension heightened when Jack walked in. She closed her eyes. Despite resolving to treat Jack as simply a helpmate while she handled most of Nathan's needs, she still felt the pain in her heart. Did he really think she'd be able to forget what had happened between them? Or when those men had attacked Tilly and threatened Emma, the look in Jack's eyes? Had it meant fear? Anger? Revenge? Whatever the emotion, it had frightened her.

Tilly finally convinced Emma to eat something, exclaiming in her shrill voice that if she didn't, Nathan wouldn't have a mother. Cringing, Emma fully felt like his mother, at least for now. The little boy couldn't be faulted for having a deceitful father, so she tried to eat, to make herself stronger for him.

"We need to leave," Jack stated flatly as he stood behind her.

She refused to turn. "Give me till this afternoon. He's not as hot today, but I don't want to leave till I think he's well enough for the trip. It's still cold out there."

Jack ran his fingers through his hair. "We may not have the time to wait, my dear."

The endearment confused her, but he had said it so casually, surely he meant nothing by it. Swallowing the knot in her throat and praying she didn't lose her breakfast, she said, "Have you seen movement?"

"Something's up. Too many damn hills around here, so I can't place the sounds right," he muttered. "Think we're close to Thompson's Station. We'll stop and get some supplies, maybe see if the doc there can look at the boy, then go.

She nodded numbly. Suddenly, her ears began buzzing, but when she tried to say something, her world turned black.

Jack caught Emma in his arms and carried her to the

other room. She was so thin, although Tilly had gotten her to eat some. He gently laid Emma on the bed and sat next to her and caressed her face. She wasn't especially warm, but, still, she hadn't fainted for no reason.

He relished that moment alone with her. He hadn't realized how much he had missed touching her. Trying to protect Emma by staying away from her had hurt him every minute of the day, and it was worse at night. Without thinking, he removed the pins and braiding in her hair to better feel the silken strands. He desperately wanted to hold her, to keep her next to him. He fought the impulse to kiss her, to plunge past her lips and taste the inside of her mouth.

Her eyes fluttered open but he couldn't read anything in them. He remained, waiting, hoping she'd accept him. At least she hadn't screamed at him or ordered him away, but the fact remained that he was a Yankee, a murderer, a traitor and a deserter and no good for her.

And she was his angel; he prayed she was a forgiving angel and not a vengeful one. To have to live without her would be his lifelong penance.

"How are you feeling?" His voice sounded strained, on the verge of cracking.

"I'm all right." Her reply was a shaky whisper, tinged with fear.

Fear he'd caused. He was angry with himself but also felt desire stirring because of her nearness. "Good. Rest some more, but not for long. We need to go soon. When we get to town, I want the doctor there to look at you, too." He wanted to kiss her, to hold her in his arms again. Searching her eyes, he silently begged her to allow him. But she offered no permission in return. Slowly, he untangled his fingers from her hair, stood up and walked to the door.

Just as he reached it, he heard, "Jack."

His heart raced as he turned.

She gave him a whisper of a smile, no more. But he was relieved by it and gave her a lop-sided grin in return. "I'll get the wagon ready." He left.

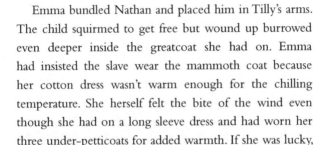

Emma bundled Nathan and placed him in Tilly's arms. The child squirmed to get free but wound up burrowed even deeper inside the greatcoat she had on. Emma had insisted the slave wear the mammoth coat because her cotton dress wasn't warm enough for the chilling temperature. She herself felt the bite of the wind even though she had on a long sleeve dress and had worn her three under-petticoats for added warmth. If she was lucky, a wave of heat would wash over her, as it had on the last three days. Her illness had continued, and when she tried to eat—which was difficult in itself—she barely kept anything down.

"Here, put this on," Jack said gruffly as he shoved his wool frock coat at her.

She took the garment, muttering thanks, but he had already walked away. Anger flared anew. He should have given it to her sooner to guard her health for the sake of his son. Slipping into the warm coat, she felt better instantly, even though she cringed at wearing anything Yankee. Closing the lapels tighter, she inhaled the faint traces of Jack's sandalwood scent. Her emotions began to battle again–her longing for Jack seeming to win the fight. If only...

Abruptly, she was lifted onto the wagon and gasped in surprise. The heat of Jack's hands on her hips and memories of when he had touched her naked flesh came back to her in a rush. But the memories disappeared just as quickly when he sat her on the seat.

"We gotta get moving," he said, hauling himself up next to her and picking up the reins. "I heard a large number of horses close by." With a signal from Jack, Petey began pulling the wagon.

Jack kept the wagon to the trees, trying to remain hidden, but a buckboard traveling across leaves and sticks couldn't help but make noise. Goliath's lead was tied to the rear of the wagon, but he was saddled as well.

Emma gripped the seat, feeling unsteady. Jack was so close to her that her emotional barriers faltered. But he wouldn't even look at her, leaving her torn by anger, desire and loss. She closed her eyes and fought not to cry again.

"See, ahead," he whispered to her. "Movement in the trees and there, in the field."

And she did see. Horsemen ran out from the trees to their right, up and away from them, whooping and hollering as they fired their weapons at a distant target. But she heard gunfire in response. It sounded close and she shuddered. Jack must've thought so too, and he snapped the reins to make Petey go faster.

They continued until the sounds of battle began to fade. Just as Emma started to breathe easier again, she realized their cover was gone. Jack had steered them out of the trees and down the hill to the township below.

Evening was falling as they rode into the quiet village. Emma could barely read the signs on the buildings. One she could read said, "Thompson's Station General Store" in gold-colored paint above the door. Jack stopped the wagon and leapt off the seat.

"Stay here," he said and walked into the store.

Emma turned to check on Nathan. He was wide awake,

looking at the buildings and listening to the few people on the street. Tilly also was awake but said nothing. Emma's father was asleep. He had been sleeping a lot recently.

Without a word, Jack came out and stepped back up onto the wagon and took them down the street to a two-storied clapboard house. A small wooden sign swung in the breeze. "Doctor Elijah Thompson" was stamped across it. Jack lifted her off the wagon, but she steeled herself against his touch.

Elijah Thompson looked up as his wife brought Emma, Nathan and Jack into his study. The man's eyebrows rose at the unexpected intrusion. "What do we have here?"

"Dr. Thompson," Jack stepped forward, offering his hand. "I'm Jack Fontaine. I've brought my wife and child. We've been travelin' and they've both been ill. We still have a long way to go. I need you take a look at them."

Thompson stood slowly, his legs stiff with age. He was perturbed. "Young man, now see here, I..."

"Sir," Jack's tone changed, dropping to almost pleading. "I need to get them home to my family in Lou's'ana. With all the troops in the area, I fear I'm runnin' out of time. I can't have anythin' happen to them. I beg you."

The elderly doctor sighed. "Follow me."

He took Emma and Nathan to his medical office at the right side of the house and closed the door on Jack's face.

"Come here, little fellow," he coaxed the child, sitting him on the table. The doctor looked at Emma. "What's been wrong with him?"

"Slight fever and crankiness."

The old doctor chuckled. "Your first?" When she nodded, he looked in the boy's mouth and ears. "His teeth are comin' in. Always a problem, especially for new parents. Here," he handed her a small bottle after he dampened a rag with it. He made a noise at Nathan and opened his mouth. The boy mimicked his movements. "Good lad." He rubbed the boy's gums. "Put a dab of this on his gums. It'll deaden the pain." Handing Nathan a flat wooden stick to play with and placing him back on the floor, he then turned to Emma.

She bit her bottom lip as his eyes narrowed, taking in her coat.

"Your husband sounds like a good Southern boy, so you wanna tell me how you got that coat?"

She swallowed. "Found it on the road. It's cold out, so I took to wearing it for the warmth." He seemed skeptical.

"And how are you feeling?"

"Fine."

"Uh huh," the doctor said, tilting her head one way, then another, scrutinizing her.

"I've been having spells of feeling a bit ill," she admitted slowly. "Lightheaded, sick to my stomach sometimes, hot and cold, but it passes."

The doctor took her wrist and pressed against her veins, quiet for a moment. "Sit."

She sat on the table.

"Feeling sensitive to touch or smell? Food unappealing?"

She shook her head no—a lie. She had a broken heart and frayed nerves, but she doubted there was a medicine for them.

"Your last flow?"

"I beg your pardon?"

"Your last flow, my dear. When was it?"

<hr />

Jack peered out the window during the night, too on edge to sleep. The doctor had told him about Nathan but

nothing about Emma. All he'd said was that she needed her
rest and not to worry. Glancing back at the bed, he saw
her nestled in the blanket, her brown hair mussed by sleep.
It hadn't upset the doctor when she had passed out in his
office. The man had simply laughed and patted Jack on the
shoulder, sauntering off to tell his wife they'd be staying
for dinner.

Later, the couple had put Jack and Emma in the same
room, believing them to be husband and wife. It made
things even more difficult for Jack because he wanted
Emma, plain and simple. He'd missed her, but he'd seen
her looking at him like a wounded animal. It was probably
because he had rejected her, but how else could he have
protected her from her father's wrath the last time? And
now, there was no other way to keep her reputation safe
than by claiming she was his wife. But he had to stay away
from her despite his desire. So he sat near the window and
waited for dawn.

Stuck inside the doctor's house, in a small hilltown
in Tennessee, Jack was alert to every sound and every
movement outside. Come hell or high water, they were
leaving at sunrise. What they'd avoided the previous day
was only a prelude to a bigger battle and probably a closer
one too. He didn't have enough ammunition to fight their
way out if either army descended on them.

As dawn colored the sky pink, a horse raced toward the
house and stopped. The rider jumped off and pounded
on the door. Jack could barely hear the doctor and the
horseman talking.

Fear crept up Jack's spine. Putting on his jacket, he went
down the stairs and found Thompson packing his medical
bag.

"Oh, Mr. Fontaine," the doctor greeted. "I must go see a

patient. Sorry. I gave your wife the gum-numbing tonic for your boy's teething. As to her—" he shut his bag.

"Honey, Mr. Samson is going to wear out our porch if we don't be movin'," Thompson's wife said from the doorway.

"Right," the doctor muttered.

"What about my wife?" Jack said, grabbing the man's arm as he tried to leave.

"She'll be fine. Her illness is perfectly normal. Just keep her fed and rested. Safe journey," he walked out. "Oh, and Mr. Fontaine, be careful out there."

Jack nodded. As the doctor walked out, Jack saw cavalry, riders dressed in grey, entering the town. Hell was about to break out, and they needed to go.

When he went to the bedroom and found only Tilly asleep on the cot, he shook her awake and asked, "Where's John Henry?"

———⚬⚬⚬———

John Henry woke confused and lost. It was dark and he couldn't figure out where he was. Everything looked odd and out of place. The room had a bed and dresser with a washstand, but they weren't his. Getting dressed, he searched his mind for an explanation and walked out the door and down the stairs, still disoriented.

As he wandered through the house, he convinced himself he was dreaming. He went out the back door, through the yard and into the woods. If he was dreaming, before long, he'd wake and all would be right.

The cold air made him feel alive, and he quickened his pace. Ahead of him was a group of horses, haltered and tied to a line. Something made him cautious and he slowed.

He heard the click of a gun behind him and he stopped.

"Who goes there?"

John Henry smiled. "Colonel John Henry Silvers of the King's City Militia."

"King's City?" The gunman walked up to his right side, still aiming at him.

"Yes sir," he answered pridefully. "Best set of rifles east of Richmond."

The guard's brows knitted but he didn't lower his rifle. "Come with me."

John Henry did as he was told and soon entered a Confederate camp, where the guard took him to a walled tent.

"Sir, I think you should see this," the guard said, standing outside with John Henry.

A muttered curse and the sounds of someone inside tripping over things came through the canvas walls. The flaps parted and a young man, pulling on his uniform short jacket came out. "What the hell is it, private?"

"Found this man, sir, coming from town, claiming to be a colonel with the King's City something or other."

The officer rubbed his eyes. "Father?"

John Henry smiled. "Charles."

"Father, what are you doing out here?" Charles asked dumbfounded.

Finally, John Henry felt like himself again. No longer lost in confusion. "Had to find you, lad."

Charles frowned, as he stepped forward, motioning to the private to return to his post. "Really, father, there's a war on. Why aren't you at home? Where's Billy? You left my sister alone at Rose Hill?"

"Charles," he dropped his voice. "Your buddy Jack came, and because of him and his Yankee colors, he got Rose Hill burned and Billy killed. He's a traitor."

"What's this I hear?" A deep voice reverberated behind Charles.

John Henry looked past his son to see a tall lanky man with a receding hairline. His face was pale, with high cheekbones and a thick dark brown goatee. His jacket displayed more silver embroidery than his son's.

"Father, General Forrest, the 'Wizard of the Saddle'," Charles introduced his commander. John Henry noted his son's obvious admiration for the man. "Gen'ral, my father, Colonel John Henry Silvers, of the former Rose Hill Plantation in Virginia."

"Glad to meet you, sir," John Henry extended his hand.

Forrest eyed him. "I heard you speak of a traitor to the cause?"

"Yes, sir," he replied, smiling. "A Yankee amongst us. A good ole Southern boy turned against his brothers."

Forrest grinned and nodded to Charles. "Looks like we'll be having company for dinner, Silvers. Why don't you find out where this lost brother is? Time to bring him home and see if we can't make him see the error of his ways, or at least pay for them."

"Yes, sir," Charles responded quickly. As Forrest left, he turned to his father, his brows furrowed.

John Henry continued to smile. It was time that Yankee Jack Fontaine paid for his crimes.

"**We have a great many wounded;
the same old story – men mutilated in
every possible way...I am sick at heart at
these scenes, and there seems to be little
prospect of a change.**"

~ Kate Cumming, Nurse, Army of Tennessee,
CSA, Diary Entry, June 27, 1863

CHAPTER THIRTY

March 5, 1863, Thompson's Station, Tennessee

Despite Emma's protestations, Jack gave up looking for John Henry. The man had wandered too far off. Jack's search ended when he saw what he guessed was over a thousand Confederate soldiers who had arrived at Thompson's Station from the south side of town. Their commander had lined them up in the hills, where they extended for more than a mile. More troops gathered, most on horseback, but some who dismounted went to a fence running along the gully at the foot of the hills. Sharpshooters dispersed throughout the town to better warn their comrades of federal soldiers approaching.

The hairs on Jack's neck stood up. Pushing Tilly into the bed of the wagon, he handed her Nathan and turned to Emma.

"Sweetheart, we need to go now," he stressed, reaching for her.

"But my father," she retorted. "I won't leave without him." She let out a scream when he grabbed her waist and lifted her up to the wagon seat.

"We can't wait any longer, Emma." He gestured toward the hills, sweeping his hand in the direction of the buildings nearest them. "Rebel troops. They're getting into position. Most are on horses, Emma. Cavalry. Fast and furious. From where they're stationed, the federals must be coming in from the North. I will not put my son in harm's way. Do you understand me?" But she only shook her head; he could tell she was readying her argument. "Do you understand me? We leave now."

Throwing the reins to Emma, Jack jumped onto Goliath. She glared at him but as he nudged Goliath onward, he swatted Petey's rump, knowing Emma would avoid leaving if she could.

Jack kept an eye on the ground before them, trying to judge which way to leave town. To the left, he saw additional cavalry amassing. In addition, a battery was forming, with cannons aimed toward the north on both sides of the Columbia Turnpike at the end of town.

Jack gritted his teeth. Goliath sidestepped under the tension of his rider. Petey snorted and Emma struggled with the reins to keep him in line. They were just outside town and the only ones on the street. Jack's frustration grew.

Emma was looking beyond him, her face paling. "Jack."

He turned around. Riders, five of them, heading toward them fast. He reached for his revolver, even knowing it would do little good against five armed soldiers. His son and Emma were in danger already.

"Stay quiet," he warned her and rode a few feet ahead of the wagon, where he waited.

The riders halted, except their ranking officer who approached. "Jack Fontaine."

Jack's spine stiffened. "Yes."

"Captain Maury, at your service," he replied, a sly grin on his face. "Your presence is required."

"For?"

"To answer accusations of you being a traitor, spy, and murderer."

Jack heard weapons being cocked and Emma's gasp.

The escort took them past Confederate lines, beyond the trees to their base camp. Emma drove the wagon, at a loss about what to do. Maury had assured her she was safe in their protection from the traitor. But, he did suggest she wait till they got the federals to retreat before sending her on.

"Can't ever trust them Yankees to be civil'zed to a lady," he warned. He directed her to General Van Dorn's walled tent and helped her off the wagon. As she took Nathan in her arms, she walked over to the tent and set him down, with Tilly to watch him. Bile rose in her throat and her heart beat frantically.

Two tents down, Jack slid from Goliath's back, and a soldier tied his hands together before shoving him into the tent. When the soldier exited the tent, he was carrying Jack's revolver and walked away. Another armed soldier stood guarding the tent.

What was she going to do? If her father was around, she was sure she could get him to intervene on Jack's behalf. He'd done so earlier. But where was he?

In the distance, she heard guns firing, which startled Tilly. Emma turned to the slave and motioned her to be quiet, pointing to Nathan. The little boy was more interested in some of the tinware lying on the ground—plates and cups that'd been rinsed but not put away.

"Ma'am," Maury called, pulling his horse behind him, "I need you to be stayin' here. You'll be safe."

"What if you lose?" Fear gripped her; if the fighting came their way, could she get them out of there fast enough? And what about Jack?

The Confederate smiled. "Believe me, under Generals Van Dorn and Forrest, us losing ain't goin' t' happen," he drawled confidently. "I'll leave a couple of my men here to see to your needs whilst we fight."

He turned, gathering his reins and pulled himself onto his saddle.

"What about Jack?" she asked, panic beginning. "What will you do with him?"

"I canna say. He your husband?" He looked at her.

Emma bit her bottom lip. One voice inside her said she should say yes, but the stronger voice reminded her firmly that Jack had rejected her, had taken her body without any promise for the future. From the look of things, he truly was considered a traitor to the South. And he had betrayed her as well, with Caroline. What would prevent that from happening again? She remained silent.

"I see," Maury said, a puzzled look on his face. "It'll be up to the generals to decide." He pulled the reins to the side, his horse turned and they rode off.

As he disappeared within the trees, it suddenly hit Emma what she'd done. Her indecision could cost Jack his life. Nathan giggled behind her because of some trinket he'd picked up and another pain shot through her. Because of her, Nathan might lose his only remaining parent.

For six hours, the battle raged. Jack could hear men yelling, gunfire, cannons roaring and the guard outside his tent pacing. He considered trying to escape, but the soldier was carrying a loaded rifle. Men like him itched to be in the battle as much as they feared it. That fear caused them to act impulsively, such as firing on anyone for little or no reason. Jack knew Emma and his son were only two tents away. The last thing he wanted was for the soldier to hurt one of them by mistake if he missed Jack.

The binding around his wrists was tight. Despite his attempt to wiggle out of it, it held strong. Because of his struggling, the hemp rope cut into his skin. He slid down the pole he was tied to and sat.

He hoped Emma still had the directions to his parents' land. At the very least, he knew he could count on rebel officers to be gentlemen and have her and his son escorted there safely. One thing was sure, it was a southern home and his father was no doubt well immersed in Confederate politics. He spat, disgusted. If nothing else, he would make a final demand—that she and the boy be taken there. He knew what fate held in store for him. He couldn't defend himself against the accusations with which he was charged. After all, they were true. And his punishment would be death.

Head bent in resignation, Jack was filled with remorse. It occurred to him that he never told Emma in words that he loved her. What a fool he was...

<hr>

The battle at Thompson's Station ended before nightfall. Union General John Coburn's troops advanced to the center of the village, but Confederate forces were too strong and outnumbered them. General Coburn's aide told him their ammunition had dwindled faster than expected. Coburn braced himself.

General Nathan Bedford Forrest knew exactly when to attack, and as his troops rode into the Union lines, he approached the federal commander. General Coburn surrendered. With a cocky grin, General Forrest took Coburn's colors and arms and rode back to camp.

Van Dorn walked out of his tent as Forrest reached it and slid off his horse, laughing.

"I see you're all ready to go celebratin'," Forrest commented.

Van Dorn twisted the end of his mustache, still glistening from the water he'd used to clean the filth of gunsmoke off his face. "Yes, I do believe so. And, in fact, I believe we have us some entertainment, according to Lieutenant Maury."

Forrest raised an eyebrow. "Really?" He pulled out a cigar and lit it.

Van Dorn smiled. "The traitor you were informed about."

"Always a good time. You get yourself all gussied up for that?"

"Of course not." Van Dorn threw his shoulders back and pulled his jacket straight. "The man was taken while holding our informer's daughter hostage. She's with us presently."

Forrest laughed. "General, if you ever stop chasing the ladies, you'll live to a ripe old age."

"Perhaps, but what good would life be without the ladies?"

The two men walked down the lane as the camp began filling with the wounded and prisoners. Confederate cavalry cooled their horses and relaxed at their tents, unwinding from a day filled with the horrors of war.

When the two generals reached the walled tent, Van Dorn motioned at the guard to bring out the prisoner.

Forrest chomped on his cigar. "Where's Colonel Silvers?"

"Right here, sur," a soldier said, escorting the elder man to him.

"Colonel, appears we've found your southern deserter," he drawled.

John Henry righted himself, chin in the air as he cleared his throat. "Good, good."

"Daddy!"

They turned and Forrest snorted. So this was what Van Dorn was talking about. A woman, with coppery brown hair falling from a braid and her dress billowing, raced to the old man's side. One thing the "Wizard" noticed was that she was wearing a Yankee officer's frock coat, minus the obnoxious brass shoulder pieces. Probably given to her by the traitor, he smirked to himself.

"Gentlemen, my daughter, Mrs. William Bealke," John Henry introduced.

Van Dorn bowed. "Mrs. Bealke."

"A widow, thanks to that bastard I told you of," the old man added.

"Father, please," she pleaded. Forrest noticed her ivory-colored skin was drawn tight across her thin face, but her eyes were puffy and her lips pale. Had travel made her ill? No doubt being a hostage to a ruffian had taken a toll.

The guard dragged the restrained prisoner, still wearing Union blue, out of the tent.

"Jack Fontaine," Van Dorn stated. "You've been accused of traitorship to the southern rights of independence. That you murdered Mrs. Bealke's husband, destroyed southern property and are a spy for the Union, down here under false pretenses."

The prisoner gazed at the Confederates who had gathered for the quasi-military trial and raised his chin, a posture that, to Forrest, seemed to indicate he had been falsely accused. Perhaps so, the general thought to himself, but this was war. When it came to charges such as Fontaine faced, there was no time or inclination to consider other possibilities.

The woman stared at him, her eyes widening. "Jack, say something," she pleaded.

She turned to her father. "Daddy, you know…"

"It's only just, my dear. He's southern born and raised. To turn his back on his own countrymen at our time of need and to seduce my now deceased daughter, marrying her only to shun her while she carried his child is unacceptable." Emma gasped. John Henry looked at her. "And then to take you, my darling Emma, after he killed your Billy, I shudder at your condition now."

Emma was stunned, her embarrassment complete.

Colonel Silvers turned to Forrest and Van Dorn. "In addition, I heard him tell part of a Yankee unit who stopped us that he was on a mission to find our army's strength and report it back to his superiors…"

"Daddy, he said that to get those men off our trail…"

"Emma, my dear little Emma, he's so cast a spell on you," her father said softly. "Where do you think he went before he was supposedly injured? He returned to his army, to report his findings."

That remark prompted Van Dorn to speak up. "When might that have been, sur?"

"Just after Christmastime, north of here, near, where was that? Oh yes, Murfreesboro."

Listening to this exchange, the soldiers around them

began cursing and judging Jack. In their opinion, he was guilty and deserved to be punished.

Jack closed his eyes. Nothing he could say or do would help against John Henry's accusations. He had used the excuse of spying. He had taken Emma while she was in mourning. He hadn't reported to his side, the Union, willingly, but he wouldn't be able to convince anyone of that. If Jack had been traveling alone, he would have tried something, although he wasn't sure what. With his hands tied behind him and armed soldiers circling, it appeared he had no recourse.

"Well, I do believe," General Earl Van Dorn began. Jack knew the bastard. He'd grown up not far from his family's land across the river in Mississippi. Arrogant womanizer. And Van Dorn recognized him as well. The Fontaine family was well known in the Deep South. Van Dorn's expression made it clear that Jack would not be released.

"As our traitor here hasn't said a word denying these accusations," Van Dorn continued, "they must be true. His sentence is..."

"No! Please! I have his son," Emma cried.

Jack saw Van Dorn appraising her, and it made him furious. If that son-of-a-bitch touched Emma, Jack would kill him.

"Ma'am, you have my deepest sympathies. I'll personally make sure you get to a safe location, wherever that might be. I give you my word." He turned back to Jack. "But, as I was saying, I sentence you, Jack Fontaine, to die by firing squad for betraying the Confederate States of America and for killing one of our people."

A cheer rose. Jack saw John Henry grin, General Forrest

nod his head and Emma's face go white. She broke free of her father's hold and ran to him.

"Tell them it isn't true," she begged.

He gave her a slight smile. "Take care of Nathan for me. Go to my father. Please, Emma."

His refusal to deny the accusations registered in her eyes. He hated himself for it, but it was him against the Confederate forces there, easily several thousand men. All was lost.

Anger contorted Emma's face as she stepped back. "You bastard," she whispered.

No tears. No desire for him. Inside, his heart broke. But what he'd done was for the best, for he knew the Southerners would make sure she and his son would arrive at his father's safely. However, when Van Dorn sauntered over to Emma, took her hand in his, and spoke softly to her, Jack's hands clenched. He'd kill the man!

As Van Dorn led her away, Forrest puffed on his cigar, not taking his eyes from Jack. "Maury, get the firing squad. And tell them to be neat about it," a smile spread slowly across his face. "I'll be taking that jacket when you're through with him." And he walked away with a chuckle.

Maury moved Jack to a tree behind the tents as three soldiers arrived bearing rifles. The men looked war weary and tired, perhaps too tired to fire straight, Jack mused. A few more men followed, including John Henry.

"Jack?"

Charles appeared before him, just to the side of the firing squad.

"Charles," Jack said, looking at his grey uniform. He squinted. Jack couldn't figure out the intricate swirls of embroidery on Charles' sleeves, but they obviously meant he was an officer.

"Son, let him go," his father said sternly. "He needs to make his peace with God."

"No, this is wrong." Charles turned to his father. "Stop this, father."

John Henry looked at him. "No, son..."

"You know better than half of what you said was a lie. How do you think you made it this far? Because of Jack. And he'd never hurt Emma. You know that," Charles sputtered.

John Henry suddenly looked like the man Jack had taken from Virginia. A puzzled expression had returned to his father's face as Charles continued addressing him. Jack just shook his head.

"Aim."

The squad pulled up their cocked rifles. Jack inwardly scorned the Confederates. What a waste of ammunition it was to have several men shoot him. One man would do. Jack had no intention of trying anything now that he believed Emma and Nathan would be safely escorted to his father's as promised.

From the corner of his eye, Jack saw Emma on the general's arm and heard Charles pleading with his father.

Suddenly John Henry began choking as though he was drowning. His face contorted in pain and surprise as he gripped his chest and crumpled to the ground.

"No, father!" Charles screamed at the same instant the command to fire was issued.

When John Henry cried out, it startled the firing squad and scattered their aim. The impact of bullets striking living tissue sounded like rocks hitting a pillow, and the force knocked Jack off balance and to the ground.

He hit it hard, especially with his hands still tied behind him. He couldn't move and was barely able to breathe with

the pain. He was vaguely aware of Emma's scream and
Charles begging John Henry to move. Before passing out,
one of Jack's last visions was of Charles, calling loudly for
his father.

———∿∿∿———

Jack breathed deeply. Cold March air invaded his nostrils
and its briskness woke him suddenly. With a gasp, he sat up,
his eyes struggling to focus on the scene around him. White
tents glowed by campfire light. The sound of crackling
flames and men talking filled the air.

He stretched, his body aching throughout. Moving his
arms brought a fresh wave of pain on his left side. Glancing
downward, he saw a rip in his jacket, just above the flesh
wound beneath and realized the wound had been bandaged.
He was to have been executed so why was he bandaged?
What the hell had happened? He remembered the firing
squad and John Henry collapsing. He remembered people
yelling, the firing squad and hitting the ground himself.

Suddenly, he heard a noise to the left, and it sounded like
metal hitting dirt. Slowly, he turned and saw Charles, jacket
off despite the cold. He was digging a hole—a difficult
task in late winter with the ground still frozen. Jack was
confused. Why would a Confederate officer dig a grave?
Especially by himself? Was it for Jack? But, he wasn't dead,
as he could tell from the searing pain he felt. Then who was
the grave for?

A body lay no more than twelve feet away. Wrapped in
heavy canvas, the inert form held Jack's attention. Rising,
he walked over to Charles.

The man was concentrating so hard on his work that he
didn't notice Jack.

"Charles?"

He looked up at Jack, face drawn, and he stared. Jack saw no light in his friend's eyes. Something was amiss.

"So, you are up," Charles stated, continuing to shovel.

Jack blinked hard and nodded. "What, I mean, who are you digging for? For me? Apparently, your firing squad missed. And where is Emma?"

Charles shoveled a little more before answering. "My father, Jack, I'm digging my father's grave."

"What?"

Charles stopped and wiped the sweat from his brow. "He wasn't well, Jack. You had to know that. Why he accused you of what he did, I don't know. And don't explain it to me. I don't want to know. Not now." He swallowed hard and loudly. "And, whatever was wrong with him must've ate at him, the war or home..." His voice began to falter so he closed his mouth and pushed the shovel in for another mound.

Jack felt as though the world had changed but that he hadn't changed with it.

"He started to say somethin', maybe to save you. Or accuse you of more," Charles laughed acidly again. "A man he called a traitor." He looked up at Jack, his eyes filled with pain. "Did you kill Billy?"

Jack shook his head, unable to find his tongue.

"And what about my sisters?"

Yes, what about them? Jack's mind whirled. Charles' tormented gaze bore into him. He deserved to know the truth about all he'd lost fighting for "The Cause."

"Caroline...We had," he paused. "Problems. I sent her home. She died while birthing our son. Emma..." He looked around. "Where is Emma?"

"She's gone. Father's dead and you—" he glanced up and down at Jack. "Everyone. The troops, command, the surgeons are all gearing up for battle. But me? I'm busy with my father's dead body. Emma was too distraught to stay. With another round of battles coming, it's not safe for her here anyway, not even to see to a funeral for our father, let alone a burial.

"No!" Jack lashed out. "I need her!"

"Did you seduce her, too?" Charles glared. He threw the shovel down, his hands clenching into fists.

"I love her," Jack stated loudly, not moving away even though he knew Charles was on the verge of striking him. "I always have. I can't explain about Caroline." Not in a way Charles would have wanted to hear. He glanced at the nearly empty camp. "How long was I out?"

"Most of the day."

Jack's right upper chest stabbed with white-hot pain, and he gritted his teeth, trying to subdue it. When the pain subsided, he said, "Did you bandage this?"

Emotions flashed in Charles' eyes. Hate. Anger. Sorrow. All combined, each struggling for control. It took him a minute to unclench his hands and shovel the ground again, and then he snorted. "Best I could do, though why I did it still escapes me, considering my father's accusations."

He threw another clod of dirt to the side. "You're lucky. Only one bullet hit because everyone's aim was thrown off when father collapsed and Emma screamed. You got a deep gouge, so I cleaned it the best I could. Most of the surgeons weren't going to waste time on a traitor." He shrugged and continued shoveling.

Jack nodded. "Thank you."

Silence fell between them, broken only by the sound of the shovel in the dirt.

"I need to get to Emma. Where is she? Where's my son?" He turned toward the road.

"I wouldn't go there." Charles' words stopped Jack. "You may have gotten off but Emma's pretty upset. She was trying to blame you for our father's death." He paused, his brows furrowed. "She was rambling on about being abandoned, Jack." He drove the shovel into the ground again. "Been thinking she may be right. Caroline turned mean as we grew up, makin' sure she was always the favorite, mostly at Emma's expense. And I, being the only son, got lots of attention." He shrugged. "Then momma died, and Caroline and Billy too. Since I've been in the war, I haven't written her to speak of, and with Rose Hill gone, the few letters I sent probably never made it to her. And now our father is dead." He shoveled again.

"Well I'm here now, so I'll ask again—where is she?"

"I done told you. Gone," Charles stated drily. "Left yesterday."

Jack had spent too long thinking he wasn't good enough for Emma and that he had nothing to offer her. He was a traitor to the South but mostly to her. First he had betrayed her love because of Caroline's manipulations. Then, on this trip, he never should have touched her. He'd only made things worse after refusing to offer her his hand. No doubt she believed he had used her and needed her only for Nathan. She didn't know he loved her. Because of her, he had thwarted death on the battlefield before. Now that it had happened a second time, he needed to redeem himself and refused to let her go. At least, not without telling her he loved her and begging her to stay with him.

"They thought you'd likely die, too. Heard them tell her you were a goner with a chest wound. Hell, you looked dead, with that jacket all torn, blood everywhere and you white as a ghost, laying all still." He shook his head and dug deeper with the blade of the shovel. "I was so busy with my father's body, I never had a chance to check on you. By the time I got everything arranged, she was gone.

Jack shifted, causing another shot of pain from his wound. As he gritted his teeth against it, his mind raced.

"Damnation," he muttered. "Charles, where did they go?"

"She doesn't want you, Jack." His voice was cold.

"I love her Charles." Jack walked up to him and grabbed the shovel to make him look at him. "I need to find her. She's got my son. And my heart. I can't live without her."

Charles frowned. "A son and her, I don't know Jack. That's family. Responsibility. Said you never wanted that. Being saddled with Caroline was one thing. Just let Emma go. She'll take your son to Bellefountaine and be on..."

"She's taking him to my father?" He grabbed Charles' shirt.

"Isn't that what you wanted?"

Yes, he had told her to go there because he was going to die and his old man would protect them, but he hadn't died. Evil reigned at Bellefountaine. Without Jack there to smooth the path and persuade his father to get them out of the country, Jack couldn't bear to think what might happen. His head hurt. He let go of Charles and pushed against his temples. "I must leave."

"Why? If all you need is a mother for your son, find another woman. Emma deserves more than that. I won't let you hurt her by just using her for that," Charles snarled.

Charles' statement hit Jack hard. He did need a mother for his son, and Emma was already acting that part. Like so many widowed men with children, he was expected to remarry—no man raised a child alone. But he wouldn't do that to Emma. He needed her, wanted and loved her too much to just marry her for Nathan's sake. He'd put it off before, thinking he had nothing to offer but now, he'd give her all he had, including his heart, if she'd take him back.

"I love her," he restated.

As he turned to look for his horse, Charles snorted. "Dammit, you're just as determined as she is. Look, if you're going after her, let me tell you something. I know she loves you. It's written all over her face. But after everything, it's goin' to be harder to win her than just tellin' her you love her too. She can be quite stubborn. About the only way I see you getting anywhere with her is if you're willing to fight for her, make her yours truly..."

"Yes, that's exactly what I want and will do." It wasn't just a mindless response. She was his heart.

Charles sighed as though he thought Jack had lost his mind. "Then good luck, Jack. You're going to need it."

Jack struggled to mount his horse, fighting the pain, but once on Goliath's back, he nodded to Charles. Nudging the horse forward, Jack knew he'd need more than luck. He'd need a miracle.

"One's heart grows sick of war, after
all, when you see what it really is; every
once in a while I feel so horrified and
disgusted – it seems to me like a great
slaughter-house and the men mutually
butchering each other – then I feel how
impossible it appears, again, to retire from
this contest, until we have carried our
points."

~ Walt Whitman, USA, Letter to his mother,
September 8, 1863

CHAPTER THIRTY-ONE

Bellefountaine Plantation
Louisiana, March 1863

Early spring in Louisiana included humidity that
Virginia lacked. After rain in the pre-dawn hours,
the air felt heavy, almost uncomfortable in the sunshine.
Emma fanned her face, trying to dry the moisture that had
formed as she sat on the second-story veranda overlooking
the Mississippi River. Despite the pretty view, her stomach
was roiling, which she attributed to the weather.

Tilly appeared at her side, carrying a glass of watered
sugar-laced raspberry vinegar. It was a repulsive concoction
but it soothed her insides.

"Where's Nathan?" she asked, sipping the vile drink.

"He be playin' in the nurser' wit that lady," the slave replied, removing a rag from a basin of water and wringing it out. She put the damp cloth around Emma's neck.

Emma moaned. "Thank you."

As Tilly backed away, Emma's thoughts returned to her arrival at Bellefountaine. Mrs. Fontaine had been so thrilled to meet her first grandchild that she rarely left him alone. At another time, Emma might have felt threatened by the woman's doting, but now, relief filled her as her energy fled with the heat and the nausea it caused.

She sighed and sat quietly. Too tired to move, she watched the river, focused on it, forcing her mind to stop tripping over memories best buried. It was an impossible task, she discovered. If she slept, and slept she did at first, they emerged, prodding her emotions. Tears often threatened. Everyone was gone. Dead. Her mother, Caroline, Billy and now, her father. She feared she'd lose Charles as well.

And there was Jack.

Her breath hitched as her throat constricted. The only thing that made life worth living was Nathan. His sweet cherub face, with that easy grin and those sparkling emerald eyes made him look like an angel. But because he was the spitting image of his father, he might have been a demon too.

If she were lucky, perhaps numbness would return to her mind and her body. She had welcomed General Van Dorn's attentions, which had soothed her and made her feel cared for.

As she was leaving the Confederate camp, Charles assured her that he would write and let her know how he was, but no letters had come. Granted her trip by military escort had taken two long, tedious weeks. A lady friend of the General's, a Miss McCoy of Corinth, was large, chatty, and bothersome and always wore strong, sweet perfume. But she had provided a welcome distraction to Emma, who was now a widow and an orphan. Dizziness threatened to overwhelm her.

Tilly pressed the cup to Emma's lips again.

"Drink, Miss Emma, you needs to drink," she coaxed, taking the fan from Emma's hands and waving it frantically in front of her.

Emma took another sip and pulled back, grasping the slave's wrist. "Enough, Tilly."

"Good morning, how are we doing this morning, Mrs. Bealke?"

She closed her eyes and resisted the urge to clench her hands. Why hadn't she heard the woman enter? "I'm feelin' better this mornin', Mrs. Fontaine." The woman's greeting reminded Emma that she'd forever be known as Mrs. William Bealke, never Mrs. Jack Fontaine. When it became obvious that Jack didn't want her, she tried to convince herself that she didn't want his name either.

Marie Fontaine's green eyes stared at her like a mother hen—one with an attitude. Emma wasn't sure whether she liked being under the Fontaines' care, but until she could arrange transportation and funding of some type, she had to rely on their hospitality. As Nathan's aunt, she could remain with them for some time.

Marie's angular face was framed by blond hair pulled back into a chignon. Her hairstyle and dress, probably adapted from the latest British trends, gave her the look of a Continental.

When she smiled, she reminded Emma of Jack. With effort, Emma returned her smile, trying hard not to cry.

"Emma, m'aime, please call me Marie."

She nodded. "Yes, but of course."

"Did you eat this morning?"

Emma nodded slowly. Breakfast had tasted wonderful. Scones with orange marmalade and tea. It wasn't her usual morning meal but she had enjoyed the sweet twist. And she'd kept it down.

"I'm glad. No doubt, it's all the turmoil you've been through that's caused you to be out of sorts. A few days of rest and a better diet should make you well again."

"Yes, thank you. I do feel better." She sat straighter, putting down her fan, but her stomach began rumbling anew. As bile started climbing, she hastened to the chamber pot and almost ran into Tilly. And she lost the breakfast she had so enjoyed. When would this illness pass?

Putting the lid on the pot, Emma leaned back, weak and lightheaded. She heard Marie murmur something to Tilly and then helped Emma return to her chair.

"I'll call Dr. Spalding." She left the room as Tilly resumed fanning Emma.

Emma closed her eyes tightly, fighting another wave of nausea. She truly believed she was going to die and hoped death would come soon.

———✺———

Louisiana's warmth and humidity continued into the afternoon, and a light rain began to fall. Emma had no tears left to accompany the rain. Dr. Spalding had arrived just before midday and examined her, the memory of which still made her uncomfortable. He had been invasive and his questions too personal to suit her. However, she had heaved again, confirming his diagnosis.

Emma was carrying Jack's child. Biting her lower lip, she placed her hand on her stomach, which was still flat.

Although her corset fit, her breasts felt heavier, larger, and her nipples had become sensitive.

"Miss Emma," Tilly said softly, handing her a cup of tea.

Emma took the cup but didn't drink. Her nerves were still on edge. Should she be excited about carrying the traitor's bastard?

"Miss Emma?"

She hadn't noticed the slave was still at her side. Swallowing the knot in her throat, she tore her gaze from the river and focused on the girl. Tilly looked nervous and was wringing her hands.

"What, Tilly?" she snapped, sounding like Caroline. She inwardly cringed.

"Well, ma'am, if'n you don't wanna carry, I can give you somethin' to stop it."

Emma's eyes widened. The slave knew of a potion to make her lose the child? Her gut twisted in revulsion, but something told her not to dismiss the idea. Could she bring herself to do that? She'd always wanted a child. And she had wanted to bear Jack's, but after what he'd done, could she bring herself to do so? Emma's indecision made Tilly even more nervous, and it showed in her eyes as she fidgeted, waiting for a response.

"Tilly, thank you. I'm not sure."

"All yous gots to do is lets me know, and I'll brin' it to ya," she stammered.

Emma nodded. It was a repulsive option—one of several she faced regarding her future. As a widow, she had the chance to strike out on her own, move to where she wanted and make a life for herself. Problem was, she had brought her charge, Nathan, to his paternal grandparents' home. In Louisiana, a state that still adhered to Napoleonic law, their hold on the child was greater because they had the resources to raise him. She, on the other hand, was homeless and penniless—Nathan's unfortunate aunt. Could she leave him? With a child on the way, her life as an independent woman would be short-lived, even after the war, because she would be expected to marry again for the child's sake. After losing Billy, who she didn't truly love, and Jack, who she loved but didn't fully trust, could she even think of being intimate with another man, let alone live with him? Her head throbbed the longer she debated about what she had and what she wanted.

Her thoughts were interrupted by the faint but growing sound of someone approaching, and she strained to see who it was. A tall, dark-haired man dressed in tan trousers and riding boots, a pristine white shirt, sapphire blue brocaded waistcoat and black fitted jacket walked her way from the other end of the veranda. His sky-blue eyes sparkled in the noonday sun, and he had an air of confidence about him.

"Ah, mademoiselle," his rich, deep voice drawled as he took her hand, bringing it to his lips. "So nice to finally meet you." He smiled warmly at her.

Emma stared at him, feeling her face flush at his touch. The man before her was strikingly handsome. Like Jack. When she said nothing, he laughed apologetically.

"How rude of me to disturb you. Let me introduce myself. I'm Francois Fontaine, at your service." He bowed.

She blinked rapidly, trying to recall the social graces–her manners had been neglected since the war began. No time for pleasantries when the enemy was all around. "Excuse me, I seem to have lost my manners. I'm Emma Fon..., I mean, Mrs. Emma Bealke." Had she really almost called herself Emma Fontaine?

He gave her a sly, devilish grin. "If I can be bolder, Mrs. Bealke, may I call you Emma?"

She relaxed and returned his smile. The man was wickedly attractive. "Yes, if I may be granted the same favor."

"Wonderful," he exclaimed. Looking around the porch, he asked, "Shall we be expecting Mr. Bealke soon?"

Her grin disappeared. "No, sir, I am a widow." Then she realized that because she wasn't wearing widow's attire, no one could tell her marital status. *I'm so sorry, Billy.* It was a fault she'd have to correct soon.

"I do beg your pardon," he said, his own smile fading momentarily. "Is there a possibility I could entice you to take a walk with me? The grounds are lovely. We have several magnolias blooming and flowers back in the garden as well." He offered his hand. It was bare, but, then, why would a gentleman on his own land wear gloves when it was barely past noontime?

Pulling her bottom lip under the scrape of her teeth, Emma worried about whether her stomach would behave if she went. Oh bother! She placed her own bare hand in Francois' palm. The warmth of his hand invaded her skin, making her tingle. It felt wonderful. But she reminded herself that such thoughts were inappropriate for a widow and because of Jack. And that was the issue, wasn't it? She felt more loss over him than Billy.

Emma rose and smoothed the skirts of her borrowed dress and crinoline.

"Bellefountaine is primarily a sugar-producing estate," Francois told her as they strolled the grounds, her arm in the crux of his, his free hand resting on hers.

Under the shade of a parasol, she avoided the sun and a slight breeze blew across the land. For the first time in longer than she cared to admit, she relaxed. The tension in her body seemed to ease thanks to Francois' deep and sensual voice and their quiet walk. The guilt that had plagued her at first slowly seeped away.

"You said your family's been here a generation?"

He chuckled. "Several, actually. Came over here under the French. You'll see more of Francais in my father, though."

"When will I meet him?"

"Soon enough, m'aime."

She had also heard that endearment from Marie. For once, she felt a part of something but knew her status was precarious. All depended on Nathan, she was sure.

The land was rich and vast, several thousand acres. Even now, during the war, she looked past the garden into the fields and found slaves busy at work. How had they managed to keep so many, considering?

Closer to the main house, Emma noticed the slaves they passed had lighter skin color. Nothing unusual about that, but she noticed something else too.

"Ah, Colette," he called softly to a slave girl.

The young slave, her skin a light cocoa, hair black, straight and long, sauntered up to him. Emma frowned. Colette, who wasn't much younger than Emma, was way too forward with her master. Despite the fact that her stomach was round with child, she walked seductively, her hips swaying.

Francois talked to the girl in French. Emma saw Colette lower her eyelids invitingly and nod. As she walked away, he offered Emma his arm again. Gingerly, she took it.

"We'll have tea, non?" He guided her to a gazebo in the shade of tall, flowering magnolia trees.

The space was small and to get to the chair, she brushed past him. Her breast slightly touched his arm, sending tingles down to her lower belly and creating a pool between her legs. The reaction scared her and she quickly sat, praying she wouldn't touch Francois again. He was so handsome, his voice so sensual, her body had reacted instinctively. Her hands clenched. This was wrong. He was Jack's brother!

Yes, but Jack is dead. Her mind stumbled. Memories flooded her. Jack before the firing squad, her father collapsing, guns exploding and Jack falling. General Van Dorn's reassurance that Jack was dead and condolences over her father as he hastened her away from the activity of soldiers preparing to leave. She had faltered, was nearly hysterical, a feeling that had enveloped her all the way to the transport...

No, stop it! She steeled herself, refusing to fall down that hole of despair again. Jack was gone.

Francois took his place and smiled at her.

Trembling inside, she fought for control. It had to be the child making her feel so...She licked her lips, trying to calm her nerves. "So, Francois, why aren't you fighting?" Ah, yes, the war. A safe topic.

He added a pinch of sugar to his tea. "I have fought. I was wounded and sent home." He shrugged. "Now I am covered by the Twenty Negro Law and protect my family's property while my father is in the Confederate government in Richmond. Because I am the only remaining son, all falls to me."

Emma nodded and sipped her tea. Politics. But peering over the rim of her cup, she frowned. He didn't look as though he had been wounded.

Two young slave girls came to the table, both about ten years old. One carried a plate of cakes, the other had fruit. Like Colette, their skin was light; in fact, they looked like weathered white women. Their reddish-brown hair was straight and silky, but it was their eyes that were most striking. They were green.

April 1863

Emma stood as patiently as she could while the seamstress pinned the skirt's hem. The bronze silk ballgown seemed a bit extravagant during wartime with supplies so scarce. It also made her feel foolish–she was in mourning, not there to enjoy herself. But Marie had insisted, saying social events raised funds for the war, especially for the wounded. Therefore, many societal rules could be bent, including those that kept widows in mourning tucked away.

Thankfully, her morning sickness had subsided. She had no idea why it was called "morning" because it lasted all day. Her stomach still looked flat, but the corset felt snug. In the mirror, she saw that she had filled out, which made her look healthier than when she had arrived.

"You will dance all night, as beautiful as you are," Marie complimented. "Francois will have to fight the other men away from you."

Emma smiled timidly. Francois had been quite attentive, and his motives had become increasingly apparent. His manners were impressive, as was the way he walked and dressed. He was muscular and sensual. He'd kissed her once–a peck at the barn. It was nice. Not as electric as Jack's but still nice. She feared he'd ask her to marry him. Her hand fell to the slight bulge under her petticoat. Francois had persuaded her to admit that she carried Jack's child and he gave her a wide grin, telling her he'd be honored to be his nephew's father. How could she say no?

Very easy. No.

But he didn't propose. That afternoon, he had taken her for a picnic on a hilltop overlooking the Mississippi River.

After he jumped off the driver's seat of the carriage, he had walked to her side and placed his hands on her waist to lift her to the ground. Her waist had thickened, though the mirror and dress still showed otherwise.

"Soon you won't be able to do that," she told him glumly.

He held her chin between his thumb and fingers, tilting her head to look into his clear blue eyes. "Never. I'll always be able to hold you." He grabbed the blanket and basket. "Being with child makes you adorable."

He grinned and she laughed despite herself. At only three months, she still didn't appear to be in the family way but that would change. Would he?

Spreading the blanket, Francois patted the space next to him. As Emma sat, he handed her a glass of champagne. The bubbles tickled her nose and she giggled.

"Francois, you'll make me forget there's a war if you keep this up."

That devilish grin spread across his face. "Good, I hoped all my efforts were working." He lifted his glass. "To the future."

She nodded and her glass touched his. As they drank, his eyes never left hers.

"You are an astonishing lady."

Tilting her head, she squinted. "How so?"

He tore off a hunk of bread, lathered it in the whipped butter and handed it to her. She was starving—something new to deal with. Hunger seized control and she took the bread, her mouth watering as she bit into it. The bread was one of the best she'd ever tasted and the butter made it even better. She hummed, savoring it.

Francois laughed. "I see you are hungry."

She swallowed, biting her lower lip. "Please, excuse me. I

don't know what came over me to have devoured that so quickly."

His good humor didn't fade. "No reason to be embarrassed, m'amour. Your child is voracious. That is good."

Her brows knitted. "Oh, and you are a doctor, as well as acting patriarch?"

"Emma." He leaned back. "Many times, our slaves have babies. The Fontaines protect their own, whether that be blood or property. I'd not let any of our women go without adequate care during their time."

Had her father held the same conviction? She tried to remember Rose Hill but nothing came to her. The house was gone, the slaves as well, she imagined. Suddenly, melancholy threatened to consume her...

"Oh, mon chere, I apologize," he stated.

She let his endearment and the sound of his voice soothe her. *No!* She should still be mourning Billy and couldn't help but think she should include Jack as well. Her vision blurred.

Quickly, he pulled a white handkerchief from his pocket. "Darling, I didn't mean to make you cry. I wanted to give you an afternoon of happiness..."

"Oh, Francois," she sniffled, dabbing her eyes with the linen square. "I fear I'm turning rather melancholy..."

She couldn't look at him, convinced he'd be stoic about it, just like her father was when her mother turned to tears. Instead, Francois moved closer and pulled her into his arms.

"Oh, Emma, it is good," he murmured. "I will keep you safe."

The comfort of being in his embrace chipped away at the emotional wall she'd built around her. One she had made to protect her from getting close to anyone other than Nathan. Except for him, God had taken everyone else she held dear. Now, though, there was another man who had begun to invade her heart, and she couldn't fight it. Didn't want to. She leaned back against Francois' chest, closing her eyes and enjoying his touch.

A fleeting image came to her–Jack. His emerald gaze and seductive smile. Then he vanished. Her heart clenched. She missed him so. Deep within, a flutter startled her. The babe. A grin spread across her lips until the muscular wall behind her moved. Francois. No, this was wrong, to be in the arms of another man so soon. She should be in mourning for her husband but had failed him and society by falling in love with Jack and succumbing to him. By taking Jack away from her too, God had reminded her not to stray again. Her anxiety grew, and with a strength she hadn't felt in a long time, she broke away from Francois.

"Emma, Emma," he called, befuddled.

"No, Francois, no, this isn't right." She stood, the soothing surroundings falling away as she tried to distance herself from him. "I am still in mourning..." A sob escaped her.

He stood and looked at her. "Apologies. I had not meant to intrude, but I thought you could use some company."

She forced a smile. "Thank you, I'm just so lost. I've no family, no home, nothing to return to Virginia for and my only responsibility is Nathan. And he is your family, too," she sighed, her brows furrowed. What was she to do? She carried another's child...one who'd be called bastard...

But Francois took her hand and kissed the back of it gently. "Your home is here, with me. And you have a family– Nathan and the little one inside you. You're probably tired. I've seen this amongst our darkies when they're in your condition. Come, let us return to the house so you can rest. Later, maybe we could discuss the future." He tipped her chin up. "You're a beautiful woman, ma chere. Jacques must have loved you deeply to bring you this far for safety's sake. He'd want you happy. Let me try to help you be so."

Emma searched his gaze. Every feature on his face showed her how sincere he was in what he spoke. Biting her bottom lip, she gave him a brief nod and slipped her arm into his.

Could she let go of the past to find a peaceful life for her and her child? Would God finally release her from His wrath?

Over the next two weeks, Francois became more attentive to Emma, acquiescing to her slightest need, from finding her blackberries and rich cream to a newly stuffed mattress that eased the ache in her lower back. He was so attractive, with that wicked smile and those light blue eyes, brilliant against his dark hair. Soon, she stopped comparing him to Jack.

But nights remained difficult. Jack still haunted her dreams, although not as often. He was gone. Dwelling on memories of him would make her ill if she didn't fight them.

To try to stay focused on her changed life, she allowed Francois to get a little closer to her. He did not kiss her again and he never pressed too hard for more, but his place in her heart was growing. And that frightened her.

On a bright and sunny afternoon, Francois took Emma for a picnic in a shaded grove near the river. In the distance, a boom sounded periodically–Union boats going upriver. It unnerved her but Francois persuaded her to ignore it, saying it was far away and that they were safe. The Yankees would never attack Bellefountaine. It was an illusion, she was sure, but with her second glass of wine, she put thoughts of the war out of her mind. She rested her head on his shoulder as he sat behind her so she could lean against him. Comfort and peace spread over her.

"Emma," his voice was low as he whispered in her ear. "Marry me."

Stunned by Francois' unexpected proposal, she stilled. At one time, she'd thought he'd propose but when he hadn't, she allowed herself the luxury of just living. But now, her heart began thudding loudly in her chest. She should have known he'd ask her after all the attention he'd showered on her. She carried Jack's child, so it made sense, but Francois, despite his good looks and seductive nature, would never truly have her heart. He had chipped away at her defenses, getting closer to her, but she didn't love him. Liked, yes. But she had given her heart to Jack. A marriage with Francois would be one without love. Lust maybe, because she couldn't fight the attraction, but was that enough? Could she live alone and try to raise the child by herself? What other man would have her? Then again, how many men would be left after the war?

"You know, I'd gladly raise my brother's child as mine," he added softly.

She felt tears forming. The child needed a father. Francois was Jack's brother. This was Jack's family home. These people would protect her and Jack's child. A home. Tears blurred her vision. They were not of joy, but of loss. *Jack.* She bit back a sob. "Yes," she whispered and as Francois smiled, leaning to kiss her, she secretly wished she had had the strength to say no.

Later that afternoon, after a restless nap, Emma walked

to the kitchen. Her stomach demanded food and the babe inside her craved meat. She could've sent Tilly, but going herself would do her good as she thought again about Francois' proposal. He was a good match— wealthy, good home and not fighting in the war. He said he'd been injured but it had not confined him, and he had both his arms and legs. So the possibility of having another child remained.

The knowledge that she didn't love him still plagued her though. She wasn't sure whether she could let him bed her without feeling as though she was betraying Jack. That's why she couldn't sleep. She hoped responding to her hunger might clear her mind.

As she drew nearer the kitchen, she saw the slave women bustling about in haste. Something was wrong. By the time she was at the door, multiple pots of water had been set to boil, along with lots of linens gathered.

"Oh, there you are," Marie stated, walking into the kitchen. Unlike her usual wardrobe, she wore a simple work dress and apron. "Come along and see what you'll go through in the next six months." Grabbing a pile of linens, she nodded to Emma to follow her.

They walked back among the slave shanties. The shanties were made of white clapboard and looked like additions to the house rather than slave dwellings. The doorways were open to allow breezes and fresh air in. But screams filled the air of the one they walked to.

Inside, prostrate on the bed, lay Colette. She wore a simple chemise, bunched above her protruding stomach. Her bare legs were bent and spread open, exposing her cunny. Her black hair was tangled and wet with sweat like the rest of her. Two older women sat on either side of her, holding her hands as she screamed again, sitting up somewhat and pushing.

Suddenly, Emma stood alone, watching as Marie went to the bed, coaxing the slave. The baby's head emerged as Colette raged louder. Jack's mother encouraged her to push, and, face shining, she did. The infant slipped out and onto the linen-covered bed.

The room erupted in motion as the women took the child and cut the cord extending from Colette to the baby's belly button. They cleaned mother and child.

"It's a girl," Marie stated proudly. "Come, Emma, see. Isn't she a beauty?"

Emma walked slowly, fear and awe gripping her. The tiny infant looked almost the color of tea with lots of cream added. A thatch of hair on her head was light brown. Suddenly, she cried out and the room burst into laughter. The babe opened her eyes and they seemed to catch Emma's. They were sparkling blue.

"**We must destroy this army of Grant's
before it gets to the James River. If he
gets there it will become a siege, and then
it will be a mere question of time.**"
~ General Robert E. Lee, CSA, conversation
with Lieutenant General Jubal A. Early, Spring
1864

<hr />

CHAPTER THIRTY-TWO

St. Francisville, Louisiana
April 1863

Union control of the Mississippi River north of
Vicksburg, Mississippi and south to the Gulf of
Mexico had made the last part of Jack's return home a
nightmare. Not that the beginning of his journey through
southern Tennessee and northern Mississippi had been any
better. He had to avoid being discovered by both armies
and was glad he was responsible only for himself and
Goliath. Although losing Goliath would slow his progress
considerably, it wouldn't prevent Jack from continuing to
make his way to Bellefountaine.

Despite Jack's painful chest wound, he had made relatively
good time until the spring rains came when he was in the
middle of Mississippi. Torrents drenched the countryside,
turning abandoned former farm fields into mud. Many
times, Goliath could barely proceed because of the way the

mud sucked at his hooves. The most valuable tool Jack had was a hoof pick. One day, the downpour was so bad that it brought both man and horse to a complete halt.

Emma was constantly on Jack's mind. He knew Van Dorn's rank would ensure her safe passage to his parents' home, but how quickly? And once there, would she stay? Especially after she discovered the dark secret of his past? He should have told her, forewarned her, but how? His desire to make sure she and Nathan were safe had overruled everything else. One thing was sure—Pierre Fontaine would do anything to protect his family. Anything. And his father owned enough land and wielded enough influence in politics, with many connections both in the United States and Europe, to do so.

It was the legacy Jack should have inherited but one he had adamantly refused. The rift between him and his father could never be mended, not by Jack's standards. But he had counted on his father to take Nathan and Emma under his protection until he could get to them.

But what of Emma? Would she reject him? Could she ever forgive him? For most of the journey home Jack cursed and berated himself. Poor Goliath had heard it all but continued to plod onward. The horse's fortitude helped Jack keep one foot in the real world.

He sneezed. *Hell and damnation, this illness would never leave him!* As if the rain and the armies hadn't been a big enough impediment, along with the stinging chest wound, he had come down ill two weeks ago. He had figured it was from being wet all the time, spring temperatures dipping occasionally, and insufficient food. Two days of hovering on a hillside, burning with fever, had cost him more than a week of travel. As his strength had waned, he fell asleep in the saddle, only to waken when he fell off Goliath.

It was pre-dawn when the boat pulled up to the dock at St. Francisville.

"Thanks." He slid his Union dollars into the boat captain's hand and tugged on Goliath's reins.

The horse's hooves made a loud clacking sound when he walked up the planking to solid ground. The sky was a muted pink as the sun rose. Jack stepped onto the main street and when he saw his reflection in store windows, he cringed. He knew he was filthy but he looked worse than he thought. His stubble had grown into a short straggly beard, his hair matted against his head. The sack coat was covered in mud and mold. His face was chapped and scratched from making his way through wilderness, and his hands also were raw. No doubt he reeked to high heaven, too.

As though his appearance wasn't awful enough, Goliath looked equally unkempt, with a dull coat, his mane and tail windblown and tangled with burrs, and his legs were marked and bloody. The saddle blanket was dirty and worn, the bridle frayed. Frankly, Jack figured if anyone had been up and seen them, they would have reached for a rifle. Thank God no one was. But he couldn't go to Emma looking as he did.

He turned down the road toward Delilah's. At the two story-clapboard house, one lone light shined on the second floor. Jack picked up a rock and threw it at the window just hard enough to tap it. The curtain was moved aside and a familiar face looked out. Through the closed door, Jack heard the creak in the stairs—a creak he had hit every time he had been there.

The door cracked open. He smiled apologetically. "Good Morning, Del."

"Oh, yes, right there. Oh God, woman, that's the spot." Jack sank deeper into the tub.

Delilah laughed, dropping the wash rag and picking up the pitcher. Standing above Jack, she dumped the warm water over his head. He sputtered as he ran his fingers through his hair.

"So, tell me how you're alive, Jack." She handed him a linen sheet as he stood. "Last I heard, you were before a firing squad for desertion. Or was it betrayal?" She eyed him, her gaze stopping at his chest. "That be lookin' like something tried to kill you for wearing the wrong color down here."

He dried himself, squinting at her through the material as he rubbed his head. "There's a war, Del. Most folks are scattered, men off fighting. Too few left to gossip, so where did you hear that?"

She laughed. "A Fontaine? Darlin', you are more than the common folk. News travels fast, maybe more so now."

He grabbed her wrist hard. "And my father? Does he know?"

"Of course," she winced.

"Sorry," he apologized, releasing his hold. "It's been," he paused, "difficult."

Rubbing her wrist, she looked at him narrowly. "So why are you here?"

He didn't answer. Reaching for a pair of pants, he stepped into them, listening to her tap her foot. "Thought you'd have a companion tonight."

She didn't answer. "You be back for Fran's weddin'?"

He shrugged his shirt on. "My brother's marrying? Thought he'd be out winnin' for the cause."

She laughed as she went to him. He looked at her as he buttoned his cuffs. Delilah was a lithe, sultry, ebony-haired beauty. The parish's most expensive whore, she knew how to excite and satisfy any man. Her cream-colored skin held barely a hint of her slave heritage from some relative way back many generations. It gave her an exotic lure that made her the money and gave her the independence no other job would. Her slave blood made her unacceptable to white society. His memories of her, his escape valve from his father before the Point, had drawn him there again. She was his refuge before the storm to come.

As she traced his jaw with the tip of her finger, she shook her head. "No, he did but came home injured. A war hero. Now, he runs Bellefountaine because Pierre's representing Lou's'ana in the Confeder'cy." She leaned in to kiss him.

He hadn't been her only client back then. His father had visited Delilah as well. The repugnant thought made him step away from her to grab the glass of whiskey she'd poured for him. "Hmm," he gulped the contents. "Francois marrying..."

She tilted her head and her brows furrowed. "Yes, tomorrow. You probabl' know her, mon cher. 'Tis the lady who brought your son here. What is her name? Ah, wait, I remember. Emeline, Emma, no, yes, Emma. The widow."

The news stunned him. His ears buzzed and he didn't hear another word. Francois was marrying Emma? His blood boiled. Over his dead body!

Bellefountaine

Emma rolled her head as the morning breeze blew through the open French window and into her room, the gauzy curtains waving gently. She sighed. Comfort. She finally felt at home. She rolled over, refusing to wake completely when she hit something hard. She gasped and her eyes flew open.

"Good morning, my love," Francois murmured as he bent to kiss her.

She leapt beyond his reach and out of bed. Her floor-length nightgown flowed, exposing only her ankles and bare feet. By the look in his eyes, the sun's rays penetrated the sheer fabric. She felt self-conscious and unattractive with her growing stomach and enlarged breasts.

Francois lay across her bed, fully dressed in cream trousers, bronze waistcoat, white ruffled shirt and deep navy jacket. His eyes glowed as he grinned at her. Such a devilish smile, accented by a wayward lock of dark hair falling across his forehead. He was so handsome, she almost forgave him. Almost.

"You, sir, take too many liberties," she said, trying to control her tone.

"Ah, m'aime, please." He got up and went to her. "Tomorrow, you'll be my wife." He bent to kiss her. She turned.

"Please, Francois," she tried to twist away from him but he caught her at the waist. She grimaced. "I'm too fat—"

He chuckled. "You are with child." He nuzzled her neck. "You are beautiful."

She closed her eyes. The heat from his hands burned through the gown, imprinting on her. His hands wandered up her back and he drew her closer. One hand brushed across her slight bulge, up her rib cage and lightly across her breast, across her hard, sensitive nipple. She shuddered underneath his touch, ashamed that her body responded to him so quickly. He had tried only once to seduce her and but she had refused him. Therefore, she wasn't surprised when he tried again. They were engaged, after all, the wedding tomorrow. Tears threatened.

This was wrong. Her gut clenched. *Jack.*

"Oh, m'aime," he whispered, his fingers wiping the tear from her cheek. "Don't cry, s'il vous plaît. I will wait until we are married."

She blinked and focused. Francois' sympathetic eyes reached her soul. He obviously adored and cared about her. He'd never said he loved her, but, then again, she didn't love him. Not with her heart. She never would and he knew that. She swallowed her tears and reached for his hand at her cheek.

"It'll be better," he said softly. "I promise you." He took her lips gently.

He was so much like Jack and so very different as well. Why did God torture her so?

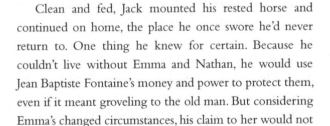

Clean and fed, Jack mounted his rested horse and continued on home, the place he once swore he'd never return to. One thing he knew for certain. Because he couldn't live without Emma and Nathan, he would use Jean Baptiste Fontaine's money and power to protect them, even if it meant groveling to the old man. But considering Emma's changed circumstances, his claim to her would not be as straightforward as he'd thought.

He gazed at sprawling Bellefountaine from the hilltop just outside the gates. Gates to Hell. Momentarily, his thoughts turned to Fanny. Was she still alive? Anger flared through him. He shut his eyes tight. It would do no good to ride into home looking for blood. His son was there. And Emma.

Francois planned to marry the woman he loved. Like

hell he would! Gritting his teeth, Jack adjusted his hat and kneed Goliath. The stallion snorted as he bunched his withers and took off. He barreled into the stable yard, scattering the slaves hither and yon. Jack pulled the reins back, balancing his weight on Goliath's flanks, stopping the horse without words. Throwing his leg over, he slid off the horse and dropped the reins. He inhaled the warm scent of horse manure, leather and magnolias. Home. Straightening his hat and his waistcoat and jacket, he marched toward the house. But at the last moment, he turned and walked down slave row. He had to know, had to face his demon before he saw Emma.

The one-room shanty on the right, close to the end, belonged to Fanny. His jaw ticked and a wave of nausea came over him as he drew closer. How much did she hate him?

The door was wide open like the rest of the hovels. The tiny window on the far side held no glass, but, with the door shut, no breeze could cool off the inside, so they left the doors open. The last step took every bit of strength he had.

"Why, Massa Jack, good Lord, son, we's be tole you be dead!" The large round black woman squealed, taking him into her arms and squeezing him tight.

"Jenny," he muttered, barely able to talk. The old matron of Bellefountaine's slave community released him but held onto his arms. Her searching eyes roved up and down.

"Yous sure be lookin' far from death." She grinned.

He snorted. Jenny had always made him feel warm and comfortable, except for now, as his tension remained.

The woman tilted her head, her eyes puddles of sadness. "Massa Jack, Fanny's gone."

"Gone? Father sold her?" That made no sense. Fanny,

delicate as a flower, with skin an appealing copper tone and curves designed for a man's hands, was a valuable commodity. Those were things Jack had never realized until his last days at home. Her beauty had attracted the attention of his father, which made his selling her seem especially odd.

"She died," Jenny stated quietly. "Long time ago."

The news startled Jack. "How long?"

"'nigh on ten, twelve years, I reckon'."

Jack was crushed. "How?" But he knew the answer or thought he did. How could she continue to live after that night?

Two young girls darted past him, past Jenny, and into the cabin, giggling. He barely noticed them, but Jenny did.

"Lilly, Maggie, you come here now," she ordered them.

The girls approached the woman, but Jack didn't notice or care. His mind and his heart were in agony. Fanny was gone. All that time, he hadn't known. She'd been only sixteen, just like him. He remembered trying to work up the nerve to kiss her, but it felt wrong. They'd grown up together, they'd played together often, as slave children and white children did. He knew it was his right to claim a kiss. As the owner's son, he could have demanded one but didn't.

However, Jack's father had something else in mind for him.

Jack was so lost in thought he only vaguely heard Jenny address him.

"Massa Jack."

"Yes, sorry."

"You need to meet them." She pulled over the first girl. "This is Lilly, and this one," she pulled over the other girl, "is Maggie. They're Fanny's girls." She waited.

The two looked identical. Their skin was lighter than he remembered Fanny's being, their hair a coppery hue. But it was their eyes that riveted him. Green. Pale green.

Staring back at him were his own eyes, a physical reminder of the depravity his father had thrust on him.

"They're your daughters, massa."

Hell.

Emma pulled on the ties of her corset again. She was determined to get into her yellow silk dress that day, come hell or high water. A giggle escaped her at the thought. She shouldn't think such things. Inhaling deeply, she tugged again and tied them. The corset held, though she could barely breathe. At four months along, she found her clothes barely fit now. Outwardly, she hardly looked in the family way, and Marie and Francois constantly reminded her she was too thin—Marie, perhaps, somewhat worried about that. But she couldn't ignore her growing middle and neither could her corset. She inhaled again. One last time...

Tilly sighed as she hooked the crinoline. "Yessum, that's it."

The slave slipped the silk gown over Emma's head and started buttoning the bodice. "We needs to get you other dresses soon." She muttered.

Emma frowned. "Not today. I can still wear this."

Tilly *harrumphed* as she hooked the sash.

Emma dismissed her and walked out on the veranda. She looked down at the yard, waiting for a moment before getting Nathan. Most of the slaves were busily at their tasks, but she noticed someone in the slave row emerging from a shanty, dressed in fine clothes. She frowned. The man was only in his shirtsleeves and had to adjust his waistcoat. He smoothed back his dark hair, except for an errant lock that broke free to settle across his forehead.

Francois.

Whatever is he doing in the slave row at this time of day? The field hands and house slaves continued in their work, not even glancing up. She wanted to turn away, pretend she never saw him there but couldn't take her eyes from him. Within minutes, he had entered the house and reached Emma.

"Good morning, my darlin'," he drawled. "You look so lovely." He took her hand and kissed the back of it.

He usually hugged her but not this time. In fact, his forehead glistened, and his shirt clung to his arms with sweat.

"Please excuse me." He said sweetly. "Had some business to take care of. I'll go bathe before the guests arrive. Are you taking Nathan to play?"

Business? In slave row? Her skin prickled. Vacantly, she nodded.

He gave her one of his dazzling smiles and kissed her. "Then I'll be on my way—"

"What were you doing in the slave quarters?" she blurted.

"I beg your pardon?"

"I saw you leaving; I think it was Lizzie's shanty. What were you doing?"

He stared at her. She could see the emotions flickering in his eyes. His jaw tightened. "I had matters to attend." He turned to leave.

"Did your business involve wearing clothing or not?" Her question surprised even her. It was a humid morning, as always near the bayou, but not enough for a gentleman of leisure to be so wet with perspiration that early.

He stopped but didn't turn. "Darlin', I think your condition is making you a touch mad."

Anger flared in her. How dare he use such an excuse to dismiss her inquiry? "Francois."

Turning, he sighed with exasperation. "You know I'm right," he smiled, tilting her chin up. He was so confident, so intense that she was nearly convinced he spoke the truth. At her nod, he kissed her lips gently. "Let me get a bath, sweetling. If you're still upset, I promise I'll make it up to you." With a quick smile, he walked away.

"I propose to fight it out on this line if it takes all summer."

~ Lieutenant General Ulysses S. Grant, USA, Dispatch, May 11, 1864

CHAPTER THIRTY-THREE

Bellefountaine Plantation
St. Francisville, Louisiana

Jack heard his little boy giggling before he saw him. Then came Emma's sweet laugh, which was like a salve to his injured soul.

After meeting the twin daughters he never knew he had, Jack needed some time to control his emotions. One question remained. Why hadn't he been told? Why? But a voice in his head made it clear. He'd fled. Left for The Point and never returned. Bellefountaine's secret had haunted him for years, and now there was no denying it.

Jean Baptiste Fontaine had continued a practice begun generations before but under different circumstances. Interracial liaisons had not been a new concept. The French and Spanish practiced it, freely and openly without ridicule. Some even married and had children. But under American laws, with the import of new slaves from Africa, interracial relationships had been banned at the turn of the century. Copulation between the races was allowed only to increase the slave population. Slave children fathered by white men were believed to be superior. And slaves they would be, for any babe born of a slave woman was considered a slave, period.

Such couplings also were ideal for sexually initiating white men without dishonoring the virginal young ladies of Society.

So Jean Baptiste simply followed the established tradition. He encouraged, even forced his sons to sow their wild oats on slave women rather than seducing innocents or visiting brothels. Jack had been told that slave women by nature were debased, and, therefore, there was no sin in bedding them. They wanted it. Desired it. The problem was that his father had paired him with Fanny. It was to be her initiation also, so that she could service her master in any way he wanted. She had no idea what that meant.

At fifteen, almost sixteen, Jack's lust took control of him. The girl he'd fantasized about was naked before him. And although his conscience protested, his body would not be denied. At first, Fanny had screamed, and he lost his nerve as well as his erection, but his father slapped her into submission and she stopped fighting. She obediently placed the head of Jack's manhood at her slit and locked her legs around his hips.

Afterward, he figured Fanny hated him. Jenny assured him she hadn't. But how could she not? He had left her carrying his twins and died after delivering them into the hell of Bellefountaine. His remorse knew no bounds.

Only three things kept Jack from fleeing again. There were his twin daughters, who he had to prevent from sharing their mother's fate. There was his son, who he had to protect from his father. And there was Emma.

She would never be his if he left. She'd marry his brother

and would have to tolerate life on the plantation with a husband who would carry on the family tradition. Jack felt as though he'd be ill.

After pulling himself together, he'd gone to the house, where he'd heard his son and Emma. He breathed deeply in an effort to calm himself. How could he convince the woman he had entrusted with his son's care that he loved her more than life? Their past had been mottled with hate, fear and distrust, and she undoubtedly thought him dead as well.

Past the trees, in the clearing surrounded by flowering bushes and magnolias, Emma sat on a large blanket. His mouth went dry. She looked beautiful. Her brown hair gleamed in the sunlight. The yellow silk pooled around her, shining like a halo. She'd gained some weight and no longer looked gaunt and tired. On the contrary, she glowed, like an angel. His angel. The one he'd fight for. The one he'd die for.

Her laughter filled the air as Nathan fell to his knees after taking a step. The cherub chirped and giggled as he tried again, stretching for a toy she held just out of his reach, encouraging him. They were his. Just seeing them, hearing them, made him feel whole.

Nathan gave up on the toy but threw himself at Emma and she fell back gracefully, tickling his sides. When Jack stepped closer, a twig snapped under his boot. Nathan looked up and cried out, crawling over Emma toward his father.

She turned, a smile still on her face until she saw him. Her expression froze.

Time stood still. The only noise came from Nathan, who grunted as he chugged closer.

"Emma."

"Jack?" She blinked rapidly and he watched her face drain of color.

He raced forward, picking up his son and was at Emma's side, fearing she'd faint. His legs nearly buckled under Nathan's weight and seeing Emma's wide-eyed look. Kissing Nathan's cheek, he put the child down.

"Emma."

Unnerved and tangled in her clothing, she struggled to stand.

"No!" With one hand holding her skirts and the other over her mouth, she turn to run, but he grabbed her, his arm around her middle. "No!" she gasped again as she began to panic.

"Shush, shush," he whispered in her ear, hoping he sounded more calm than he felt. "It's all right. Shhhh."

"Nothing's all right." She turned in his arm. Despite herself, she cradled his face. "They killed you."

He said nothing.

"Your betrayal made my father so upset, so angry, so confused," she whispered.

He watched, dreading the accusation in her eyes. "No, Emma..."

"You and this war, this awful war, killed my father!"

He shook his head. "Emma, he wasn't right for a long time. You told me he had been hurt, an injury to his head. Between that and losing his home and most of his family, plus all the traveling and hardship, I reckon it was too much for him. His heart just gave out."

Her eyes widened, making her look like a trapped animal. Afraid she'd hurt herself, or more likely run from him, he cupped the back of her head, a stupid attempt to keep her from fleeing. "He was right about some things I suppose. I am a traitor. A deserter. And I have killed. Spying—there was that is too." He looked deep into her brown eyes, hoping. "But the truth is this. I've come back for you. Emma. For you."

She began to shake her head. "No, no..." She broke away from him and stepped back, almost stumbled. Gathering her skirts, she yelled "no" again and ran to the house.

He stood, watching her, and glanced back at Nathan. The child sat on the blanket, no longer interested in the adults but playing with a set of wooden blocks.

As Jack swallowed, trying to gather his thoughts, he looked back at Emma. She was still going toward the house when she suddenly stopped. He watched in horror as she clutched her middle. Fear seized him and he ran to her as she fell to the ground.

"Emma!" He scooped her up in his arms.

Barrett, the house slave, opened the door for them and quickly moved aside as Jack walked past him and up the stairway.

"Tilly!" He yelled. For the love of God, he had no idea where Emma's room was.

The slave peeked out a door halfway down the hall. He moved quickly, following her into the bedroom. He set Emma down and Tilly reached under her skirts to undo her crinoline, letting it fall to the floor. Jack lifted Emma again to gently lower her to the bed. Her breathing was shallow, her face still pale.

"Get a doctor," he ordered Tilly. "And get Nathan." He started unbuttoning her bodice. Swiftly, he unsnapped the busk of her corset. "Come on, Emma, breathe. Breathe!"

Free of the corset's restraints, she inhaled deeply. Color washed back into her cheeks and he sighed. He reached into her glorious sable hair, freeing the strands of their pins. Slowly she opened her eyes.

"Sweetheart, how are you feeling?" He feared he'd almost lost her. Maybe he had.

She swallowed. "Jack, I don't understand. They told me you were dead!"

"Easy, darling. I was only wounded. I'm fine."

"But, but, they insisted," she panted, disbelief and anger fighting within her. "The General claimed he witnessed you die. I was so upset over daddy, I should've checked myself—"

"Shush," he soothed. "It's okay. I'm here and very much alive. Tilly's getting the doctor. Rest." With his fingers threaded through her hair, he bent closer, his lips meeting hers. She didn't protest. He ran his tongue across the seam of her lips, tasting lemonade and tears. She opened her mouth and he invaded it, tasting, stroking her tongue, inhaling her breath. She returned his fervor, tentatively at first, then with more passion.

He broke free, nibbling down her jaw, her neck, to her chest. She tasted like manna to a starving man. "Jack," she sighed.

The sound of his name on her lips ignited his passion further. His hand went to her corseted breast. She felt fuller, firmer than before or was it his faulty memory? She gasped loudly.

"Jack, please," she pleaded.

"Brother, what the hell are you doing to my fiancée?" A drawling male voice threatened.

Jack released her, slowly pulling away to stand. Her deep brown eyes shone with desire, but he had to face another challenge. His brother and their past.

It might be harder to win her than by just admitting you love her. She can be quite stubborn. If you're willing *to fight for her, make her yours truly...*Charles' words came back to him.

———❦———

Francois stood there, leaning against the doorway, arms crossed, hair askew, jaw set and his blue eyes glittering. He looked devastatingly handsome. Emma's breath caught in her throat. But perhaps Emma was attracted to him more because he was so accepting of her and her unborn child, Jack's child.

Jack's caress of her overly sensitive nub had sent tingles throughout her body, unfurling desire. It was a sensation that Francois' kisses had never caused. Of course, he'd never ventured beyond her mouth or neck because she refused his desire to do so. She knew all too well that only Jack could ease her longing. Even though she believed he was dead, the idea of any other man being intimate with her chilled her to the bone.

Staring at Jack, Emma saw he had changed during their time apart. He was lean and muscular, like a mountain lion. She'd felt his chest and arms hard against her as he carried her inside. His face was more angular, his skin bronze from the strong spring sun. His dark brown hair was windblown, as though he had forgotten his hat in his haste to get to her. At least, that was what she hoped, what she wished and prayed for.

But she was to marry Francois and should have stopped Jack from kissing her although she couldn't. She craved him, missed him. Loved him. Her heart skipped. *Oh God, no. Not that.* He'd left her before. To admit she loved him would make her even more vulnerable were he to do it again. Like everyone else had. Her mother, her sister, Billy and her father. *Oh please, dear Lord.*

Jack planted himself between her and Francois.

"Brother." His voice sounded cool.

Francois smirked. "Jacques. So ghosts do exist, non?"

"In more ways than one." Jack forced a smile. "Where is our father?"

"Away," Francois replied.

"Gentlemen," Emma said, trying to straighten her bodice and sit up. She motioned to Tilly to help her.

"Did he frighten you, m'aime?"

Jack growled.

"I'm fine Fran, please," she begged. "Jack what happened?"

"They missed, so to speak. Your brother helped me escape," he told her without looking away from Francois. "I had to find you."

"Well, we see that you have. Now, if you want to stay for the wedding—" Francois began boldly.

"Jack, you don't understand."

"You'd forget me that fast?" He turned to her. "And what of my son?"

At that, Emma moved, perhaps too quickly. The room spun. Tilly grabbed her elbow. Emma inhaled deeply before saying, "I hadn't forgotten—"

"Darlin', don't. Let me handle this." Francois stepped closer.

"You?" Jack spat. "You'll stay out of this!"

"I think not," Francois growled.

"Gentlemen!" Emma's patience was wearing thin, and she was concerned that they'd kill each other if she didn't stop them.

Behind Francois, a young slave boy appeared. "Dr. Spalding said he cain't be here til later."

Emma swallowed. "Tommy, that's fine. I'm okay."

Jack's eyes narrowed. "Tommy, come here lad." The slave

padded slowly to the white man he didn't recognize. When Jack tipped his head up, the boy's eyes were wide with fright.

"So you continued, I see," Jack uttered disgusted. "Kinda easy, isn't it?"

"You know better, Jacques." Francois' voice held menace and his hands fisted at his sides. "At least I haven't killed any of them."

"You bastard!"

Emma was confused. "What are you two arguing about? You need to get along because..." she trailed off.

Jack turned and scowled. "Why?"

She couldn't tell him. Not if he was going to leave her again. Although he had returned, there still were no words of love, of him staying, nothing. It seemed all he wanted was to seduce her and kill the one man who said he'd be there for her. No, she wouldn't tell him.

Francois nodded to her.

Jack's rage nearly boiled over. "You haven't told her, have you?"

"There's nothing to say," his brother smugly replied.

"You are not worthy of her," he spat. "Jesus, you are arrogant."

"And you are?"

"Stop it! Stop it now!" Her voice rose. Jack ignored her and confronted Francois.

"Tell her. I'm sure she's noticed. Do not drag her into this hell without her knowing," he said, low, threateningly.

"Tell me what?" For all the years she'd known Jack, he never spoke of his home, never went there either that she knew of. All she knew was he felt his father had the money and power to protect her and Nathan from the war. What was so demonic about this place?

Jack brought Tommy around to face her. "Look at him, Emma. Look at him."

She looked at the slave. "He's a child, Jack. Maybe seven, eight?"

The boy nodded. Jack's tight grasp made Tommy cower.

Jack glared at her. "Look closer," he demanded.

She squinted. His skin was lighter brown, almost beige even. And he had stunning blue eyes. Her mouth dropped open with sudden realization. "He looks like, like—"

"Me," Francois said, his voice cold. "Or our father."

Her stomach flipped. Images of slaves crowded her mind. The memory of the blue and green eyes now meant something. What had seemed an odd occurrence became all too clear. "But there are so many."

Jack snorted. "Welcome to Bellefountaine, or hell as I think of it."

The month she'd been there, she'd seen lighter skinned slaves with blue eyes. And two with green.

"There are multiple ways to use slaves," Jack stated. "Because importing slaves became illegal, what better way to increase their numbers than to encourage breeding them?"

Emma was stunned.

"As for those light-skinned slave girls," he turned on Francois. "Why don't you tell her what's in their future?"

Francois pursed his lips, his blue eyes icy.

"They're sold to the brothels in New O'leans for a high price." Jack nodded in agreement.

"No," she whispered, falling back to the mattress.

Jack went to her. "I won't allow Nathan to be subject to this. Or you. Your intended would get you with child; he's proven his ability to do so many times with the slaves."

"Jack," Francois threatened. "It's not as though you're a

saint, as Fanny learned."

Jack flew at his brother, knocking him to the floor. Francois leapt back up and returned the punch.

"Stop!" she cried.

They tumbled onto the ground, pounding each other. They rolled into a table holding a porcelain tea set and sent everything crashing to the floor. Emma yelled again as Jack pulled his brother up, preparing to hit him again. She saw the blood on them, the look of madness in their eyes.

Her ears started to buzz and the room became edged in blackness. She grabbed the bolster at the foot of the bed.

"Massa Jack," she heard Tilly shrill as Emma clung to the post.

The slave's yell finally reached the brawling men's ears, interrupting their fight, and both panted as they rose from the floor. Emma struggled to stay upright.

Jack was at her side instantly. "Darlin', you all right? You're very white."

Despite her lightheadedness, she glared at him just as Francois stated, "Brother, give her room to breathe." He went to her as well, limping slightly.

Jack remained where he stood, his concern for her evident. Francois' casual demeanor annoyed Emma. As her future husband, he should have been worried about her, too. If the room ever stopped spinning, she'd walk out on both of them.

"I came back for you Emma, for you. I can't believe you are..." he twisted, eyeing his brother, "in love with that scoundrel and that I mean nothing after all we've been through."

She wanted to scream but stood there in frustration, anger building. "After all we've been through? You act as though you considered us one, a couple, but how many times did you deny me? Hurt me? You even bedded Caroline! Married her, fathered a child with her, forsook my heart for her!" Tired of fighting Jack in her head, Emma's tongue was finally loosed.

"Emma..."

"No, you will hear me. You betrayed your home, the South, absolved all ties to your family. Fran told me you haven't inquired here in years." She saw his jaw tense... and Francois fight a grin, which irritated her more. "You betrayed me for Caroline, then you stole me from my home, let my husband sacrifice everything so you could get me with child, and, with that act completed, you denied any feelings for me! I saved your life, and for what? You hurt me, Jack. Hurt me!" She was beyond caring about what she said but finally paused in her tirade. Jack looked like a wounded dog.

Emma asked, "So why wouldn't I accept your brother's proposal? At least he's asked for my hand and has been a gentleman for the whole time I've known him, but you arrive and claim I'm yours? Ugh!" She spun and nearly lost her balance. From the corner of her eye, she saw Tilly dart out the room.

"Emma..." Jack stood.

"Non, mon frère," Francois said smoothly, stepping closer. "As you have heard, I'm the better choice."

Jack's nerves were on fire. Not only because of the fight with Francois, who had handled himself surprisingly well, but especially because of Emma's outburst. Apparently she hated him. A hatred he himself had sown. He couldn't deny any of her accusations. Now, he had to find a way to win her back or lose her forever.

"Emma," Jack started again, ignoring his brother and no longer aware of the pain from the punches Francois had delivered. "I love you. I have loved you since the moment I met you, back on that creek at Rose Hill."

She laughed scornfully. "I don't believe you. I can't. Not anymore, Jack..."

"It is the truth. I have fought heaven and hell to get here, to save you and my son from the nightmare of my family and to prove to you I love you. I want to marry you."

"Ma chere, do not listen to him," Francois said. Jack noticed he seemed to realize Emma might not wed him after all.

She stood there, wordless but shaking her head.

"Please, Emma..."

"No, Jack, no!" Tears sprang to her eyes and the color had drained from her face. Breathing heavily, she said, "You've hurt me too much."

"I never meant to hurt you. I was trying to protect you from me. What future could I offer, being a soldier at war? But I found I can't fight without knowing I've got you to live for." He took her hand. It was cold as ice. In the warm spring heat, it shouldn't have felt like that.

"And I have been here, consoling her wounded soul because of the damage you've done," Francois interjected. "I will be here. Always. I also love her." He now stood next to Jack. "Mon aime, it is all arranged—the priest, the guests, our future."

Emma's life had quickly become complicated. Francois had been at her side, willing to accept her and her baby as his, plus Nathan. He was sweet, suave, able to take care of her needs and wants, but he had a dark side. She'd known in her heart what his "business" had been in that slave shanty she'd seen him leave.

But now Jack was with her again. He was alive. He had finally said exactly what she wanted to hear for so long–he loved her, enough to go through hell and high water, or war, to be with her. But the past didn't disappear just because she wanted it to. He had betrayed her, broken her heart. More than once. He claimed he couldn't go on without her. She was torn. Her love for him remained strong despite everything else, and with his baby inside her...

Both men waited anxiously for her to decide. What should she do? She had promised herself to Francois, and he was right, the ceremony, the guests, everything was arranged for their marriage ceremony—but she didn't love him. And the fact that he continued to do what he did "for the family" disgusted her.

It would be so much simpler if she could just live on her own.

But Society would look down on her and make it impossible for her to live in peace, especially without means. And her unborn child would be considered a bastard.

Emma's head throbbed and her heart ached. She thought she'd be sick, but then there was a slight flutter deep and low inside her. It was as though the baby wanted a say in what she would do.

Torn by emotion, she heard the buzzing in her ears again. She gripped the duvet as the room began spinning. When she heard footsteps in the hall and glanced up, Mrs. Fontaine was standing in the doorway with Dr. Spalding behind her. Tilly must have gone to her. *Thank heavens.*

Jack didn't hear his mother arrive until she called out to them, "Francois, Jacques, get out of the way."

The doctor passed them and went straight to Emma. Jack frowned. He knew Emma was upset, but why did she need a physician?

"Both of you boys come here," his mother ordered.

He knew that tone. Had heard it since childhood—the voice of authority. Although he was an adult, it still caused a chill to go through him, making him feel like he'd been caught stealing a cookie. He'd bet Francois felt the same.

Dutifully, they left Emma and went to her.

"Jacques, I didn't know you'd returned," she stated coolly.

"Just got back, mama. I would've—"

"Tsk," she waved at him to be silent. To his brother she said, "My dear Francois, you and I will take a walk and let them have some time alone."

"No, mama, I can't leave my—" Francois protested.

"Yes, you will," his mother replied sternly. Looping her arm in the crux of Francois' arm, she aimed him toward the door and glanced over her shoulder at Jack. "You and I will speak later. For now, settle your issues with Emma. She has a wedding." Having issued her orders, she and his brother left the room, Francois still arguing futilely against it.

Jack knew he had only a short time to convince Emma not to marry his brother. With a brief plea to God and steeling himself, he turned to where she sat on the bed. The doctor was discussing something with her, but he couldn't hear them. Was she sick? Fear gripped him. Tentatively, he walked to them, hoping she was well and forming his argument to persuade her to be his forever.

"Drink this." Dr. Spalding pressed a cup to her pale lips. Jack's alarm grew. Jesus, if he lost her now, he'd die.

As the brown liquid seeped into her mouth, she sputtered. Jack had to bite back a grin when he caught a whiff of the stuff and saw her face redden. Straight whiskey often revived one.

"Jack?"

"I'm here, sweetheart," he said softly.

"Mrs. Bealke," the doctor said, pushing Jack out of the way and putting his finger to her wrist, "how are you feeling now?"

She looked confused and stared at Jack. He knew he looked a sight. His cheek was swollen, one eye blackened and his lip torn, but he thought he had wiped off most of the blood.

"Fine, I'm fine," she answered.

The doctor scoffed. "Mr. Fontaine, do try to control yourself. A lady in this condition must be treated delicately." He closed his medical bag with a snap.

It was Jack's turn to be confused. What condition? Emma was blushing.

"Rest. I'll be back t'morrow ta check on you," the doctor told her as he walked out the door.

Jack held her hand. "What condition, Emma? Have you been ill?"

She glanced downward. "Where's Francois?"

His brother. She wanted to know about him? "Mother pulled him away," he answered coldly.

She waited for more.

"They're walking in the garden or something." His tongue was tied in frustration. She wanted his brother instead of him. But could he blame her? *If you're willing to* *fight for her, make her yours truly...*Charles' voice sounded in his head.

"Emma," he squeezed her hand. "Please listen to me. I, I'm sorry."

"Did you willingly participate in that?" She didn't need to clarify what "that" was.

He sighed. "Not willingly. I was 'inducted' into the practice early. I was made to lie with a slave who I'd grown up with, considered a friend. She was a virgin," he swallowed the knot of regret. "I hurt her. I couldn't live with it, so, yes, I ran. It, it killed her," he chanced a glance at Emma. Her eyes didn't waver from his face, but tears welled in them. The pain caused by Jack's revelation equaled the agony in his soul, but she said nothing. He swallowed before continuing. "She had twins. I'm sure you've seen them. I, I didn't know, not till today. The whole event haunted me for years. To my father, it was a tradition and part of my responsibility to the family and so forth. I'm sure it doesn't make sense to you. Your family had no such 'tradition.'"

"No, but it wasn't perfect." She sounded sad and made him wonder just how much Caroline's greediness and arrogance had cost Emma.

"I sent you here because my father is wealthy and well known. He could send you anywhere you wanted to go. I wouldn't have suggested it otherwise." He touched her cheek. "Emma, this is where I need to be. With you. I love you."

The tears now trailed down her cheeks. Tears of joy? Or regret?

"I hurt you with Caroline. I, it—" How could he get through this? "A mistake. Terrible. Look—" He was faltering and knew it. "I've always loved you. Ever since I met you." Her hands trembled inside his. "*Marry me*. Not Francois."

The warmth of her smile vanished as did the color in her cheeks, and she withdrew her hands. It was as though a wall had suddenly been erected, separating them. "Jack, no, I, I can't."

Inside, his heart skipped. Had she still told him no? He had asked for her hand before but married Caroline instead...But Charles' advice echoed again. Jack would have to fight for Emma.

"Emma, I love you," he pleaded softly, taking her hands back. He believed that if he held her, she would feel his love.

Tears streamed anew. "No, please, Jack. If I allow myself to believe you, I'll just get hurt again, and I'm not sure I'll survive it," she sobbed, trying to pull her hands from his. "Everyone's left me. And you've left me more than once! You betrayed me with Caroline. I don't think I could take your rejection again."

Anger surged through him, mixed with understanding. Charles had told him the same thing. And she was right. He had left her twice—both when he took Caroline as his wife and when she believed him dead from the firing squad.

"I'll never leave you. I promise, with all my heart and soul." She remained silent. *Waiting for a battle to begin was easier than waiting for her response.* But she said nothing. He asked, "So you love my brother?"

She tentatively shook her head.

"But you'd marry him? A man who carries on the 'family tradition' of coupling with slaves to breed more of them to sell? Is that what you want for Nathan? For yourself?"

"But Francois has stayed with me ..."

Jack laughed spitefully. "You'd rather him than a man who'd love you and only you forever?"

Jack saw the war in her eyes as she swallowed hard. He'd give anything to make her understand. "Darling, what do I have to do to make you see? I love you and want to grow old with you, the two of us, with Nathan—"

"Jack," she whispered. "I have something to tell you."

He looked up, hopeful.

A timid smile came to her face and she tried to wipe her tears away. "What Dr. Spalding said, about my condition? It'll make you leave me again." She bit her bottom lip. "I'm with child."

His heart plummeted as he examined her appearance more closely. He thought her slightly fuller form was the result of having more and better food and greater comfort under his mother's care.

"My brother's—"

"Yours."

His heart skipped. "What?"

A smile came to her trembling lips. "I carry Nathan's brother or sister."

The news hit him hard. A baby. He grinned as his heart swelled. And just as quickly, it deflated. She carried his child but didn't love him. "Good," he said stoically, focusing on the wall behind her, frantically working to mask his disappointment.

She lifted his chin. "I didn't want to tell you unless I knew you loved me. Considering all you've gone through to be here, to tell me you love me—"

"It's true," he interjected, his gaze back on her. "Marry me, Emma. We may not be able to stay here or even want to. There is still a war going on. It won't be easy, but I promise, as God is my witness, I'll never leave you again."

The wind blew gently, the southern sun and warmth spilling into the room. He watched her, praying that God would convince Emma of Jack's sincerity.

She bit her bottom lip, a habit he had always adored. He'd gladly spend the rest of his life soothing that abused lip if she'd give him the opportunity. Slowly, she gazed up at him, her eyes glowing. "Yes, Jack Fontaine, I will marry you. You know I will follow you anywhere. Because I love you."

His heart leaped. He took her in his arms as he leaned her back against the pillows, kissing her deeply.

Through the open windows, in the distance, the faint roar of Union naval artillery upriver blasted at Vicksburg—the last remaining Confederate stronghold on the Mississippi River. The War of the Rebellion raged on.

-The End-

Stay tune for the next in the
Hearts Touched By Fire series –
THE KEY TO THE SOUTH

Join me for more fun, learning about upcoming novels, cover reveals, being on the team to see new stories first and all else an author and her muse can share! *www.ginadanna.com*

ACKNOWLEDGEMENTS

I would like to acknowledge my support team for helping get Jack & Emma ready for publication. I'd like to thank the Rom-Critters critique group, especially Ella Quinn, Kary Rader, Tmonique Stephens and Carrie Ann Ryan. Without their reading and critiquing from the get-go, this tale would never have happen. I'd like to thank Marc Kollbaum, close friend and curator of Jefferson Barracks Historic Site in St. Louis for a ton of help, too numerous to try to list! To my co-workers at Jefferson Barracks who helped, rather they wanted to or not – Jack Grothe – the Billy Yank of all time! I'd also like to thank George & Mary Rettig who helped me with Louisiana geography and family/social histories for the Fontaine family. To JJ Jennings and Mark O'Leary for their support. To my editor, Bernadette LaManna, who helped correct my grammar, my running descriptions/sentences/paragraphs, and my repetitiveness that can happen on a saga this overwhelming.

And I especially would like to thank my mother, who quietly waited for her daughters to realize that not only was our father's Sicilian heritage fascinating, so was her family – a family that has been in the USA since the 1600s and fought in the American Revolution and the tumultuous American Civil War. She is the one who introduced me to the autobiography of one of our ancestors who was a Confederate surgeon, who shared with me the family genealogy and stories she knew. It is her who spurred me to follow my historical interests (though I'd bet she would have chosen a more lucrative degree than my BA & MA in History). Thank you mom! I wish you were here to read Jack & Emma and realize it is in memory to your side of the family. History is my favorite subject, the American Civil War my particular interest.

Also want to thank Rich – He's my warrior, my knight and my love whose strength and support helps me when my muse disappears or when deadlines seem impossible and willingly puts up with my rantings.

Without all these people, **The Wicked North** would have never made it to paper but stayed as a muse running rampant in my head. Gratitude!

Novels by Gina Danna

HEARTS TOUCHED BY FIRE (CIVIL WAR) SERIES:

The Wicked North (Book 1)
The Key To The South (Book 2)
Rags & Hope (Book 3)
The Better Angels (Book 4)

THE GLADIATOR SERIES:

Love & Vengeance (Book I)
Love & Lies (Book II)

LORDS & LADIES & LOVE SERIES:

To Catch a Lady
To Dance With A Lord
To Kiss A Lady

Her Eternal Rogue
The Wicked Bargain
Great & Unfortunate Desires
This Love of Mine

AUTHOR'S NOTE

Ever since I can remember, I've loved two things –
horses and history. I got my childhood wish fulfilled when
I found my Arabian in 2009. As to history, I have had the
pleasure of not only getting my BA & MA in history and
work toward my PhD in Civil War history but also using
my degrees as my career in the museum field. I have been a
curator at the Missouri State Museum, a museum educator
at Jefferson Barracks Historic Site in St. Louis and park
guide in interpretation at the National Park Service at
Vicksburg National Military Park. And while working at
JB, I discovered the world of Civil War reenacting. Being a
living historian or reenactor, adds such depth to historical
interpretation that simple research cannot touch. To try to
go back in time and live as our ancestors did opens the
mind to being closer to what they experienced, how they
lived, makes everything more real and fabulous. It is a
hobby that is addicting and expensive – I probably own
more Civil War dresses than modern day!

All of this background helped me immeasurably in
making Jack & Emma's story more real. **The Wicked
North** took longer to write than any of my other novels
because I wanted to be dead-on accurate in my details while
drawing the reader into that era, that time when tensions
were so tight, a war that tore this nation apart erupted.

My personal library on Civil War books is extensive
but by no means complete. But to those readers who are
interested in more, I will list some of the multitude of books
I referenced in writing this novel, not in specific order –

Generals In Blue by Ezra J Warner

Generals In Grey by Ezra J Warner

Robert E. Lee by Emory M Thomas

JEB Stuart, The Last Cavalier *by Burke Davis*

Gateway to the West, The History of Jefferson Barracks Vol. 1 *by Marc Kollbaum*

The Official Military Atlas of the Civil War

War of the Rebellion, Official Records of the Union and Confederate Armies

To The Point, The United States Military Academy, 1802-1902 *by George S. Pappas*

The Civil War, The First Year Told By Those Who Lived It ed. By Brooks D Simpson, Stephen W. Sears and Aaron Sheehan-Dean

Nothing But Victory, The Army of the Tennessee 1861-1865 *by Steven E. Woodworth*

Within the Plantation Household *by Elizabeth Fox-Genovese*

Civil War Medicine by Robert E. Denney

Journal of a Secesh Lady, The Diary of Catherine Ann Devereux Edmondston, 1860-1866

The Life of Billy Yank *by Bell Irvin Wiley*

The Life of Johnny Reb *by Bell Irvin Wiley*

The Civil War by Bruce Catton

The Ladies' Book of Etiquette, Fashion and Manual of Politeness *by Florence Hartley*

Civil War Era Etiquette *by Louis Martine*

The Medical and Surgical History of the War of the Rebellion (1861-65) – Official Records

Autobiography of John Taylor, Confederate Surgeon, State of Mississippi

This is a light smattering of references used. For more, please contact me or visit www.ginadanna.com

Author Bio

Born in St. Louis, Missouri, Gina Danna has spent the better part of her life reading. History has been her love and she spent numerous hours devouring historical romance stories, dreaming of writing one of her own. Years later, after receiving undergraduate and graduate degrees in History, writing academic research papers and writing for museum programs and events, she finally found the time to write her own stories of historical romantic fiction.

Now, living in Texas, under the supervision of her two dogs, she writes amid a library of research books, with her only true break away is to spend time with her other life long dream – her Arabian horse – with him, her muse can play.

Made in the USA
Middletown, DE
16 July 2024

57383109R00245